DEDICATIONS

This volume is dedicated to Kateybug, Pie, and Orion. Meow!

I also dedicate this work to the respective crews of Wild Hunt Press and Lungga Creatives who have worked so hard at my side to make these publications a reality and not just a pleasant daydream.

And finally, to all the real monster hunters out there! Thank you to Nick Redfern, Linda Godfrey, Bart Nunnelly, Ken Gerhard, Lon Strickler, Albert Rosales, Jonathan Downes, Jacques Vallee, Loren Coleman, Whitley Strieber, and all the rest of you – and to the memory of John Keel, Brad Steiger, and Rosemary Ellen Guiley. You all make the world a lot more interesting by letting us know how full of mystery it remains.

BOOGEY KNIGHTS:
DARK WARRIORS

Aurelio Rico Lopez III

Zach Cole

Ryan George Collins

Kevin Heim

Christofer Nigro

Dustin Dreyling

Matt Hickman

JJ Lindsey

Neil Riebe

Alex Dumitru

Cody Bratsch

Cover Art:
Benjo Quinajon of Lungga Creatives

i

Preface Art:
Illustration by Glenn Lugapo. Final art and title
design by Elden Ardiente – both of Lungga Creatives

Since Benjo Quinajon did such a stand-up job on the paperback's wraparound cover, it was the opinion of the publisher that you may want to see it in its full glory, with its back page unencumbered by the mandatory bar code obfuscating a bit of the art. So, check it out!

Table of Contents

PREFACE

"Greetings, Borgs and Goa'ulds! Welcome to the Mansion of the Maquis! I am Kavikin Windbreaker, and this is my feline companion, Tarkin. We'll be your travel guide through these tales of science fiction, adventure, and exploration! Join me as we examine awesome alien artifacts and fantastic features from far futures, to reveal... um..."

The host turns from left to right, perusing the esoteric souvenirs he sees on each shelf.

The cat in the windowsill rubs his head on the host's blazer, and when satisfied with the amount of hair he's left behind, lays down and purrs. Names do not concern him.

"Is it the poor lighting in here, or do these figures look like—?"

Lightning crashes outside with a thunderous boom, briefly illuminating the entire room via an arching window in a cold white light, followed by several seconds of no light at all. Eventually the chandelier far overhead comes back on, only dimmer, seeming to cast more shadows than its illumination would suggest possible. Despite the darkened surroundings, it is apparent that the mahogany shelves go up two or three stories and are filled with books man was not meant to read and engravings man was not meant to see, obscured by shadow and dust, but no less forbidden.

The host looks down at his own hands, grasping the handle of a staff. But instead of the Cosmic Cudgel he'd been expecting, he sees that he holds a silver wolfhead attached to a wooden walking cane.

With a start, the host glances up again, and let's cry a blood-chilling howl!

"No, this can't be happening!"

Jerking his head back to stare at the fourth wall, he almost lets his sunglasses slip from his face; almost lets a glimpse of the glowing amber light tinged in crimson shine in the darkness, his eyes reflecting light they could not possibly catch.

He regains his composure, if not his control, and looks to the writing desk before him for answers.

"Mansion of the *Macabre*? Thirteen threatening thrillers about... *monster hunters*? But... *I'm* a monster hunter! This can't be right; I must be in the wrong house! I can't have been dislodged from space and time to become a horror host!"

The lack of neon-lit corridors confirms his fears. Clearing his throat and adjusting his fedora, the spectacled man begins again, glancing back to the desk from time to time to make sure the details are right.

2

"Good evening, and welcome to the Mansion of the Macabre! My name is... oh, let's go with Gavin Chesterfield." The host returns the cat's shady glance. "Guess that means you're actually *Tarquin*, rather than *Tarkin*."

The cat signals his acknowledgement by flicking his white-tipped tail and yawning.

"Join me, won't you, as we delve into a haunting world of monsters who roam the nights and terrorize the innocent. These are not their stories, though. These are the tales of those personages brave enough, *foolish* enough, to stand up to the darkness that surrounds them, and force it back, so others may sleep through the mayhem, never knowing of the dangers they narrowly avoided. These are the stories of the men and women who rise to the challenge of protecting the innocent from the boogeymen under the beds of humanity."

With a grin, the host's eyes flare up with a pale xanthic glow behind his tinted lenses.

"These are the tales of... the Boogey Knights!"

The host releases the silver cane handle, muttering about wanting gloves when handling such items, and picks up a stack of manuscripts from the desk.

"Should I *read* these before talking about them? I've never horror hosted before. The audience won't know how accurate I am, unless they read the stories before the Preface... but if that's their twisted game, they deserve what they get."

He frowns at the thickness of the first one. "Great, I can't wait to see what—eh? Oh, this is just *wrong*!" Thumbing through the pages, he sighs. "I knew this would happen. I fall out of sync with reality and now I'm introducing my own adventures as works of fiction. May as well get this over with."

"Our first daring dark adventure might be more at home in a book of sword and sorcery! It tells of three heroes' journey to some wondrous mountains, a veritable quest featuring those knights of boogeydom Mike, Dale, and Steven. I won't spoil the surprise as to what they're facing, but Christofer Nigro, the author of this S.A.V.A.G.E. (Society for Assessing Viability of Abominations as Good or Evil) case file, called it *Here There Be Dragons*, so you do the math.

"Did I mention that some of these 'Knights' may qualify as *creatures of the night* themselves? Yeah, I should probably find a clever way to hint that sometimes it takes a monster to beat a monster; but honestly, any pun I offer here will just come off as ornery.

"Next up is... Alex Dumitru's *Call me Rufus*. As long as you aren't personally a telemarketer, you should enjoy this one, as Rufus puts his experience to good use dealing with the living and the dead... and the undead. And if you *are* a telemarketer, I don't think I want you to read it anyway. Rufus certainly wouldn't."

A sneeze from Tarquin interrupts the host's analysis, as if to suggest that the offered opinion of telemarketers ought to be extended to the rest of the human race. To clarify this point, the cat hisses and swipes a clawed paw at empty space, and immediately settles into a nap.

"Ivan faces fiends, foils friends, and forces fate in *Hearts of Darkness*. How is this account of *my* story considered to be someone else's creation? The author's name is Kevin Heim. That better be another one of my aliases, or someone will be hearing from my attorney."

The host throws the top three manuscripts onto a pile on the floor and looks up again. "You see, when I'm hosting a science fiction anthology, I'm Kavikin Windbreaker, and when I'm hosting a horror anthology, I'm Gavin Chesterfield. When I'm serving as a Boogey Knight, I'm Steven Pertwillaby. When I fight spirits on my own, I'm Ivan Schablotski. And presumably when I'm writing, I'm Kevin Heim. Hey, I don't question *your* life choices!"

The pages separate on their way down, and as each one lands it is immediately engulfed in baby spiders. Tarquin nods, acknowledging the predators' territory for the time. Likely they will make for an entertaining hunt later.

"Cody Bratsch brings us *Hush, Hush, Hush*, which focuses on one of the original classic monster hunters, and makes it clear that he qualifies as a real Boogey Knight. Revealing anything more might ruin it for you, but even when you do figure it out, you'll be glad you stuck around for the full story."

Discarding another ream of paper, the host looks pleased with what he now finds on top of the stack. "Here we go – Zach Cole's *First Hunt*. This is a story of the shades of gray existing between the black and white extremes of good and evil, featuring Jeremy Walker as he is just learning the ropes of how to handle living in a world where the monsters are real."

"We have another collaboration up next, between Matt Hickman and the aforementioned Christofer Nigro. *K.A.R.U.D.* features a trio of monster hunters working the Houston, Texas area, and between Mac and Kitty and Melissa and Mack, you'd think they'd have enough to contend with just learning how many is in a trio, but fate has bigger problems in store for them."

The host then turns the dust-covered page to look upon the next tale. "An old acquaintance of mine likes to spout the virtues of science over magic, and while I tend to agree, it cannot be denied that the supernatural tend to overcome technology, not counting those professional paranormal investigators in New York. *The Works of Mortals* is a fun twist on the monster hunter story, but when it comes to science and technology vs. magic and the supernatural, I'll let you decide which is the real winner."

The host pauses for a moment, considering how to approach the next selection.

"Consumerism is scary enough by itself, but *Let's go to the Mall* takes it to a more visceral level. Ploder has been around long enough to make his own rules about which fights are worth fighting, but he may have chewed off more than he can bite this time. Dustin Dreyling presents a tale with plenty of monstrosities that leave no ambiguity."

The host continues. "Here we have another story of hunter vs. haunter with lives hanging in the balance! Christofer Nigro tells the tale of monster hunter Dale tackling graveyard ghouls in a chance encounter called *Grave Consequences*. JJ Lindsey consulted on this one, so it ought to be a winner. And I've personally worked with Dale before, so I can attest to his capability.

"Hmm, another story by Kevin Heim. I assume he's one of my identities, since this one features an occasional ally of mine, one of the original 'Famous Monsters,' as the monster hunter in a story called *Redux of the Living Dead*. 'Redux' suggests bringing something back from the past, so I imagine there's more than one classic creature to feature in this one."

Boogey Knights: Dark Warriors

"Neil Reibe gives us *Horror House*, and boy is that title ever apt! Marcella Saward is our paranormal investigator this time, though necessity has her sharing the spotlight with the residents of a certain eponymous domicile. Set back in the before-times of the 20th Century, expect the unexpected, like the characters in this story should have done!"

Tarquin stretches and pushes a pile of pages off the windowsill, drawing the host's attention to them.

Grumbling once again, the host bends down to pick up the papers on the floor and brush off the spiders. The cat helps by jumping on to the pages as he is gathering them and laying down. Knocking over the cane he'd been carrying at the beginning, the host bumps his elbow on the desk and gives up. He stands but abandons all pretenses of composure.

"Here's one where things can get a little overwhelming at times. It's what happens when the monsters get out of control. Aurelio Rico Lopez III tells us the story of Jack, a man doing the best he can to survive in a world already gone mad, in *Stray*. Hard to know if Jack counts as a hero or not, but I know I'd rather have him on my side when the chips are down."

The last few sheets of paper give the host pause, and he sighs before looking into the fourth wall. "One story left – lucky number thirteen. This one's a doozy too. It's another one by Christofer Nigro, but this one's a solo tale about Mike Nero, star of the *NERO* series of werewolf novels published by Wild Hunt Press. This standalone story is titled *And an End...* which is fitting in more ways than one. They can't all be *Happily Ever After*."

The host places the pages he's still holding on the desktop and scoots the ones still on the floor underneath the furniture. He then picks up Tarquin, who allows the offense of being held with more grace than the situation warrants but there are tuna treats to be had when this is all over, which softens the blow of the indignity.

"Look, those are the stories. They're pretty good, and I'm not just saying that because I'm in a couple of them. Now go enjoy them and let me get out of here. From the Mansion of the Macabre, this is Gavin Chesterfield, signing off!"

"Mrowr."

END

HERE THERE BE DRAGONS

Christofer Nigro
with JJ Lindsey and Kevin Heim

Case #: Undetermined
Time: June 2009
Locale: Stradshire, Romania, Europe

On the outskirts of a village called Stradshire, hidden in a secluded rural area in the Balkans, a young man by the name of Jenning Fintin is running for his life, his mission one of life-shattering importance. H was riding a large brown stallion, the fastest he could find in his backwards little village, sequestered in the middle of nowhere. As his horse sped down the dirt trails, he realized that nothing less than the lives of every single human being in his small but closely-knit little community depended upon his success that day his own life did not matter. There was but one small post office operating on the outskirts of this village, and he had to make it there in time. He held the letter he had hastily written tightly to his breast, determined not to drop it or lose it under any circumstances.

If only an Internet café existed somewhere in his village, but unfortunately Stradshire had yet to enter the 21st century. The great majority of people living there did not even bother to own a computer, and no Internet access was available in this far off bucolic region of Europe. For the most part, the people there never complained. They knew they were anachronisms to on the rest of the continent, but they enjoyed their simple lives. They relished farming and living off the land provided for them via abundant game in the local forests, and many grew fresh vegetables in their own gardens.

The diminutive village had only two small taverns, and almost every single business there was family owned and operated, with corporations and brand names like Mocha Cola and Big Kahuna Burger being unheard of. They had no need for the problems in the outside world. Their little neck of the woods knew no war, had very little crime, and most people there knew each other. The community was like a large extended family. Everyone looked out for each other, and life was as close to utopic as anyone on Earth could hope for.

Until the day that *he* came.

Yes, "he" indeed. Jenning dared not even think the man's name. He dared not think of the reasons why the mayor unhesitatingly gave up his office to the man in question. The police force in Stradshire was minimal, and the simple people there never needed more than a few constables being active. In a village where most people know everyone else, and where everyone looks after each other, there was really no need for anything like the big city police forces. There were no street gangs, no bands of thieves; even shoplifters and pickpockets were virtually unheard of there. Surely if utopia existed anywhere in the world, it existed in Stradshire.

Until the day that *he* came.

Until the day that *he* took over.

Until the day the madness started.

It must have been many centuries since something like *him* had set foot in their locale – or most anywhere else in Europe, for that matter. Though Stradshire existed very much in the past, the villa was still thankful that it thrived without some of the horrors known to the medieval world. The people were happy to have a small medical clinic that utilized modern medicine. They were pleased to have a small post office on the outskirts of the town environs that provided slow albeit direct communication with the outside world.

For the first time in his 24 years of life in this remote but peaceful region of Europe, located just seventy miles from the border of Serbia, in the Romanian portion of the Balkans, Jenning Fintin was wishing for access to cyberspace so that he could send an e-mail to the world beyond Stradshire.

Jenning's horse whinnied in complaint as the young man continued to press the beleaguered animal to run faster and farther to reach his destination. After he arrived at the post office, the desperate young man quickly dismounted from his stallion, and dropped the envelope down the appropriate chute. He hoped and prayed that the new overseer of his hometown was not aware that Jenning had left the village limits. He hoped and prayed that the individual he dreaded even thinking of would even understand what a post office was.

Breathing a quick sigh of relief, Jenning next thought that perhaps he should urge the horse to run him clear out of the village and as close to safety as possible. It was a long run from the "Little T" to the "Big T," a.k.a., a small Romanian province beginning with that letter to the larger Transylvania, and the horse would need to stop and rest several times. However, he might be able to make it. He might be able to escape from the madness on his own even if everyone else in his town could not do so.

But would it be right of him to abandon his extended family? Did they not need his support? Would help even come? Would the magazine that he sent the letter to receive it promptly? Would its editorial staff forward the letter to someone who could actually help? He only found a single copy of *Omnibus* magazine in a nearby general store, one of the rare tomes that were periodically imported there from the outside world besides stalwarts like *Reader's Digest* and *National Geographic.*

Just as Jenning debated with himself as to whether he should turn back and be with his family or attempt to escape the madness and seek out further help, the decision was taken from his hands. He heard the foreboding sound of huge leathern wings flapping, and a large shadow from above suddenly enveloped him.

"Bad young man, Jenning," a distorted, hissing voice said to him. "Very bad. Your punishment will be most severe, I am afraid."

"No! I was only checking for mail," Jenning pleaded in response. "I swear! Please!"

"The cost will be the life of your young sister, Meriam," the voice retorted. "I am sure she shall be quite tasty."

"No!" Jenning exclaimed with maniacal fervor. "Leave her alone! She had nothing to do with this! Please, I beg of you!"

But Jenning could tell he was not being heeded. And he also knew that the sound of his own voice desperately pleading was the last thing he would ever hear.

***

Mike Nero loved having a large apartment all to himself in the middle of Buffalo, New York. The city was an awful place to live, and in a perpetual economic rut; but since he worked largely online this did not affect him as badly as other residents of the Queen City who struggled to earn a living. And after all, Buffalo was *his* city. It was where he was born, and he always thought it was an interesting place to make his home even though everyone else who lived there always seemed to talk about "getting the hell out" of there as soon as they could.

However, the city was a place of mystical convergence, and he grew up there. His formative years occurred in Buffalo. The lycanthrope he eventually became by choice started here. Perhaps most importantly, the person he became when he eventually rejected the darkness that once almost turned him into a misanthropic monster started here. And though those memories were often not very fond ones, to say the least, Mike nevertheless felt an obligation to protect his hometown whenever a paranormal threat reared its ugly head. Moreover, having a large three-bedroom apartment all to himself came in handy whenever he required a meeting place for his various teammates in the Boogey Knights. It has been so ever since the latter team of wayward but dedicated monster hunters were brought together by the American monster fighting org S.A.V.A.G.E. (Society for Assessing Viability of Abominations as Good or Evil) to handle "side" missions.

Steven Pertwillaby, a.k.a., 'Agent Ambergris,' the team leader, was already there, enjoying a cup of something hot from Coffeebucks. He and Mike Nero, a.k.a., 'Agent Black,' both knew the third member for this upcoming mission would be arriving within minutes -- he had just called them on his cell phone to let them know that he was quickly approaching the neighborhood.

Several minutes after the phone call ended, the doorbell rang as expected.

"That would be Dale, unless Avon is paying me a late call," Mike quipped. "And I'm not sure who I would rather it be considering how cute so many Avon ladies are."

"As long as she can fight monsters, I'm good either way," Steven responded. "Maybe she can suggest a more colorful name for you than 'Agent Black', while she's at it."

Mike ran down his flight of stairs to open the front door, and in just a few seconds Dale, a.k.a. 'Agent Crimson,' entered the apartment.

"It's about time, Dale P--!"

The newcomer raised a flat-palmed left hand, setting his luggage down with his right. "Lemme stop you right there, Mike," he said firmly. "It's 'Dale McCammon' for now. Had to work up a new identity and lay low after a recent case with a gorgon put me back on the authority's radar."

Steven laughed. "That's fine, 'Mick,' since I'll be known as 'Gavin Chesterfield' for the foreseeable future."

"Seriously?"

"Of course not. I'm fucking with you," Steven Pertwillaby scoffed at his friend. "I already used that name earlier this year in Red Bank, New Jersey, and the police are looking for 'him' too. But where we're going, you better have I.D. in whatever name you're using."

"You know I don't do airplanes," Dale snapped back, clearly exhausted and in need of a shower. "I've never been on one in my life. So, what's this urgent case of Mike's that warranted a 23-hour car drive?"

Mike displayed his infamous half-grin. "Welp, you've been working so hard dealing with the monster problems in Wisconsin lately, I figured an impromptu vay-cay in the wondrous Queen City with your monster-slaying pals would be totally cathartic for you."

Mike's grin faded when Dale threw him one of his terrifying glares. "23 hours on the road, Mike, and four of them were spent putting down a rabid Hodag. I'm in no mood for your jokes,' man."

"Okay, okay!" Mike lamented hastily. "But, c'mon now, Buffalo isn't *that* bad. It's where I was born; it's where I hang my hat -- or, rather, where I hang my skull cap. And it's where I first joined the ranks of the Brotherhood of Fenris, so you know it's a lot more interesting and important than it actually looks."

"As I recall," Dale said, "the Brotherhood came here looking for you. They didn't start in Buffalo. And I wouldn't be so flattered that a group like that thought they could use me for evil."

Mike sighed dramatically. "Some people are so fixated on details."

Steven raised his sunglasses and rubbed his temple with both thumbs. "At least two-thirds of us don't want to be in Buffalo right now; no offense, so let's get on with it. Dale, please go shower and change."

Dale sighed and headed to the master bedroom. Before closing the door, he yelled, "Mike, is it okay if I pee in your shower stall? Okay, thanks!"

"Omfgs! That was ornery, even for Dale!" Mike Nero started to run after teammate, but Steven put his hand up in a 'halt' gesture to stop him.

"Yeah, that was bad; but we have other concerns, so please don't wolf out over a bad joke. Our flight leaves in thirteen hours, so we have to be at the airport in ten."

Whatever Steven was going to say next was drowned out by a blood-curdling scream from the master bedroom. This was followed by a soaked, towel-covered Dale trudging out of the bedroom down the hall in a huff. "Dammit, there's no hot water."

Mike shrugged his shoulders in mock-embarrassment. "Whoops. I knew I forgot to mention something."

Steven put his sunglasses back on and sat down. "Black! Crimson! We have a mission. Heads in the game, please.

***

After Dale dressed, the trio gathered in Mike's living room.

"Hope you have a 'McCammon' passport, Crimson," Steven started, "because we're all going to fun-filled Eastern Europe!"

Dale all but spilled his Nozz-a-La soda all over Mike's hardwood floor. "Say what?"

"Yes, you heard me right," Steven confirmed. "Mike, tell him what you told me."

"First off, this mission has been cleared and funded by S.A.V.A.G.E.," Mike explained while adjusting his nylon utility belt to his darkly garbed full body outfit. "Our special flight is prepared so we

13

do not wreak havoc with security at a regular European airport, despite the fun memories that may provide for future dinner discussion. This paid-for vacation is our 'reward' for doing so well as a team against that alien homicidal maniac that was laser blasting the Hel out of those rednecks a year ago. Perty will be the field commander, as usual. Once we arrive on the continent, we can thank it for all the wonderful familial lineages it brought the world through the centuries, like the Frankensteins, the Draculs, the Pitamonts, the--"

"I think we get the gist, Mike," Steven curtly interjected.

"Okay, okay," the portly but densely built Italian said. "Anyway, here's the skinny on the mission. Someone from the village of Stradshire sent a letter to *Omnibus* magazine – yanno, the one reporting on supposedly true stories of the paranormal written by people who investigate the phenomena -- pleading for help. He said that a mysterious man with supernatural abilities had taken over the village, and he didn't know where else to turn. So, he wrote to the magazine, hoping it would reach someone who might be able to help. The letter was printed in the 'Looking for Help' section of the mag – yanno, the section where people send requests for aid from exorcists if they have a demon haunting their home or when they have a gargoyle in their belfry, or some other nasty paranormal goings-on.

"He didn't go into too much detail other than that, because the letter was clearly written quickly, and the editor of the magazine did the best he could to correct all of the grammatical errors that originally made the letter largely unreadable. The missive was seen by one of Dr. Enygma's many agents, who passed the message to this world's resident sorcerer supreme."

Dale said, "Then why doesn't Doc E go deal with it? I don't like being his errand boy. And I also don't like the idea of flying, especially not over the damn ocean. I'm a monster hunter. I know what kind of things live in there!"

"I guess Doc E and his Secret Order of Defenders have their hands full with some business in the Middle East involving Pazuzu," Mike replied. "McNeil is involved, so you know that will get the Order's priority right now. But anyway, it may be good to get away from the United States for a while and visit a far-off place where we're not wanted. As for flying over the water... well, c'mon, what are the odds of

14

our plane actually getting pulled out of the air by Cthulhu or one of those mutant sharktopuses, or whatever?"

Dale leaned back on the couch and put his boots up on the coffee table, ignoring Mike's annoyed frown. "You still got your airplane gremlins, alien abductions; hell, I heard a story a few years back about some monster hunters that had to deal with a demon that was crashing planes just for kicks."

Don't forget," Steven pointed out, "that this is a private jet chartered by S.A.V.A.G.E. It will have all the wards necessary to ensure a spook-free flight."

"Yup," Mike noted. "And they won't skimp on the Dramamine and paper barf bags either. In case that was a concern of yours also."

"Yeah, we all know the risks there," Dale said while sipping his soda. "Remember that Wendigo case in Yellowstone? We had supposedly foolproof wards there, too." Dale took another sip. "Doesn't matter, I guess; we survived all that. I'm in. Still not happy about it, though."

"That's alright," Mike said. "How often do monster hunters ever get to be happy anyway?"

"Personally, I've never been to the Balkans," Steven said. "I'm looking forward to traveling somewhere new. But since there are active Ordinance operations going on in Hungary and Romania, my biggest concern is leaving a paper trail once we're over there. Soon as we touch down, we *have* to use code names."

Dale laughed. "Do we all have to wear suits and shades, too?"

"Sure," Steven nodded back. "And you even get to be Mister Pink."

"Sweet. Means I survive!"

$$***$$

Roughly 24 hours later, a large van from Lariat Rent-A-Car Bucharest was carrying the BK team to Stradshire, a quaint hamlet located in the Romanian province often referred to as "the small T with the big demon-haunted mountain." The trio had tried to catch as much sleep on the flight over as possible in the hope of offsetting the jet lag. They knew they would have to be on full alert when they arrived, in case a voodoo master or some black magick cult was truly menacing that area. If anything, the team decided that this should be a relatively easy mission compared to some of the things they have gone up against in the past. A small group of zombies should be able to be dispatched and the town liberated without undue difficulty.

The intrepid trio regretted being unable to replace any of the lives who had been lost, and they did realize that a "man with supernatural powers" was a rather vague description of what they were facing. But to someone living in a town that was a relic from an earlier era of European history, that should not have been surprising. The threesome needed to check the place out, and they would stop at nothing to see to it that any shadowy thing that may be loose in that village would be neutralized quickly enough.

All three Boogey Knights had taken a walk on the dark side and all of them barely escaped with their souls intact. They all knew quite well the lure and power of the dark side, and how the forces of light had to be ever vigilant in opposing the darkness. Their status as "warriors against the wyrd" was hard won, and the fact that all of them could have gone in the opposite direction served as strong reminders that they had to serve as examples to the world that darkness – both within and without -- can be effectively opposed and resisted.

The team expected to face a man of magick who did not escape the lure of the dark side, and who used his power to prey upon the innocent and those weaker than them. Such actions would not go unpunished so long as the Boogey Knights drew breath. Provided, of course, they didn't aggravate each other to death first.

***

The sleek silvery van drove through difficult and ever narrowing roads that were leading into an enclave deep within a forest. It was nighttime in the woods outside of Stradshire, and the land looked both beautiful and ominous. Anything could be hiding in the dense foliage, and the Boogey Knights were well aware how many supernatural beings used forests as their base of operations. "And to think a certain young chap named Goodman Brown thought *he* had things to worry about in the woods," as Mike Nero enjoyed pointing out when it was least welcome to hear.

"These roads aren't exactly made for a big ass van," Dale said. "Or, really any kind of modern vehicle. We should have gotten horses, though it's been a few years since I did any riding."

"It's a lot easier to carry our weapons in a van than on horseback," Steven pointed out. "Especially for those of us that don't have much practice at it. But I really do wish the rental place had a four-wheel drive vehicle available. Next time we should try to reserve something practical so it's ready when we get there."

"Ooh! We should get four wheelers next time!" Dale stated with mock exuberance.

"Well, let's face it, guys," Mike noted. "This is Stradshire, not Chicago."

"They riding a lot of four wheelers through the streets of Chicago?" Dale queried.

Mike scowled. "You know what I meant, Dale."

"That's 'you know what I mean, *Agent Crimson'* to you," Steven said firmly. "Code names, dammit; use them!"

"Sorry, sorry," came Mike's typical *mea culpa*. "Agent Crimson, Agent Ambergris. Geez."

"Yeah, Mike!" Dale said. "I mean... Agent... Some Color..."

"Black!" Mike corrected. "Yanno, like the bottom of your socks? Or, the color of your soul? *That* color."

"Nothing wrong with my soul," Dale replied. "Just got a few miles on it, is all."

"A few light years is more like it," Mike retorted quietly.

Steven kept his eyes on the road, such as it was, but his glare was still felt by the others. "Knock it off, or I swear I will turn this mission around!"

The driver's side back window, where Mike was sitting, suddenly shattered and the van skidded ninety degrees to left before screeching to a halt in the muddy tracks that passed for a road.

"I swear to Dionysus!" Steven shouted. "If you two can't control yourselves while I'm trying to navigate this goat path, I'll--!"

Another bullet pinged off the windshield, leaving a spiderweb pattern of cracked glass instead of breaking through.

17

"Oh shit," Steven murmured. ""Weapons to the ready!"

It was then that Dale noticed a spatter of blood on the left shoulder of his black leather jacket. He turned to see Mike slumped over with a gaping bullet hole in his right temple. His eyes and mouth were wide open as if he were struck down while in mid-sentence.

"Mike's down! Shot right through the fucking head!"

"Silver?" Steven asked.

"I don't know," Dale quickly replied as he brandished his gun and began looking for signs of the mystery sniper.

With a reflexive grunt, Steven tumbled out of the van and shifted into his lycanthropic form. Years of practice enabled him to morph with relatively little effort. As a werewolf, his fur offered better cover when hiding in foliage and his range of vision included the infrared.

"I see a heat signature!" he growled. "That rise to the right, in the shrubbery!"

Dale used the van for cover, aiming around it, but without any extra-human senses he realized that he may not be able to pick the shooter out of the darkening, late afternoon woods.

"Take some shots at him!" Steven exclaimed in a guttural shout. "Keep him focused on the van and I'll try to slip around behind him."

Dale fired a short salvo of shots toward where he suspected the shooter was hiding, at least enough to distract him while Steven slunk into the woods.

Running primarily on instinct in lycanthropic form, Steven stalked through the trees, avoiding any source of light and staying upwind of his prey. It was easy enough to home in on the thunderclaps of the shooter's rifle – especially with enhanced hearing. Steven was only dimly aware that, as a human, he could probably identify the caliber and make of the weapon; but as his wulver self, it was just another obstacle to avoid in the hunt for his quarry. Once he had circled around, staying in his prey's blind spot, he allowed one more shot to be fired and then lunged in the direction of the sound.

***

The sniper, Vlado Maximoff, rushed about the foliage in the fading late afternoon light, stopping to hide behind some thick brush. He was

18

hoping his green-hued raiment, combined with his lifelong knowledge of these woods, would provide some camouflage from his pursuers. But the new master of his isolated hamlet had warned him not to count on that. He had no idea what the attributes or capabilities of any given interloper who came down the sole road leading into Stradshire would be.

A former constable involuntarily turned assassin, Vlado was simply ordered to fire on anyone who passed a certain perimeter on that road, and that is what he did. The sudden appearance of *him* in the town offered the ambitious lawman the chance for more power than a mere constable of a small town could ever hope for. Thus, he was one of the very few residents of Stradshire who deliberately tried to get on the town conqueror's good side. That was *one* of the reasons he was determined not to fail the mysterious despot at his all-important post.

Upon finding what he considered to be good cover, Vlado readied his rifle and peered out through the masking greenery. It was then he found himself looking into the reddish, animalistic eyes of the transformed Steven Pertwillaby.

"Jesus shit!" the sniper screamed in his native Serbian.

Vlado jumped up out of the concealing vegetation with an extreme start, nearly dropping his weapon in the process.

The werewolf fell onto the constable-turned-assassin as soon as he broke cover. Flattened, the breath was knocked out of Vlado before he could even cry in pain. He brought up his arm in an attempt to slam the beast with the butt of his rifle, but a swipe from its claws knocked the weapon away. It was then that Vlado turned to notice that the human he'd been shooting at was standing over him with the barrel of a gun pointed in his direction.

Dale cocked his gun and told the sniper not to move. "I won't even aim for a kill. I'll kneecap you and leave you for my buddy there to make kibble out of... unless you've got something real interesting to say. Like, who you work for, or why you opened fire on us?"

Vlado looked back and forth between the armed man behind him and the fanged, hirsute man-monster in front of him, its lips curled back in rage. The appearance of desperation came over his countenance. Vlado realized that the only chance he now had was his old service revolver that he had hidden in the shoulder pocket of his green overcoat. Using the stealth techniques he learned while serving years earlier in the French Foreign Legion, Vlado surreptitiously maneuvered his right hand towards the pocket where the handgun was concealed.

Beads of perspiration began rolling down the constable's brow as his mind was barraged by a series of fears and doubts. These were no ordinary interlopers. One, at least, was clearly not human. They were both thoroughly pissed that he had managed to kill one of their number.

Would the bullets in his revolver even do any serious damage to the werewolf in front of him? Could he possibly shoot the man standing behind him before getting shot himself? Even if he chose one target and succeeded in a hit or kill, the other would then do him in. Vlado realized that there was but one course of action open to him if he wished to escape the wrath of either of these two interlopers… or that of his feared master, if the two let the former constable go after ratting *him* out.

Since Vlado's opponents seemed to favor English, so too would be his defiant words to them. "I will not compromise the master! He will kill you himself!"

"Boring," Dale sniggered. "Guess there's no reason to keep you from becoming a chew toy then."

Vlado then put his renowned combat reflexes to good use.

With a swift motion he drew his revolver under his own chin and pulled the trigger. The former constable's brains exited the top of his skull with a thunderous boom. Both the lycanthropic Steven and the gun-wielding Dale found themselves spattered with the contents of Vlado's cranium.

"Well that was gross." Steven wiped his face on his sleeve as he shifted back to human. "At least we know it's a cult. Not too many types of bad guy can inspire that degree of fanaticism."

"I'm thinking vamp," Dale said. "Probably a Master. You know how they like their bug eaters."

The duo returned to the van, which was still running, and peered into the back seat. What they saw didn't look good.

***

Several minutes later, Steven and Dale emerged into a clearing while carrying the corpse of their friend and teammate. Both seemed out of breath as they carefully placed the body down in the grass. By this point, the sun had gone down, and a bright waxing moon was visible in the inky sky.

"Shit," Dale said as he took a few deep breaths. "How the hell does a werewolf get fat? All the ones I ever had to deal with had that supernatural metabolism going on."

Steven did his best to conceal his own gasping. "Dale! Is this really the time for that?"

"God damn bullet sponge here deserves it for that dumb fucking socks joke." A look of concern came across his visage. "He... is going to revive, right?"

"He would if we could lay him under the rays of a full moon. But it's only a waxing moon in the sky. Those weakened lunar rays will likely not be enough. So, I'm really hoping he has a certain item in the lead-lined pouch of his utility belt."

"I noticed you going through his belt. I thought you were just lifting his wallet. What were you looking for?"

Steven shrugged off the sarcasm of his teammate as he pulled a roundish stone made into a pendant from a specific pouch on Mike's belt. The sigh of relief he breathed upon finding it was fully audible.

Dale looked unimpressed. "You left his wallet and stole a rock?"

"This, Dale, is the moonstone Mike acquired a few years back from a solo mission I'd rather not get into right now. It was actually brought back from the Moon itself and inscribed with Norse runes making up a prayer to Máni, a planetary intelligence the Norsemen worshiped as a goddess personifying the Moon."

Dale took on a perplexed countenance. "A moonstone? Like the one that astronaut brought back in the '70s that made him wolf out? I heard about that. He was the son of that newspaper publisher that was always badmouthing--"

"Yeah, that's the one. This particular moonstone is infused with lunar radiation and mystically enchanted. It's designed to give Mike the equivalent of full moon exposure under a waxing or waning moon, so his transformations are less difficult, and less likely to result in a severe flare-up of the wasting illness once he reverts back to human."

"Kick ass. So, how does it work?"

"Pure Fucking Magick; I have no idea how it works, or why it even works, but it does. According to Mike, this stone should heighten his shamanistic lycanthropy 30-fold, or multiply the effect of the moonlight, or something like that. It's magick, alright? The rules are made up! First, I need to hold it up and let it absorb as much moonlight as possible. If it were a new moon, there would be no chance for him. But with a waxing moon just a few days before a full lunar phase, it should take just a few minutes."

"Still kills me that you're a werewolf that doesn't believe in magic," Dale said.

Suddenly, the moonstone began glowing a bright crimson. Its mineral composition started drinking in the moonlight, triggering a radioactive reaction. As the lunar rock illuminated, the pock marks of the stone and the inscribed runes became much more visible.

"Nice!" Dale exclaimed. "Sort of like those glow-in-the-dark toys I had as a kid. You hold 'em up to a lightbulb for a few minutes, and…"

"Yeah, sort of like that," Steven interjected as he continued to hold up the glowing rock. "The energies and mineral components of this stone are supposed to absorb the moonlight and amplify its effects, giving Mike the equivalent of a full moon ray bath. I think he could speed up the effect by reciting a quick spell to Máni, you know, if he was conscious... or alive. Everything I know about this came from Mike himself, and it only applies to shamanistic werewolves that perform their own rituals. If I put this rock against my forehead, it would change me instantly, and I might go into a rampage, but just touching it does nothing to me without a full moon. We just have to hope this amplified moonlight is enough to get him going without the help of spells."

Dale stepped up for a closer look at the illuminated rock's effects. Steven blocked his teammate's forward progress with a stretch of his arm.

"You may want to step back a bit, since this stone is radioactive due to being on the Moon's surface. Its radioactivity can't hurt a lycanthrope, even in human form, and a few minutes of exposure shouldn't be too dangerous, but still…"

"Good call," Dale said as he stepped backwards a few feet. "You never know if you're gonna get cancer or superpowers. Not gonna roll those dice."

Steven placed the tight nylon loop of the pendant around Mike's neck. He then stepped away next to Dale to allow the energies to – hopefully – do their regenerative work. For several minutes, the moonstone kept glowing and even pulsating, but their fallen comrade remained still, his eyes and mouth as wide open as before. The bullet wound to the side of his head looked as open and bloody as when he first received it.

"Are you sure this is going to work?" Dale queried with a tone of unease. "I mean, I know you checked, and the bullets weren't silver, but still, he took that slug in the skull, right into his brain. What's that do to a werewolf? Is he gonna come back ready to ride the short bus? I mean, more so than he was before?"

"We made sure the sniper's rounds weren't silver, so there shouldn't be any permanent damage from the wound." Steven paused to consider. "I've heard that some werewolves can suffer brain damage from lead bullets, like this guy I looked into named Crayne; but his lycanthropy was from a curse, so again, different rules. With Nero, we have two things going for us. First, his lycanthropy has a divine source, so even without his active participation, it should still work to heal him."

Dale waited about ten seconds before asking, "So, what's the second thing?"

Steven smiled a little before giving his answer. "Odds are, Mike's brain is too small for a bullet to hit."

"Wow," Dale shook his head. "And you got after me for calling him fat?"

"What I was originally going to say is that the bullet probably made a clean break in the skull, due to the shape and caliber. If it had been fired from a shorter range, it would have been messy, and the fragments it could have left in the brain might be a problem for even magickal healing to deal with. There's no exit wound, either, so Mike didn't lose nearly as much of his noggin as he could have."

"I take it that getting the bullet removed first isn't an option right now either?"

"Afraid not." Steven's reply was notably solemn. "Our first aid kit didn't come with a *Brain Surgery for Dummies* book. Professional non-surgeons like ourselves would only make any such attempt a major epic fail. And I doubt we could trust any hospital in that village, presuming there even happens to be one with the proper facilities. We have to rely on Mike's healing factor to expel the bullet when he transforms. *If* he transforms. C'mon, Mike. What the hell are you waiting for? Suck up those lunar energies and wake up, already!"

"You know, he's gonna freak out when he comes back," Dale said. "From what I hear, this kind of resurrection can be... traumatic."

Steven frowned. "Unfortunately."

"Also, I'm pretty sure his body voided the bowels at death, which should be embarrassing for him."

"It did, "Steven said, a grimace in his face. "Werewolf sense of smell's not always a plus."

Suddenly, after what seemed like an eternity (but was actually about fifteen minutes), Mike Nero's fingers began wriggling. This was simultaneous with his eyes blinking once and his mouth beginning to take deep, almost desperate inhalations.

"Something's happening!" Dale exclaimed. "Looks like he's coming around."

"This looks like it may well be the start of his... rejuvenation process," Steven responded. "Still, we had best prepare for... well, anything."

With that said, Steven quickly morphed into his werewolf form to give himself the added power of the lycanthrope. Dale, for his part, reached into his leather jacket and took hold of his gun.

Mike Nero's body was now undergoing a series of what appeared to be spasms as his cellular structure became saturated with the invigorating lunar energies collected and magnified by the moonstone. He then began coughing incessantly before abruptly jumping into a sitting position. Both Steven and Dale watched the troubling tableau with a combination of interest and caution.

The gaping wound in the side of Mike's skull began bleeding profusely once more. He opened his mouth and emitted a raspy cry of pain. His body began to spasm again as the pouring blood was suddenly accompanied by the semi-flattened piece of lead that had once been a bullet popping out of the wound. Mike managed to focus his gasp into a faint shout of agony when that happened.

"Um... gross," Dale said.

As the bullet was kicked out of his cranium, Mike's strange but familiar metamorphosis began. Fur started sprouting from his dermal pores as his jaws elongated into a canine muzzle. His cries of pain became increasingly less human and more like the yowling and baying of a dog as this occurred. His teeth and fingernails began extending and taking on a razor-pointed aspect.

Just before his facial skin became fully covered with a silvery gray coat, Mike Nero's gaping bullet wound ceased bleeding and started closing up rapidly. The effect was much like watching footage such a dermal injury healing recorded over the course of a few months that was heavily sped up.

Just above the wound his ears elongated into a pointed, canine appearance. His bio-mimetic black garments unraveled as his body took on an incredible amount of accrued mass, finally congealing into an all but invisible "collar" of cloth around his neck. His utility belt and nylon skull cap stretched to fit the new morphological contours.

In short order, Mike Nero was no longer human, but the beast he had long ago christened Beowolf, a slight mutation of the name of his favorite hero of Norse legend. His now massive semi-humanoid lupine form snarled in rage and pain as the metamorphosis was complete and he jumped to a bipedal stance measuring nearly seven feet in height. Steven and Dale flinched only slightly, still prepared for the worst while hoping for the best.

"Grraaarrh! What. The. Fuckkk…!" the werewolf snarled. "My skull… is… ringing!" The lycanthrope then focused his senses, picking up the familiar sight and scents of his comrades-in-arms. "Steven… Dale… what the… what…?"

Steven stepped forward with just a smidge of caution. "You were shot in the head by a sniper. Dale and I got him. Glad you brought the moonstone along. I used it to heal you under the light of the Moon."

Beowolf looked at the radiant, pulsating stone pendant around his neck, feeling the soothing energies still flowing into him.

"Well… shit," the werewolf said. "That sucks. And it fucking hurt!"

"A bullet to the noggin will do that," the still lycanthropic Steven replied while fighting to keep his lupine temper in check. "Especially the healing part. I think you'll be okay now. I would stay in wolfen form

25

for another twenty minutes or so, just to make sure your healing process is complete."

"Yeah, that was one nasty wound you got – erm, *had* – there, dude," Dale said as he walked up to his two shaggy allies.

"It sure as Hel felt like one," Beowolf said as he got his animal rage under full control.

"So… are we off to the village again?" Dale queried.

"I would say we are," Steven replied as the trio headed back towards their van.

***

Steven and Dale stood on the edge of the small lake, the rays of the waxing moon and stars reflecting off the surface in a glittering sheen. The body language of both made it clear they were fighting boredom as fiercely as any dangerous monster they had ever crossed paths with – either solo or as a team. Close to their feet was Mike Nero's discarded and carefully washed nylon utility belt.

"It would serve him right if it turned out some nasty ass lake monster was down there," Dale remarked.

"Come on," Steven replied. "When you die, poop leaves the butt. It's pretty much what happens to everyone. You can't blame him for having shit in his pants when the bio-mimetic material turned into a collar. I didn't hear you volunteering to remove his clothes before he resurrected."

Dale looked unimpressed. "Whatever. Let him take his time. Better than having to smell him, I guess." He looked up at the stars. "You know, there are a ton of lake monsters in this part of Europe. You don't suppose..."

Dale's spiel was cut off when Beowolf's massive lycan form emerged dramatically to the surface of the water, splashing his teammates so they were partially spritzed.

"No, I don't suppose that at all," Steven said as he began patting himself dry.

"Lame," Dale remarked quietly while he did the same.

26

Beowolf continued to splash as he tramped through the waters and rejoined his comrades on the grassy shore. He then scooped up his utility belt and turned his large, muzzled head to Dale.

"There!" he said in a very rough voice, indicative of the difficulty a werewolf has with producing coherent human speech. "Squeaky clean."

"Except now you smell like wet dog," Dale commented.

"Yea, probably," Beowolf replied. "Here, get a waft of it!"

The lycanthrope shoved his furry arm close to Dale's nose.

Dale pulled away, his face contorted with disgust. His hand drifted to the shoulder holster under his leather jacket. "You want to get shot again, Fido?"

"Hah ha!" Beowolf chortled inhumanly for a few seconds before bursting into a coughing fit. "Shit, I hate how much it hurts to laugh in this form."

"I take it you're clean now?" Steven asked.

"Yea, 'cept for my clothing. It was in collar mode around my neck, and I tore it off." The hulking man-wolf then glared at Steven and appeared to make an attempt at smirking, something his canid muzzle would not readily allow.

"Hey, Perty, you heard about the shit hitting the fan? Well, this is the shit hitting the face!"

Beowolf tossed the soiled "collar" of bio-mimetic clothing at Steven, who caught it with his right hand.

"Are you sure you don't want me to shoot him?" Dale asked.

"If you shoot him now, we waste even more time resurrecting him." Steven turned back to his outstretched arm... and the malodorous collar hanging from his right hand.

"Hey Nero, you heard about 'Wash-N-Wear'?" With a flick of his wrist Steven sent the collar flying into the water. "Now you can be a 'wash-n-wear-wolf! Fetch!"

Beowolf scowled to the extent that a lupine muzzle was capable. "That was ornery."

"Dale's just lucky I didn't revert to human while I'm starkers," Beowolf said. A moment later, he had reverted to homid form, now stark naked since he had torn his clothing collar off. "Whoops, no such luck! I just totally did!"

Steven shook his head while Dale curled his lip in disgust. He was clearly still thinking about shooting Mike.

"Bwah-ha-ha!" Mike laughed for a moment until he abruptly realized why reverting to human form while soaking wet in the evening during the autumn season of Europe was not exactly a good idea.

"Geez! It's freaking cold as Nifleheim out here!" Mike hollered as he covered himself and ran for the damaged van.

"Whatever you need to tell yourself, Tiny," Dale rejoined.

"That's because of the cold!" Mike shouted from the interior of the van. "And you shouldn't have been looking anyway!"

A few seconds later, Mike's voice shot from the open backseat again, this time directed at Steven. "Speaking of which... I know the van's axle is broken, so it can't drive anymore. But can you at least start the motor so I can warm up in here while I dry and get dressed?"

"I suppose so," Steven replied, "since it's not good for much else anymore. I'll start the motor and crank the heat; you dry off."

"Many thanks, Kemosabe," Mike quipped as he dried and dressed himself in one of the spare uniforms he always brought on a mission. "Luckily the sealed pouches on my utility belt are airtight and coated with lamination that makes the whole belt very easy to scrub clean. Otherwise, my herbs and other paraphernalia would be soaked and useless."

"Yes, lucky that. And don't think I'm unaware that 'Kemosabe' actually means 'one-who-creeps or spies,'" Steven griped. "If I was going to watch you bathe, I wouldn't have needed to be sneaky, you know."

"It does?" the still shivering Mike said through slightly clattering teeth. "I know a completely different translation in Apache. You shouldn't be too quick to be offended... *Perty.*"

Dale snorted, eliciting an evil glare from Steven.

A moment later, the sartorially restored Mike Nero emerged from the back of the van, fully dried and no longer shivering. He also had an annoyingly casual beam on his face, as if people died and came back every day. Though, in the circles the Boogey Knights walked in, that is not exactly far from common. Hence, they counted their blessings whenever someone (or something) that came back from the dead was *actually someone they wanted to* for a change.

"Well, dudes?" Mike said with his usual degree of teen-like elation. "I'm ready for our trek into town when you are. My head no longer hurts, so I'm guessing that I'm all healed up now."

"Awesome," Dale lamented. "Just remember, now that I know you can resurrect, it's a lot less trouble to just shoot you to shut you up."

Mike gritted his teeth as he followed his teammates down the chosen path.

"Oh, and Dale?" Mike said. "As to why I'm fat despite the werewolf metabolism thing? I dunno, and that sucks. But I guess even lycan metabolisms work in unexpected ways. Notice how some older lycanthropes look awesome for their age, but others look deceptively frail and even withered… until the transformation, that is?"

"I've seen just about every kind of werewolf and shapeshifter," Dale replied. "So, I guess you're one of those it sucks to be, though I kind of figured it had to do with your wasting sickness."

"Pretty much," Mike conceded.

Dale paused for a moment. "How the hell did you know I complained about your weight. That happened *after* you went and got yourself Old Yeller-ed."

"Well," Mike responded, "with you being you, and me being, well, me… I just figured you would have made such a complaint."

"Fair enough."

***

Steven gave further instructions to his two teammates as they arrived close to an area of the forest that led to a clearing. Within that clearing was a small road that provided a direct route to Stradshire. Each of them grabbed whatever weapon they thought would be most appropriate for wiping out supernatural evil and began their lengthy trek towards the obscure little village. After a while, they could see the post office where Jenning just barely managed to send the letter to *Omnibus*.

They continued to walk onwards, using flashlights to lead the way in the dark. Upon approaching the village, they could see that the many homes dotting the landscape were quite modest, and none were larger than a single story in size. No buildings of any real measure could be seen. No one walked the streets. The lampposts, which were the only modern feature to be seen in this town, were illuminated and the cemented streets were visible under the lights. Not a single vehicle was parked anywhere. Horse stalls were evident all over.

"Wow, these people really do live in the past," Mike observed aloud. "I guess we can't stop at a Big Boy Byrne's for a meal."

"There could be an all-night tavern," Steven noted, "but don't expect it. Small European communities tend to close up at night, especially in areas where it's dangerous to be out in the dark. We just have to hope something's open where we can ask for information … preferably in English. But we have to be cautious because we have no idea exactly what we will be facing here."

"I'm still thinking vamp, probably a Master, what with Renfield back there," Dale mentioned. "Could be some kind of wizard or cultists though. Either way, I've got just the thing." He jerked a thumb over his shoulder at the shotgun slung across his back.

"Or, if that doesn't work..." Dale opened his jacket and produced a long knife engraved with sigils. "This will work wonders against supernatural threats, but I prefer to deal with them long range if I can."

"Just put it away for now," admonished Steven. "The last thing we need is to alert the wrong people that we are in town."

"That's a cool blade," Mike stated with notable interest. "Where did you get it from?"

"You really don't want to know," Dale said with a decidedly unpleasant grin. "Besides, we've already been shot at, so clearly the wrong people already know we're here."

"Unless dude was merely stationed there, and not actually sent just for us," Mike suggested.

"Then at the very least we know they're expecting someone," Dale said. "And when he doesn't check in with whoever put him there, this Master of his is gonna know what's up." He concealed his blade and continued strolling.

"Guys, I believe I spotted what may be the local tavern," Steven pointed out. "It's located just up the street there and I think I hear noise coming from it. We may be able to find something out in there."

"Why didn't the guy who wrote that letter leave a return address so we can go directly to his home?" Dale queried.

"Possibly because the dude knew he wouldn't survive delivering the letter and he figured a return address would be pointless," Mike answered grimly. "He was smart enough to just use "W. Planina" on the envelope."

"Yup", Steven confirmed. "S.A.V.A.G.E. got the name of the town by decoding the letter. I've seen a few cyphers working in the military, and that kid was pretty creative with his encryption."

Moving over to the tavern, all three of them walked in. It was populated by just a few people who were quietly seated and drinking, clearly keeping to themselves. All were dressed in clothing reminiscent of a much earlier era to most of the rest of the Western world. The architecture of the tavern's interior was likewise quaint and "old world" in design. One man was tending the bar, an older gentleman with graying hair and a large moustache. The three Boogey Knights walked up to the serving station of the bar.

"Howdy," Steven saluted as Mike and Dale looked around, noticing that each of the patrons stared at the three strangers with a look of both surprise and concern.

"You three are not from around here," the man said with a heavy accent. Thankfully, most people in "The Little T" province of Romania spoke English, but their accent could be hard to understand at times.

"Yes, we are visiting some friends," Steven mentioned. "And we heard that something… unusual was going on here."

The bartender suddenly looked very perplexed, not to mention fearful. "You should not have come here. Your friends, whoever they are, would never have asked you to come and visit during the past few months. If you are telling me the truth, and you really do know people here, then your visit was quite unexpected… and quite unfortunate."

"Why exactly is that?" Steven asked firmly. "This seems like a nice enough little village."

"It once was," the bartender said with a melancholy tone. "Until *he* came."

"And who is that, exactly?" Steven inquired.

"It is best you do not ask. It is best that you try to leave here, if you are able. This is not a good place anymore. If my family wasn't here, I would have attempted to leave myself. But attempting to do so may cost my family their lives."

31

All three of the erstwhile warriors looked at the bartender. "We may be able to help with… *him*," Steven told the fear-stricken older man.

"So, that fool Jenning actually did manage to get word out," the bartender realized aloud. "When he never returned, and his younger sister was taken, we had assumed he failed. But what can the three of you do to help us?"

"What happened to the girl?" Mike broke in and asked, suddenly sounding alarmed and more than a little angry. "Where is she being held? And by whom?"

"And what exactly is going on here?" Dale queried.

The bartender suddenly turned white as a sheet as he looked towards the door of the tavern. The three warriors in front of him shifted their gaze in tandem with the barkeep. Standing in the doorway was a tall man, standing over '6'6" in height, with flowing flaxen hair and clad in what appeared to be a suit of bluish leather armor. His eyes seemed to glimmer as he stared directly at the bartender.

"Bad man, Alphonse," the mysterious individual said an authoritative, grating voice.

"I told them nothing at all!" Alphonse exclaimed, his brow now covered in perspiration and his entire body trembling profusely. "I told them to leave!"

"You knew what a bad young man Jenning was," the mysterious figure said. "Were you in on his plans? If so, the life of your lovely little daughter is forfeit."

"No! Please!" the jolly-looking bartender was now hysterical. "I told them nothing! I told them to leave! I swear on God's holy name!"

Steven moved away from the bar, slowly approaching the cobalt-clad man before them. The stranger's eyes seemed to shimmer even more as the hunter of monsters made the move, and it was now possible to tell that the man's irises were a bright green, the brightest Steven had ever seen on a human being. If human is what this individual in sapphire armor truly was.

Behind Steven, Dale reached for his shotgun and slowly brought it around to hold it at waist level, pointed in the direction of the newcomer.

"What are you threatening him for? *I'm* the one looking for trouble," Steven stated matter-of-factly.

Every single patron in the bar looked absolutely petrified. Would the man in azure armor accuse them of being in on Jenning's plan next? And is it even possible these three strange people could possibly oppose their new master in any meaningful way?

"You three are from the world outside of this town," the man said in his icy, rasping voice. "I could smell your arrival. There is quite an interesting stench to the three of you."

"You will not go near that girl," Mike said in no uncertain terms. "Tell us where you took Jenning's sister. *Now.*"

The man suddenly broke out in laughter. "Did you just presume to make a demand of me?"

"Damn right I did," Mike replied.

The cerulean-armored man erupted in laughter again, his laugh even louder and more raucous this time.

The BOOM of a shotgun being fired indoors drowned him out, but only momentarily. The mysterious man did not even look down to see that he wasn't hurt by Dale's volley. There appeared to be a barely noticeable indentation in the armor where the bullet struck, with just a slight wisp of smoke wafting from it.

"You clearly have no idea who you are speaking to, do you?" the now angry being in blue-tinted garb lamented, his voice taking on a deep, venomous tone. "My name is Drogg, and it is the last name you shall ever know."

"Well, fuck," Dale whispered, visibly shaken at the ineffectiveness of his specially-blended buckshot. He looked back at the stranger. "You wanna answer the damn question?"

The man called Drogg looked over at the bartender. "Have your daughter come to the usual place after I deal with these interlopers. Otherwise, I shall take everything and every*one* else that you possess or *will ever* possess from you."

Steven stepped in closer to the man, with Dale rushing in alongside him.

Drogg turned and walked outside of the tavern. Alphonse the bartender said a silent prayer to his Deity that these outsiders would be capable of dealing with their town's new self-appointed mayor, but he doubted it. Yet his daughter's life depended on whether or not these three men were capable of succeeding.

33

Now confronting Drogg outside of the tavern, Mike ran up to the tall, navy-attired man and put his hand on his shoulder. "Tell us where you have the girl! This is the last time I'll ask politely."

Drogg turned around. "Since you asked me so politely, fool, I can do naught but answer." The tall, armored man patted his stomach and beamed a vile sneer. "She is in here. And she tasted quite scrumptious."

Mike's full-faced countenance took on an expression of primal rage for a split second before releasing it. "You're... going... to... *pay*... for that, you asshole!"

Mike raised his fist and took a powerful swing at Drogg. The flaxen-haired man's head turned with the impact of the haymaker, but he did not go down. He then casually turned his head back to the dark-garbed man who had the unmitigated temerity to strike him.

"You... dare to lay a hand on me?" was Drogg's angry, rhetorical query.

The long-haired man in sapphire then pushed Mike with a single hand, the casual shove sending the portly but powerfully built monster hunter clear off his feet and soaring backwards through the air. He landed on a horse trough many yards away, his weight and momentum reducing the old wooden construct to countless shards of wood.

Steven and Dale rushed Drogg while he was distracted with sending Mike airborne.

"Time to end this," Steven decreed.

Both Steven and Dale grabbed Drogg and attempted to force him to the ground with their combined might. In response, Drogg lifted his arms and threw both men against the door of the tavern, the force of impact shattering the front window.

Mike was already back on his feet, and he noticed the waxing moon in the sky above. "You certainly are strong. You're likely something a lot more than human. But guess what? So am I! Watch this, asshole."

His anger knowing few bounds at this moment, Mike quickly concentrated intensely upon an image of the glowing full moon while reciting an emotionally charged prayer to the wolfen Norse deity Fenris. A few moments later, right before Drogg's eyes, he morphed into the form of a huge bipedal man-wolf. The creature known as Beowolf then bared his vicious teeth and growled at Drogg. The enraged lycanthrope looked forward to tearing the azure-clad man to shreds.

"Now... let's see how *you* like being torn to pieces and *eaten.*"

Instead of looking on in fear, Drogg merely grinned and broke out in raspy laughter again. "Do you believe that what you just did was impressive? Observe and learn the extent of your folly, for I have a surprise for you as well."

Drogg spread out his arms and was suddenly surrounded by a nimbus of greenish energy. Within several seconds, his '6'6" form accrued an enormous amount of mass from sources unknown and morphed into the form of a dragon who was at least 25 feet in length.

The reptilian monstrosity had skin that was a deep cerulean in color, not coincidentally matching the shiny armor worn by the man the creature had disguised himself as. The dragon's true form likewise possessed four legs with enormous yellow talons, a long whip-like tail, two bat-like wings, and two large yellow horns protruding from his dinosaur-like skull. The beast's lizard-like countenance was completed by a huge maw with multiple rows of dagger-like teeth and iridescent green eyes that showed no visible pupils.

Looking majestic in his enormous true form, Drogg opened his mouth and hissed loudly, almost seeming to smile as he extended a thick, wriggling serpentine tongue.

If Beowolf's canine muzzle was capable of frowning, he would now have done so. *Oh. Shit. He was one of those.*

Despite his fear, the werewolf snarled loudly in defiance and rage.

"Fucking hell," Dale said. "I... uh, I didn't come loaded for a goddamn dragon!"

"Fucking hell is right!" Steven looked at the sight before him in wonder. "Mike's already played his hold card, so the element of surprise is shot, and I don't have anything that beats a dragon!" He stopped moving, as he suddenly realized he'd been subconsciously backing away from Drogg.

"Wonderful," Dale replied. "How can we stop something like that?"

"I don't know," Steven replied. "The last time I fought something that big, I had to trick it into falling into an active volcano... but this guy has wings!"

Beowolf's now half feral mind was fuming with ire over the thought of those young girls who were killed, and his anger prevented him from backing off from the superior menace in front of him. After allowing the animalistic rage to consume him entirely, the man-wolf ran towards the dragon and leapt twenty feet into the air to grasp onto the reptilian horror's neck. Hissing in anger, Drogg moved his neck around in a furious attempt to dislodge the errant werewolf, who viciously clawed and bit at the dragon's cerulean flesh. Trickles of blood streamed down the dragon's neck where Beowolf's teeth were embedded, but the lycan was as yet unable to inflict serious wounds on the reptilian beast's scaly blue armor-like hide.

Now thoroughly enraged, Drogg twisted his long neck and slammed Beowolf to the ground, knocking the wind out of the werewolf. Beowolf growled and still managed to rake his claws against the reptilian's facial skin, trying desperately to tear into one of its large, gleaming eyes. Before he could do so, however, the dragon sunk the long talons of one of his dinosaurian feet clear through the lycanthrope's left shoulder, effectively pinning the struggling werewolf helplessly to the ground. Drogg then opened his fearsome maw and prepared to bite his much smaller foe's head off.

Determined to prevent his teammate's demise (likely for good this time), Dale passed his mystically enhanced dagger into Steven's hand. "Gut that mother!"

Steven grabbed it and jumped into the air, transforming into his werewolf form at the same time. Using both hands to hold the blade, he drove it deep into Drogg's neck. Blood flowed freely and the dragon started writhing his neck angrily. Swinging his enormous head forward, Drogg head butted Steven into the air, the werewolf landing roughly several yards away.

With Beowolf still pinned to the ground and helpless to aid his teammate, the dragon opened his mouth wide while facing Steven and began forcefully exhaling. The great beast's teeth began sparking as flammable gastro-intestinal fumes were forcefully expelled against them and suddenly the creature's mouth was ablaze.

"Aw shit," Steven mumbled as he realized that he was about to be barbecued.

Acting quickly, Dale pulled out his shotgun and fired multiple shells straight into the dragon's open mouth. "Let's hope it's softer on the inside."

Drogg sputtered and coughed out a large wad of blood and phlegm, and then turned his attention to Dale. Exhaling further, the dragon sent a torrent of brightly colored orange-yellow flame at the third mortal today who had dared to raise arms against him.

Dale leapt for cover as quickly as he could, with the flames hitting a nearby house, setting the front of the mostly wooden edifice ablaze. Moving downwards to his knees, Dale let off another shot from his shotgun, this time aiming for Drogg's luminous left eye. He hoped the creature would be most vulnerable there. But his aim wasn't quite perfect due to the dragon suddenly shifting the position of his head, and the buckshot bounced off the creature's razor-sharp teeth rather than piercing either of his eyes.

Summoning all his might, the still pinned down Beowolf used his claws to tear as far as he could into the scaly skin on the back of Drogg's foot. This caused the creature to reflexively move his injured limb upwards, thus freeing the werewolf. Rolling away and getting back on his feet, Beowolf ignored the searing pain in his perforated shoulder blade and again leapt at the dragon. This time the hirsute warrior landed on the giant reptile's back. The werewolf ripped the dragon's flesh open with his claws but was still unable to deliver a truly serious wound to the amazing saurian.

Moving his neck backwards, Drogg swung his horned head at the werewolf, hitting his adversary and knocking the lycan off him. Beowolf landed hard on his back, blood pouring from his skewered shoulder and staining his grayish fur crimson. As the lycanthrope struggled to his feet, Drogg slugged him with his powerful tail, the force of the swipe pummeling the man-wolf over two inches into the muddy earth. The dragon then began moving towards the insensate werewolf with astounding speed for a beast so large, determined to snuff the life out of Beowolf while he still lay stunned on the ground.

"Steve!" Dale shouted, now back on his feet. "Do you still have my knife?"

Steven stood back up, taking a loping stance appropriate for his still lupine physiology. "Sure do. Lemme see if I can aggravate that wound in his throat with it! Soon as I get clear, take the shot!"

The werewolf warrior raced back to the dragon on all fours, holding the dagger in his mouth. One tuck-and-roll later, he regained access to the earlier slash across the wyrm's neck. Unwilling to release the prey he had already downed, the dragon tried to whip his tail towards this irritation, but Dale took that opportunity to shoot the reptilian ravager in the snout. The fleshy nostrils flared in pain and the creature responded by turning his long neck around.

From his own vantage point, Dale could see the swollen venom sacks in the back of his huge adversary's throat release their viscous fluids onto the recoiled tongue. The monster hunter quickly rolled on his back and over to his feet again, taking advantage of his superb reflexes to evade the fusillade of venomous fluid, if only by a hair's breadth.

"It spits acid!" Dale shouted out at the dragon: "What're you, fucking Reptilicus?"

"Acid Loogies? How many tricks does this damn creature have?" Steven asked aloud.

Aiming squarely at the cut that Steven was actively widening, Dale let off another volley from his shotgun, this time managing to deeply penetrate the exposed meat, and only barely nick Steven's clawed hand pulling back a scaly flap of skin. Drogg roared in pain as dark ocher-colored syrup poured out of his injury.

"You... will... pay... for that!" the dragon hissed out in echoey, barely decipherable words.

Again, exhaling forcefully in Dale's direction, the young warrior realized that the dragon was again about to spew forth a plume of deadly flame. But before the reptilian monstrosity could do so, a still-bleeding Beowolf again leapt upon the beast's neck and raked Drogg's left eye with his claws.

"Finally nailed the bastard's eye!" the lycan groaned to himself as he lost his grip and dropped fifteen feet to the ground.

The dragon still spewed forth a lethal stream of flame but the unexpected pain and inability to see clearly caused the shot to run wild and set ablaze a horse trough over to the side of Dale. As the dragon again roared and moved his head back and forth in another frantic attempt to dislodge the still clinging Beowolf, Steven stabbed the great beast's throat multiple times with Dale's sigil-inscribed knife, hoping the skin underneath would be soft enough for it to do some serious damage. Steven's lycanthropic strength was sufficient to make several new holes before he had to jump clear to avoid a monstrous reptilian leg reaching up to knee him.

Roaring again in pain, the dragon pushed his neck back and hurled Beowolf off him, again causing that werewolf to land hard on the ground a few yards away.

Now unable to see clearly until his wounds healed, and with blood still dripping from his throat laceration, the dragon decided that the best thing to do at this point was to flee the area. He could not kill these three right at this moment, and they would doubtless bring other warriors here to battle him. Drogg grudgingly realized that he would have to leave this human town and retreat back to the lair that he usually made home.

His attempted foray into this reality from his own was much more dangerous than during medieval times, when those of his species and others related to it walked much more frequently and comfortably in the world of mortals. The reptilian ravager now realized that he needed to become more familiar with the modern world of humanity and its unique set of challenges before he could again become master of a sizable section of it.

Yes, he would take the time to learn about the contemporary age of the human world, and after he did, he and the rest of his kind would again reign supreme. And he would once more have the opportunity to enjoy the delectable feast of a young virgin girl and hoard invaluable treasures of the earth, among other pleasures he could find in the mortal world and nowhere else.

Spreading his leathern wings, Drogg the mighty dragon took to the sky like something akin to a dinosaur with the flight capabilities of a bat.

He turned his longish reptilian neck only briefly towards the three warriors who drove him away and quickly hissed, "*There shall come a reckoning!*"

Dale continued to fire shots at the creature, hoping to hit his wings and drive him back to the ground, but within moments Drogg had managed to depart the village entirely. His saurian form looked astoundingly graceful as it rose far into the air, moving out of the Boogey Knights' line of sight with a speed rivaling that of an eagle.

Beowolf reverted to human as he slowly and painfully rose to his feet, favoring the mostly closed but still painful shoulder wound he had taken during this battle. *Much better than almost literally losing my head to the jaws of a dragon, though.* He then willed himself back to human form, his bio-mimetic clothing unraveling from the form of a cloth-like collar that it took when he morphed into his more massive lupine form to fully cover his default incarnation.

Dale ran over to him alongside Steven who, still in his "wolfed out" mode, was cleaning the blade of the ocher-colored blood it had spilled.

"Are you okay?" Steven asked his teammate.

"I'll be okay, I think," Mike replied, stretching his arms to help deal with the pain in his shoulder. "My chest wound will take some time to heal, but it's at least closed now. Still, I feel like a wreck."

"A wreck?" Dale asked sardonically. "You're lucky you're anything after jumping it head on like that. I don't think even you could come back from a pile of ash. Or dragon shit."

"That beast killed young girls," Mike replied with barely checked rage in his voice.

"Yeah, I know," Dale agreed as he stowed his shotgun. "Still, you came close to buying it for good this time."

"I think we all did," Steven stated very matter-of-factly. "For a minute there, I was wondering if we would make it through this one. The Boogey Knights aren't really the team I'd call first for a dragon attack. Maybe that vampire detective from L.A., but not us."

Dale took a deep breath. "You know, I always thought the 'Knights' part of our name was more metaphorical. Never expected to have to slay a dragon."

Steven sighed. "Dale, please."

Just then, before that exchange could continue any further, Alphonse walked out of the bar, followed cautiously by the patrons who were inside. "You three… are alive? But what of Drogg? He said he would kill my daughter!"

"Drogg left," Steven tried to reassure the understandably shaken man. "And I don't think he's coming back. Like any bully, he's only tough when he knows he can win. My son knows more about dragons than I do, though; I'll get his take on the matter when I get the chance. He can tell us a lot about them, and how we can effectively deal with Drogg if he ever does come back for his 'reckoning.' But I don't think we'll be seeing him again, here or anywhere."

Alphonse looked at the sky and said a prayer aloud. "Thank you for answering my prayers, o Lord. And please take care of Jenning and his sister now that they have passed into your heavenly realm. And thank you for not letting Jenning's terrible sacrifice be entirely in vain."

Steven looked back to his crew. "He's not talking to us anymore, so I think it's time to head home. And by 'head home,' I mean find a different way back, because I am *not* filing insurance papers for that van we trashed. Let the rental place chase down S.A.V.A.G.E. for the money."

"Speaking of," Steven continued, "we might need to hire a donkey cart to get us off this mountain. If we head to the airport in Sofia, we'll be dealing with Bulgarian security, so no one will be looking for..." he trailed off, mumbling to himself.

Dale turned to the barkeep. "Hey, Alf, you know any place we can get some horses? Maybe a pack mule or something?"

"I think we can arrange that," Alphonse said. "But might I suggest you first get a room for the night? You must be quite tired. And there are plenty of rooms at the inn. No one has come to this town for months."

"Sounds good to me," Dale replied. "After all this, I could use a shower and a couple days' worth of sleep."

"And while we're at it," Mike added, "is there any place to get pizza in this town? And do you happen to sell Mocha Cola? If so, I think it's Dale's turn to buy!"

"Sure thing," Dale said, slipping Mike's wallet unnoticed from his back pocket and dropping it into his jacket. "Drinks are on me."

END

CALL ME RUFUS

Alex Dumitru

Shelly Easton was about to be devoured. She had not been expecting it, had not prepared for it, and at the tender age of twenty, had very little in the way of a life to flash before her eyes. What was before her eyes instead was a headset, its little black microphone in front of her mouth. From the front it made her look cartoonishly surprised, like a little black oval saying, "Oh puddytat, you gonna get it now." It had not slid off because of the bun she had put her blonde hair into.

But she was not concerned with how the equipment allotted to her from California Dreamin' Travel Corp made her look. She was more concerned with the salivating, dripping maw mere inches from her vulnerable frame.

She had never thought of a mouth as a maw before. Had never had to unless she was watching Animal Planet. But this one was quite certainly a maw, like the kind on anglerfish. Full of crooked, long, needle-like teeth that did not so much fit together as they rioted themselves apart with each opening of the thing's jaw in front of her. The long arms that held her up by her own were not arms either, but whipping, slapping, impossibly strong tentacles akin to the limbs of an octopus.

But it was squid tentacles that cut at your flesh and burned like these ones did. She knew that from Animal Planet too.

Alex Dumitru
Call Me Rufus
Boogey Knights: Dark Warriors

The lights that had once illuminated the offices of the tele-sales department of California Dreamin' Travel had once been bright fluorescents that had bathed her cubicle and those around her in a soulless glow. But since the things had shown up – right when the humming, low and soft, had started – the lights began to strobe and flicker. This cast the rest of the ensuing horror into a vaudevillian stop motion around her, her friends – well, her co-workers, at least – were being ripped, torn, and maybe even... swallowed.

The thing that held her fast, aside from its prodigious amount of teeth, had a thick worm-like body, covered in fleshy ripples and wrinkles. It terminated at the floor into a tree-trunk of gnarled and knobby tentacles that roiled about it as it moved. It had no eyes. Neither did its companions.

But this disability had not stopped each of these beasts from zeroing in on their prey as they sat bewildered at their phones. Some of them had continued trying to get the people they had called to attend a ninety-minute presentation on time-shares so they could qualify for their all-expenses paid, four-star Caribbean cruise even as they heard what was happening around them. The screams... and the roars.

Shelly desperately wanted to shut her eyes, but they remained locked open. It was more than I could bear. I hadn't been thrilled when I got the call from them, spinning me their bullshit like a spider spins silk, but when I heard the fear in the voice of "Kandice" about her quota, I thought something might have been up. My kind of something. My daddy taught me these things.

It had been a boring night, I had just finished working out, and was contemplating cooking something or going to bed when the phone rang. Now I was here. Better than chili or another dreamless night. I blew some hair out of my face, lifted my shotgun to my shoulder, kicked my duffel towards it, and grinned.

"Excuse me," I said. I love starting that way. Almost as much as, 'Hey, asshole!'

The "head' of the creature menacing Shelly Easton turned to look at me. I don't think it so much "saw" a man wearing jeans, a Slayer tee, and work boots any more than it saw my scraggly excuse for a beard or my long black hair. Hell, even my shotgun, or anything else I was carrying in my duffel bag.

"Now," I continued, "let me put your mind at rest that this is not a sales pitch, so you can just... relax."

I pulled the trigger and watched the left side of the Mawhead's face detonate with a wet geyser of flesh and... whatever else was in there. It dropped Shelly Easton and shrieked. The others surrounding it, all busy until I came in, decided to look up from their food. About thirty, maybe thirty-five, blood-slicked mouths pointed at me in unison. In the sudden quiet I heard the moaning of the dead. Never a good sign. Several of the Mawheads sucked in tubules resembling insidious, pointed tongues.

Not good, I thought.

See, unlike Shelly Easton I knew the difference between tentacle and tubule. Tentacles, which I hate, are for catching, grabbing, and shredding. Tubules, which I hate *so much* worse, are for injecting. Injection of *what* will be left up to the biology of the animal. With these, I figured it was nothing good.

The satisfying *chik-chuk* of my shotgun broke the momentary silence and the Mawheads all bellowed in unison before heading for me. I pulled and the rest of my first target's head left the premises. It flopped to the ground, twitching. The others were rolling in with a slick swiftness.

Good. Anything is better than those damn sluggish "Sascrotch."

BLAM! Another load of buckshot ripped through one of the oncoming wave, and it splattered against the ceiling made of that shitty tile stuff you see in every sad little office. Another shot went straight down one of their throats and I had the sick satisfaction of watching its ass blow up. I laughed.

I then felt one of their tentacles slip around my boot. It had tried to go behind me.

"*Fuck* you!" I shouted jovially.

I was almost drowned out by the blast but didn't care. Class was in session, and I was gonna teach these inter-dimensional douche-nozzles a lesson.

The tentacle spasmed out instead of around and the Mawhead thumped to the floor.

Decent carpeting for a place like this.

Three shots left in the Persuader. I was going to need a plan sometime soon. I swung around and brought the stock of the Mossberg into the teeth of one of the beasties. They collapsed in and flew down its throat. Satisfaction again.

It reeled backwards and I glimpsed Shelly sitting there in a pool of pus and her own blood from the wounds in her arms. The expression on her face as she leaned against her desk suggested that she was stunned. Didn't blame her. Most folks aren't able to take this kind of thing. Just me and a few others, really.

As it came back down, I jammed the Mossberg into the folds of flesh in the trunk and pulled the trigger again. These things were softer than they looked, and they looked pretty squishy to begin with. It ripped in half from the barrel's persuasion, and I was finally gooped. Gooped with authority, in fact. I felt wet, but at least it wasn't pulling any Ridley Scott shit and burning.

The remaining creatures fell back at the sight of the others being cut down. Mossbergs are good for that, especially the .500. I kept it pointed at the swarm. I hoped to hell they couldn't count and had no idea that this thing only held eight rounds since I had blown six. One of them tested its luck. Make that seven, now. One left in there, a lot more out here. Usually in this situation I shake up the other guys' nerves with a good cobalt stare. But these fucks had no eyes. Shit.

I hoped they would realize that within a certain radius they would get hurt. So, I

took a step to my left, towards Shelly. They backed up. Good.

I took another slow step, and they moved some more. Farther away now. Very good.

"How are you doin'?" I asked Shelly. She didn't say anything.

"Hey!" I shouted. Shelly twitched and looked up at me. Her eyes were very round in the stuttering, jerking light.

"W'sup?" I asked again.

"Y-you… who are you?" she asked.

I grinned. "Call me Rufus. "Rufus Church. Pardon me if I don't shake your hand or nothin'. Sorta busy."

"S'okay. I'm Shelly Eas-"

45

"Yeah, read your name tag. Wanna get the fuck outta here, Shelly Easton?"

She nodded. Her headset jiggled a little. She was very much somewhere else, which was good. This was not a good place to be right now.

The Mawheads were getting impatient, and they were going to call my bluff any second. They had gotten very quiet, just hissing and slithering noises. The muzak was still playing and I could hear Amy Winehouse talking about how they tried to make her go to rehab. I hate this shit. Give me something a little harder any day.

"You're gonna have to stand up, okay Shelly?" I said.

She nodded and started to get up. Her arms brushed the desk, she winced, and then just like that she was back. Her breathing started to speed up, her mind started to reel in her skull, and her sanity started to stretch before snapping. I've seen it happen a million times. Holding up the shotgun with my right, I reached into my pocket with my left. I got my lighter and flicked it open. My duffel bag was at my feet, next to Shelly from when I had booted it.

"Get ready to grab that bag and run when I tell you. Got me?" I said to Shelly.

She needed a glass of water applied to her face, but she was still hearing me. And I was about to help with that anyway. If my hunch was right, this would give us enough surprise to get out of the immediate threat of the Mawheads and give me time to come up with something better. I flicked the wheel and was rewarded with a flame as long as a porn dick. So, it was pretty long. I held it up to the ceiling and waited. The sensors in sprinklers are really sensitive these days.

Just a few seconds later I was rewarded with a gush of cold water. It came down all over the office and made the whole place look like it had developed a thunderstorm, lightning and all. Just like I'd hoped. The Mawheads whipped around in confusion, and I looked to Shelly. Cold water: applied.

"Run!" I barked and grabbed her arm.

She scooped up my bag and we were off. We went out through the door I had entered. In the lobby the water was coming down too. And the Mawhead that had been chowing on a secretary when I came in still

46

had a machete in his skull. I snagged it and we kept moving. We passed the front doors and Shelly started pulling on my arm.

"It's over here! The door's over here!" she yelled.

"Yeah, I know," I replied.

"We have to get out of here!"

"I ain't done here."

Running while carrying a Mossberg, a machete, and with a telemarketer hanging on one arm is slow enough. Making conversation can make it more difficult. So, when I spotted what looked like a break room, I ducked in and pulled her with me. I slammed the door and took my flashlight out of my pocket, clicking it on.

"Shitty table, folding chairs, and snack machine," I muttered to myself.

Check, check, and check. It was a break room all right.

"What are you doing here?" Shelly Easton asked me.

"Taking a break?" was my response.

I looked up. No sprinklers in here. Weird. We were both soaked anyway. I wrung out my hair, setting the shotgun and the machete on the table.

"How did you even know that would work?"

"What?"

"The sprinklers. How'd you know?"

"Oh. No eyes. Figured maybe they'd hunt by vibrations. Y'know, like in 'Tremors' and shit. So, I set off the sprinklers. Smokescreen."

"What's 'Tremors?'"

I sighed. Nobody watches the classics anymore.

"Never mind."

"Rufus?"

"Yeah?"

"Why are they here?"

"Dunno."

"Why are you here?"

"To fuckin' kill 'em. And you offered me a cruise. You got a quarter?"

She looked at me blankly for a minute, so I clarified. "I want some Cheeto's."

"You're... hungry?"

"Fuck that! You ever read the back of a bag? Naw, it's for them. Don't know why, but the more unnatural something is, the more they like Cheeto's."

"Bait?" she asked.

"Bait," I confirmed.

"But the power's out."

I nodded. Then I put the stock of the Mossberg through the glass and got me some Cheeto's. Shelly didn't seem too pleased, though.

"I thought you said they hunt by *vibrations!*"

"Well, that won't help. Besides, it was just a theory."

Then something hit the door. It was a solid thump. Too solid.

Shelly screamed. "It's them!"

Another thump. Harder this time. Like...

"Fists," I said.

I grabbed my bag from Shelly, set it on the table, undid the zip. I started reloading the Persuader, thinking about how much I really, *really* hated tubules. Especially if I was right. Then I scooped out my most trusted companion, my greatest weapon and resource in my work, the thing every monster hunter, amateur or pro, should carry at all times: Duct Tape.

I strapped the light to the Mossberg's barrel, tucked the machete into my belt, and made my way to the door. Shelly was starting to sob.

"Chill the fuck out," I said. *Chik-chik!* "I *got* this..."

I reached out to the knob just as the door shook with another impact. My hand touched the brass and turned it. I knew what would be there before I opened it, though. If it was a survivor, it would have tried the knob first. So...

The door swung open. What looked at me in the glare of the flashlight was the only thing I liked encountering less than telemarketers: a zombie telemarketer. He was still wearing his headset, even.

It moaned at me. In the second before I pulled the trigger, I had time to take a few mental notes: Splits in the skin, black ooze seeping out, heavy decomposition, glowing eyes. Not quite a member of your run of the mill Romero troop, then.

BLAM!

Headshots still worked, though. I know I should have used the machete, but my main advantage against these fucks is that I don't follow their rules.

Shelly let out another scream as the zombie dropped. I stepped out into the hall, swinging my light back and forth. Nothing else there. The water had stopped flowing, just dripping intermittently.

I wondered how many of the Mawheads had used their tubules and how many had been too hungry to bother. Were the zombies for getting even more food for the Mawheads? Was that why they were nowhere to be seen? Were they making plans too?

So many questions and only seven rounds left. I turned to motion to Shelly that the coast was clear. She was standing in the doorway watching me with those big round eyes again.

"Why'd you have to shoot him?" she asked.

"Zombie," I said. Should have explained everything. Apparently, it didn't.

"Can't we fix it?"

"Y'ever hard-boiled an egg, Shelly?"

She nodded.

"Y'ever tried to fix *that?*"

She shook her head. She got it. She looked back to my duffel.

"What else is in there?"

"Help yourself," I said. "But make it fast."

A few moments later she walked out with my dad's old .44. My dad loved him some Dirty Harry shit. One time he asked a werewolf if it felt lucky right before capping the poor bastard.

My duffel was over her shoulder, and she looked pissed. I knew that look too. It happens if you see this shit, don't go crazy, and have something personal in it too.

"Was he a friend of yours?" I asked, looking at the Z.

"Not really. His name was Mark. He was always trying to get into my pants. But he didn't deserve that."

"They rarely do. You know how to use that?"

She smiled. "Point and shoot?"

"Good enough. Y'know, for zombies and shit. Let me handle the big ones. And careful, that thing will kick your head off if you're not ready for it,"

"Okay."

I chambered another round, my favorite sound in the whole world. I grinned. "Let's rock."

I knew after blowing Mark away that I had only a few seconds until the others came looking to see what the noise was. And I was right too. Shuffling at the end of the hall. Both ends. Zombie kill box. They lurched with an artificial, jerky movement that made them look like malfunctioning Muppets.

"Oh, no! You do not pull that Japanese shit on me!" I shouted and Persuaded the one at the front of the lines.

I didn't hit his head, but the contents of the shell blew out his neck, and the head didn't really have a chance after that. He crumbled and the rest kept coming. Shelly opened up with the .44 and I was right behind her.

I've always hated zombies. They're the reason my dad retired. His arthritis was making it difficult for him to reload fast enough, and he wasn't as light on his feet as he used to be. Couple close calls later and I was a solo act. They just keep showing up too.

I emptied three more shells into the advancing group and three more sets of headlights stopped glowing. I heard the shots behind me but didn't have the time to look.

Another shot and the wall behind one of the ghouls lit up with goop made luminescent, lit from my flashlight shining through his middle. He stumbled to the floor, his legs not working anymore. I dropped to a quick crouch and gave his head a crack with the stock. They were getting close.

I slung the Mossberg over my shoulder and pulled out the machete. One reaching hand went skittering off into the dark, the owner drooping to her knees when the blade thunked between her eyes. I should have been having fun, but these guys just aren't challenging for me anymore.

I took out the last few of them on my end without any more difficulty. I turned, getting ready to take out the others. With a rookie telemarketer on the other end things couldn't help but be worse, right?

50

Shelly Easton stood, gun in both hands, chest heaving, gore on her shirt, in front of a mound of heavily decomposed and brained bodies. The gun had been turned around and the butt was slicked with brain and blood. She didn't know how to reload, but she knew how to rock and roll apparently.

"You, um…you alright?" I asked.

She nodded.

"No bites or anything?"

She shook her head.

Then she looked at me, locking her eyes on mine, and spoke.

"Where are the rest?"

"Let's find out," I said and dangled the bag of Cheeto's I had stuffed into my pocket from my fingers.

Shelly smiled and reached up to her headset. Taking it off, she tossed it onto her pile of zombies. She reached up, shook her hair out and tossed a bobby pin away too.

"You sure you're okay?" I asked again.

She handed me the gun and the duffel. "Show me how to reload this and I'll be great."

I crouched down, unzipped the duffel, and went through the process of using a speed loader, but slowing things down so she could watch me. The lady was looking over my shoulder, and by the time I had finished demonstrating she was a step behind me.

She had been wearing a variation of business casual: nice blouse, earrings. But it had been casual Friday at California Dreamin', so her jeans hadn't been a violation. When I wiped off the stock and handed it back, she had taken off the blouse to reveal she was wearing a white tank top underneath it. It was still wet and slightly spattered with gore. Why was I suddenly turned on?

"More of those in the bag?" she asked.

I reached in and gave her another, words briefly eluding me. While crouching next to me she put her hand into the bag and began pulling out more ammo and stuffing them in her pockets. I was getting a little dizzy.

Shelly stood back up, her eyes glinting a little in the flickering light from the doors down the hall. At that moment the emergency lights kicked on, and she was in a brief silhouette. I took a deep breath and stood with her. I had pulled out my two favorite Glocks, Lucy and Ethel. My mom is the huge *I Love Lucy* fan. Not me. Really.

"Ready?" I asked.

"Fuck yeah," she responded.

Somewhere deep in my mind, Queen started playing for some reason.

We turned and walked back towards the offices. When we got there, I looked at the Mawhead corpse that had been eating the receptionist and smiled. They had no idea what was coming. Me and Shelly raised our feet and kicked the door in. The water on the floor sloshed and the decent carpeting squelched, but for some reason I heard that and also "Don't Stop Me Now" at the same time. I hadn't heard that song since my parents renewed their vows in '06.

Aside from that, the office was quiet. The lights still flickered, but no one and nothing moved.

"Are they gone?" Shelly asked.

I reached back into my pocket and grabbed the Cheeto's. I shook them briskly. Thirty or so heads bristling with teeth popped up like grotesque, deep-sea whack-a-moles.

"There you are, you ugly fucks!" I shouted.

I chucked the Cheetos at them and pulled Lucy out of my pocket.

Mawheads surged at us, but they were no more a match for small arms fire than they were for the Mossberg. Their heads began popping under the persuasion of Lucy, Ethel, and Dirty Harry. I thought briefly of Theseus and the Minotaur as we entered the maze of cubicles, still firing. It occurred to me that Theseus had never had the advantage of a Glock against such a beastie, and I made mental note to book a trip to Greece sometime.

Halfway through, one of the walls came down with a thud and I was suddenly pinned. The tentacles were slithering up at me, and the comic duo were separated as my arms were wrenched out to either side. My legs wouldn't respond under the slippery bulk of the thing holding down the cubicle wall. Teeth leered down in front of me, and a thick, white protrusion snaked out. Have I mentioned how much I hate tubules?

It had a look like an inchworm, pebbled on one side, but with a long, bone-white needle of a stinger at the end. My arms were screaming from the little teeth in the tentacles, and I was struggling to get my feet out from under. The tentacles dug in deeper, and Lucy and Ethel dropped from my hands.

But suddenly another hand was in front of my face. One that, until recently, had been working phones. Shelly grabbed the Mawhead by the end of its tubule and pulled. The thing lurched and followed like a huge, hideous puppy. She pressed the .44 under the jaw of the thing as it tried to rear back and squeezed the trigger. I only heard the shot as I pried myself from under the wall.

I rolled out of the way as another Mawhead came surging at me and I found myself in a soaking cubicle. No way out but through the Mawhead. My mind started to race, but then I remembered my dad and his number one tenet: "There is no such thing as an unarmed man."

I grabbed the computer monitor up from the desk, one of the cheap and heavy variety, not a flat screen. Raising it above my head I screamed like a caveman with a boulder and brought it slamming down onto the beast. Goop sprayed out and sparks flew.

"Eat that, you Lovecraftian fuck!"

I turned, grabbed the chair, and hurled that at the next one, knocking it back. By the time it had recovered I had already landed on it with two handfuls of pens. Yuck spewed from each puncture but I just kept making them until it stopped moving. I stood up and saw Shelly pouring lead into another one. I ran for Lucy and Ethel, snatched them up, and ran to her. As one slicked up behind the fighting telemarketer I gave it both barrels.

"*Ghraaaaaaaaghghg!* was all the banter I had left for that one. My adrenalin was up, my arms were sore, and there were still more of them.

"I'm out!" Shelly cried.

Her pockets were pulled up, chamber on the .44 flipped open. I tossed her Ethel.

"Only a few left!" I shouted back.

A few shots later, the office was quiet again. Almost. Somewhere, someone was sobbing. Or were they laughing?

"You blew it, you blew it!" the voice said, and we both realized it was behind us.

We looked, and at the end of a long passage that ran down the tail end of the cubicles stood a man in a soaked business suit. His voice was muffled from his hands over his face, and he was shaking his head.

"You all *blew it!*" he snarled, taking his hands down.

The man was bald, and his flabby features were sunken in, sad looking.

"You know this guy?" I whispered to Shelly.

"Mr. Corbough?" she said, lowering Ethel a little bit.

"They were going to give me *power!*" Mr. Corbough shouted. "But you people couldn't sell worth a *fuck!*"

His jowls were veined in a way that just didn't look right. And his voice still sounded like he might have been gargling something while he talked. As he got closer, we saw water leaking from his mouth.

"They told me it was going to be just like the *Mary Celeste,* or the Aztecs... or, was it the Mayans? Who gives a shit?" He laughed harshly. "But they just... got too *hungry*. Then they just... *came through...*"

"What the fuck are you talking about?" I asked.

Corbough looked at me with eyes that were too bright. And too green.

"No such thing as a free cruise," he said. "Fucker got me with that tongue thing. Like one of the worms at the bottom of a... tequila. Like in... meh..."

He trailed off and I saw the end of the tubule trailing from his leg like toilet paper stuck to a shoe. By the time I looked back to his face, Mr. Corbough was well on his way to joining the ranks of the living dead. I sighed and looked at Shelly.

"You wanna?" I asked her. "He's *your* boss."

She lifted Ethel back up, pointed it squarely between his eyes, and he started twitching.

"This is for everyone who didn't hang up on you, you lying sack of shit!" she said.

BLAM!

We walked out with the feeling of a job well done that I usually don't share. My truck was sitting where I left it. My duffel was a lot lighter, and my first aid kit was in there. I opened the door, pulled out the kit and started bandaging up Shelly's arms, then mine.

"So, do you just... do this?" she asked me as I worked.

"Yup."

"So, you're good at it." She did not phrase that in the form of a question.

"Yup."

"But you do it by yourself?"

"Yup."

"And it's... what? Some dark compulsion? Are you avenging your family? Or, what?"

"Mom and Dad live upstate in Chestnut Falls. I run a video store in the next town over."

"You work at a video store?"

"I *manage* a video store."

"Wow. But what about Ne-"

"Fuck Netflix."

"Ooookay. Not touching that. So, this is... a hobby?"

"No legal limit on monsters, not to mention they never go out of season," I said while finishing up my bandages. "Could you hold that there?" She put her finger where I requested. and I finished taping it down. "Thanks."

"No problem."

I looked at her again. She was blonde, she had suddenly become a badass, she could handle a gun with no training while wearing a wet tank top. And last, but not least, she was the sole survivor of a horrific event. I had gone my whole life waiting for this girl to follow the monsters out of the world of B-movies. And here she was.

"So... you wanna go get a burger?" I asked her.

"I'm a vegetarian," she responded.

Well, shit. Nobody's perfect. Still...

"So... you wanna go get a veggie burger? Harder to find this late, but doable."

She laughed, then handed my duffel bag full of guns, knives, and other high explosives back to me before going around to my passenger door. As she got in, I made a note to myself to ask Dad how he met Mom.

"So, where to now, Mr. Church?"

"I told you, baby," I said while turning the key. "Call me Rufus."

END

Valentine's Day isn't my favorite holiday even when I do have a special someone to share it with. This year I met someone special, alright. He's so special he even haunts my dreams!

HEARTS OF DARKNESS

Kevin Heim

February 14, 2014

Things were not going as well as I'd hoped, though in many ways, it's my fault for hoping for anything better. There are few clichés as well known in the world of monster hunting as, "Don't read aloud from the Book of the Dead!"

It doesn't have to exactly be the Book of the Dead to qualify as a bad idea, but in this case that is exactly what the title translates to, from Greek. That's right; I read a passage from the *Necronomicon*. Out loud!

So really, I should have expected nothing less. I found the book in… wait for it… a cabin in the woods. Yes, I am very aware of how stupid taking the book sounds, but there were other forces at work, and it made more sense at the time for the tome to stay with me than to let something else gain access to it.

What exactly was it that was trying to get the book? Okay, I know how this sounds, but I think it was aliens from Zeta Reticuli. It was in the White Mountains, where such extraterrestrials have been sighted before. I probably should be telling that story, except that was on New Year's Eve, and today is Valentine's Day. Plus, it may prove embarrassing for a certain cryptozoologist and her fiancé, and I promised Dr. Victoria Waddell I wouldn't say anything that could get her fired.

So yes, there was a thing out there that I never got a good look at. I called it the "Creeper in the Woods," but I'm pretty sure it was one or more alien beings, and I don't trust anyone to wield the power of the *Necronomicon* safely, human or otherwise.

Obviously, that should have included me. I thought the index would have been safe to read. I was only going through it to see why aliens might be interested. Now here I am, being stalked by what I can only assume is the literal Boogey Man. Good thing fighting boogeymen is kind of my specialty.

I say the Boogey Man, but really, the term is used so loosely that could mean anything from Bigfoot to Jack the Ripper to a sentient shadow that animates objects to maintain permanence when the light should banish it. This boogeyman is more in the Creepy Pasta vein.

It's been like, five years since Slenderman broke the Internet, with plenty of copycats following. One website, BugOut.com, changed its format shortly after, replacing its stories and videos of people freaking out in public to hosting stories and videos of urban legends and monster attacks.

The new format worked, and they gained a lot of popularity (i.e., advertising revenue) as people wanted to get in on the ground floor of the next Creepy Pasta. One of the early hits was a character called the "Fraidy Man." He was a typical boogeyman figure, but he could only attack people while they slept, at least that's how the stories started. Some writers described how he looked, but then his original creator, Westley Roberts, said "Fraidy" could change his shape inside the dreams he uses to go after people, so he could look like anyone or anything.

Fraidy, as he was now known thanks to that post, was then linked to lots of unsolved murders where people seemed to have died violent deaths while asleep. The stories got even wilder, attributing strange events from over a hundred years ago to Fraidy. Fraidy was now Jack the Ripper. Fraidy was now the Phantom of the Opera. Fraidy was now the mean old school nurse that terrified one author when he was a child.

The zeitgeist had spoken, and a Fraidy movie was quickly greenlit by New Line, hoping to have the next *STAB!* Franchise in theaters. It all went to shit when Roberts was found dead in his house in Indiana. Naturally he was in his own bed, mutilated, with the word FRAIDY written in three-foot tall letters, painted onto the bedroom wall with Westley's blood.

Two neighborhood kids were arrested but no charges were ever filed due to lack of forensic evidence. Having a real, active unsolved murder attached to the stories played great with the sickos, but no businesses wanted to be associated with that kind of press, and when all the ad revenue dried up, and rumors of lawsuits started to circulate, the page's owners deleted everything. Even the links back to BugOut were erased from other sites, and that takes some serious Net Ninja skillz. Google doesn't even show dead screencaps.

Whoever wanted to make Fraidy go away worked really hard at it. The fact that Westley had started out as a computer programmer in Wisconsin before moving to Silicon Valley with a DotCom startup, only to be left penniless and homeless when that company collapsed right after his arrival just added to the mystery, even though all of that went down years before he moved to Indiana and started working with BugOut.

That brings me back to… me. A month and a half ago, I read the Table of Contents to the *Necronomicon,* out loud. I also skimmed through the Index, but only mumbled a handful of words, as I could hardly pronounce every little syllable if I'd wanted to. How is this connected to the Fraidy Man? One of the more popular stories about him was that he used to be a real person but was turned into a dream demon by the *Book of the Dead*, and now he wants to find the book and use it to come back to life. I assumed the brainiac that came up with that particular legend was basing the *Book of the Dead* on the one from the 1990s *Mummy* movies, since those movies attributed life restorative abilities to the *Book of the Dead*, and death curses to the *Book of Life*. But who says urban legends have to be rooted in facts, or make sense?

Then about three days ago, I found the book in the wrong place on my bookshelf. Now, I know keeping a book like that in my own apartment is a bad idea, and I was planning to take it to the Theurgy Society's New England headquarters as soon as possible for safe keeping. The Theurgy Society is a secret organization based out of London, England, but they set up branches around the world to use whenever and wherever a threat of a… cosmic nature has a possibility of manifesting. I was a member of Theurgy back in the '80s when they were preparing for the Harmonic Convergence of 1987, and they contacted me again to help make sure the world didn't end when the Mayan Calendar ran out in 2012. Yes, a lot of it is conspiracy-theory doom-prepping, but the fact is that if groups like the Society didn't take action, the world really would have ended several times over by now.

These days there is a prediction that the Ragnarök of Norse mythology will happen later this month, which means they are manning the proverbial battle stations again. And by 'proverbial' I mean 'literal'.

My buddy Pete Fitzhume and his father, who is also Pete Fitzhume, are the caretakers of the Deary Center in Ripton, MA, where all Theurgy records and archives for the area are stored. They have the facilities to keep esoterica like my *Necronomicon* relatively safe, but Ripton is on the far side of the state from me. Finding time to drive at least three and a half hours each way, means losing a potential day of work (and two full tanks of gas), so I've been procrastinating for a while. There's a whole lot of nothing in that part of Massachusetts, and my PT Cruiser isn't great on road trips, so I haven't made it a priority yet.

Besides, I didn't see the rush to hand the book over, since nothing happened when I read those little portions out loud. December 31st, nothing. January 1st, nothing. February 1st, still nothing. It wasn't until the 11th, three days ago, that I began to worry I may have made a mistake.

I've seen a lot of weird things, and done a lot of weird things, so it's not uncommon for me to have dreams that most people would consider nightmares. I didn't even think it unusual for the Fraidy Man to pop up in one of my dreams, assuming it was *just* a normal dream.

And it was almost that easy for him to trick me. In the dream, he goaded me into fetching my copy of the *Necronomicon* and reading a passage. I started for it but balked at actually pulling it off the shelf. I didn't even look directly at it, since I was fully aware that the book was dangerous. I didn't have to believe in the Fraidy Man to know about his desire to find a way to return to life within that tome. So, I slid it under a stack of magazines on the same shelf and probably said something very clever before the dream ended.

When I woke, I was in my guest room where the bookshelves are. I was lying down on the floor, but I had clearly moved there from the couch in my living room, where I fall asleep almost every night watching television. I used to have other people living with me, like family members or roommates, but now it's just me and a couple cats in a three-bedroom apartment in Salem, Massachusetts. I don't have to worry about oversleeping because if I'm not up by 6:30 AM, I'll have one cat doing lunges on my bladder while the other tests how scratch-proof my nose is. In a way it's sweet, because in all other respects Kali and Oddball don't get along, so any sign of solidarity between them is an accomplishment.

I got up off the floor and, after feeding the cats, made a pot of coffee while considering the odds that I was sleepwalking into the guest room while dreaming about walking into the guest room. I used to get up a lot earlier, but since starting with Alert, I don't have regular hours, and mornings are "business casual" unless I get called in. The HybraDyne plant I used to work for in Kingsport is getting shut down, and I was part of the first wave of layoffs.

By the end of March everyone from the Kingsport lab will be unemployed or transferred to the company's robotics division in California. I'm still under a Non-Disclosure Agreement so all I'm really free to say is that I hope they have a good surplus of guidance system components, because their net will be pretty useless if the satellites come crashing out of the sky. Remote automation requires an uninterruptible signal, and the components I used to make for them were essential to that task.

So, this is me sounding bitter. I do have a weekend job at Miskatonic University, in Arkham, but when Dr. West isn't on campus, it usually doesn't provide more than four hours of work, cleaning his labs and offices. Being his technician barely even pays for my weekly coffee addiction. In addition, I have a consulting contract with Alert, a paranormal investigation and elimination firm, also in Arkham, and I'm hoping they'll pick me up full time now that I'm available.

Alert is actually an acronym, standing for After-Life Experiment Research Team. Marketing showed that people were more likely to call us if they didn't know what the letters mean though, so A.L.E.R.T. became Alert. Despite being on the fringe of what society accepts as legitimate research, the company does a lot of work in the Massachusetts North Shore area. I've looked into more creaky floor boards and raccoon dens than I have actual paranormal phenomena, but work is work.

For now, my primary source of income is my military pension, and that's pretty underwhelming.

Point is, I have anxiety dreams all the time, mostly related to money but often enough they are tied to uniform inspections, homework, missing the bus, and other minutiae of everyday life that gets blown out of proportion in dreams. One time I dreamt my son was dead, and another time I dreamt that my best friend from college had been brought back to life through questionable means. Both of those were horrifying, and played on real, albeit subconscious fears of mine, so meeting the Fraidy Man and avoiding the *Book of the Dead* did not register high on my list of bad dreams. The only thing that really disturbed me was the sleepwalking, but not enough to get me to do a WebMD search. I really just didn't give it much thought.

I also didn't care enough about the nightmare to mention it when I checked in with the Alert guys to see if they had any work for me. That was also a mistake, because Fraidy not only popped up in my dream again Wednesday night, but I could have gotten a referral bonus for bringing in a demon based on an urban legend before people started getting hurt.

Wednesday night, people started getting hurt.

My bedroom is cluttered (and that's putting it very mildly) and I don't have a lot of space between the doorway and the bed, so I pretty much took two steps and hoisted my leg up to kneel on the foot of the bed. It's on a frame with drawers in the bottom, so it starts two feet above the floor, then there's a big honking box spring mattress before I get to the memory foam mattress and the down mattress cover. That's a good four and a half feet to get to the top; if I'm sore I literally have to climb the frame and mattresses to get in bed, which explains why I'm content to fall asleep on the couch so often.

Wednesday wasn't one of those sore days though, so after changing into shorts and a loose tee-shirt, I just hopped up and plopped down face first onto the comforter. There's only a four-foot clearance above the mattress so I can't even kneel straight up without hitting my head on the ceiling, and I've grown accustomed to lying down, rolling towards the head of the bed, and wrapping myself in a sheet as I move, like a human burrito. It works for me.

It didn't work this time. As soon as I was horizontal, I found myself submerged in a thick liquid. Thicker than water, to be sure, and just like the saying goes, it turned out to be blood. Of course, this was another dream, but I didn't know it at the time. I was inexplicably face up in a pool of blood, surrounded by ravenous-looking humanoids. They looked like a cross between vampires and zombies, and they were clearly feral. The monsters in the movie version of *I Am Legend* came to mind.

For many people this would have shock value, if not actually inducing terror, but… I mentioned I was in the military for twenty years, right? Didn't mention which branch though, and that's because it doesn't officially have a name. The important part is that it's the department within the Department of Defense that deals with monsters. To be more precise, I have been surrounded by hungry vampires before, and I've been surrounded by hungry zombies before. Being surrounded by hungry "zompires" was quite frankly new, but not that impressive.

"I hope this isn't the best you've got!" I shouted to no one in particular. I wasn't 100% positive this was a dream, but I did know that someone was behind it. If they were really going to attack me, the zompires wouldn't be waiting for me to respond to their presence.

"We aren't here for you; we want the child!" The head zompire (?) said to me. He was standing upright and wearing black clothes under a black robe, in stark contrast to the others, who were all hunched over and wore nothing but shredded remains of normal street clothes. His voice was like a loud whisper, as though the wind was yelling at me, and there was just the hint of a European accent, though nothing distinguishable.

He gestured to my chest, and I saw a baby covered in blood laying on top of me. I had a brief flash of panic, wondering how I can conceal the baby from them, before I realized that I was definitely dreaming. The baby hadn't been there before, the head zompire wasn't there at first either, and the blood wasn't pungent enough to be real. I also still hadn't been attacked, which was growing more nonsensical by the moment.

"There is no child; you're fighting over a shoe." Sure enough, when I looked down again, a bloody shoe was on my belly, sliding off into the muck. "And if you're really looking for fresh blood, why are you so interested in a puddle of honey?" The viscous fluid remained just as thick, but it was now clearly agave nectar. I knew it wasn't real honey, but I was okay with a minor mistake like that, especially when I had just turned a baby into a sneaker. Besides, it kept the reddish tint, so it was more believable as a perceived mistake rather than a shift in reality.

Yes, I was feeling smug when I should have been figuring out who was attacking me and what their agenda was. I started to stand so I could fight if the situation called for it, but the zompire leader kicked me in the chest and I was left sitting, leaning back on my elbows.

Only that didn't happen either. I fell backwards, my arms catching nothing solid to support my torso against. With no leverage I just fell, quickly smothered in the sticky syrup. I was unable to breathe and unable to swim. But again, I reminded myself I was dreaming, and I wasn't going to be beaten in my own head.

I curled up into a fetal position and 'found' a pocket of air inside my T-shirt to allow me to breathe while coming up with a plan. That's when the clawed hand grabbed my head and held me down. Physical contact hadn't happened yet, so I wasn't sure if the monsters *could* touch me till that moment. The fact I was being held down, even in a dream, meant there was a chance that I could be hurt. Maybe I'd suffocate in my sleep, or strangle myself with a sheet, or some other means of accidental death in bed. Being asleep didn't mean I wasn't in danger.

I still needed to breathe, because those are the rules my mind expected, so I kept one hand on the collar of my tee, pulled up to my mouth. With my left hand I reached up and grabbed a finger. I assumed he would be too strong to break his grip while struggling against the thick syrup, but I doubted he'd keep his hold on me if I bent his pointer backwards and broke it.

It worked, but not because I believed it would work. He was too startled by the resistance and pain to bend the dreamscape to his will right away. I know this because I felt the hand turn into a large spider with bristles on its legs after I was already pulling myself up by the arm. The arm quickly became a tentacle, but I'd already witnessed the frantic scramble to keep up, the same thing I'd been doing earlier in the dream.

This had to be a coordinated attack by someone adept at dream manipulation. It was then that I remembered the previous night's dream, when the Fraidy Man had guided me to my bookshelf.

Suddenly there I was, standing in my living room in front of the bookshelf again. And the Fraidy Man, still wearing the look of the zompire king, smiled at me from the reflection in my window. The window is inset on a narrow stretch of wall with bookshelves on either side of it. In the real world I keep it covered with heavy curtains so sunlight doesn't come in. I'm not much of a fan of sunlight, so seeing the glass, and especially the reflection of someone that wasn't in the room with me, pissed me off. My apartment, my rules.

"You're pretty good, Ronnie!" The Fraidy Man was in my head, so I'm sure he knew that being called Ronnie was a childhood irritation for me. "I might have fun tormenting you for weeks before I tire of you."

"What torment? You're dreaming if you think you have the upper hand on me!" I was raising my voice a bit, which I knew wasn't necessary, but I get very defensive when accused of something I didn't do, which it turns out includes being accused of getting scared. "You just made a bunch of stuff happen that should have frightened me. It didn't work. Go home, Fraidy; you're drunk."

He lunged at me through the reflection, but it wasn't exactly fast, and I easily grabbed both his arms, holding him there. "If I head-butt that window, will you be shattered with the glass? I really want to find out!"

Fraidy finally looked as though he knew he didn't have the situation under control. Most monsters I've encountered in my life either run off of pure instinct, or have some kind of power complex, thriving on the sensation of being able to dominate other beings. Monsters are a lot like people in that respect.

"I'll swallow your soul, bitch!" he practically screamed at me, but his struggles to escape my grip betrayed his panic.

He no longer spoke like an angry gust of wind; it was more like an exaggerated puppet. If the voices of Grover and the Cookie Monster were blended into one over-the-top growl, it would be a decent impersonation of this guy. "You sound like you're having a nightmare on Sesame Street when you lose control; it's cute."

Then I remembered watching *Smile Time* on television ten years back or so, and I decide not to give him any ideas. "Screw this. You're in my head, now... bitch!"

I pulled his arms towards me, making him lean his face through the window. In retrospect he could have made his arms longer, or jerked me into the window with him, or any number of other responses. I didn't realize it, but he was playing me.

When his shocked face got close enough, I looked down and thrust forward, crushing his nose with the top of my head. I felt some kind of impact, but it wasn't solid, like bone on cartilage should be. Turning up to look at what happened, I saw the image of a grotesque demon, possibly built out of human bodies, carved into his face. Not face I realized; it was just plain flat skin, save for the etchings. I tried to make sense of it and noticed that there were letters carved onto him, nestled among the pictures.

Thinking I might have stumbled across some kind of weakness, I read the syllables I could make out. "Ca'n Dar, Katardi, Natura--"

I stopped and pulled away from the page in front of me. The bastard wasn't there; it was that damned book of the dead again! Only this time I was holding it up, opened to a page roughly in the middle. And I was wide awake now, my bare feet cold against the floor in mid-February. He tricked me into reading out loud, and I fell for it, even after I knew that was what he was going to do.

I slammed the book shut and took it into the kitchen, where I used an entire roll of Saran Wrap to entomb the fiendish folio in cling free plastic (okay, it was actually the generic Sam's Mart brand plastic wrap). For good measure, I put it in the freezer, a tried-and-true method of neutralizing scary books that I learned from Joey Tribbiani.

Thursday morning, I drove to Arkham to wait outside the office of the paranormal investigators and heard on the radio that a freak earthquake had disturbed portions of Essex County in the Massachusetts North Shore. Few people felt the tremors, and it didn't register on any seismographs except for one in Beverly, and even there it only measured 0.3 on the Richter scale. I didn't feel it myself, but I was in the midst of a battle with an imaginary dream phantom, or whatever, so I had an excuse.

One thing they never told me about fighting dream phantoms is that there is no refresh stage during Rapid Eye Movement sleep, probably because I remained at least marginally active physically, instead of enjoying that sweet, sweet sleep paralysis. I was pretty exhausted and wasn't paying that much attention to the radio. Turns out, they also reported that at least twelve graveyards were either damaged in the earthquake or desecrated by opportunistic flash mob vandals. Each of them had one grave upturned, and they happened to be the oldest graves in each of the cemeteries.

What did grab my attention was, right as I was pulling into Saltonstall Street near Miskatonic University's campus, the morning show hosts were interrupted by a more serious announcer. The news anchor, normally not in the studio that early, stated that three people were reported dead and seven more injured in the vicinity of Ravine Lane in Arkham, in what was being described as a massacre involving drug users, perpetrated against the city's homeless.

Ravine Lane was only ten minutes away from me, so I cut a left and headed over to check it out. They built a community center there something like four years ago, before I lived in New England, but last year it was a homeless shelter. Now it's officially closed, and unofficially still a homeless shelter just with no heat or electricity.

I couldn't get too close, since it was considered an active crime scene, but I saw covered bodies being moved into ambulances, and people were being triaged and treated for their injuries on the spot. Not enough ambulances to get everyone to the hospital at once, I guessed. They all had wounds consistent with being bitten by animals or zombies, but from the brief snippets of conversation I heard, there was only one attacker, and he or it moved really fast.

I have some experience with zombies, and despite what the movies and video games claim, they don't move fast. Their greatest weapon is surprise... and strength of numbers. Right, so their two greatest weapons are surprise and strength of numbers... and general disbelief. Anyway, a single zombie couldn't have done all this unless it found these people while they were asleep, and the ones it killed should have already been reanimating by then. This couldn't have been zombies.

Whatever it was had to be incredibly strong; one victim had been thrown into a tree. It also had to be fast; they had all fled in different directions right after the first one was attacked. And even though it bit some people, it left plenty of meat and blood, so it seemed to be killing for sport or to spread a disease.

I know of plenty of types of creatures that meet two of those conditions, but not all three. Werewolves eat their prey and are hard to confuse with humans when they are big enough to toss people around. Vampires drain their victims, and rarely bite anyone they don't intend to kill or enthrall. Ghouls, wights, revenants, sasquatch, gremlins, pixies, infiri, killer robots from the future, deep ones, oompa loompas, killer klowns from outer space, and toddlers were also easily ruled out. Okay, maybe not the oompa loompas, but I think they only hunt in packs.

Then I remembered my dream last night, and the partial incantation I read in my sleep. It was possible that I'd summoned a demon, or partially summoned one, and that could mean any number of nasty things might be roaming the woods around Arkham. Or did I raise the dead, only for the Fraidy Man to take possession of the body, and now he was running around killing people with a body I prepared for him? Whatever it was, it was bad, and I may have played a role in making it happen.

I kept an eye on the EMTs and their patients to make sure none of them started turning into undead monsters, and then I called Scáth (pronounced "Skaw") Hazzard, the head of Alert. Scáth was hired to take charge of the Miskatonic Valley region two years ago, primarily due to an insurance foul-up regarding his last name. It turned out his great-grandfather Wilbur had a history of taking on criminals and weird threats, alongside a team of scientists and vigilantes back in the 1940s.

This helped secure Scáth a place in management that he may not have been 100% qualified for. He stepped up though, and the fact that Arkham hasn't already been sucked into a dimensional vortex validates his position within the organization.

Scáth told me to bring in the book, but when I mentioned that the Theurgy Society has a location in Ripton that can safely handle containment of such artifacts, he sounded relieved and suggested I take it straight to them. I agreed immediately, since making the trip on Alert business meant I'd be on the clock. Getting paid takes some of the suck out of wasting a whole day driving to no-man's land and back.

When I put a call through to Pete Fitzhume, Jr, I had to leave him a message. I wasn't about to risk driving to Ripton in *my* car if there wasn't even anyone on site, so I went back to Salem to grab lunch at my favorite pizza place while waiting for a callback. Since I'm not an active member of the Theurgy Society, I'm not entrusted to hold onto a key to the club house, though it would probably be smart for at least one other person in the area to be able to unlock the door.

Pete gave me a call around noon, but it turned out he and his father were both visiting his uncle Emmet in Washington D.C., just in case the upcoming "Viking Apocalypse" turned out to be the real deal. They wouldn't be back in Ripton until Saturday at the earliest. I left the Flying Saucer Pizza Company to return home so I could get on my computer. My super high-tech flip phone isn't the best at surfing the World Wide Web, but I got it for free by mailing in four cereal box tops, so I'm satisfied with it.

Once home, I logged into Facebook and contacted the S.A.V.A.G.E. messenger group. Yes, the letters stand for something semi-clever, but this is one of those cases where the acronym came first and the meaning came later, so it's a bit awkward. "Society for Assessing the Viability of Abominations as Good or Evil." Long story short, it's a network of monster hunters and experts founded by Professor Charles Savage, so it's easy to see why that particular acronym was forced onto us. The vast majority of data is still stored in an old online forum, but for chatting with other members Facebook is just more convenient.

S.A.V.A.G.E. is also where I first met Dale Parker and Mike Nero, my fellow "Boogey Knights". It's a terrible pun and I immediately regretted naming us that, but it caught on, and started getting used by other hunters who worked together to fight 'boogeymen' under the S.A.V.A.G.E. umbrella. I started using the site while I was active duty, and since I wasn't allowed to do any freelance work at that time, I used the alias 'Steven Pertwillaby' for my online account, but my handle is "Crazy1van". Dale, Mike, and I have only worked together a few times in person, and there was a case involving vampires that caused something of a rift between us, but we have helped each other on several cases since then, even if only by providing tactical information. I wasn't sure I needed Mike or Dale, but if anyone was going to be able to help me out, it would be one of these self-proclaimed Boogey Knights.

I sent out a message requesting aid from anyone with experience fighting dream demons or handling the *Book of the Dead*, with the topic *CALLING ALL NIGHTMARE WARRIORS*. Username "Chozen1" got back to me within 15 minutes and had plenty to say about Fraidy. He promised to meet me in 24 hours and recommended I keep the *Necronomicon* somewhere so that I couldn't get to it when I went to bed that night, like a safety deposit box or the Moon.

I didn't have access to either one, so I put it back in my freezer, but only after placing it inside a 24-inch by 18-inch by 8-inch ForeverWare container, and then filling that container with water. I doubted Sleeping Ivan would be able to read a book that was encased in ice.

After eating five pounds of tater tots and a tub of Rocky Road ice cream (I had to empty the freezer to make room for the book's container), I went to bed, ready for anything. The Fraidy Man appeared all right, but this time he just showed up sitting in a lounge chair wearing a Christmas sweater and sipping some flaming drink from a goblet. Oh yes, and the room where we were meeting was on fire, as was Fraidy. His face looked like an undercooked meatloaf, but I was sure it would brown quickly enough in this heat.

"Not bad, concealing the book where you can't reach it." He still sounded like he was gargling Muppets. "I applaud the effort. You can't stop me, of course, but now we have this time to chat. Have a seat."

I thought about how the portion of the room behind me must be nice and cool, with a comfortable chair in reach, but when I moved to find a seat, it was all flames and burning furniture. "I guess the 'control' I exhibited last night was just a ruse on your part?"

"Yeah, I guess so. Now, *sit!*"

I felt my body propelled into a beanbag chair, the vinyl melting everywhere I touched it. I was plenty uncomfortable, but I didn't feel like I was sustaining third-degree burns.

"Okay, so you have me at a disadvantage. You seem unable to hurt me, though. Aren't you supposed to kill people in their sleep?"

"Don't believe everything you read on the Internet, kid. If I wanted you dead, you wouldn't have survived the first night."

"So, you think you can make me help you resurrect the dead? Build a better body? Go on a murder spree?" I struggled but couldn't stand up or even roll over and fall out of the seat. I was stalling, but he could tell I was stalling, which could only mean he was stalling too.

"Nice little life you set up for yourself in New England, Ronald. I just want a part of the action. Bed and Breakfasts, maple candy, lobster bisque, elm str—"

"Oh, shut the hell up! If you want to tell me your evil plans, go for it. Otherwise, can we just fight? You smell like a tire fire and sound like you have puberty stuck in your throat. I won't even go into how you look. So just bring it on, or is the Fraidy Man really a fraidy cat?"

"You may have a lot of guts, but you aren't much in the brains, are you? This is *my* show, and you'll dance when *I* pull your strings! You can't taunt me into releasing you, and if I can't hurt you, I can definitely manipulate you." The exposed polystyrene beads in the seat suddenly turned into spider eggs, and thousands of tiny arachnids swarming up over me and into my mouth, ears, and nose.

Spiders. Why did it have to be spiders?

Naturally I responded by panicking. I thrashed about, completely disoriented. I tried imagining I was standing up straight, leaning against a wall, even floating on my back in a swimming pool. Nothing changed; I was still engulfed in spidery goodness, and I was agitated enough that I had to open my mouth to scream, allowing in… a flood of spiders.

I decided to try something different. Spiders have always been a phobia of mine, but it's really about the size and multitude than the threat any one individual creature could pose. Put a spider in my hair, and I'll freak out until I get it out, but if the spider is on my arm, or somewhere else I can see, I'm not nearly so bothered. So, if I tried thinking of the swarm as a plethora of individual spiders, maybe they wouldn't give me the wiggins?

No, I was wrong; so very, *very* wrong! Making them into one-at-a-time spiders made me contemplate just how many there were, and that overwhelmed me completely. If this was a normal dream, I would have woken in a cold sweat right then.

"Before you slip fully into despair, consider how this night's going for you." His voice seemed to be coming from directly in front of me, but I wasn't about to open my eyes with all those creepy crawlies on my face. "You and I are going to make history tomorrow night, and it will go much easier for you if you cooperate.

I felt like I was passing out, which had me curious as to whether people can pass out within dreams, but Fraidy decided to play one more card before letting me fold.

"And just so you know, those deaths last night are on *you*! Pleasant dreams!"

I woke to the sound of angry cats who were certain they were going to die if I didn't get into the kitchen and feed them immediately. Oddball, a tuxedo that was not above punching noses when the giant food dispenser overslept, was sitting on my chest. One front paw was already raised ready to strike. He wasn't using his claws though, so at least he wasn't that desperate yet.

Kali was at the foot of the bed. The American longhair/Maine coon mix had a plastic bag with her, and she was happily licking the plastic, knowing that I detested the sound. She was of a very different mindset than Oddball. Oddball always insisting that I wake on time, a time which became earlier and earlier; maybe Oddball's internal clock only allowed for a 23-hour day. Kali, on the other hand, usually left me to wake in my own way. Her specialty was herding me to the bedroom at night, because she knew that the earlier I got to sleep meant the earlier

I'd wake up and feed her. If she was on the bed trying to get me up alongside Oddball, I must have slept way later than I should have.

One look at the alarm clock confirmed it; 11:23 am. I felt my swollen nose and discovered that Oddball had indeed been using his claws. I had simply slept through the assault. I rolled out of bed and stumbled to the kitchen, poured myself a cup of Amaretto Roast, and fed the cats. The coffee was brewed automatically on a timer set for 8:00 AM and was already well on its way to being cold. I thought about reheating it in the microwave but didn't. I was at least partially responsible for three innocent people dying; I didn't deserve hot coffee.

I was expecting "Chozen1" in about half an hour, so I got a quick shower and started up the desktop computer to see if there was anything new regarding Fraidy. The computer took a while to load Windows, like it always does, and I got dressed during the interim. Going straight to Messenger, I found three new comments waiting for me.

"MyOhMya" informed me that the book was a trap, and I never should have opened it. "MarMik" told me that the cabin where I found it was a trap and a mysterious agency seeds remote locations like that with occult artifacts just so people like me would find them. "Stabbo" (I knew this one was Dale Parker) commented that defeating a nightmare creature was all about lucid dreaming. None of this exactly revealed new insights into what I could do about Fraidy, but I definitely need to explore the idea that someone planted the book in a remote cabin on purpose. If this whole Dream Phantom thing was a setup, somebody had a lot to answer for.

My visitor came to town in an old, *really* old, Oldsmobile. I think the color was called *Curdled Cream*, but hey, it had Michigan plates, so if he drove here in that thing, it's clearly a better ride than my 2003 PT Cruiser Turbo. We had agreed to meet at the Ravine Lane center in Arkham, and I was fifteen minutes late, but that was okay because he was two hours behind schedule. I had the book, still frozen in seven inches of ice, in the hatchback of my car.

I stepped up to shake his hand and immediately withdrew it, recognizing the prosthetic on his right arm. "Are you the 'Chozen One'?"

"Call me Dusty. Are you 'Crazy One-van'?"

"Call me Steven," I countered, and gestured towards the woods adjacent to the building. "This is where the people were attacked Tuesday night. I'm not sure what it was, but the Fraidy Man suggested I summoned it via the *Book of the Dead*."

"Nothing good ever comes from *Anthropodermic Bibliopegy*, Stevie. Grimoires bound in human skin will always lead to trouble. Now, why don't you hand the book over and I'll take it from here. Sending these skin-jobs back to Hell is what I do."

I didn't know what "Anthropodermal Bibliography" meant, but I assumed the "anthro," "dermal," and "biblio" parts meant man-skin-book, and I didn't think I wanted any further clarification than that.

"Not even the copies of the *Necronomicon* at Harvard or Miskatonic have skin on them. Does that make it more magical than normal?"

"Look… Steve, I don't have all the answers for you. I know that book is bad news, I know that Fraidy will keep hounding whoever has it, and I know that it's my job to keep it out of the wrong hands. Right now, that means *your* hands. So, load it into the Delta and I'll be on my way. Your problems will be over, and I can get back to work."

I wasn't sure this guy had the right attitude, but he seemed to know what he was doing, and honestly, I wouldn't mind not having to deal with the Fraidy Man anymore.

"Back to work on what? Do you destroy these books for a living? Translate them so you can find the counter-spells to their powers?"

"What? No, I work retail. I had to take off four days of work to make this trip. The book is going into my meat freezer for safe keeping. Now let's get moving; chop, chop!"

"Wow. No, that's not how I do things. This is already a problem I have to deal with. At least three people have died because of me."

"Geeze, don't be so melodramatic. Everyone dies, and that nightmare monster is the one that caused it, not you. Now come on; I got this. You asked for *my* help, remember?"

"For a 'Chozen One', you're kind of a jerk, you know that?"

"Sure, and for a 'Crazy One', you're a real uptight douchebag. What's your point?"

"My point is, I don't want to let the book go if it may be needed to trap the dream demon or return some undead monster to the grave."

74

I closed the hatch on my car, making it clear I wasn't passing the ForeverWare container to him anytime soon. I was pretty sure he couldn't lift it himself with only one hand. That's kind of insensitive of me; I guess I am a douchebag.

"Alright, what if I get you a hotel room and we set up some kind of dream stake-out so we can tag-team Fraidy when I fall asleep?"

"You don't really know how dreams work, do you?"

"Yes, but okay, I don't know how dream demons work, and I thought maybe this was something you knew how to do. You have experience fighting dream phantoms, right?"

"That doesn't mean I'm some kind of 'Oneiromancer'. It means *Dream Magician*, try to keep up." Dusty snapped his fingers at me like I was a dog that wasn't following one-word instructions.

"What about the monster that's ripping people up? *In the real world*? Some corporeal creature is out there, and whether you take the book or not, we have to stop it first!"

"Look, the truth is, I've been to Arkham before, and I wasn't a big fan of your quaint New England town back then. Did you know there are weird cults and dark gods linked to this place? I don't want to spend any more time here than absolutely necessary! There was this guy last time, and he was reanimating the dead *on purpose*! Like, with science! Nothing about reanimated corpses should be *science*! I am not staying overnight in the Town of the Living Dead!"

I decided not to tell Dusty that I work part-time for Dr. Herbert West, which primarily involves assisting with his reanimation experiments.

"Alright, what if we get a hotel room in Salem or Danvers?"

"You mean Salem, where the Sanderson Sisters came back from the dead; or Danvers, where the haunted Danvers State Hospital was? Holy Hell, man, do you have any cities that *aren't* haunted by witches and ghosts out the wazoo?"

"So, let's just wait for dark, see if the monster returns, and then head somewhere far from the Miskatonic Valley. We could head north and hang out in Derry, or south and stay the night in Providence."

"You know Michigan is *West* of here, right? Staying coastal does me no good at all."

"Fine, you can hit the road after we fight the monster. But Fraidy said he and I would be changing the world *tonight*, so tonight is when I'm going to need help, because he didn't sound like the book was going to be a factor anymore."

"Well problem solved! You come with me to some motel West of here, and Fraidy will track you down wherever you are. If he's after you, he'll show up, and if he's after the book, he'll still show up."

I couldn't really argue with that logic, not without revealing more than I wanted to tell the self-proclaimed "Chozen One", so we agreed on Oakhaven, Massachusetts, near the Connecticut border. I didn't have the heart to mention that Oakhaven also had a reputation for witches, ghosts, and a few other oddities (specifically, Turkeys of Unusual Size). As far as I knew, the Stabe Motel had no spooks, specters, or spellcasters. Heck, they didn't even have Wi-Fi. There is some nice topiary work framing the parking lot though, and a garden bed circling the building. Guess they thought a green and pleasant exterior would make up for a run down, internet-less interior.

***

Two and a half hours later and we're here. The traffic on I-95 was light, but 90 and 84 were a bit worse than my TomTom had predicted. Dusty had to settle on getting drive-thru from a rest-stop McDonald's, since there are no Weenieville franchises in New England. I'm pretty nervous, even without toting the *Book of the Dead* with me and awaiting an attack by the Fraidy Man and/or some undead creep. My craptacular PT Cruiser overheated several times on the way here, and once Dusty heads back to Michigan, I have to drive back to Salem with no one watching my back in case it breaks down.

We put the container in the bathtub, with the book still frozen inside. I grab a few buckets of ice from the machine on the second floor; we're on the first floor, but the one near our room doesn't work. Inconsequential, but I'm already in a bad mood, and this does nothing to improve it. Dusty flops onto the bed closer to the window and disconnects the artificial hand from his arm.

"How did that happen, anyway?"

76

Dusty looks up from the knapsack he brought in with him and gives me a little bit of a sneer, but I also see a hint of pride in his eyes. "I... cut it off with a chainsaw."

I know my eyebrow has got to be scraping my hairline as I contemplate this revelation. "What the hell, dude? Did the Fraidy Man control you in your sleep or something?"

"No, it was just asking too many *personal questions*." His glare could have frozen the *Necronomicon* without the use of a freezer. "I forgot my gas can." He tosses me his keys with his left hand. "Bring it in here, will you? I have a feeling I'm gonna need a full tank."

I'm pretty sure he's being cryptic on purpose, just to see if I'll ask more questions. When I get back into the room with the can, I see that he has a chainsaw on his bed, with a fixture that lets him attach it to the stump on his right arm. I also see a leather harness he must use to support it, which makes sense; if he tried to cut through anything that offered the slightest resistance the chainsaw would just bounce off and probably hit him, were it not properly braced.

"Okay, that's pretty hardcore there. Not sure how effective that will be against something that only exists inside a dream, but at least we're covered if one of us gets locked in the bathroom."

"I suppose you believe Wes Roberts died of natural causes and his blood just happened to burst out his body into a pattern that resembled words?" Dusty puts on the harness, which included a sheath that he holsters a sawed-off shotgun in. "Fraidy has gotten out before, and I'm sure he plans to do it again. My guess – he's going to possess you, manifest physically via your body, and I'll have to kill you to banish him. No offense."

"Um, that might not be in line with my own plans, all of which involve me not being dead by dawn." I lay down on my bed, fully clothed and on top of the sheets. "If I fall asleep and grab him in a dream, can you wake–?"

"No. You don't have any power over him, so long as he stays in your dreams. Only the book can destroy him, and for that to work he'd have to be human; or, I'd have to bring it into a dream with me to confront him."

"Kind of sounds like that's exactly what he wants you to try. He's been all about trying to get access to the *Necronomicon* all week."

Dusty checks that his shotgun is loaded, purposely not making eye contact with me.

"That's why I'm expecting to have to kill you. Hey, you hunt monsters, eventually you come up against something you can't win against. Happens to everyone eventually. At least you can rest in peace knowing you helped take the bastard down with you. It's not a 'win,' but it's better than a 'lose.' And I'll be sure to update the S.A.V.A.G.E. boards with tales of your heroic death."

"Geez, if that's really your whole plan, shouldn't you at least put down a tarp or something? This isn't much of a kill room."

"What do I care? I don't even like this state. Besides, the room's in your name, remember?"

So much for reasoning with him. Time to play my trump card. "You know, there's a prophecy about me…"

"A prophecy, really? That's groovy." Dusty rolls his eyes, then turns on the television. "Did you think my handle was 'Chozen1' because it was the only way I could work a 'z' into my name? Half the hunters I've heard about have prophecies about them, and the other half are their sidekicks!" He looked disinterested after that. "We get free Skinimax, right?"

"Okay, not to brag, but I can't be possessed, so the Fraidy Man won't be manifesting through my body. Your plan won't work. There was this spell back when–"

"If you can't be possessed, how did Fraidy get into your dreams? How did he make you read the book? Why are you even worth his time? He's a demon, or ghost, or tulpa, or whatever, but he's not a fool. He knows he can use you or he *wouldn't be trying to use you!*"

With a loud *CRASH!* the motel room door is flying in at us, knocked off its hinges by a powerful kick.

"I picked him," the Fraidy Man bellows at us, "because he read from the book, and I knew he'd bring *you* in." Fraidy stands before us in the body of the motel's landscaping guy. He's wearing dark green bib overalls with the Stabe Motel logo in the center of them, over a sweatshirt that was yellow before the man's blood stained it red.

What catches my attention most is how he's armed himself. He has an extended cultivator in one hand, and a five-tined hand rake built into a gardening glove on the other one. Whoever this man used to be, he clearly cared about horticulture. It's too late for him now though; the deep lacerations across his face make it clear that he died before Fraidy moved in.

Dusty is already aiming his shotgun, one-handed, at the newcomer. "Well, hello, Mister 'fancy plants!' It's two against one, and this time the odds are in *my* favor!"

He fires off a volley, perfectly aimed (at eight feet away, it would have been pretty hard to miss, even if he wasn't left-handed). Fraidy flies backwards, arms and legs splayed out, and lands on his back in the parking lot. "I take it back; he *is* a fool. Or was."

Dusty sounds as cocky as ever, but I notice he reloads anyway. Good thing too, since Fraidy is already standing in the doorway again, arms outstretched. "I felt that! Feels good to feel again! Gimme another round!"

"My turn!" I growl as I leap across the room, claws reaching for the dream demon.

Did I mention I'm a werewolf? It doesn't really come up that often, as I have near total control of my lycanthropic form. But today is February the 14th, 2014. Not only is it St. Valentine's Day, it's also the first night of the Full Moon, and I have plenty of pent-up hostility to unleash on this asshat.

I take a hit on the snout from the cultivator Fraidy is wielding, but it's not made of silver, and I'm still high on the endorphin rush of transformation; so, I don't give it another thought. It does divert my aim a touch though, so as my face turns to the right, I get a mouth full of Garden Weasel. Eating a power tiller is a bit much, especially since it's running, and I yelp around the blood spraying out of my mouth as I try to dislodge spinning tines from my jaw.

I fall crashing into the TV stand, and whatever softcore flick Dusty had been watching abruptly goes silent. I hear gunfire and a lot of swearing coming from the bathroom. Fraidy's frontal assault was a diversion, and Dusty must be taking on whoever was sent to recover the *Necronomicon*. I want to help, but my mouth is still getting mulched.

I bite down hard, with enough force to bend the aluminum iron alloy tool. It's also hard enough to shatter several teeth and separate my jaw. It works; I pull the mutilated cultivator out of my mouth, but I'm also near to passing out from the pain, and I can't conceive how I'll be any use in a fight.

I still have my claws, and I know I'll heal from any damage not caused by silver, given enough rest, so I stagger to my feet and look for Fraidy.

The monster must have taken me for being out of the running, because he's passed me, heading for Dusty. The "Chozen One" is already engaged in a game of dueling chainsaws with… what looks like an uglier version of himself. No, make that an undead version. I'm guessing that was the thing I conjured up in Arkham, because he made some kind of armor out of human skulls, which makes sense given the number of graves that were opened that night.

They're trying to kill each other with jabs about the other's incompetency, and I'm thinking the zombie-looking one might actually be some alternate version of Dusty. They seem pretty evenly matched. And they seem like they've battled before, so I'm trusting that the real Dusty is capable of beating him, else he wouldn't have survived the last time.

The Fraidy Man looks to be waiting for an opening in which he can strike with no fear of retaliation. He may have been throwing around a lot of bravado about getting shot, but I don't think he can afford to have his new body too damaged before he gets to the book.

Normally I'd lunge at him and try to rip his head off with tooth and nail, but my mouth is pulp and I'm wheezing from all the blood in my lungs. There's not much chance I can sneak up on him. Instead, I stay low and take a swipe at his hamstrings.

Just my luck, he's wearing leather boots. As he spins around, I discover that they are steel-toed boots, too. Thankfully, he kicks me in the ribs, since I'm pretty sure that if he went for my head, I'd slip straight into unconsciousness. Instead, I curl up in a fetal position, as expected, but really so I can lash out with my legs and hit both of his knees hard enough to bend them backwards.

I can see the pain and surprise on his face, and that makes the broken ribs worth it… kind of. I mean, no, I'm never a fan of fractured bones, but it's nice to see that he isn't, either.

I'm still wearing shoes, so I can't rake my hind claws through him, but I can kick straight up into his chin as he heads for the floor face first. With luck his jaw is just as messed up as mine is now.

He spits out the tip of his tongue, which is pretty gross, but it isn't covered in blood like I was expecting. That body is already dead, so he can be damaged, but I don't think he can really feel pain. Most likely he's the same kind of undead that Dusty 2.0 is, a spirit inhabiting a recently deceased corpse.

"Change seats!" I try to yell, but it comes out pretty garbled, and I doubt Dusty has a clue what I'm saying.

I jump up, land on my feet, and launch myself at Dirty Dusty, catching him in the chest with my shoulder. Like the real Dusty, he heard me but didn't seem to notice that I was up.

Dirty stumbles into the shower stall (who knew a fleabag motel like this would provide a tub and a shower?), but rights himself quickly. "You'll never–"

I disarm him, literally, by slicing off his right arm at the elbow. I'd love to claim I said something clever as I did it, but my brain is half-lupine right now, I'm in the heat of battle, and my tongue is still shredded, so I just pick up the chainsaw he dropped and toss it behind me.

"Thanks!" responds a voice that sounds… like a Muppet. Dammit!

Fraidy had been doing pretty badly against Dusty one-on-one, but the addition of a chainsaw to his arsenal seems to have evened the odds.

I reach a clawed hand into the mouth of the still-struggling Dusty Double, and just pull till his jaw comes unhinged... and keep pulling. When it rips off entirely, I grab his head and bend it back, so he's looking at the shower nozzle behind him. The corpse he possessed is much older than the one Fraidy is using, and the meat tears easily.

I consider removing his head entirely, but that's not as easy as it sounds, even in that state. Besides, I don't know if destroying the host body will just allow him to float away and find a new one, or return to Dreamland, or animate a doll somewhere. That actually happened on a case I did last year, so we had to immobilize the body rather than annihilate it. But there's no single set of rules that can be applied to things like these.

Instead, I swing him around by his one remaining arm and thrust him into the path of Fraidy's chainsaw, fowling his latest attack on Dusty. Both ghouls collapse on the floor in a heap and curse me a thousand times over, but I was in the military; I've been cursed out by the best.

Dusty and I take away their toys, as well as their arms and legs. I like that Dusty isn't fazed by me being a werewolf; most monster hunters go straight for the 'sorry, but I can't take the chance that you'll eat somebody' line of thinking, and then I'd have another fight on my hands.

I try to shift back to human, but under the full moon, it's nearly impossible, even when I don't have a broken jaw. I head to my car as a werewolf, hoping no one sees me, and return with bungee cord. I'm pretty sure there was no one else on site except the manager, and odds are he's already dead, but I don't like taking chances. Okay, I don't like taking *unnecessary* chances.

We tie them together back-to-back. The Fraidy Man, in between swears and hexes, insists that we're only delaying the inevitable. "This won't kill me, and once you destroy this body, I'll be back inside your head, till I can maneuver you into reading–"

"Okay, stop right there. Who said anything about destroying you?" Dusty turns to me. "Hey Steve, you wanna drag Jack and Shit out to the swimming pool for me?"

I nod and follow his direction, still unable to annunciate any quips of my own. It sucks not getting to join in the witty banter; that's always the best part of any fight scene.

Dusty meets me there, pulling three large bags of Quikrete quick-drying cement he removed from the maintenance shed. "Good thing that gardener was so well stocked. We have everything we need to make a hole, fill it with deadbeats, and cover it up so no one will even notice. They should stay well preserved for a good long time."

Maybe Dusty wasn't such a jerk after all. I mean, yes, he's a jerk, but I'm glad he's a good jerk. And I'm glad I can't talk, so I'm not saying this out loud, since it's nowhere near the level of smack talk that's been thrown around tonight.

"You two are *mine!*" Fraidy screams just before getting buried in cement. "I have a contract, and I always collect my bounties!"

Wait, what?

As the night has progressed my body is already healing, knitting torn ligaments and mending broken bones, the biggest advantage of being a werewolf. I am able to talk again, finally, though not well – at least not until the jaw sets completely. Plus, I think some of those teeth are gone for good. Once my mouth heals, I can't just shove them back in and hope they'll take root. Bones can mend, but they don't regrow, at least not with my flavor of lycanthropy.

"Rhat did you shay? Bounty? Rawr you shome kind of Monster Hunter Hunter?"

"Just you 'Destined One' types. Every time some mook dies leaving a prophecy unfilled, an angel gets its wings… ripped off!"

Dusty whacks him on the top of his head with a trowel. "So, this was all a trap to lure us into one spot? I can't believe we were monster-baited!"

"And I would have gotten away with it if it wasn't for – gleck!"

I look at Dusty, incredulous. "Rhamn, I'd have thought you'd let him finish the line!"

"Nope, I'm done screwing around with these two." He forces broken cement rubble into Fraidy's mouth, *urinates* on both undead, and laughs like a drunken frat-boy who just found an untapped keg.

I pour in the last of the Quikrete, and smooth it out to match the bottom of the swimming pool. As I climb out of the pool, I see Dusty is already loading his belongings into his car.

"By the time the Sun rises I need to be on the road home, and you better come up with a story to explain what happened here. Good luck with that, Scooby!"

***

Moments later and he's heading West, trying to beat the dawn. I have a little while left to figure out what I'm going to do. The manager and gardener were dead, and now buried, and there were no other guests besides us, so I'm probably running an arson-gone-wrong play here, once I can speak clearly enough to call some friends to help. I didn't know either man, but I'm sure they didn't deserve anything like this. I'll have to make sure there's enough evidence to prove they were murdered, so at least their families will have some kind of closure.

It's been a rough week, but at least all this is over, and I survived another Valentine's Day. Plus, Dusty took the… *crap*!

The *Book of the Dead* waits for me in the bathtub, still shrouded in plastic and sealed in a bin. Dusty completely forgot to bring it with him, and I forgot it was here too. Looks like this might not be over for me after all.

END

CREDITS

Stabbo The Magnificent/Dale Parker = created by JJ Lindsey
Mike Nero = created by Christofer Nigro
Scáth Hazzard = created by Aaron Oliver
Dr. Victoria Waddell = created by Yvonne Dittrich

HUSH, HUSH, HUSH

Cody Bratsch

Ireland 1885

Little Toby O'Connor had been sitting up in his bed for half an hour, trembling with terror.

Despite being in his own room of his own house with his parents sleeping just down the hall, the twelve-year-old boy had never felt more vulnerable. There was a strong chill in the air, exceptional even for an autumn night such as the one Toby found himself in the middle of. It had been going around the small village he lived in for several months.

Now it seemed that the source of that chill had found its way to Toby O'Connor. He felt it deep down in his bones. Hence, Toby was aware that despite being by himself when he first fell asleep, he was no longer alone in his room. Or at least that was how it felt.

Toby had endured nightmares in the past of shadow people looking in on him from outside his room's window. Their dark frames were revealed by the dim light of the streetlamp just outside his house. However, any distinct characteristics and details were still shrouded in darkness. This time was not like those nightmares, for it felt all too real. Toby could feel the cold on his skin, the breath from his mouth, and the heavy, fear-filled beating of his heart.

Wide awake and unable to move, he laid with the covers pulled up to his chin, in a state of near-panic. Unlike those dreams, he was absolutely certain he could feel the presence of someone or some-*thing* actually in the room with him.

"Please, God," Toby let out in the quietest of whispers.

The blue-eyed, chubby-faced kid with long, messy brown hair slowly scanned his room for any possible signs that he was not alone. It was about the only sort of movement Toby could get himself to do voluntarily, rotating his head and eyes around to look for whoever or whatever might be lurking in the darkness. He saw the box filled with toys he used to play with when he was younger, as well as his chair and desk next to the window. Toby could also just barely make out the rug lying across his stone floor. He could also see the pictures he used to draw hung up on his wall, which was also made out of stone just like the majority of the house.

It was small, like most of the other homes, businesses, and other structures in the tiny village.

Toby's house was exceptionally small and rundown-looking, almost appearing like a tiny cottage that time had forgotten. Still, it was his home and it had been for all his life. In that time, he had always felt safe and secure there, especially with the very caring parents he had. However, that sense of security had been shaken several months prior. Now, sitting in that room on his bed that autumn night, it was completely gone.

Despite that, Toby had found nothing, save for some shadows dancing on his walls, which he knew were nothing to fear.

"It's... fine," Toby said to himself. "Only tricks of the light shining in from outside."

He was just barely able to come to such a logical conclusion. A mix of adrenaline, exhaustion, and a healthy dose of fear-induced paranoia made it hard for Toby to think or even see straight. Toby had not jumped out of his bed and ran out of his room screaming his head off only because he was unable to. That icy, uncomfortable grip of fear forced him to stay in one place despite all his wishes saying otherwise. Toby had tried more than once to scream. However, that same paralyzing terror seemed to have a grip on his throat as well.

Yet, despite the state he was in, how truly scared he was, Toby O'Connor had every intention of breaking free of the grip his fear had on him. The terror of whatever may or may not have been in his room with him was not going to hold him there forever. Although he was terrified, Toby knew that, for his own sake, he would have to move. He had just enough rational thought left to realize this. The boy did his best to get himself out of his paralyzed state and start moving at last. However, when Toby finally succeeded in doing so, it was incredibly slow, and he was not preparing himself to run for the door.

Instead, Toby slowly pulled his bedding off him, making him feel the chilling nip in the air all the more as he went to look under his bed. He had to know for sure if there was actually someone there. He could not just let the feeling of an intruder in his room go without having some sort of confirmation. Besides, he thought that knowing for sure if someone was there or not would give him enough motivation to get his feet moving, depending on what the answer was. Toby had looked everywhere else; the only place left was under the wooden frame of his bed.

Come on, Toby. You only need to look under there. Then you can either run or go back to sleep... or, you could just run even if there's nothing under the bed anyways. You won't know until you look; now do it.

The child took several deep breaths before moving faster than he had that whole time. He threw himself over the side of the bed and pulled up any bedding blocking his sight. He hung upside down and looked for any signs that someone was under there hiding. Toby kept breathing deep and heavily as he scanned under his bed, his eyes taking time to adjust to the darkness. Even when they did, he still saw nothing at all, despite there clearly being more than enough room for someone to be under there.

Yet all he saw were a few books, stray pens, and pieces of clothing that had been randomly thrown and scattered under the bed. Toby sighed with relief, letting out all the anxiety and fear that he'd been building up before as a small smile came over his face.

See? There's nothing. There's no monsters or burglars or anything here; nothing at all.

Toby was wondering if he should still leave his room anyway as he started to push himself up. He got to where he was no longer hanging upside down over the side of his bed but was now on his hands and knees preparing to turn onto his back. That was when he saw something that nearly stopped his heart and made his blood run cold.

He was paralyzed once more, save for the trembling running through him and the shivers going up and down his spine. There, hidden in the darkest part of his room where the outside lamp light could not reach, Toby saw a pair of eyes and the outline of a smile.

The horrifying sight of those eyes and that creepy smile were only about ten feet away and they were so high up they gave the impression that whoever they belonged to was very tall.

Beside the fact that they belonged to someone who had invaded his home so willingly and was in his room with him, something else seemed especially frightening to Toby.

It was hard for him to pin down, especially given his state of mind and the situation he was in, but the eyes seemed off somehow. They felt other worldly, unnatural, like they belonged to something not human at all. The smile was just disturbing, being filled with crooked, yellow teeth, some being more like distorted fangs than anything human.

Even worse was how unnaturally wide the grin seemed to be, not looking at all like a normal person's smile. Despite the oddities of it, the snicker and the eyes did seem to convey some sort of very human emotion. They seemed to convey joy, happiness, and a sick sense of naughty pleasure as if whatever freak they belonged to was glad that Toby was seeing it. In fact, whoever or whatever this disturbing thing was, it appeared to let out a few sniggers as it tried to hold back a full fit of laughter. It was like the impulse some kids felt but fought against when they got caught doing something they were not supposed to.

As unsettling as all that was, it was about to get even worse. Toby was able to make out more details as the seconds ticked by, which felt more like hours to the frightened boy. Indeed, this intruder looked to be very big, very tall, and quite broad shouldered. The shape seemed to give off a sense that this stranger was, in fact, human; a man even, yet it still felt like something else entirely at the same time.

However, Toby did not actually need all these physical signs to realize that the thing he saw was not of this Earth; at least, not in the way that human beings and animals were. He knew deep down what this otherworldly monstrosity was and what it had come for.

It had come for him! Just like it had come for several children the nights before. Toby had to get out of there fast and he knew it. He had to force himself to take action, break free of his frozen state that his fear forced him into, and run for his life.

Too bad he never got the chance to even try.

Only a few seconds after Toby had visual confirmation of the entity's presence did it spring forth faster than the eye could see. In the same swift movement, the eight-foot-tall man-like creature scooped Toby off his bed and into its hands, lifting him high into the air. Its jagged, claw-like fingernails dug into the boy's arms as it shrieked in a voice that sounded like it came straight from Hell. Toby screamed like he knew it would be the last one he ever let out.

"*Mommy! Daddy! Help me! Please! Please, help!*"

However, the boy was cut off when his mouth was forced closed by some invisible force, muffling any noises he made. Toby looked upon the hideous face of the paranormal entity that had him in its clutches. It let go of one of his arms and brought a finger to its mouth in a shushing mannerism.

"Hush. Hush. Hush."

It was then that the door to Toby's room swung open, his mother and father rushing in as fast as they could. The mother dropped the lantern she was holding as she screamed in horror at what she saw. The father, holding a late 19th century Snider-Enfield rifle, had the same horror on his face, but acted on it as he raised his gun.

"*No!*" the father screamed. "*You'll not take my boy from me!*"

The creature shrieked its unholy noise before flying backwards into the darkness at high speed. The father got off only one shot, but the thing, whatever it was, had already vanished – as had his son, who was never to be seen again.

***

It was 8:00am the very next morning. A horse-drawn coach was making its final approach to the small rural village located, almost randomly, in the middle of the Irish countryside. The driver had the coach stop on a hill overlooking the town. It was also here where a five-foot stone border, standing next to the dirt road the horse and coach stood upon, began.

"All right," the disheveled-looking and ruggedly dressed driver barked in his thick Irish brogue. "This is as far as I go. I'll not be messing around in that town. Not with the things I've heard about it."

Less than a second later, one of the coach's side doors opened. Out stepped a much more gentlemanly dressed man. He was tall, about six-foot-one, thin, and looked to be middle-aged, either in his mid or late fifties. The man wore a white dress shirt with a black dress vest over it and a long black coat. He also wore a red scarf, which hid his black bow tie underneath. Finally, the man also wore gray dress pants, white gloves, and black boots, carrying with him a cane and an umbrella, the latter laying upon a big black leather bag he held in his hand.

The man looked around with his light blue eyes for a moment before exhaling a deep sigh. He then turned to the coachman, who got his first real good look at his passenger. He saw the slightly sunken-in cheeks of his face, which itself seemed to be a little long and otherwise perfectly slim. His nose appeared somewhat more pointed yet fitting for his features. He also seemed like he had only recently started to lose his well-groomed graying hair, which was on display before the man placed a bowler hat on his head. Yet the thing that stuck out most about this man was his stare.

It looked so intense, so focused, so intimidating in how far it seemed to extend. It almost looked like he was not even staring at the coachman or even the world around them. It was more like he was gazing right into the coachman's soul, like he had seen so much in the world that all he could see now was what was beyond it. Be it into the core of another's very being, or into the spirit realm itself, this man gave off the impression he could see it all. It actually made the coachman a bit more unsettled than he had already been about the town.

"Thank you, my good man," the departing passenger said in a pleasant, genuine tone spoken in his natural Dutch accent. "Have a splendid rest of the day."

The driver only gave a quick half-smile and nod before making his horse turn to leave. The well-dressed man stepped to the side of the road, giving the horse and coach enough room to turn around and be on their way. He watched them depart for a moment before walking up to the stone barrier on the other side of the dirt road. There the man removed one of his gloves and ran his bare hand across the cold, smooth stones that stuck out from the side of the wall. Then his eyes followed its path, which led directly into the town.

Well, I had best start walking, then.

As he went along his way, his mind never wandered once, thinking only about what he came to this town to do. He had been called upon for a very specific task, one he had performed variations of several times before. The man did, however, think about other things when he was not on a job such as the one he was about to undertake. His mind was rather open whenever he had the free time for it, whether it be researching things he was interested in or interacting in a social environment

When he was researching, however, for projects or classes for the university he taught at, or actually teaching said classes, or was on assignment for the university, he was all business. He was especially serious when it came to the kind of tasks such as the one he was about to take on in this little Irish village he was approaching.

It was not an undertaking the university had sent him on, nor were any of the similar quests of this kind he had gone on before. Nevertheless, he took them even more seriously due to the nature of these excursions and the strong implications they had for the whole world. That was why he made no fuss when the driver dropped him off outside the town.

The man hardly ever complained, knowing that there would always be obstacles that came with this life he had chosen to take on. The man usually took the majority of these difficulties in stride, feeling it would all be worth it so long as he completed his tasks successfully. He reached into one of the pockets of his coat and lightly rubbed a golden cross he carried with him as he quietly prayed for success, much like he usually did before these types of missions.

Between thinking about the task, what variables could go into solving it, and praying that he could, it felt like no time at all before the man was standing just outside the town itself. Upon entering said village, he saw that it was just as messy, rugged, and somewhat rundown as it had looked from the hill above.

The small buildings looked as if they lacked any recent upkeep, ranging as they did from being composed of cracked stone or rotting wood and so on. Shopping stands, wooden frames with raggedy tarps over them – all in disrepair – littered the sides of the streets, looking as bad as everything else the man had seen.

Even more in disarray than the town itself were the actual people living there. From what the Dutch gentleman could see, they seemed incredibly miserable, even more than people in their position probably would be. They all looked distraught, eyes full of sadness, and with a horrified countenance on their dirty faces.

They don't even seem to care if they live or die. Also, no children around. Or, at least, very few of them from what I've seen.

The man looked again and saw that there actually were some children scattered about in the streets. "Some" was the key word, for it seemed like there were far fewer kids than there should have been, even for a town as small as the one he was in. From what he could tell, their adult guardians kept them on very short leashes, almost literally in some cases. They all appeared desperate to hold onto their kids, as if they would fade into dust if they did not. If there was even one stray kid by themselves on the street, a parent would come up and reprimand them for going out alone before taking them home.

Some of these kids had frightened expressions on their faces, almost as if they were afraid for their very lives. Then there were others who had expressions suggesting that they did not know how to respond to the traumatic experiences their village was apparently going through. The majority of adults who had no children with them wandered around with even more solemnly blank expressions. It was as if they had lost their sense of purpose; like they did not care what they did or did not do in life, as the man had previously observed. Perhaps that was indeed the case and was thus the cause of what took away their will to keep the village intact.

It's worse than I thought. Luckily, I'm not too late. There are still children here, which means there's a chance to fix this. I only hope I can do so before any irreversible damage is done to this poor town.

"Van Helsing!" a voice called out across the way.

The Dutch gentleman turned around, spotting a man with a gray Irish tweed cap and in a suit and bow tie walking up to him. Under his cap was a head of red hair with a somewhat bushy beard to match. In comparison he looked to be the best dressed resident of the town and the one who kept himself the tidiest. Even then, though, he still looked like he had seen better days.

"Are you Professor Abraham Van Helsing?" the red-bearded man asked in a traditional Irish brogue.

"Yes," the Dutchman replied. "Indeed I am."

"My name is Rory McConnell," the man in the suit said as he extended his hand. "I'm the mayor here. It's a pleasure to be making your acquaintance."

The man identified as Professor Van Helsing respectfully accepted the mayor's hand. "Likewise, I'm sure."

"I..." Despite all the time he had spent preparing for this meeting, Mayor McConnell was still not entirely sure how to go about it. "Look, I'm not going to mince words with you, Professor. I'd like to extend our hospitality to you, give you time to rest, for food, drink, lodging and all... but... with all our town has had to put up with already... I– I was hoping we could handle this... *situation* as fast–"

"Take me to the latest crime scene as soon as possible," Abraham interjected. "If you would please."

Rory McConnell was quiet for a moment, as if a bit taken aback by the professor's willingness to get started. He quickly shook himself out of it and nodded in compliance.

"Yes, of course, sir. We'll be on our way then. Follow me, if you would."

Rory then led the university teacher through the depths of the town to the intended destination Abraham had asked for.

***

The door to Toby O'Connor's bedroom opened up, allowing Professor Van Helsing, Mayor Rory, and Thomas O'Connor to enter. Thomas was a thin man with green eyes, a bushy brown mustache, and short locks of brown hair who wore a stained white dress shirt and an opened brown vest. He looked as if he had seen much better days. Nonetheless he was intent on being as helpful in the ongoing investigation of his son's abduction as he could be. Thomas and Abraham carried two large lanterns with them as the trio of men stopped in the doorway for only a moment to look around.

"This is the room where it happened?" Abraham asked as he turned to Thomas.

"Y– yes, sir," Thomas just barely managed to say as he looked away.

It was all he could do to keep from breaking into sobs of utter grief and sadness. It was only the night before that his son Toby had been taken from him. His wife, Alley, was in an even worse way, being bedridden from the depression she was forced to endure from losing her only child. Abraham looked to Thomas with pity and sympathy, even putting a hand on his shoulder. This made him look to the professor, never losing the emotionally distraught expression on his face.

"You have my sympathies, Mr. O'Connor," Abraham said. "I am truly sorry for the loss your family has experienced... but you can still do something about it. You can help me see to it that this does not happen to anyone else in this town again."

Thomas heard the tone and inflections in the professor's voice, which sounded sincere while still being professional. His countenance also evoked a look of genuine sympathy while retaining the same professionalism he put into his words. The level of dedication this Abraham Van Helsing seemed to have about him made Thomas force his emotions down as much as he could. Once he was sure he had them under control, the O'Connor patriarch nodded his head in agreement.

"Okay, Professor," Thomas said. "You have my full cooperation."

"Good man," Abraham replied. He then looked around the room, his eyes falling to the near left side. "Set up your lantern on the floor over there, but please try not to touch anything."

"Right," O'Connor agreed while he did as he was instructed.

"You stay put, Mr. Mayor," Abraham said to Rory, who nodded in compliance.

Abraham then walked up to the bed, which had not been touched since the night before. The bedding and pillows were still messily scattered across the room. Professor Van Helsing paused for only a moment as he looked down regretfully at the bed that once belonged to Toby O'Connor.

Poor boy. I am sorry I was not here to stop what happened to you. But you will be avenged, that I swear.

Then the university professor set his lantern and black leather bag on the nightstand next to the bed. Abraham pulled out several tools to aid in his examination of the room. He had already had his suspicions of what was behind this kidnapping and the others that had occurred in the town recently, but he wanted to be certain. The professor put on a small pair of spectacles, some disposable examination gloves, and grabbed a small test tube filled with a green substance. After shaking it lightly, the chemical compound inside the tube started to glow.

"You say that no one has been here to investigate this abduction yet?" Abraham questioned.

"No, sir, Van Helsing, sir," Rory replied. "We have some men here whose regular job it is to investigate and examine such scenes, but I believed it would be best to wait for you since you were arriving today."

Abraham listened while he also scanned the room very closely. He would crouch down, move a hand gently over the walls, and even looked on the floor as if he were expecting something to run across it at any moment. The professor also took close care to examine the hole in the wall. It was this same hole Thomas had made when taking a shot with his rifle at the thing that abducted his son.

No blood stains... or any kind of stains at all, save for the marks left by the bullet.

"And what time did this all occur last night?" Abraham asked.

95

"Abo- about midnight, sir," Thomas said in a voice shaking with emotion. "I... I'd heard all the stories of what had been occurring across the town for the last month or more. But... I never thought--"

Thomas' voice caught in his throat, his emotions trying to overtake him once more. Neither Ror, nor Abraham, faulted Mr. O'Connor for this. Rather, they understood the grieving man's feelings all too well. The two men exchanged a knowing glance before looking back to Thomas with pity.

"I understand your position, Mr. O'Connor," Abraham said. "That is why I will do everything in my power to see that the full truth is brought to light and justice is ensured for your child."

"Th– thank you, sir," Thomas replied. "Thank you very much, Professor. That *demon* that did this must be stopped, whatever the cost!"

"Agreed," Abraham concurred as he went to examine the far-left wall. "Were you able to get a good look at what took your son?"

"Oh, I most certainly did," Thomas said. "It may have been dark, but something like what I saw... it is impossible that a man wouldn't be able to tell what it was, no matter how dark. That is why I'm telling you this thing that took my son was no man. It looked like a man, if just barely... but it had the face and body of the Devil himself."

"If you saw it, then would you be able to describe it in better detail?" Abraham asked.

"It was eight feet tall," Thomas said. "It had a wide body, as if it were big enough to lift the bed with the simplest of ease. Its– its face was like that of a human skull, but with rotten flesh in the final stages of decay. It was also greatly deformed, having one swollen eye socket and one that drooped lower than the other. And its eyes... its horrible red eyes... it was like Satan himself were peering into your very soul.

"It wore these tatters. I think they might have been a brown coat. I- it looked like it had just been taken off a dead man. I have to wonder if it might have been.

"Part of me also wonders if it was actually that tall, or if it was somehow able to lift itself above the floor and look bigger than it actually was."

"This spectre could very easily be either or," Abraham said. "If it is what I think it is, anything would be possible."

Thomas and Rory looked to Abraham with conflicting expressions. They seemed to want to ask the university professor what he meant. At the same time, they also appeared to be afraid of the answer.

"And... what *do* you think it is, Van Helsing?" Rory finally asked.

"It has been known to take several different forms in the past," Abraham went on. He then stopped at a particular spot on the wall. "Eureka!"

Abraham then walked over to his bag and pulled out an empty test tube, a box of chalk, and a little chop stick. Then he grabbed a single piece of chalk and hurried back over to the wall. The professor began wiping the chop stick over a small section of the stone piece of the cottage.

"It has used several different methods in the past to steal children," Abraham explained. He then examined the wooden implement before opening the test tube he had with him and putting the stick inside. "Some of these methods are viler and more grotesque to the human eye than others. However, the target has always been the same: infants. Our offspring are always what it comes after, eviscerating whoever and whatever it must in order to get to them."

"Damn it, man, quit being so vague!" Thomas shouted in a burst of emotion. "You already know what cursed abomination has come into our town, so just say it!"

Abraham looked to both Rory and Thomas with an intense stare that almost seemed like it could kill a baby bird.

"You both know damn well what it is I am referring to!" Abraham said. "You know, or else you would not have requested my assistance here."

He then walked over, grabbed the arms of both Thomas and Rory, and pulled them over to the wall.

"What is the meaning of this?" Rory said in outrage. "Release me, Professor, at on-"

Abraham slapped both men's hands on the wall.

"Do you feel that?" Abraham asked. "Of course, you do. That residue is ectoplasm; a supernatural viscous substance that exudes from the body of an otherworldly entity entering our world from the realm beyond."

Thomas and Rory looked as if they had just seen the face of God and it instilled them with the greatest of fears. Even when they looked to each other and back at Abraham, they never lost those awestruck and terror-filled expressions.

"So, p– Professor," Rory said, "y– you're really implying... that this was a spectre of some sort? A phantom? An apparition? A human spirit returned from the grave to haunt us? A ghost?"

"Do not play the fool with me, Mr. Mayor," Abraham said as he released the two men's hands.

He then marked out a vaguely human, but abnormally large shape in the wall. Next, he moved to the floor and marked some spots where the ectoplasm had fallen. He also found a particularly large puddle under the bed. Abraham then turned to Rory and Thomas, looking as serious as ever.

"You both know what this apparition is," Abraham said. "You know full well this is no wayward human spirit or regular spectre. This is a demonic entity spewed from the pits of Hell itself for the sole purpose of stealing innocent children from their mothers and fathers."

Abraham paused and stood expectantly as he was waiting for Rory and Thomas to respond. Much to his annoyance it seemed as if Mayor Rory was refusing to say anything, whereas Thomas appeared as though he was genuinely unable to say it. He was pent up with far too much emotion.

"You know its name, but refuse to speak it," Abraham went on. "So, I will say it for you. Your town... your village... has come under siege by the evil of the *Boogeyman.*"

***

Abraham and Rory had left the O'Connor home and it was not too long before they were in the mayor's office at the town hall. It was how one would expect an elected figure's workspace to look, if maybe a little bit messier and more disorganized. This did not surprise Abraham given the state the rest of the town was in.

As Abraham accepted a seat Rory had offered him, the scientist thought even more about the horrible situation the town and its residents were in. He watched as the mayor walked around the desk, removed a bottle of Irish whiskey from one of the drawers, and sat down himself

"So, you know already what this thing is, Van Helsing," Rory said. "And you've seen what it's done to the town. It wasn't always like this, ya know. Nothing in this town was as you see it today. Before, we were a bustling community of potential. I sure as shit wasn't drinkin' while on the job back then neither.

"I tell you, this place was actually quite respectable. We all kept it up pretty good, all things considered. We were not just some backwards town that time forgot like you'd think we were by looking at it now. Hell, I'll even be as bold to say we were the best village this side of Ireland. But then that damned Boogeyman--"

Rory stopped as he got a faraway look in his eye, terror creeping on his face just at the mention of the demon. "When it came for our town... for our children, good or naughty, indiscriminately, that's when it all changed. That was when our whole town started going to shit, to hell in a hand basket. Losing our children made us all start losing our own souls, our very wills to live."

"Yes, I understand," Abraham responded. "I've heard of a great many cases regarding the Boogeyman and similar spirits doing the same things elsewhere and getting the exact same results. I will confess, though, that I have never actually dealt with the Boogeyman directly before. In fact, it is quite a rarity for me to go up against any sort of spirits or demons, maybe doing so only once in a while here and there. I do my best to stand against the forces of darkness, true, but my expertise lies in combating... *different* types of creatures of the night.

"I shall even admit that I probably would not have taken this case if I had not already been in this area on business for the university. Still, I must ask you; are you certain that you want me to handle this and not someone else? I will still do everything I can if you ask me to. As I have said, this is not my regular field, but I can give you the names of people much more qualified-"

"It has to be you, Professor!" Rory exclaimed as he stood up. "We've waited too long as it is! Plus, everyone already knows your track record against all these monsters and beasts spawned from Satan. We can't wait any longer! You've seen the state of our town! It can't get any worse than this; we can't let it."

Rory fell quiet, but his facial expression betrayed what he was feeling. There was a strong hint of fear and worry in his eyes as he shook ever so slightly. This caused Abraham to raise a brow.

"I surmise it is something far more personal," Abraham suggested. "You have a child of your own you're worried about. You fear they may be at stake next, am I correct?"

Rory began to weep as he looked up at a large, painted, golden-framed portrait hanging on a wall in his office. Abraham looked as well and what he saw was the mayor beside a lovely young lady with fair skin, red hair, and blue eyes. Between them was a younger daughter who looked much like her mother, except that she had many freckles across her face.

As Abraham studied the picture, Rory stepped out from behind his desk and walked over to a bulletin board set up on the side of the room.

The university professor looked away from the picture and watched as Rory pointed to an image posted on the board. There were several pieces of paper pinned up, but the particular piece the mayor drew attention to almost looked to be a rough sketch of the village as it would be seen from overhead. Noticeably, there were several red Xs drawn over many of the rough drawings of the houses in the center of the town. Only three residences at the very core of this display were left unmarked, one of which Rory was pointing to on the chart.

"Your home," Abraham said knowingly. "It is right in the center of this madness brought on by the Boogeyman. Yet it would seem your house has yet to suffer the tragedy that has stricken the majority of your town thus far."

"But it's only a matter of time," Rory said as he looked to Abraham intensely. "I know this is not your field, Professor, but you're closer than anyone or anything else nearby that could be of help. That is why I sent for you, practically begged for your aid when I heard you were in this part of Ireland. I'm sorry to put you in this position. I would have thought of something else, but--"

The mayor of the small village got even more emotional, openly weeping as he poured himself a shot of his whiskey. "Our town is running out of time. Everyone hates me already for not acting on this sooner. I cannot in good conscience blame them, but it still plagues me to think about it. Just as the Boogeyman still plagues my town as we speak, Professor, waiting to strike like the cowardly demon it is.

"Then there's my sweet little Hannah. I cannot bear the thought of me and my wife Maggie losing her."

Abraham silently contemplated what to do before reaching a decision and standing up. "Then I will see to it that you do not have to."

Rory was wiping his tears away when he looked to the Dutch gentleman in a state of near jubilation.

"You shall take our case then?"

"I most certainly will. Your village has suffered long enough, and I will do everything within my power to see to it that it suffers no more... and that your family stays whole. I lost a daughter myself once and I would not wish that horror on even my most hated enemies. So, I will help you however I can, Mr. Mayor."

"Oh, many thanks to you, Van Helsing, sir," Rory said as he shook Abraham's hand so enthusiastically. "I knew you were a good man, and you would help us in our time of crisis. Your reputation of being a good-hearted, wonderful soul proceeds you even here. Why, all throughout the world tales have been spun of your legendary battles against the forces of evil. Thank you ever so much for continuing that reputation by agreeing to take this case here in our little town."

"I thank you for your kind words, sir, but anyone who calls himself a good man of God should be willing to help whenever and wherever he can in whatever way possible."

Van Helsing then pulled out his golden cross necklace from his coat pocket and rubbed it between his fingers. "I only pray that any efforts I put forth tonight will bear success enough so your town will sleep soundly in the nights proceeding."

"I have every confidence in you, Professor."

"Thank you, man," Abraham replied graciously.

"So, where will you start?"

"Hmm... I am not entirely sure at the moment," Abraham responded as he walked over to the bulletin board. "Although, if I had to guess...

the Boogeyman is most likely to target one of these three houses here in the center of all the havoc it has wreaked thus far."

"Do you think it might be my house?" Rory asked nervously.

"I already know that you do. You fear that it is, not that I blame you. However, if I were a betting man, which I am usually not, I would say that sounds most likely to me right now as well. It seems too much of a coincidence I would arrive here on this day when you fear for your daughter's life more than ever."

"Do you think it's a prophecy of some kind, or destiny maybe?"

"Who can really say for sure? The Lord does work in mysterious ways. Still, I do think I should be preparing myself for a potential showdown with the Boogeyman at your home estate tonight. Midnight, if I am not mistaken?"

"That's when all the others happened, yes," Rory answered nervously.

"Right then," Abraham replied. "We will need to make preparations at your home immediately, then. We will need men and supplies. I shall write down everything required for this undertaking."

"You shall have it all," Rory said emphatically.

"Good to hear," Abraham responded. "We will also need men on standby with the same supplies at the other two houses, just in case. I shall take no chances in allowing this Boogeyman to slip by when he is so close, and I have the opportunity to take him down."

"Right. If need be, one of the other teams can send a man to retrieve you from my home."

"Very well, then," Abraham said as he turned to Rory. "I will need to get a few things in order before we meet again this evening. Is there lodging I may take up somewhere in town until then?"

"Most certainly. There's an inn on the far side of town. You can't miss it."

"Then I shall go there, make notes, and prepare."

"Very well. Take care until tonight then, Van Helsing, and thank you again."

"Your continued gratitude is most appreciated."

With that the two men shook hands once more before Rory showed Abraham out of his office. As he was leaving town hall, the professor found himself looking at the gold cross in his hand once more, the very one that used to belong to his daughter.

God willing, I shall not fail this town like I failed you.

***

Midnight had come, though many had futilely prayed throughout the day that it would not. As the hour grew nearer, all prayers turned to begging God that no innocent lives would be lost that night. Many could not get themselves to sleep that unsettling evening. Their children were just as restless, the mass paranoia extending even to them.

Of all who felt worried and fearful, it was a particular young girl who had felt it the most leading into the midnight hour. When the time came, she was lying in her bed, having only just finally gotten to sleep after spending fearful hours awake in her dark room.

Her only light came from a small lantern placed on a nightstand next to her bed. The ten-year-old, red-haired girl laid in her bed, her blankets aiding the flower-patterned white nightgown she wore in keeping her warm. Her head laid on a fluffy white pillow.

Across her bedroom, there were a few large dressers for her clothes. She had some shelves for her books and dolls, among other things, and even a small desk in the corner. It was all spread across the white-walled, wooden floored, second level room that seemed like a small village unto itself. It was more than any girl could ever want.

Yet, despite how wonderful it all seemed, none of it was enough to soothe the troubled soul of the young lass. She had been kept awake throughout the evening by the possibility of what might happen to her that night. The only reason she had managed to get to sleep at all was because her fatigue had gotten to the point where she could fight it back no longer. Even then, the sleep the girl managed to get was restless as could be and occupied with frightful, nightmarish images.

Because of how restless her sleep was, a part of her realized that she was only dreaming, but the nightmares still frightened her. What terrified the child all the more was that those nightmares would soon be coming true.

The signs were shown that this might come to pass, for the air began to feel all the colder as the howl of the wind outside got louder. The sound of leaves and small debris being blown around outside and hitting the girl's house added to the unsettling atmosphere. Even worse was a

104

small fog that appeared to be rolling in from the outside. It somehow added to the feeling in the air that no one was safe.

Despite being asleep, the girl still saw and even felt all this occurring around her home, as if her dreams were a premonition of it all.

Then darkness forced itself upon her room as the lantern was suddenly snuffed out by unseen forces. The air became colder still as the room darkened to an almost unnatural degree, even for such a late hour. All the spaces underneath the girl's bed seemed to be getting even darker, the pitched black shadows creeping out from underneath the elevated frame. It was then that the girl awoke, although it was almost impossible for her to tell since she was still seeing glimpses of her nightmares.

It became all the clearer as her eyes began to adjust to the darkness... and they did not like what they saw. Rising up, seemingly from the depths of Hell itself, came the form of what looked almost like a man, but was clearly an unearthly entity. Its body was hidden under a long, brown, torn, and tattered coat that seemed as old as time itself. What she could see through the darkness was its skull-like face, warped and twisted in the worst of ways. Horrifying red eyes filled the sockets of the sinister skull, grinning madly with a lipless smile.

The girl breathed heavily as she looked on in utter fear at the demonic thing oozing out from underneath her own bed. When the eight-foot-tall apparition fully stood, it reached one of its disgusting hands for the girl, who started to whimper and weep with fear.

"*Now!*"

Queued by the voice shouting from the darkness, the whole room suddenly lit up bright as could be. The Boogeyman froze, his eyes darting erratically about the room in surprise. The demon was surrounded by several men, who seemed to be armed with various tools.

"Drop it!" Abraham Van Helsing barked.

"Come, Hannah!" Rory cried as he ran up to his daughter's bed.

Grabbing his little daughter and pulling her away, Rory managed to get the girl in his arms just as a metal net fell upon the Boogeyman. He pulled his offspring all the way to the other end of the room where his wife Maggie was waiting for them. She looked down upon Hannah, holding her face in her hands as she inspected her child.

"Oh, thank God," the relieved mother let out tearfully as she hugged her daughter tightly.

All attention was soon turned to the demon known the world over as the Boogeyman. Despite being a phantom-like entity, the net made of chains had actually seemed to fall across the entity as if it were an actual corporeal. The weight of the bonds dropped it to the floor as it cried out in a voice like a hundred banshees howling at once. The men who were supposed to charge forth, tackle, and pile up on the Boogeyman hesitated, for the very sight of the thing terrified them, despite its apparently vulnerable state.

"What are you waiting for, you fools?" Abraham asked over the entity's howling.

"How is the net holding that thing?" one of the men asked in disbelief.

"I told you!" Abraham let out in frustration. "It is made of iron forged in the courtyard of a church and blessed by a priest. Satan himself could not escape that net if he wanted to. Now *go!*"

Still the men hesitated as they looked upon the fallen form of a being so otherworldly and horridly demonic that it truly felt as if it should not exist at all. Yet it was there right before their eyes despite how impossible it felt to them.

"Good God in Heaven," one man muttered.

"How could a good God let something like this be?" another man asked, sounding just as stunned.

Smoke flowed from parts of the Boogeyman's body where the chains touched, causing the sinister entity to cry out all the more. A closer look and it seemed as if the chains were leaving burns all over the phantom's body.

"The net!" Abraham called out.

It was too late, for soon the Boogeyman rose as it threw its hands to its side and let out a terrifying shriek. The iron chain net was sent flying through the air across the room. Several men screamed out, some even dropping the iron bars and clubs they were given for the task.

"You've got to stop it!" Rory shouted as he hugged Hannah close to him. His wife and daughter looked just as fearful as they all huddled together. "Please, don't let that thing take my daughter!"

Somehow, the mayor's pleas appeared to work on at least some of the men. Several of them rushed forth at the Boogeyman with their weapons held high. However, this was not some random barroom brawler they were facing, and they were about to find that out the hard way. The Boogeyman looked at two men coming at it from the left. The otherworldly entity then threw its hand forth and the two men were instantly taken off their feet and blown back by some invisible force of supernatural origin.

They crashed across the room's floor and one of the shelf-covered walls while three other men jumped in to take the Boogeyman. The vile creature saw them coming and thrust its hand forth, sending them flying back much like he had the two before. The trio collided into four other men behind them, sending them all down to the floor. The Boogeyman then shrieked as it levitated into the air and over the bed before landing right in front of the fallen men who were struggling to get back up. They stood for what would become a massacre of terrifying proportions.

The Boogeyman's horrible fingernails expanded six inches and sharpened into pointed claws. These newly grown weapons were then slashed across the throat of two of the men. Blood sprayed like water from a fire hose as the men gurgled and gagged, grabbing at their slit necks. Immediately following this, the Boogeyman grabbed another man by the arms and tore both limbs off in one savage pull. The other men tried to do something, but either the Boogeyman was too fast. It bit into one man's face before burying its claws into his gut, tearing out his innards in a graphic display of gore.

More carnage and disembodiment befell the men, who could do nothing but suffer bloody ends at the Boogeyman's taloned hands. Their blood, flesh, bones, and organs flew all about the room, leaving it a red display covered in human body parts and viscera. Some of the blood and tissue even splattered on Rory and his family as they stayed huddled in their corner. The mayor tried to make Hannah look away, but she could not help staring on as the Boogeyman ripped the men who tried so hard to protect her into pieces. By the time it was over, the room was a terrible mess, yet the gruesome tableau was still not finished.

The Boogeyman turned to the McConnell family with an evil thirst in its devilish eyes that only snatching a child would quench. The ghastly being started to move in on the McConnell's; not so much walking as simply moving forward in an unnatural way. The McConnell's were terrified beyond belief, for they knew just what the Boogeyman wanted, dreading it to High Heaven as the demon continued drawing closer.

"No, please!" Rory begged. "Not our girl... not my little Hannah!"

"Don't take my baby away from me!" Maggie begged tearfully.

Their words fell on deaf ears, for the Boogeyman shrieked as its right hand stretched for little Hannah. The girl screamed as loud as she could right before Abraham Van Helsing came up from behind and shoved an iron spike through the Bogeyman's body. The creature screeched in anguish as the sharp object pierced the middle of its back and came out through its chest. The entity's new wound burned to the point it began to hiss smoke, the sight of which made the McConnell's cringe. Abraham took advantage of the Boogeyman's painfully stunned state as he pulled a pouch out from an inner pocket of his coat.

He opened it up and started pouring its contents around the Boogeyman, revealing them to be salt. The scientist soon completed the circle which the Boogeyman now floated in the middle of. Abraham took a moment to catch his breath, his chest heaving heavily as he looked upon the nightmarish being up close and properly for the very first time.

"You are certainly unique from many of the other creatures I have bested over the years," Abraham said aloud. "But just like them, you shall soon meet justice as God would have it."

The university professor then pulled out a copy of the Holy Bible and began to read from its pages in the Latin dialect. Instantly, the Boogeyman's body violently twitched and convulsed as it cried out in agony. A strange, yet strong wind seemed to be emitting from the entity itself, which wafted throughout the room, the shreds of its coat blowing in different directions.

It grabbed for the stake in its body, which only burned its hands while it desperately struggled to pull the impaling object out. The Boogeyman shrieked as the wind howled on, even blowing out the bedroom window in a shower of glass. Undeterred, Abraham continued to read scriptures from the holy book.

The McConnell's watched on in terror and amazement as the events continued to play out, Hannah and Maggie crying all the while.

"*Van Helsing!*" Rory screamed, though he was drowned out by the wind's howl.

Abraham kept on reading from the Bible, having to fiddle with the pages somewhat because of the raging gale. He refused to let it become a major obstacle for him, for Abraham was determined to put this dark spectre down as he had so many agents of evil in the past. With intensity burning in his eyes, the scientist glanced away from his holy book only once to see the Boogeyman try to rush forth at him. Instantly, it was stopped by some unseen force field, one put in place by the markings put in the salt on the floor, which was mysteriously undisturbed by the swirling winds. Abraham was unable to hold back a smirk of satisfaction before he looked to his Bible and continued to read from it.

At the same time, Hannah turned to the Boogeyman as it let out an extra loud screech of anguish. She saw, much to her horror, that the phantom kidnapper was fighting through its pain to pull the spike from its chest.

"Daddy!" Hannah cried.

Rory turned to see the Boogeyman completely wrest the spike from its bulky torso before lifting it high and aiming it at Abraham Van Helsing.

"No!" Rory shouted as he rushed to Abraham's side.

He pushed the professor over and across the bed just as the Boogeyman flung the spike – which burned the hand that held it – at Rory. The mayor tried to move himself to safety, but the sharpened weapon still tore through the sleeve of his coat, his shirt beneath it, and the flesh of his left bicep. His wife and daughter screamed in horror as they saw blood flow from the wound on the politician's arm.

Abraham watched as Maggie and Hannah ran to Rory's side in an attempt to aid him. When the university professor saw what had happened to the town mayor, he looked to the still trapped Boogeyman with the darkest of glares.

The professor brought up his Bible and continued to read from its pages. Instantly the Boogeyman held its hands to its chest and began to shriek again as it twitched and shook about as though it were in a massive amount of pain. Large waves of shadowy blackness expanded from random points of the phantom's body as if it were being torn from the inside out. The Boogeyman tried smashing its way free from the force that held it where it was, but nothing it did would break the invisible field that the salt somehow made.

Abraham's voice intensified in tone and volume as he continued to read while flashes of thunder and lightning began to erupt at random. As the professor was nearing the end of the final verse, he looked to see the Boogeyman turning its hate-filled, luminescent red eyes towards him. With one last glower of defiance, Abraham finished his reading and his otherworldly foe instantly burst into many pieces of shadow that soon dissipated into nothing.

Instantly afterwards, Abraham hurried over to join Hannah and Maggie at Rory McConnell's side. He started examining the injury on his arm just as many more men burst into the room.

***

The next morning saw Abraham exiting through the front of the town hall, Rory and Hannah following close behind. The university professor looked at them both and gave a pleasant smile accompanied by a small bow and tip of his hat.

"Oh, no need for that, sir," Rory said. He beamed joyously, despite his arm being in a sling and full of stitches. "With what you did for our village, we should be doing all the more for you."

"That's quite all right, Mr. Mayor," Abraham replied. "I was glad to be of service."

"Please, just call me Rory," the mayor said. "None of my friends ever have to address me by my title."

"Well, I'm glad to be in such good company, Rory," Abraham said.

"Won't you stay for a while?" Hannah asked.

"Oh, I am sorry, child, I wish I could," Abraham responded. "But a man who leads the life I do must know when it is time to move on. Unfortunately, that time seems to be perpetual. After all, one never knows when evil may strike again in the world. I must always keep myself as available as I can to answer the call to arms against the forces of darkness. Besides that, I do have other responsibilities. I am, after all, still a university professor."

"Well, we certainly understand that," Rory said.

"Whether it may be the Boogeyman again or something else," Abraham went on, "I must be ready to face whatever creature of the night falls upon this unsuspecting world."

"The Boogeyman?" Hannah asked. "But I thought you–"

"No, my child," Abraham said. "I am afraid I cannot permanently deter the Boogeyman. It is quite possible that no one truly can. It is a spirit that has plagued various parts of this world for many a century, manifesting in a great diversity of forms. It can be exorcised as I did last night, but it is debatable if man will ever have the power to truly banish it from entering this plane of existence permanently."

Abraham saw that Hannah was starting to become upset, prompting him to crouch down to her level. He then lightly put a hand under her chin and turned her head up some so he could look her in the eyes.

"However, I do not think you shall have to worry about him coming back here," Abraham said sincerely. "At least, not for a good long while. Spirits such as the Boogeyman are a cowardly lot, preying on the innocent and then running off with their tails between their legs whenever they are bested."

This got Hannah to smile and even laugh a little, which in turn put a smile on Abraham and Rory's faces as well.

"Why do you think the Boogeyman came here, Mr. Van Helsing?" Hannah asked.

"Who can say for sure what reason, if any, goes into a demon's train of thought?" Abraham said as he stood up again. "That is assuming they have one at all. Perhaps we shall figure it out one day and perhaps not. Mankind has made many other grand discoveries in the past. We may one day even find a means to permanently banish demons from this world altogether."

"You really think so?" Hannah asked excitedly.

"It is possible," Abraham answered. "A man in my position cannot discount anything. Furthermore, it is good just to be as hopeful as one can be. Remember that for me, won't you, Ms. McConnell?"

"I certainly will," Hannah replied.

"Then my time here truly was worth it," Abraham noted before turning to Rory. "I guess I shall be on my way then."

"Thank you again for all your help, Professor," Rory said. "Many times more thank you, even though it will never be enough."

"Oh, but it is," Abraham assured his new friend.

"Goodbye, Mr. Van Helsing," Hannah said.

"Goodbye and Godspeed, Ms. McConnell," Abraham replied pleasantly.

With a final tip of his hat, Professor Abraham Van Helsing turned away and headed out for whatever he might have to face next. As he walked along, the professor pulled out his daughter's golden cross necklace. He rubbed it between his gloved fingers, gazing at it to remind himself of something. No matter what may come his way, so long as he remembered why he did what he did, he would always be ready for it.

END

FIRST HUNT

Zach Cole

The name's Jeremy Walker. Six months ago, my girlfriend, Jessica, was killed by a werewolf. That was my first exposure to the supernatural. Before that, I was just a college graduate who was planning on proposing to the love of my life.

Not only was my girlfriend murdered by the werewolf, but I got scratched. The virus or whatever it is that spreads the "curse" entered my body and left me as a werewolf myself. Well, a Lycan. According to Tark, it's a special sort of werewolf that is able to change from a man to a wolf at will.

"Who the hell is Tark?" you may ask. He's the guy who found me after my run-in with the werewolf. He helped me recover and rein in the beast that is now inside me.

"You know, there is more than just werewolves out there," Tark says, sitting in his favorite recliner in the living room of his cabin.

I sit next to him in a recliner of my own. It's newer than his and just as comfy. I put down the book I was reading on meditation.

"Why not?" I reply. "It'd be stupid for one type of supernatural creature to exist and not any others. Are you getting at something by telling me this?"

Tark chuckles, looking away from the fireplace and towards me. "You know me well, Jeremy. What I'm getting at is that you have a gift.

A gift that could save lives. There are individuals that hunt the creatures that are out there killing people."

"Like the werewolf that killed Jessica," I say, my face hard as a rock.

Tark nods solemnly. "You have the ability to stop something like what happened to her from happening to anyone else."

I turn towards him. "You want me to become a monster hunter?"

"No. I want you to save people."

I look down at my feet, mulling over it for a moment.

"You're right," I finally respond. "I don't want anyone else to suffer like I have."

Tark smiles. "Glad to hear. Luckily, I know of a job."

I don't reply. I just give him a "go on" look.

"Have you heard of the Owlman?" Tark asks.

"A half bird, half owl creature, yeah?"

He nods. "Story goes two teenage girls were on holiday with their parents in April of 1976 in Mawnan Smith, near Falmouth in Britain. One day, they walked down to the old remote church, more than a mile from the village center. That's when they saw it. A bird man, wings and feathers and everything. It was just sitting atop the church tower. The story goes they were so scared by the sighting that their father decided to put an end to their holiday and leave Cornwall immediately."

"It didn't attack them?"

Tark shakes his head. "No, but keep listening. In July of the same year, two fourteen-year-old girls decided to go camping in the area. They were very aware of the story of the Owlman, and they spotted a giant owl with pointed ears. They further described it as being the size of a man with glowing eyes and black, pincer-like claws. The discovery of this cryptid soon made headlines and it was named the Owlman of Mawnan Smith. The creature was quickly branded a hoax, as many things are when they seem impossible to the human mind.

"But it seemed most of the reports led back to one man: paranormal researcher Tony 'Doc' Shiels. Shiels was known for taking part in a project to find monsters. It's been said that he saw the Loch Ness Monster and took a picture of her.

"People soon dismissed the claims of there being an Owlman haunting the church and its surroundings, explaining that they had probably only seen a very big owl, if they saw anything at all. Since then, several scattered sightings have been reported, the last being in 1995. Though in 2000, a loud, owl-like sound could be heard at night in the Mullion church yard. However, since its first sighting back in '76, the story seems to have been forgotten by the people of Mawnan Smith."

"Why are you telling me all this?"

"Because, my boy, the Owlman isn't gone. It's migrated here to California. And it's killing people."

***

The information I just received was a lot to take in. I've researched various cryptids since I was turned into a monster myself. Not a lot of them seem believable. None of them do, actually. But here I am, turned into a werewolf and being told the Owlman is real now. It made me wonder how many other cryptids are real.

I suppose I'll soon find out.

"I was a hunter myself," Tark said, going through the files of the Owlman's kills. "And I never once thought that I'd be hunting the Owlman. It seemed like such a peaceful creature. And why is it here?"

"I'm no expert," is my only reply as I blankly stare at the pictures of mutilated bodies.

I grab my head and clench my eyes shut, trying to block out the images of Jessica's ripped open body.

A hand on my shoulder makes me jump. I look into the worried eyes of my mentor.

"You alright there, son?" Tark asks.

I nod. "I'm... I'm good."

His eyes linger on my own for a moment before turning back to the photos.

"So... what's our play?" I ask.

"It seems to be nocturnal," Tark replies, "so that's when we should start looking for it. In town."

"In town, huh?"

Tark nods. "I know another hunter that may wanna help us out, too. I'm rusty and you're new, so we'll need a veteran hunter on our team."

A phone call and an hour later, a knock sounds on the door. I'm startled awake. I was sitting in my recliner and was starting to doze off.

"Glad you came," Tark says while opening the door to his cabin.

"I actually just caught wind of this case, myself," a familiar voice tickles my ear.

My eyes pop open and my head swivels toward the door. That's when I see him… Jessica's brother, Josh.

He gives me a smile. "Hey Jerm. It's been a while."

"Sorry," I respond, avoiding eye contact with him. "I haven't felt like socializing much lately."

He waves me off. "No choice now!"

I let out a chuckle, my first real one in the six months since Jess was murdered. I'll admit, I've been moping around and deeply depressed ever since. I've tried everything aside from being with another woman to get out of it, but I just don't see that happening. Maybe I never will…

"I say we scout around for it tonight," Tark said.

"Same," Josh agrees. "I actually even have an idea as to where it may be hiding during the day."

"Great," Tark responds. "We'll head over there just before sundown and see if we can encounter the creature before it leaves its hidey hole in search of food."

Yippy, I think, my face deadpanning.

***

We didn't have to go far to find the creature's hiding spot. It was in the very same forest that Tark's cabin resides in. We stand before an old, run-down house on the other side of the woods. The setting sun on the place sends an eerie chill through my spine. I'm beyond scared. As terrified as I was when I encountered the werewolf six months ago.

Why did I agree to this again? I wonder.

I look down at the pistol in my hand. This was the first time I've held a gun in my life. My dad wasn't big on guns. Never took me hunting. He just wasn't that kind of guy. He was more interested in uncovering things that have been long dead, like lost civilizations and what not.

I look to Tark and Josh, each of them having a weapon of their own. Unlike me, armed with only a small caliber handgun, they're armed with heavier hitting rifles. Tark has a hunting rifle while Josh holds an AR-15.

"You sure bullets are going hurt this thing?" I ask nervously, eyeing the pistol in my hands.

"Well, not really," Josh replies, killing any confidence that I might've had. "No one knows anything about this creature other than the stories. Unlike many of the other creatures I've gone up against in the past, I know nothing about its weaknesses."

"So, we can only hope that these will do the job," Tark says while waggling his rifle at me.

"Let's get going," Josh insists. "We don't have long before the sun sets, and it goes looking for more food."

We make our way toward the house.

"What I don't get," I mention, "is why this creature needs so much food. It killed six people, leaving them bloody messes, in only two days. Supernatural or not, that's weird for any creature. It shouldn't need to eat that much."

"That's a very good point," Josh concurs, stopping in his tracks. He pats me on the shoulder before turning to Tark. "I think we should be extra careful going in here."

Tark nods his agreement, tightening his grip on his rifle.

Josh slowly opens the door. Tark shoulders his rifle and enters the dark insides of the house. I shuffle nervously inside behind my mentor. Josh takes up the rear.

The inside of the house is dark, but my eyes adjust quickly, thanks to my new… condition. It's very run down. The floor is rotted in places. Vegetation has crept inside, covering most of what's left of the surface and is trying to make its way up the wall. The place must've been abandoned for years, or even decades.

Creaking draws our attention upward. We spot a staircase. Like the rest of the house, it's decaying and covered in vegetation. We slowly make our way up. Thankfully, it holds. We have to hop over a gap where the flight of stairs has rotted away. The top floor is completely decayed. The walls have been knocked down and there's a gaping hole in the roof.

That's not what holds our attention, however.

Amongst the ruins of the upstairs sits the creature we're after. It's curled in on itself, looking to be sitting on something. I squint, focusing on our surroundings. My eyebrows shoot up as I realize what we are standing in.

"This is a nest," I say.

Tark and Josh whip toward me, both saying, "What?"

My face sours as I repeat my realization. "We're standing in the Owlman's nest."

***

Our heads snap towards the creature curled in on itself as it begins to stir.

"Shit," I mutter, aiming my pistol at the bird man.

"Hold your fire," Tark whispers to me.

I do, taking my finger away from the weapon's trigger.

The Owlman unfurls, revealing its horrible visage to us. It has the build of a man but is covered in feathers. It has long, gangly arms ending in three fingered, black claw-tipped hands. Its feet match its hands, except for having only two claws and somewhat resembling the pincers of a crab. Its wings fold against its back as its owl-like head swivels in our direction, staring at us with beady black eyes. It opens its beak, letting loose a horrible screech.

A cold sweat breaks out across my forehead. Every instinct I have is yelling at me to turn tail and get the hell out of there. But I don't. Instead, my eyes drift from the creature itself to what lay at its feet. White, ovular objects. Eggs.

"It's not an Owlman," I say. "It's an Owlwoman."

"And it's dying," Tark declares quietly, lowering his weapon.

"I understand now," Josh says, lowering its own weapon. "Well, most of it."

We watch as the creature sits back upon its eggs, eyes still locked on us.

"It didn't need all that food for itself," Josh continues. "It needed it for its brood. And whatever it ate before, which was probably woodland animals, wouldn't make the cut."

118

"So, it went after bigger prey… people…" I say, my fear turning to anger.

"Still doesn't explain why it came here all the way from England," Tark says, ignoring my statement.

"It's possible it came to the U.S. to mate before finding a suitable nest," Josh says.

While Josh and Tark exchange theories on why the creature was here, out of the place it was born or haunted or whatever, I took a step towards it. The thing watched me but didn't move. So, I take another step. And another. Until I'm standing just a few feet away from the creature. It hisses as I raise my pistol to its head. Yet, it still doesn't move.

"Woah, what the hell are you doing Jeremy?" Josh yells.

"It killed people," I say and pull the trigger.

The bullet rips from the gun's barrel, exploding through the Owlwoman's head. It flops to the ground, brain matter and blood oozing from its skull. The two people behind me just stare on in horror as I move the carcass of the creature out of the way.

"What are you doing, boy?" Tark asks.

"They'll grow up to be killers, too," I answer, lifting my foot and stomping on one of the ovals.

It squishes beneath my shoe, followed by a sickening crunch that signals the death of the developing creature within.

"The fuck, dude!" Josh shouts, grabbing my shoulder.

I shrug out of his grasp, crushing another egg beneath my foot.

"They'll grow up to be killers!" I yell. "All of them! Just like their parent!" I squish another egg under my foot. "They deserve this. So, they don't rip people away from their loved ones! So, people don't turn out like me!"

The last egg crumbles beneath my foot, followed by a shriek and a crack.

The monsters were all dead.

***

"I thought that was what we were supposed to be doing," I say.

We're now back at Tark's cabin, in the living room. I sit in my recliner. Tark sits in his. Josh paces back and forth in front of me, steaming mad. He turns to me, looking as if he were about to explode. He calms as I stare back at him. He tears his eyes away from mine.

"Listen, dude," he says, "you're not the only one who lost Jess that night."

"I know that," I growl.

His anger returns, his eyes staring daggers into mine. "Then start fucking acting like you know! She was my fucking sister!"

My gaze shifts to my feet. "You're right. I'm sorry."

"The creature was just following its instincts," Tark points out, speaking for the first time since we returned to the cabin. "It was no different than a tiger or a bear. Not to mention it may have been one of a kind. Now, thanks to you, it's extinct."

"What does it matter?" I grumble.

Tark shakes with rage, looking as if it were about to burst forth. He clenches his eyes shut, trying to control the anger.

"It may have been too soon to expose you to such things, it seems," he says after a few moments of silence. "You have to learn that you cannot let anger control you. Not every creature out there is evil. Some, like we saw today, are just animals doing what nature tells them to do."

I stay silent, knowing I'd set them off if I said anything more.

Tark frowns. "You'll learn in time. And time is something we have plenty of."

END

K.A.R.U.D.

Christofer Nigro and Matt Hickman

Near a sewer opening in Houston, Texas late 2010s

It was quiet at this time of the night at a certain decrepit neighborhood in Houston where a certain manhole cover was located (it will be the opening scene of the horrific tableau that is about to unfold, in case this file is being read by a moron). The large metallic disc was poorly attached to the portal leading under the street and easy to lift, something the homeless people of the city were well aware of since they often used this opening to come and go from the abandoned subterranean subway system so many of them made their dwelling place. This entrance to their habitat was also well known to residents of the city who made it their business to know everything about the metropolitan geography, including the trio within a red four-door 2010 Chevrolet Camaro that pulled up to a curb about ten feet from the manhole of note.

"It's gonna be disgusting down there," Melissa Grace, the driver with rainbow hair and garbed in a black parade jacket, said in a voice that many had told her resembled the titular girl from the animated TV series *Daria*. "Are you really sure you want to go down there without a hazmat suit, Mac?"

That question was addressed to the sole male of the threesome who sat shotgun beside Melissa. This gentleman was white, appeared to be in his mid-30s, fairly muscular in build, and his apparel was characterized by a U-shape earring in each of his lobes, dark blue jeans, a blue T-shirt with the band Van Halen's logo on it, and an open leather trench coat covering that. Yes, this was the Mac whom the Goth girl driver had spoken to, and both man and monster alike were loathe to fuck with him; especially not monsters, whom he happened to kill for a living. A good job if you could get it, and if you happened to be capable of surviving a single night of it – which was an even taller order than getting such a whacked-out vocation.

"Hey, I've stalked monsters in worse places than the sewers," Mac replied as he grabbed hold of his trademark baseball bat and prepared to exit the scarlet vehicle. "Be glad I hooked up with you two long *after* that time I had to make my way through a cave to hunt a group of nesting harpies. The whole cavern was filled with rotting food, decaying human corpses, and the bird ladies' own shit."

"Eeewwww!" responded Kitty Gruber from the back seat, as the slightly chunkier woman pulled the collar of the fluffy pink jacket she wore over her nose as a metaphorical gesture. "Even imagining what that cavern must have smelled like makes me want to yak up two days' worth of lunch."

"So, yeah, the sewers will be almost tolerable by comparison," Mac said as shut the passenger door and headed towards the rusty old manhole lid a few feet away. "Besides, it's not really a sewer but several miles of unused underground tunnels intended for a subway system that never happened. Pretty much like the one they have in New York City. It's perfect for both serving as a refuge for Houston's homeless population... and, unfortunately as a covert dumping ground for cannisters of corporate toxic waste. Much like what happened in the underground region of New York back during the '80s, which is why we now have the same problem here that they did there. Some assholes never learn, so they need to be taught a lesson until they do."

Kitty hit the keys on her laptop with great rapidity as she searched the Internet for info on that incident. "That whole awful shebang is reported in a few places, but is considered an urban legend, just like the alligators that live down in the New York sewers are supposed to be. Those companies know how to cover their asses, and the story is way too crazy to be treated as real by the average person even though it totally is. So…"

"So, yes, it's up to me to deal with the "K.A.R.U.D.," Mac replied as he struck the front portion of the bat to the palm of his free hand to make his point clear.

"The *what?*" Kitty asked.

"Oh, that's an acronym for Killer Anthro-Reptilian Underground Dweller," the dark-haired Mac elaborated.

"Um, according to these reports and the file that Nero guy got you when he found out about this, a different acronym was used for these things back then," Melissa noted.

"Yeah, I know," Mac replied, "but I like this one a lot better, since it sounds like 'crud,' which is what this whole affair is full of. So, I coined the new one. Also, changing the name keeps government and corporate algorithms from getting a 'hit' on our own files. That can happen no matter how good S.A.V.A.G.E.'s[1] firewalls are."

"And since this shit is going on in Houston, Director Nero insists that we're the Boogey Knights unit that has to handle it. I bet he would've had us fly up to his home base in Buffalo if the vampire infiltration going on there now required an outing into the sewers to take them out!"

"You'd be surprised at some of the places Mike has had the pleasure of going to deal with monsters," Mac noted, "so, I really don't know. The point is, these toxic mutations have now popped up in the city we live in and protect. The homeless population is being both slaughtered by those mutations and transformed into more of them, and we've been elected to take care of it. Which is fine by me, since 'Lucille' here has been begging for a workout." Mac tapped his bat pseudo-affectionately to make it clear to what he was referring to with that name.

"Who?" the red-haired Kitty enquired while sticking her attractive face out the back window. "Ya know, if you wanted to give your bat a lady's name, you could've picked one of the two girls you're committed to. That would have at least been flattering, to have something you wreak such carnage with named after one of us. But… 'Lucille?' *Seriously* now?"

---

[1] S.A.V.A.G.E. = Society for Assessing Viability of Abominations as Good or Evil.

Mac sighed. "Never mind. It was a joke, and you wouldn't get it since it pertains to some crazy guy I had a run-in with after I got stranded for a few weeks in this really fucked up alternate timeline. Anyway, it's time I went into the hole."

Kitty snickered loudly while Melissa said, "Woohoo, mama!"

Mac shook his head. "Plenty of time for that later, girls. Right now, I have some nasty things to kill. I'll be right back, though."

"You better be," Kitty remarked. "Because the sight of your bat covered with yucky mutant blood is gonna get us all hot and bothered. Then again, there's another stick of yours we'll be lots more interested in. Unless, of course, you happen to transform into Mackenzie, in which case we'll gladly make do with what she has instead."

Geez, those two, Mac thought to himself as he pulled open the loose manhole cover. *If I didn't love them so much and find them hotter than the surface of Venus, it'd be lots more difficult to overlook how some of their worst puns can remind me of being on a mission with Mike Nero instead of them. Then again, having a werewolf at my side on a caper like this would be helpful. Still, it's nothing I shouldn't be able to handle on my own, especially with The Girls backing me up. I'll just keep telling myself that enough times that I'll actually start believing it; that should get me through this shitstorm like it has all the others I've been through.*

Mac strode through the darkened cavern with his trusty hardwood bat in hand and ready to swing, while exercising caution so that he did not accidentally strike one of the still-human residents who may inadvertently surprise him. After all, this was their home, not his, and he was here to save as many of them as he could while cutting off the threat of the K.A.R.U.D. before it escalated to the point where the cannibalistic creatures began preying on humans who lived above ground too. Just as it had occurred during that mess in the Big Apple a few decades ago, where a few ordinary but thankfully intrepid people managed to rise to the occasion and save the day… but not before a lot of human flesh was devoured and innocent lives altered in a most horrifically literal sense.

Then again, look on the bright side, Mac mused to himself to keep his mind focused away from the crazy situation of facing such a threat virtually alone. *If Nero was here, he would now be bitching about how capitalism is to blame for all of this, and insisting we would be making the businessmen and local bureaucrats who caused this latest mess our next targets, so at least I don't have to listen one of those spiels of his now...*

Mac stopped walking as he heard a loud "Ow!" after he stepped on something.

"Who the fuck just went crushin' ma leg?" came a weary voice from directly below him. "Was it ya'll again, Bert?"

"Naw, man," came an equally knackered voice from beside the first. "Was probly Cletus this time."

The bat-wielding monster hunter looked down to see that his foot had accidentally trodden on the left leg of a homeless man wearing tattered clothing who rested next to two more like him. They carried quite a stench, but Mac was willing to tolerate that, as he was filled with nothing but sympathy for the plight of these men.

"Sorry, dudes," he said. "This wasn't the fault of your Cletus, but just me."

The first man looked up to reveal an unshaven face with several missing teeth. "And who in the holy hell are you? You don't look like no under dweller I ever saw down here before. Are you some fuckin' copper come to give us a hassle? Or, some reporter come to interview us 'bout how horrible it is to have to live down here, so that nuthin' gets done again?"

"Neither of those," the slayer of things monstrous replied while lowering his bat. "My name is Mac. I'm actually down here to hunt the creatures that have been hunting all of you lately."

"I'm Ned, by the way," the under dweller said. "And do you mean the reptile-looking bastards that been eating us and that some of us turn into after they done bitten us?"

"Exactly them," Mac clarified. "Have you seen any in this area of the tunnels?"

"No," Bert answered for his friend, "but the three of us were chased by one in another section earlier. We settled down here for a nap so we wouldn't be nowhere near the places they're usually found. Cletus here beside me had a close call when one of them grabbed him durin' the chase, but we pulled him away. Ain't that so, Cletus?"

The apparently snoozing third man of the group made no response. "Cletus, did you hear me, man?" Bert queried as he shook his friend awake. "This stranger here says he's come to help us since the cops ain't done shit, and…"

Bert and Ned alike screamed in horror when Cletus looked up to reveal a visage with bulging yellow eyes and a wide frog-like mouth twisted open to a degree beyond human capability and filled with razor-sharp teeth. The growling sound the creature made as he salivated at the sight of his two (former) friends was as terrifying to their ears as were the altered facial features of the man they had previously known so well to their eyes.

"Get down!" Mac yelled to Bert and Ned as he swung his bat.

The inhuman countenance of the thing that was once a homeless man named Cletus was bashed in by the force of Mac's blow. The large spew of greenish blood and assorted gore produced by the attack spattered against the dingy gray wall behind Bert and Ned, as well as on their still screaming faces.

Mac finished off the still twitching mutate with two more decisive blows until its remains moved no longer. He then turned to the still wailing men.

"Shit, not Cletus!" Bert bellowed.

"Not Cletus!" Ned repeated.

"Shut up and listen!" Mac hollered at the two. "I realize that something really horrible just happened, but you have to pull your shit together and get the hell out of this tunnel. As in, up that manhole over to your left! Go somewhere, anywhere but here or in any of the project tenements within three blocks of here, since these tunnels probably intersect with the cellars. These tunnels are no longer fit for human habitation!"

Just then, Mac's body seemed to start trembling as his muscles contorted and his bodily contours began morphing. *Oh, here it comes. At least this didn't start happening* during *a battle…*

Bert and Ned became panic-stricken again as the old friends grasped each other in a tight embrace.

"Fuck, Ned! That Mac guy musta got infected! He's changing into one of them now!"

Mac did indeed transform into something altogether different than before… but also very different from one of the reptilian cannibal mutates spawned in the Houston tunnels by toxic waste exposure. Not to mention something altogether more pleasant for the two under dwellers to behold. The shifting of shape occurred quickly and with minimal pain and discomfort, as it always did when Mac experienced certain conditions of stress. Looking down at the two homeless men was not a creature born of toxic hell, but a rather attractive woman with long brown hair and large breasts that formed two bulges underneath Mac's Van Halen T-shirt.

"Whoa, Bert!" Ned shouted. "Will ya look at that. Mac's got tits now! Am I hallucinatin', maybe 'cause of the toxic guts that got all over me when Cletus's head was popped open?"

"No, you aren't," came a feminine voice from the equally womanly body that once belonged to the man named Mac. "But it seems Mackenzie decided she would come out now. Sorry if the change startled you, boys."

"What the fuck?" Ned muttered. "Are ya'll sure you're not some toxic sewer mutant of some kind or other?"

"Yes, I'm sure," Mack (now with a 'k' for the shortened version of the first name). "This started happening after I was exposed to this mystic object I found back in my teens during an early monster fighting mission. It caused another aspect of mine to manifest both physically and mentally; the female side that was always a part of me. Neat, huh?"

Ned and Bert looked at each other with twin expressions of utter incredulity.

"We gotta be dreamin'…" Bert opined again as his hands sunk into his palms.

"Well, if that's so," Ned replied, "then I think that maybe this time we done gone to Heaven instead of Hell."

Mack could not help giggling to herself over Ned's reaction despite the seriousness of the situation she had to contend with.

That was quickly spelled out when a vent on the side of one of the underground walls just above Ned was knocked out by one of the mutates as it launched a surprise attack on the man. The homeless resident of the tunnels screamed yet again as he was effortlessly lifted upwards and into the air shaft that had previously provided comforting heat to those who slept beneath it.

"Bert, grab his legs!" Mack yelled as she reached into one of her coat pockets to extract a Browning BDA .45 ACP.

Despite being in another state of panic, Bert did as the lady requested, holding onto Ned's legs a hard as he could. The unexpected extra weight interrupted the smooth abduction of the hapless man, but Mack knew that would end no more than two seconds later when the reptilian cannibal redoubled its efforts. It never came to that, however, due to the chestnut-tressed woman pointing her firearm into the vent at an angle where it would hit neither Bert nor Ned. This allowed the large red glow of its mounted laser scope to center on the forehead of the hideous mutation several feet within the shaft. The trigger was pulled and for the second time in ten minute a mutate's skull exploded in a mass of greenish gore.

Bert slid the shrieking Ned out of the vent to find him covered in another large spatter of one of the creature's sickly-colored bodily fluids and brain matter.

"Oh God, don't let it take me!" Ned bellowed.

"Calm down!" Mack demanded, raising her soft but firm voice for the first time that night. "The more you scream, the more you're gonna draw those creatures here! That's what I want, of course, but not until after both of you retreat from these tunnels!"

"How... how the hell did you make a shot like that?" Bert could not help himself from asking that as he wrapped an arm around Ned to forcibly calm him.

"I've always been a crack shot thanks to the training my grandfather gave me," Mack explained. "He was one of the best monster hunters who ever kicked an ass. It's a shame he wouldn't have accepted... this part of me."

Mack struggled to wipe the somber look of regret from her pretty features, as this was not the time for melancholic venting, and those were not the proper shoulders to lean on. They were hapless humans in need of her help.

"Alright, help him up and get him out that manhole," she said to Bert. "No more just standing there!"

"Sorry, um... ma'am, but I was chest admiring the lady that rescued us... I mean, *just* admiring the *hero* that come saved us!"

"Mmmhmm. Now, stop admiring and start *running!*"

Bert did as commanded, helping the still frazzled Ned move along with him.

"By the way," Mack called to them. "There will be a woman named Kitty in a wooly pink coat guarding the manhole you're going to come out of with a gun. Make sure you yell 'don't shoot, we're humans and Mac helped us get away!' as soon as you pop out, so she doesn't mistake you for one of those things and blow you away!"

"Good advice, so I'll take it!" she heard Bert's scratchy voice shout back as he reached the metal ladder leading up through the manhole.

Mack then placed the gun back in her coat pocket, raised the baseball bat into swinging position, and began trekking down the tunnel into the inner reaches of the subterranean environment. Her keen ears and eyes were scanning for any possible sound, but nothing save for her own footsteps could be heard clacking on the concrete ground.

She knew that would not last long.

***

Nero got his intel soon after discovering those toxic barrels were being stored down here, so they've only been down there a few weeks, not years, like they were in New York. But about two dozen homeless people have been reported missing so far, and that's bad enough. It's still like catching cancer in its early stages, though, so I should be able to get them all without needing extra help, right?

Mack did her best to self-reassure until she heard the scream of a woman, followed by a few wails that were decidedly non-human. *Head's up, girl!*

The monster hunter that was currently a lady ran down the tunnel as fast as her strong legs could take her, following the echoes of those screams. She turned the corner to see a middle-aged woman in raggedly clothing besieged by two of the cannibalistic[2] mutates. One of them held her to the ground as she frantically pummeled at its frog-like face to

---

[2] Yes, I know it can be argued that these mutates are not actually "cannibals" if you want to get all nitpicky and technical, since cannibalism is defined as the eating of other members of one's own species, and these creatures are quite likely no longer human. I get that. But since the word "cannibal" sounds scary, and the K.A.R.U.D. were once human, let's just go with it instead of quibbling over details, ok? Thanks, bruh!

little avail, while the second was attempting to get around the first so it could more easily get its share of the impending feast.

Less than a second later the first mutate had its brains blown out the back of its distorted head courtesy of a bullet from Mack's firearm. As the second one looked up and roared a challenge to her, the monster hunter pocketed her gun and raised her makeshift hardwood bludgeon.

"Woohoo! I'm now up at bat!" she screeched while rushing towards the literal example of toxic humanity before her.

The lady under dweller remained on the ground flailing her arms about and screaming, "Oh god oh god oh god…!" as if still in shock.

Mackenzie leaped over the hapless victim with a lithe move she could only perform as gracefully while in female form. This jumping move culminated with the slamming of the bat across the mutate's face as she swooshed by it. The creature's jaw was broken, as evidenced by pieces of its teeth and a stream of green blood dribbling out its mouth. It remained on its feet and swung its powerful arms at Mack, trying either to strike her down or slash her with its clawed fingers. The monster hunter countered the frenzied attack with another blow from the bat, this one to the mutate's skull. A third such blow crushed its cranium into a mass even more distorted than usual.

The monster groaned in a horrible but piteous fashion as it coughed up green blood and fell to the ground unmoving. Mack turned and reached her hand to the still furiously trembling woman on the ground.

"Come on, lady!" Mack shouted. "I'm here to help you! I've gotta get you out of here before the rest of those things get here…"

Mack just barely pulled her slender fingers away in time to avoid getting them bitten off by the no-longer-quite-human lady as the latter chomped at them. The under dweller opened her mouth wider than any human jaw should have been capable to screech at her savior and to expose a set of sharpened teeth.

Shit, I hoped I could save her! Mack thought to herself as she smashed open the homeless woman's now misshapen skull before the nightmarish metamorphosis could complete itself.

That was when the hunter of monsters heard the distinctive wailing sound of a group of mutates echo down a side tunnel connected to the one where she stood. Three of the monstrous mutates emerged from it ahead of the others. They were fully transformed, having dispensed with

130

all their human clothing to reveal bodies resembling a bipedal lizard with grayish-olive skin and the aforementioned horrific visages to complete the horrendous features.

"All right, bitches!" Mack shouted while raising her bat. "Have at thee, or something like that!"

One of the mutates charged, and Mack deftly ducked under its swinging claw. She countered with a blow to its long-toed, spade-like right foot with her bat, crushing the inhuman digitals and causing the mutated beast to slouch over in pain. She then stood up to her full height of just under six feet and smashed the monster's skull with her hardwood bludgeon. Its skull was spattered into a mass of emerald gore as it fell unmoving to her feet.

The other two mutates exhibited a remnant of their previously human intelligence by attacking their foe in unison. Mack held the bat in each hand like a staff to act as a barrier against the double assault. She was strong, but the mutates were stronger and they forced her back against the wall. Before they could bite into her, however, the monster hunter raised her legs and put the soles of her sneakers against their gray-green torsos to hold them back. She then pushed with all her might while their slavering, gaping maws opened hungrily as they struggled to sink their teeth into the woman's tasty flesh. Mack managed to halt the creatures' further progress but was unable to push them away despite giving it her best.

The struggle continued for over twenty seconds with the screeching mutates slowly gaining ground on their intended prey. Suddenly, their foe's monumental effort of will was aided by an exhibition of much greater leg strength, and the reptilian duo found themselves pushed several feet backwards. The two human legs returned to the concrete floor beneath them to reveal the once-again male form of Mac Evans.

"Yes, Mac is back!" he shouted in elation. *And just when I needed the extra strength and durability in place of the extra agility and speed I gain when Mackenzie comes out.*

The well-built young man ran forward with his bat and smashed one of the mutates beside its grotesque head, breaking it open with a great spurt of sickly-hued greenish blood. The second one bellowed in rage and hunger as it charged at him immediately after he had dispatched the other.

"Don't worry, I saved some for you!" Mac exclaimed as he swung the hardwood stick with all his considerable might.

A few seconds later the creature lay twitching on the fetid ground with its exposed cerebrum splattered on the concrete beside it.

Before Mac could take a breather, however, he heard more of the familiar inhuman wailing coming from down the side tunnel. That was likely the remainder of the mutates, and it was still unknown how many of the homeless population who called these tunnels home other than Bert and Ned managed to escape. His repentant concern was soon replaced with a need for self-preservation and termination of the threat.

Since their monstrous caterwauling suggested about a dozen of them were on their way, the hunter of monsters realized the bat would have to take a back seat to his Browning BDA to finish the job. That was always his choice of handgun since he learned that it was the preferred weapon of a certain legendary detective from Miami, a lawman who also happened to be friends with his equally legendary grandfather.

Mac tossed the bat aside and drew his powerful firearm in a double blur of motion. The menace he was now facing was born of science gone wrong, not sinister mystical forces, so ordinary lead ammo would do the job – there was no need to resort to the ammo he carried that was comprised of silver, wood, cold steel, or rock salt pellets.

If only the bat was small enough to stuff into one of the bottomless pockets of this enchanted trench coat I managed to pick up from Santa Domingo during a mission to Cali. Oh, well, it's still one of only two in existence, so why complain about its shortcomings?

"Come and get it!" he shouted like a chef proudly announcing the completion of a prepared meal.

The first two of the dozen monstrosities – both resembling and differing from the Deep Ones he had faced in the past during a mission to Innsmouth – sauntered out of the side tunnel to face their quarry. Within two seconds both creatures had their brains emptied from their no-longer-human skulls via the monster hunter's .45. A third one slid around the bend at much quicker speed, obviously learning from witnessing the gory fate of the first two. It was a good but futile move, as Mac still blew the cannibalistic monstrosity's guts through a newly created cavity in its lower back.

"Come on, come on, there's plenty for all of you here!" Mac shouted to hurry the remaining nine along to their scheduled termination appointment.

The next two K.A.R.U.D. swiftly turned the corner, and Mac was as quick to hit the trigger as before. Unfortunately, this time the act was accompanied by just a clicking noise followed by nothing more, as opposed to the thunderous bang followed by a copious display of sickly green gore he was expecting. The clip was empty of ammo, and that sucked.

Shit! That really sucks! Mac mused in agreement with this omniscient author. "Well, I guess they're won't be plenty for everyone after all," he remarked with grim irony.

With another move that was almost a blur of motion Mac pocketed his empty .45 – which not even he had the time to reload – and slide across the smooth concrete ground to evade the talon swipe of the closest creature. He calculated this so he slid towards where he dropped the bat, which he quickly armed himself with again.

I guess I'm gonna have to take the rest of them with this old thing. No other choice!

Mac stood firmly with the bat in position to strike with a ferocity he had rarely exhibited before, as that was his only chance of getting out of this situation alive and uneaten. Suddenly, however, he noticed what resembled a small ceramic coin with odd symbols etched on its sides roll between the two mutates who were closest to him. The coin suddenly stopped of its own accord, as if "trapped" between their own electro-biological energies. This was punctuated by what looked like a tiny but visible arc of static appear between each side of the coin and the respective leg of the creature it stopped between.

Both mutates began yowling in agony with smoke rapidly rising from both of their bodies as if they were being steamed from the inside. A few seconds later both burst into flame, seemingly from the inside out, and their conflagrated carcasses fell to the ground in two flaming heaps. The remaining six toxic beasts screeched in confusion, horror, and rage at the fate that had inexplicably engulfed their scaly comrades-in-cannibalism.

Well, inexplicable to them, perhaps. For Mac's part, he recognized that coin as a mystical artifact of ancient Babylonian origin that was part of Melissa's magickal paraphernalia. He also knew that meant he was no longer fighting alone.

Melissa and Kitty were now visible standing between the four remaining monsters and their paramour Mac. Each of The Girls had their own firearms brandished and pointed at their targets.

"Those Babylonian fire coins do a righteous job at inducing spontaneous combustion in humanoids," Melissa said with a proud smirk. "I'm glad I picked a few of them up on eBay before the sellers realized what they actually had!"

"I wonder if you could use them to barbecue steak," Kitty snarked as she shot one of the three remaining creatures through its grotesquely extendible throat.

"Nah, it's more likely just reduce them to cinders, which would put a damper on our barbecue," Melissa opined as she blasted out one of the second creature's bulging eyes.

"I thought you girls were supposed to stay back to look up more info and to guard the manhole!" Mac admonished them as he bashed open the head of the final standing mutate with a might swing of his bat.

"Just consider yourself lucky that we don't always stick to the plan, babe!" Kitty remarked.

"Yea," Melissa concurred. "If we did, you'd find yourself stuck to those things' gastric lining tonight instead of between the two of us in bed."

Mac sighed as he brought the bat down on the twitching creature he had just felled, reducing its head to a sickly green mush and ensuring it would never stand again.

"Well, I guess that's all of 'em," Kitty said.

"You almost got yourself killed," Melissa lamented to Mac. "Naughty boy. We're going to have to punish you when we you get home."

"I can live with that," Mac replied with a grin.

"Wait," Kitty said. "You didn't get bit, did you, babe?"

"I am officially bite free," Mac gladly announced. "Until you two get me home, I suppose."

Kitty sniggered. "Okay, but what do we do about those disgusting toxic waste bins that are somewhere down here? Wait for the government to come pick them up?"

"Fuck no!" Mac replied. "We'll have a S.A.V.A.G.E. team come in and remove them. I doubt my suggestion of leaving them in the bedroom of whoever signed the order to store them down here will be taken up, but I'll make it anyway, just as a way of venting."

"Won't the gov-gov bitch about that?" Melissa queried.

"Let them," Mac responded. "These toxins are not just a dangerous but mundane carcinogen hazard. This stuff is actually mutagenic, so that puts it in monster hunter jurisdiction. If the government complains, we'll see to it that the story gets in the hands of the wrong journalists."

"Well, that's better than expecting us to store those bins in our basement, or something like that," Melissa said.

"So, shall we get out of these tunnels, make the call, and then head for home?" Mac asked with a smile.

"We couldn't do it fast enough for me!" Kitty said. "We need to shower all this gunk off with the quickness."

"On the plus side," Melissa noted, "our shower is big enough to hold three."

The trio shared a giggle and Mac walked towards the manhole egress with an arm around each of his partners in both love and monster hunting.

Though he did not mention it, his smile was forced in an effort to conceal his remorse over the lives he failed to save this night despite his best efforts. The hazards faced by monster hunters were immense, and not all of them were in the realm of physical danger. Mac Evans knew this as well as any other who took this rare and extraordinarily path but the difference between *knowing* and *accepting* a harsh truth could often be huge.

END

THE WORKS OF MORTALS

Ryan George Collins, Esq.

"Some people say a man is made out of mud,
But a poor man is made of iron and blood."
~Merle Travis, "Sixteen Tons"

Max checked his pocket watch, then glared at the door, tapping his foot impatiently. He had gotten up at the crack of dusk, preparing everything for the arrival of his guests, and they had the gall to be late for the grand unveiling of his discovery. It was half-past midnight already, and there had not been so much as a wisp of fog or a gust of cold wind announcing their arrival.

Sighing angrily, he glided casually down the hallway of his lavish gothic mansion for the third time that night to make sure everything was presentable. As his gliding brought him past the room where his discovery lay, he paused there for a moment to check inside. It was most vital that everything be in order before presenting it.

He opened the door only a crack and peered into the room.

His discovery had not moved, nor had anything else. Everything was as he had left it.

Good.

Max returned to the grand hall at the entrance of his mansion, and a flash of lightning illuminated one of his guests in the doorway. He jumped in surprise and was glad he did not have any blood in his veins

136

to betray his embarrassment through blushing. It was a bit silly to be startled so easily, especially by one of the blood brothers he was expecting, but Max chalked it up to anticipation about the grand unveiling and did his best to obscure it.

"Ah, Sami, you made it," he said. "Please, enter."

Sami did so, changing from his human disguise to his true form. He left a trail of feathers behind him as he flew in and perched on the nearby hat rack. Sometimes Max envied Sami for his looks. Max was born of European stock, and while he was certainly not ugly, his looks were nothing compared to the beautiful complexion his South African friend could sometimes adopt. Sami's hypnotically stunning human form was just a façade, though. Most of the time, he appeared as a bird not entirely unlike a hamerkop. In his true avian form, he would only be stunning to an ornithologist.

"How was your trip?" Max asked.

"Longer than I would have liked," Sami replied as he preened his wings. His South African accent was noticeable, but mild, all things considered. "I would have rather flown, but that would have drawn attention. Too many bird watchers in this country."

"I know what it is like to draw a crowd," said a new voice with a mild yet noticeable Chinese accent. This newcomer was a stiff-bodied Chinaman with rigid arms and attire which had gone out of fashion when the Qing Dynasty fell. The skin on his face was slightly decomposed, and when he entered, he moved in short hops as a rabbit might do.

"Welcome, Xū," said Max. Unlike Sami, Max did not envy Xū's looks in the slightest.

"Much obliged, and to you as well, Sami," Xū nodded. "Is all our company met?"

"Not yet," Max replied. "We're still waiting-"

"-Fer me, I believe," said a new voice carrying a heavy Scottish accent.

"Ah, my dear Mary," Max said with a grin.

"Har-dee-har," Mary answered sarcastically. "Never heard tha' one before." Mary was quite a beautiful woman from the waist up, but her lower half was more likely to be admired by a game hunter than a potential lover. Though her lovely green dress mostly obscured her deer legs, they could not obscure the clacking of her cloven hooves against the stone floor as she entered. "Got anythin' ta drink, Maxie? I'm parched."

"I have a bottle waiting for us," Max said. "B negative, aged 54 years, acquired fresh this past week from a former business associate. Come. We shall drink as I show you my discovery."

Max guided his guests down the hall to where his discovery waited for them and paused before opening the door. He could not resist the urge to be a bit dramatic before the grand unveiling, and a big smile crossed his face. "My friends, my kindred spirits, I give you... the Works of Mortals!"

The door swung open at just the right speed to time itself perfectly with Max's words and revealed what was originally the drawing room repurposed to accommodate the thing on the mahogany table.

What it was, the visitors could not guess. It was shaped like a person, that much was apparent, but it was not like any person any of them had encountered before. It lay prone on the table, though it just barely fit, as it would have been nearly eight feet tall were it standing upright. It was naked and lacking in any anatomical features that would denote its gender, but the overall build was masculine in appearance.

Strangest of all was how it was put together, for it was indeed put together and not a naturally formed being. The skin was stretched over muscles that were oddly shaped, but not all of it was organic. Machinery ran throughout its body, in some places exposed either by a lack of skin or by protruding through it. Broken portions of baked clay adhered to its body in random patches.

Whatever it was, it showed no signs of life. Its thick eyelids were closed, and its ribs did not expand to accommodate breathing.

"What on Earth is this?" asked Xū, his voice conveying the amazement everyone else was feeling.

"This is my discovery, of course," Max beamed. "I found it while I was out last week. There's another mansion on the other side of town that I usually don't pay much attention to, but my search for a decent meal brought be near enough to it for me to notice something was different."

He found the bottle of B negative, opened it, and poured goblets for his guests as he continued. "By different, I mean the place had been almost completely burned to the ground. Only the older stone portions of it still stood. The masonry work is most impressive. Anyway, my natural curiosity got the best of me, and I had to go and take a closer look for myself. And what should I find in the basement? Nothing less than this charming fellow, along with the remains of a notebook." He passed around the goblets. "I hypnotized a few vagrants to carry him here, then I killed them to collect their blood and started reading through the notes."

"And did the notes say anything about this… thing?" asked Sami as he dipped his beak into his drink.

"Oh, did they ever!" Max took a sip of blood to wet his whistle before continuing. "Mind you, the notebook was damaged in the fire, so I can't tell you the whole story, but it would seem this was an attempt by someone to make a sort of golem. From what I can tell, some scientific fellow and his assistants pieced the thing together from corpses, filled in certain parts they didn't have with machinery, and finally placed it in a cocoon made of clay to finish it."

Mary examined the thing more closely. "Whit in the de'il's unholy name would they do that fer?"

"Whether you mean 'why encase it in clay?' or 'why make it at all?' I wish I could say, but I have no clue," Max shrugged. "As I said, the notebook was fairly damaged as well. Everything I've told you just now is all I could get from it. I suppose it might have been one of those experiments mortals do just to see if it can be done. It's a favorite pastime of theirs, you know. Whatever the case, the intent was to bring it to life, of that I have no doubt."

"Well, it clearly didn't work," Mary said. "This fella's deader than all 'f us combined."

"Which begs the question," Xū interjected, "why bother bringing it here and putting it on display for us?"

"Because I think the mortals were on to something," Max said. He raised his goblet to his lips, realized that it was empty, and so retrieved the bottle to refill it as he continued. "My current theory is that something went wrong while they were trying to give it life, and that's what caused the fire which destroyed the structure. It must have been some freak accident, because everything I've read in the notes seems fairly sound."

139

Xū shook his head as he hopped over to warm himself at the fireplace. "I marvel at how you still insist on dabbling in science when you have supernatural powers at your command. What good is science in the face of magic?"

"Especially failed science such as this," Sami added as he alighted on the prone giant's torso to get a closer look of his own. "A dead end is a dead end, if you ask me."

Max was starting to feel a sense of discouragement. His friends were clearly not as excited about this as he was, so he became determined to persuade them to his line of thinking. As such, he launched into an impassioned diatribe.

"Well, let me ask all of you something: What is science but another name for discovery? Why do you suppose the mortals progress and propagate while we immortals stagnate and dwindle in number? Because of their discoveries, that's why! And how do they make those discoveries? Through science!"

He began to pace about the room as though he were an actor on the stage delivering his big soliloquy in the final act.

"Science is how they figured out our weaknesses. Meanwhile, we have rested on our laurels believing that our powers will win out in the end, and where has that gotten us? They know a hundred surefire ways to repel us, but we have no way to repel them! What can we hang on our walls to keep them from staking us? What can counteract the poison of silver, iron, and salt? What would sustain us if the mortals were to go extinct? We need their blood to survive! We have got to think about those questions and figure out how to answer them!"

He pointed at the golem. "I don't know what purpose that hideous thing was made for, but it was an attempt by mortals to make life. That alone may be a significant discovery for us and our kind. If *we* can succeed where they failed, who knows where it might lead us?"

Mary helped herself to the bottle of B negative. "A'right, Maxie, ye think ye're so smart, answer me this: How d'ye intend to bring th' blasted thing ta life with a burnt notebook and nae equipment?"

That took all the wind from Max's sails. "I… don't… know…" he answered slowly, as if he were embarrassed to admit his cluelessness after delivering what he though was quite a rousing speech. "But just because I'm not sure doesn't mean I won't find out. Being immortal means I have plenty of time to experiment."

"Did you try lightning?" asked Sami, who was now perched upon the golem's chest.

"I haven't tried anything yet," Max admitted. "But lightning, Sami? Really? Isn't that a bit cliché?"

"Perhaps, but it's cliché for a reason." Sami tilted his head in thought, then shrugged as best as could without human shoulders. "Why not?" he said, speaking more to himself than to his companions. "It's worth a stab."

No one had time to object before Sami channeled a current of electricity into his beak and pecked at the giant's chest, transferring the charge from himself into its body.

A shockwave radiated out from the giant which knocked everyone off their feet. Sami remained on the creature by digging his claws into its skin.

When the shock had passed, Sami became aware that he was now bobbing up and down very slowly like a boat on the ocean. It was not his own movement, but the steady rising and falling of the giant's chest as it breathed its first breaths.

Sami cautiously hopped towards the giant's head and was thrilled to see its eyes open.

"It worked!" the bird shouted in triumph. He turned to face his companions, who were just beginning to pick themselves off the floor. "I did it! It's ali-*aack!*"

Sami's words were cut off as the giant's meaty right hand shot up and grabbed him tightly. Slowly it rose to a sitting position, its ghastly yellow eyes examining the bird in its hand and the three beings who stood before it.

Its dry clay-infused lips cracked open, and in a booming guttural voice, it uttered a word filled with the most intense hatred anyone in the room had ever heard spoken.

"Srti...goi..."

Its vice-like grip on Sami's fragile feathered body tightened, and in an instant the bird was crushed.

Gears whirred and clicked as the giant got to its feet, tossing the bird into the fireplace so the body would be properly incinerated. For a moment, it stumbled as it tried finding its balance, but the gyroscopes in its cranium kicked in and did exactly the job they were meant to do. Not even as it was stabilizing did it take its hate-filled eyes off the immortals before it.

"Stri...goi..."

The man-made golem began marching towards them. It moved slowly, but its stride was great enough to cover an immense distance quickly.

"Stri...goi..."

Mary shuffled behind Xū and Max, making them a barrier between her and the giant. "Call it a hunch," she said, "but I think this fella may 'ave a bone ta pick with oor kind."

"Strigoi!"

The giant charged the trio with horrific fury. Max and Mary were out the door in an instant, but Xū was not so lucky. His stiff body only allowed him to hop awkwardly, and the giant caught him quickly.

Unable to struggle very much and stunned that he could not change his form and escape, Xū tried the only weapon he had left at his disposal: hypnosis. His eyes glowed as he stared into the giant's wretched yellow eyes.

"Release me," Xū commanded.

The circuitry in the giant's skull generated sparks that flew from an open cavity above its left eye. It did not obey the command.

The last word Xū heard was the same word the giant had been repeating since Sami had awoken it.

"Strigoi!"

"This is why ye shouldn't be messin' wi' science, ye bugger!" Mary yelled at Max as they ran for the door. "This is whit always 'appens! Somethin' gaes wrong and nearly kills ya!"

"I am *not* responsible for any of this!" Max shot back. "I was going to take my time studying and experimenting! Sami is the idiot who went off half-cocked and electrocuted the thing! If you want to blame someone, blame him!"

"I can't bloody well blame 'im if he's dead, now can I?"

Something hit Mary from behind and knocked her off her hooves. Max came to a stop halfway between the door and where Mary had fallen and turned back to see what had happened. Mary was sprawled upon her stomach, pinned down by the permanently dead form of Xū. The poor Chinaman's stiff body had been forcibly bent and twisted into a pretzel, and the agonized expression on his frozen face meant he must have felt at least some of it.

The giant lumbered down the hall behind them, his eyes burning with rage at his targets.

"Strigoi!"

Mary struggled to get up, but between the extra load on her back and the slipping of her cloven-hooved feet on the stone floor, this task proved impossible to do on her own. "Dinnae jist stan' there, Maxie! Help me!"

Max hesitated, unsure of how to act. Helping Mary was the right thing to do, though doing the right thing was not really in his nature as one of the Undead. She was his friend, but they were not really that close.

The giant's intentions were crystal clear by now. If Max left Mary where she lay, it would almost certainly stop and finish her off, which might give him enough of a head start to escape, but…

But what?

Max clasped his hands together and did his best to sound sincere even as he continued backing towards the door. "I'm afraid there's just no time, Mary! Thank you for your sacrifice! I'll tell your story!"

With that, he ran outside, locking the door behind him as he fled.

"Ye ruddy little gobshite!" Mary screeched at the traitor she had thought a friend. "I'll find ya in Hell so I can kick yer bleedin' arse fer all eternity!"

She continued spouting such threats and curses even as the giant ripped her to pieces. Max had transformed into a bat the moment he had cleared the front steps, knowing that flying would put more distance between him and the giant than simply running. His keen bat ears could hear the doors splintering as the giant burst through them, but he did not dare to look back and see if it had noticed him.

Even in his flight, his mind had worked out a theory as to why the mortals had made the giant. It must have been a weapon, yet another tool in their arsenal for slaying his kind, and it was terribly efficient at doing so. Sami, Xū, and Mary had all fallen to it so easily. Max knew that it was pure luck which had allowed him to escape the giant. Well, luck and a sense of self-preservation so powerful that it transcended sentimentality.

He had escaped, but to what end? Suppose the thing figured out how to follow him or found him again as it continued killing immortals. Was he just going to keep running away from that monstrous brute for the rest of his unlife? Was that any sort of way to spend eternity? Besides, he would have to find a place to hide until dawn, and since he did not know if the giant needed to sleep, what would prevent it from finding him in the day and finishing him off?

No, there were too many variables. He could not just fly away and hide. Max had to end this as quickly as it had begun.

He circled back, using his echolocation to see if the giant was still following him.

It was. It still lagged far behind him, but it had not given up its pursuit. How it was able to keep track of him at such a vast distance was something Max would have been impressed by if his very existence was not at stake, but it did confirm to him that retreat was not a permanent solution.

Max turned again and continued his flight to the town. One way or another, this conflagration would be over before dawn.

The giant marched down the empty street, yellow eyes searching for his prey. It had lost sight of the bat somewhere in the town square, and even though it was simple-minded, it still knew that nothing could just disappear without a trace, not even the Undead. Its prey still had to be here somewhere, and it was compelled to keep hunting until it found him.

The man-made monstrosity searched, marching ever onward into a rolling fog bank.

Suddenly, a fist shot out of the fog and struck the giant in the face. The golem turned to retaliate, but its own fist simply passed through the fog, striking the ground without hitting anything else.

A foot appeared behind the creature and struck it in the small of its back. The giant whipped about and wrapped its arms around nothing.

The monster growled in anger as it squeezed its eyes shut and tensed its muscles. The whine of an engine charging stirred from within its core. With a sudden burst, a shockwave of electricity radiated from the giant's body.

144

The fog vanished, and Max appeared in front of his opponent. He was hovering a foot off the ground and was stunned that the burst of lightning had turned him back to a corporeal form. He decided that he would figure out how that was possible after he had won.

"Strigoi!"

The giant lumbered towards his foe, but Max was not done yet. He extended his hand forward, and at this command, his familiars appeared. Bats filled the sky and rats filled the street, surrounding the golem in a tumultuous swarm.

The giant was overwhelmed at first, disoriented by the onslaught. It stumbled, and for an instant, it looked as though it might fall.

The gyroscopes in its head whirred loudly, and the monster remained perpendicular. It swatted its massive hands and stomped its mighty feet. With each move, multitudes of vermin were crushed. After only a few seconds of this, those familiars who still lived decided they had had enough and fled back to the holes from which they had crawled.

"Cowards!" Max shouted at the fleeing creatures, not realizing the irony of his accusation.

The monster reached out and wrapped one meaty hand almost completely around Max's head. Every instinct in the vampire's body fired at once. He tried to transform into fog, a bat, a hellhound, anything that would help him escape his adversary's vice-like grip, but his body refused to alter. As he wondered why, he received an answer as he felt pain like needles in in his flesh wherever the giant's hand held him. His skin burned the way it might when touched by silver. He realized in an instant that the giant had silver filaments embedded like hairs in its palm.

This turned out to be Max's final realization, for as soon as he had it, the giant closed its fist and crushed his head.

The golem dropped Max's limp decapitated body on the road, where he would dissolve in the sunlight at dawn. With the last of its enemies slain, the monster took a moment to be still in the cool night air.

As it stood, a thought entered its simple mind. It occurred to the giant that perhaps its job was not yet done. When it had awoken, it knew that it had to slay the blood-drinking creatures before it, but now it wondered if there were more such creatures out there in the world. If there were, if the four it had killed that night were not the only ones, then its task was far from over.

A large bat flew overhead, making a beeline for the west.

Though the giant did not really know much about the world and how things worked, it knew an enemy when it saw one.

"Strigoi…"

The giant lumbered after the bat, knowing exactly what had to be done.

"So, I guess your odd little experiment worked, Ulrich," said Myra.

"It did more than work, Myra," Ulrich nodded. A satisfied smile crossed his face as he and his companion watched the giant leave from the safety of a nearby rooftop. "It performed gloriously! It was the most brilliantly executed plan ever conceived!"

"If you do say so yourself," Myra quipped. She sat on the edge of the roof, feet dangling over the edge. "I do admit it was clever, leaving the monster in that burned out building with just enough clues to entice the suckers into signing their own death warrants. It was a long shot, but it paid off. Terribly sadistic of you."

"You're too kind, my love."

"So, what will your little creation do now, I wonder?"

Ulrich slung his feet over the edge alongside Myra. "He will carry out his purpose, of course, scouring the land for undead blood drinkers to usher off to Hell where they belong. The best part is there's not a thing they can do about it now. Max was right about one thing: his kind are terribly stagnant."

Myra drummed her fingers on the ledge. "What will he do when there are no more left?"

"Who can tell?" Ulrich shrugged. "I suppose on that day, he will finally rest."

"Aren't you worried he might turn on us one day? We're not exactly innocent of taking blood, either."

"I don't know if he'll ever turn on us, but that makes it more exciting, don't you think?"

Myra smiled. "I can't argue with that. Anyway, there's still plenty of hours left in the night. Shall we go for a hunt now that we have no competition?"

Ulrich took her hand. "Darling, you read my mind."

The couple leapt from the rooftop, changing as they did so.

It was a pair of mighty wolves that landed on the street and howled triumphantly at the night sky.

Before running into the nearby forest to stalk and hunt whatever caught their attention, they each took the opportunity to urinate on Max's body.

Werewolves were petty like that.

NOTE: In case you were wondering, Sami is an impundulu (lightning bird), Xü is a jiangshi, and Mary is a baobhan sith. Each one is a variation on the vampire myth from South Africa, China, and Scotland respectively.

Hey, they never said what kind of vampire should appear in this story.

EDITOR'S NOTE: Also in case you're wondering, the badass, vampire-hunting man-made monster in this story is called Venator. That is Latin for "hunter."

END

LET'S GO TO THE MALL

Dustin Dreyling

Foreword

I find myself in a predicament.

I think I've bitten off more than I can chew. That's not easy, since I'm half rat. *Wererat,* to be specific. Lycanthrope. Like Gaga says, we were born this way (she would know, too; she's not all human herself). Not every one of us is a werewolf, though. Many animals are represented in our freak menagerie. I've met wolves, leopards, mongooses, squirrels, snakes, turtles, crows, bears, and all kinds of weird shit. There are no animal tribes or families or any crap like that. Lycanthropes are all individuals, species be damned. I've met a few other rats, but none of them were like me. They each had different abilities from mine.

I make things burn. I make things smolder. I make things explode. A long time ago, some mates of mine gave me the nickname "'Ploder." As in Ex*ploder*. Yeah, they weren't the brightest, nor the most creative bunch. I'm not from the U.K. or Australia, by the way. "Mates" refers to the time I spent being a pirate. Those were the days! They seem so long ago, now, as I'm getting pretty old.

But not too old to slay supernatural scum, something I've taken up as a hobby-turned-lifelong-mission. Not necessarily saving *all* the innocents or anything like that, but I do what I can to keep the unseen forces in check, so they stay that way. At least I try. I fuck up from time to time. But when I do, I burn it all to the ground!

Yes!

That's right, other me.

I love to burn things to the ground. I have severe problems. As a pyrokinetic with pyromania *and* being an extraordinary creature capable of getting away with a lot of things is a curse and a blessing. I'm a bad man-rat from time to time. I like to think that more often than not, I torch the right things and/or people. But I happen to be a troubled guy. Ever hear the sound of glass shattering from intense heat?

Music. Pure music to my ears. I strive a little too much for it sometimes. I always stake a building out ahead of time before I raze it; I'm not a monster inside, just on the outside.

That's not true! Lies! We live to scorch. Live to sear. Live to incinerate. That's who we are as Ploder.

Shut up, you damn Smeagol wannabe. Nobody is talking to you, asshole. Stay in there, I'm in control right now, and I'm talking to these good people here. They want to hear about the hijinks we got into last week with the mutagenic freaks. That's why I'm doing this narrative in the first place. I'm talking about our current predicament. Oh, you're all ears now, huh?

He loves it when I talk about our quality time together.

"Burn her like a rat! Burn her like a rat!"

Calm down, quit quoting Texas Chainsaw Massacre 2. *I never should have let me watch that movie.*

Anyway, so here goes. My predicament. From the beginning.

I

Tandy (not his real name) just puked all over the elephant man trying to stomp us into the ground on the rooftop of a popular bank's Minneapolis headquarters. Wait, I guess that would be the roof, not the ground, huh? Anyway, he upchucked really good; the ravenous little buggers that reside in his belly being just as nasty and hungry as they always are.

They promptly cover the twelve-foot-tall elephant man from head to toe, and the pachyderm-headed mutation simultaneously shrieks and trumpets as the worms that Tandy blasted from her stomach begin to devour the poor freak. He's trying to swipe them off with his hands but isn't having much luck. I wince as he bothers with using the trunk distending from his gray-skinned face, resulting in a few of the fuckers climbing on and tearing into the proboscis of our gene-spliced opponent.

All the hand swatting in the world doesn't stop them from tearing through his trunk, which drops to the gravel-covered roofing atop our spontaneous battle arena. I'm amazed he hasn't charged us yet; instead, he was too busy eyeing up the two giant tusks protruding from the monstrous thing's animal-freak-face. Those would give one or both Tandy and me a bad day.

Don't question fortune like that if you're ever in my situation. Just strike.

The elephant asshole charges.

Torch him! Light him up! Gyahhh!

For once, I listen to the crazy fucker tearing at my mind. He's always there, the pyromaniac part of me. And this time, I let him go. His elation releases endorphins into my system seconds after he lights up the poor bastard towering over me and my rotund black friend – the latter of whom vomits starving lamprey-faced nematodes on PCP.

Elephant man ignites like he's spontaneously combusted, which I'm sure he appears to have been to anyone who may be watching. I'm not concerned with this, however, given the ridiculous nature of the situation. I can just hear the incoherent ramblings now.

Officer, a giant rat man, or was it a man-rat? Anyway, a rat guy and a black dude that ralphed these nasty worms were fighting a huge elephant-headed dude who spontaneously combusted! No foolin', man! Just fucking ignited before my eyes. What? I've only had a few shots of Jägermeister, why?

Yeah, real convincing testimony. I just presumed the Jäger part.

Then the tall bastard picks me up in his flaming mitts and *throws* me off the building. Yeah, you're damn right *"shit!"* I sail in an arc down towards the streets below, wind tickling my big rodent ears.

The better to hear you with, my dear!

Shh. I'm still talking, dick.

I crash through the windows of a penthouse suite on the top level of a business-oriented hotel high-rise, located far from anything entertainment flavored. I imagine it's where rich corporate fat cats go to score with hookers and whatnot. The carpet eats my epidermis as I skid to a halt after smashing through the huge picture window. I'm not ignorant to my luck that the window even broke. My full-on wererat form does add quite a bit of incredibly dense, muscular mass to my body, but still. I could have just bounced off of it, had I not hit it right, and those instances of bad fortune are hard to recover from with only seconds before becoming a pancake on the sidewalk.

The breeze is eager to torment me now that I had made an entry point and assaults my ass end, which is sticking out towards the broken window. The chill May air was angry that evening. The breeze made my rear sphincter pucker. A song's lyrics loops over and over in my head, and my stunned brain fails to recognize the tune.

"Any way the wind blows..."

From where I lay, smashed into the penthouse's carpet, I hear two things that my mind uses to try and push me back into action. One is a scream from a woman in the room, the other is a guy nearly matching her octave for octave with his own shriek. I also hear, albeit faintly, an elephant crying out in agony, along with a crazy voice talking some shit at the top of his lungs. In case you didn't figure it out yet, I have *excellent* hearing. And I guess that's three things.

"How you like that, you big-eared bitch?"

Tandy's not quite baritone voice is just the tiniest bit shrill at peak volume. I only laugh a little, the agony caused by the chuckling makes me hate Tandy a little bit more.

Bringing my attention back to the immediate concern, I look up at the king-size bed in front of me. The guy and girl are still in a very precarious sexual position, having stopped mid-thrust. The guy withdraws and scoots back to the headboard, the woman following suit. They just sit there and stare at me, naked. I can't help but notice her boobs heaving as she pants, and the eye-burning sight of the guy's still present erection.

Why does it curve that way? Does he have a broken boner?

Shut up, idiot, it's not an actual bone, it's just spongy tissue that fills with blood and gets hard. Like a sperm whale's head. And I don't know, he and I aren't that close, ya dillhole.

What? Do you hear yourself, nerd? You just talked about boners and sperm whales in the same breath. And I'm the psycho part of you.

The naked fucker tries to run but I don't let him. I'm on my feet and pouncing on dude before his fuck buddy can move. I slam my fist into his head, earning a large amount of pain for my efforts to avoid slaughtering him. He goes limp instantly.

I ride his body to the floor and spring off it, landing on the bed with the screaming woman. I whip her in the face with my four-foot-long rat tail and she gets bitch slapped into la-la land, dropping to the pillows at the head of the huge bed.

After looting the wallet I see laying on the bedside table, I run and leap out of the broken ass window I crashed through only seconds before, stretching my body out in a way that I hope will give me better results. I fly across the street and crash through one of the windows of the bank skyscraper I was flung from in the first place.

I find myself in an office, the gray cubicles making me happy I'm not one of the poor schmucks who have to look at this crap every day. I dash across the floor, leaping up and over many of the improvised offices in the process as I reach the elevators and stairwell. I debate being lazy for a second before I run up the stairs.

I retrace my original route to the rooftop, running through smashed doors and broken walls, finally arriving at the 'special privileges' elevator for the higher-ups. The doors are still pried open from our original visit, and I jump up through the open maintenance hatch inside the elevator car once more, gripping the sides and pulling myself up almost effortlessly before shimmying up the elevator cable like the badass showoff in gym class. Back when they still did rope climbing.

Do they still do rope climbing?

"She makes me feel kinda funny. Like when we used to climb the ropes in gym class."

And now the douche canoe is quoting *Wayne's World*. That's my existence, folks. A batshit crazy second personality quoting movies and trying to get me to set everything and everyone ablaze.

You know you like it, hypocrite. Lies, it tells, lies!

Seriously, quit with the Gollum shit. That's been played out since the movies.

Peter Jackson makes some cool looking flicks, but the dialogue and acting are ridiculous. She looks like a damn elf, but why did he have to subject us to three movies about Legoland and Kate from *Lost* with pointy ears? Oh, and some dwarves and a hobbit, too. Smaug was fucking awesome though.

Just don't even get me started on the ravine scene from his take on *King Kong.*

Shit, here I am, talking about damn movies. At least I didn't go off about Jackson's other flicks, like the infamous *Dead Alive* and *Bad Taste,* never mind the insanity that is *Meet the Feebles.* That is one messed up mama Jama! And then he makes some dramatic crap that I hate more each time I watch it. That goes for *Lord of the Rings, The Hobbit,* and *King Kong.*

But I digress…

My internal monologue is rendered moot when I reach the top floor. Although I was *not* thinking about Peter Jackson's movies at the time.

No, what I was thinking about is none of your business, reader; don't even ask.

We were thinking about burning sex offenders off the FBI's registry website. Starting with the letter "A."

Quiet, don't talk about our secret hobbies!

I run up the stairwell to the roof and plow through the pneumatic door, jumping clear of the swiftly closing portal cover as it slams shut, locking us out once more. Elephant man is lying on the roof, burning. This makes me happy, the raw bloody spots in my mouth where my back molars punched into both sides of my tongue still very present in my mind. One of the big asshole's punches made me bite down on my own tongue *extremely* hard.

Tandy is standing there on the roof, smoking a Black and Mild.

"'Bout time you got here, brutha."

His pronunciation of the word "brother" tips me off to the sarcasm. Not that it wasn't evident, given the circumstances.

"I got held up in traffic," I said, throwing my hands up in the air, grinning.

"Shit, are we done here?" Tandy's valid question makes me smile once again.

I nod. "We are, my friend, we are." I look at the corpse of elephant man. "As soon as you dispatch the cleanup crew."

"No problem, I had some more anyway," Tandy says, and promptly barfs his lethal stomach contents all over the still smoldering corpse of one big elephant freak.

The massively jawed little creatures, still covered in what smells like Tandy's bile, get to work devouring the remains of the charred hybrid of man and pachyderm.

What's next? Four turtles and a rat? You get us into the dumbest shit, buddy.

I'm not your buddy, guy.

I'm not your guy, friend.

I'm not your friend, buddy.

Did we seriously just do that? We better burn something soon or I'm going to explode, guy.

Ha, friend, *couldn't help it, could you?*

Where was I? Oh, yeah, Tandy smoking and the smoking corpse of the elephant man was being devoured by Tandy's bile worms. He's just standing there, leaning against the perimeter wall of the rooftop, puffing on his fragrant number once again. Then I see him prick his ears up to his left side a millisecond before I hear it too.

Wings. Getting closer to us.

I'm slammed into from behind by a soft, feathery form, the light alternative to scales and fur grazing my face as I'm thrown to the unforgiving graveled rooftop. A multi-syllabic string of curse words pops out of me with the wind that is knocked out by the action. I glance up behind me and see a sharp beak and huge, forward-facing eyes.

Owl-man, huh? Someone really likes TMNT. Are you sure you aren't behind this?

Laughter bounces off the walls of my mind. He's a smartass, I'll give him -- me -- that.

Before owl-man can escape, I pounce on him, burying my front teeth in his neck. I feel blood flow over my face and down my body in a torrent, my prey crying out in surprise and pain as its lifeforce cascades down my neck. My furless tail wriggles in delight as my opponent drops to the roof, its neck still gushing. I step back and off the nearly dead owl freak and look at Tandy.

"Hey man, do ya mind getting one more?"

As I ask him this, he starts gagging in a way I am more than familiar with.

"Thanks, partner," I say.

II

Two days later, we are sitting at our place, drinking coffee, and watching a movie. Some silly Stephen King farce of one of his short stories. It was a story about different levels of monster rats, called *Graveyard Shift,* and the film version perverted it into a giant bat story with abysmally bad acting and script. It reminded me of *Maximum Overdrive,* a movie Steve himself directed, admittedly in the midst of a coke binge if the Internet is to be believed. The movie is a classic, but it's horrible.

Why do you always talk about movies? What is your problem? You need to get laid, me. Stat.

Yeah, don't I know it, pyro voice, don't I know? All in due time.

Again, we were eating breakfast and watching *Graveyard Shift*. I had just finished my bacon, and Tandy asks me a question out of nowhere.

"Why do you call me Tandy, Plo?"

I spit out my coffee in a cliché retort, and look at him immediately after, raising one eyebrow like the famous Rock from WWE and now Hollywood fame. I don't care what anyone says, I like the Rock. He's just fine as an actor; there are plenty of lameass actors who *aren't* former wrestlers and get better recognition than he does. Don't you dare throw *Doom* at me, though.

Shut up with the fucking movie references, jackass. Get on with the story before I self-immolate us!

Shit, right.

So the movie gets interrupted before the official dick of the film gets what he deserves, the news pushing the panic button like they do. Apparently, a group of "men in costumes" were attacking the Mall of

America. Men in costumes. So, it's automatically *men* in this day and age? Shit. I've met a ton of women who were badasses. Badassery knows no gender, true believers. Badassery just is.

Whatever, so the point is, more of the half animal, half people creatures were running amok in the MoA. Cool, I haven't been there in a while.

I look at Tandy, whose real name is Jasper, so I couldn't resist *Last Man on Earth*-ing him with the nickname. I know, I'm out of control with the references; I'll try to stop, I promise. But it's hard. Life as a wererat who kills supernatural menaces isn't very glamorous. I don't have a lot of girlfriends, but I don't really need the companionship, either. They just get in the way or become a weakness and a liability.

Two hours later, Tandy and I have woken up Grblyxx, my favorite imp, and we are loading up the car for a road trip. Grblyxx is not a morning imp, so we tread lightly for the first couple of hours after waking him, narrowly dodging the flames spewing from his mouth as soon as his peepers popped open. He grumbles and bitches about a little bit of everything, and demands we listen to the band Devildriver.

I am acquainted with the band. I connect to the Bluetooth speaker in the living room and begin playing the most popular songs on my favorite music app, regardless of its many flaws. The larynx-shredding vocals please me, and I crank the stereo some more, earning a grimace from Tandy.

"What? Too metal? Who do you like, *Paht-na?*"

I stare Tandy down, the Rock eyebrow back in full effect. He makes a funny expression with his lips before he answers.

"You know I wanna hear some Wu-Tang," he says in a pouty voice, under his breath so I can barely hear.

"Wu-Tang again?" I ask, taking the bait.

"Aw yeah! Again and again!" he shouts with delight on his face, despite Dez Fafara's chainsaw vocals pummeling our eardrums.

Tandy dances for a couple of seconds, then stands up straight. I laugh and it seems to encourage my freakish sidekick. There's a spring in his step as we load up my "key lime" colored Mitsubishi Eclipse, circa 2011, while the resident imp of the house rocks out. The zippy sports car is tight on space, but we travel light and Grblyxx is two and a half feet tall at the most. The worst part is his wings, but so long as he keeps them tucked in, we should be good.

I fry up some more bacon and eggs and Tandy makes toast for all three of us, even though Grblyxx never eats anything that didn't move on its own at some point. Plants do not count. I'd just say he's a carnivore, but he'll occasionally eat fruit that grew on a tree.

Well, it moved when it fell from the tree, didn't it?

I never respond to his argument, wanting to point out the fruit he eats is picked off the tree by people, and he would literally have to go and watch an apple tree or whatever and wait for something to drop. Then he could eat it. I've thrown this is his face once, and my left butt cheek still smarts where he torched my ass in retaliation. Not a good sport with logic. I mean, I was being facetious, but still, yeesh. What a grouch. I'm mostly immune to fire, but Imp flames still hurt like a bitch.

We eat breakfast and get some coffee in us, and then we are off. We leave the secret lair and get onto Interstate 694, headed west. I crank up some Wu Tang, the oldest from their school that there is, *Enter the Wu Tang (36 Chambers)*. Tandy squees -- you know, the noise that fangirls make when they squeal in delight at something? I see Grblyxx laughing his ass off silently in the backseat. I'm thankful for the silent part. Those two get ugly when they fight, and I don't need Tandy puking in my car again. That's how I lost the Supra I used to rock -- destroyed by mysterious devil stomach worms.

We bank to the south, transitioning from 694 to Interstate 35E, taking the new route through and past the outskirts of Saint Paul – Minnesota's capital city – and follow the highway down to where it intersects with Interstate 494. This takes us straight to the Mall of America. Or, it would if the exit ramp wasn't blocked off by cops.

"Shit," I grumble. I turn down the Wu for a second. "Change of plans, buckos. We're going to have to sneak into the fucking place."

"The fuck we are, Plo! I *am* a demon, remember?"

His high-pitched voice slaps me like a reality check. Duh. Imp magic is actually pretty useful in our lifestyle choice. Hunting supernatural delinquents can be difficult when the boys in blue or worse are aware of their presence. Fortunately, Grblyxx can hide us in plain sight.

We head down to the next exit not cordoned off by flashing lights and cars, about five miles further down. I backtrack towards the mall as far as I can before being cut off by authorities on the scene. I park at the loading dock of a small business and kill the engine of the Eclipse. Tandy looks at me and sighs.

"You're going to turn into horde mode, aren't you," he says, not a question.

"Of course, my main man. You know how this works." My grin feels excessive, but I don't reduce the fervor behind it.

"Great."

Tandy isn't a fan of horde mode. That's where I literally fall to pieces – cue the Patsy Cline – and transform into a mischief of rats. Each is a singular, sentient version of myself but much smaller.

Sentient does *not* mean smart. They can figure out simple switches and machines, but that is about the extent of it. Each piece of me has to steal some of the intelligence pool that is my brain, diminishing the overall horde I.Q. a little more with each extra body I break down into. It's usually around a couple dozen rats total, I've found this ratio to be best for retaining rational thought and cognitive perception.

Tandy just doesn't like rats. Which is really funny when you think about it. I am a freaking wererat, but it's the little rats that get to him. I get it. Hordes of little things overwhelming oneself tends to be a little frightening. Like if *Gremlins* were real. Nasty little fuckers, man. I was several hundred years old when I saw it in the theater back in 1984, and *I* couldn't believe what I was seeing. A horror movie wrapped up in Christmas, with some cute merchandising thrown in to grab the kiddies' attention and their parents' cash.

I wasn't surprised when kids were getting scared to death. I had a couple of zinger dreams myself the week after I saw that movie. I just hope those kids didn't have dreams like me. Getting dismembered by a giggling horde of the creatures was not good times in REM land, even for a mean bastard.

On a sidenote, a werewolf I met once told me that movie wasn't entirely untrue. There was an… incident, once. That moon poochie was silly. Given his name, he seemed to think he fought the legendary Grendel. Or maybe he thought he was Christopher Lambert.

I get out of the car, Tandy exiting the other side of the zippy little vehicle. Grblyxx climbs out of the car by scrambling up onto the roof. My very audible hiss of disapproval at his black claws scraping up the paint job earns me a sadistic grin in retort as he stands up fully on top of the Mitsubishi and stretches both his limbs and his extra limbs. His red skin looks sleek and slippery in the cloudy daylight, and I'm a little in awe at the being from a different plane of existence.

I don't freak out, there are a few people nearby and we are not out of their line of sight, but I can see the little horns on his impy head glowing blue. This is a sure sign that he has already disguised us. Blue is basically the cloaking spell, for lack of a better term. Usually, I hear him chant to start the spell, but I must have missed it this time. Normally, he throws his hands up and shouts, "*Operuit caligo!*"

"So, what's the plan, Stan?' Tandy is looking at me, his arms folded in an annoyed way, a pouty look on his adult baby face. "I'm ready to do this!"

"So am I," I say, and suddenly feel myself burst into pieces.

Tandy's disgusted cry instills happiness in all 25 of me as we all hit the pavement and scamper off in the direction of the Mall of America, my portly sidekick with digestive issues and demonic familiar following close behind me.

III

The collection of rats that make up my person manage to get into the loading dock area beneath the Mall, a huge bay of spots for the many deliveries that happen each day in this mecca of enclosed shopping. We easily get past the cops swarming the property, and with all of our jaws we chew a nice entrance hole in a grate, slip through into the office checkpoint, and out the back door to the loading dock. I reform myself, the sensation of all of those bodies sliding together making me feel a little dirty like it always does -- like I'm playing with myself in public or something. Nobody can see me cloaked except Tandy and Grblyxx, but they are on the other side of the door I open after reforming into my human visage. No need to go full wererat just yet.

Tandy whistles at the immense space, and we head through another side door next to a roll up metal door. Past that is the dock area and the maze of hallways that run behind the scenes of the giant complex. We round the first corner and are greeted by the slain bodies of several employees... well, pieces of them, anyway. Blood is everywhere, limbs and organs spread around like they were randomly tossed here and there by whoever butchered the poor people. I see a big ass footprint in the nearest pool of blood, followed by a few more of different sizes and shapes. They trail down the corridor, seemingly oblivious to the evidence they left behind when these things stormed through here.

I can't help but notice the diversity of prints on the floor. Canine, for sure. A big one, too. I think an alligator or croc, maybe; and definitely a huge rodent of some kind. We know our own. The others are harder to identify, as I'm not a wildlife biologist or anything. Either way, there are some big fuckers in there raising hell. Although, the lack of gunfire is telling me hell was already raised. Past tense. I'm expecting a slaughterhouse up there.

We take the freight elevator nearest all the blood up to the main floor. The doors open to pretty much what I expected. Bodies are everywhere, civilian and authoritative alike. Shoppers, local cops, state troopers, and S.W.A.T. members litter the floor. Mangled weapons lay all over the place as well, each of them bent into useless configurations.

Strong S.O.B.s, so watch your ass.

You seriously thought it was necessary to tell me that? Me?

I hear growling, like the deep, distrustful sound an angry dog makes when staring down someone it doesn't like. It echoes throughout the tomb that used to be a shopper's paradise. Still in human form, I can't pinpoint the exact floor it's coming from, but I'm pretty sure it's the one above us.

Grblyxx finally speaks, and I notice the blue light of his horns has disappeared, meaning we are visible once more.

"It's right above us," he whispers and points up through the floor over our head. "Second floor. Change forms now, Ploder."

Knowing better than to doubt my imp friend, I change. My body increases in mass as my musculature grows and my head painfully elongates in some kind of science-defying process; blood drips here and there from the rapidly forming and healing wounds caused by the transformation from human to full wererat. I stand a foot and a half taller but tend to crouch like a hunchback more in this form for some reason.

Long whiskers shoot out from the sides of my face as fur covers my body almost instantaneously. The sensations from them remind me of how primitive my human form is in the sensing department. I'm now aware of the currents and vibrations in the air. Sounds register as well, but not like hearing, as it's more like *feeling* sounds.

My ears are back, and I instantly pinpoint our surly opponent upstairs. I smell him, too. Definitely the canine. I can't pinpoint the breed, as not an expert on dog scents, but I can smell the drool, so I'm going to guess some kind of rip-your-face-off guard dog breed, like a pit bull or a bull mastiff or something. Again, not a dog expert.

But now I can also hear and smell its companions. Three of them. One is definitely reptilian, as I can smell the scales and that scent that lizards, snakes, and crocs all kind of share. I'm gonna guess crocodilian by the prints I saw earlier.

The rodent of unusual shape (I'm not getting sued) is now very identifiable. A fucking red squirrel. I hate those assholes. They are mean as hell. I'm not looking forward to this inevitable face-off. It's funny, I don't even wonder how the hell giant, mutated freaks like these are even possible, never mind how they came to invade the Mall of American.

I'm used to ridiculous shit, anyway, so I can't really talk, either. The freak scale is normal for me. But I still can't place the scent of the last creature up there. It's swampy smelling, something that probably lives in muck on the bottom.

"Ploder, what's the plan?" Tandy is tapping me on the shoulder.

Grblyxx stands behind him, wings half ready for flight at a moment's notice. Tandy looks slightly scared; he's paled a little bit since we got off the elevator. I bet even he can smell the things above us. I hear his stomach gurgle loudly. In fact, I'm pretty sure the whole mall could hear it. The indication that his devil worms were stirring sound like the world's loudest percolator brewing.

"Well, now it's damage control," I say in regards to his gastrointestinal sounds.

Then we hear a stampede tear across the floor above us, along with growls and bellows echoing louder than Tandy's stomach gurgle.

"Get ready to puke on 'em, Tandy. I think they're going to be very predictable."

I pull out my weapons, a sickle with a serrated blade, and a claw hammer with an adjustable claw that I usually place in the sticking straight up position, like a spike. I'm not from the Soviet Union, either, so don't go reading too much into that. They are my favorite two-weapon combination. Years and years of experience has led me to this conclusion time and again.

Tandy has his Colt .38 pistol in his hands, yet again pulled out from God knows where. I never see him actually draw that gun; it's just suddenly in his grip. It boggles my mind, but also means I don't have to worry about him in combat. He knows what he's doing by now. Which is good, because the freaks upstairs end up being just as predictable as I had hoped.

The first one to hit the floor is the crocodile freak. It stands about eight feet tall, dwarfing us, and issues a throaty bellow at me that I can smell. My ears twitch in pain, the decibels cruel on my advanced hearing.

Tandy retorts for me, as gallons of hungry worms pour from his mouth and cover the poor sucker. Bellows turned to whimpers as the worms devour it alive, easily cutting through its scaly armor like nothing. Then it does the smart thing and treats the revolting spew of death like fire. Stop, dropping, and rolling succeeds very much in crushing nearly all of the puke worms going to town on the thing's scales. I'm mildly impressed, mostly because no one ever thinks to do that. They can't eat you if they're squished and dead, after all.

My recognition of the croc-man's ingenuity quickly fades when the dog freak drops down with the red squirrel asshole by its side. The rodent-faced freak charges me, bounding up and down in the air instead of just a bull rush. It confuses me enough that it lands on me a split second before I'm able to get out of the way. Sharp claws dig into my shoulders as the heavier freak slams me into the hard tile floor of the mall. I swear at it profusely, crying out as it suddenly plunges its front incisors into my chest, puncturing my lung and cutting off the string of expletives I had prepared for it.

I hear Tandy cry out as the dog freak slams into him on humanoid legs, very much a rip-off of the half-shell heroes of the '80s and '90s. Someone is very uncreative. Tandy goes flying across the floor, his pistol sliding well away from him after soaring out of his grasp. A demonic sounding bark tears out of the freak's throat, loud as death metal on crappy ear buds directly in your waxy canals, but with a bass I could feel even from where I was underneath Squirrelface.

"Fuck this," I mutter.

Then my weaponless hands seize squirrelface and I let go internally. The furry head lights up as my pyro personality takes over, pyrokinetically immolating my opponent, and myself as well. I'm immune to my own flames, but not anything I'm wearing.

So much for the remains of those clothes.

My vocal cords threaten to shred as I half roar, half scream at the poor fucker as I incinerate his head.

"Burn! Burn, you motherfucker! Burn until your flesh is nothing but charred carbon!"

My voice is barely human sounding, as wererat vocals are not as refined as a normal man's would be. Squirrelface bucks and thrashes as my flames consume him, reversing our positions as it rolls over.

Then its legs come up between us. A massive impact hits me in the chest and I am sent sailing through the air. I can see the final animal freak drop down from the balcony as I sail up over it, before crashing into a pillar and hitting the second floor hard. My revulsion supersedes my pain, however.

It's a leech. I fucking hate leeches.

I'm roused back to my senses by the sound of a flame burst. As I climb back to my feet and look over the railing, I already smell what I'm expecting to see. The crocodile guy is on fire, being consumed by bluish flames. Grblyxx still has the remnants of his breath weapon lingering out of his mouth like a pilot light. He is about twelve feet in the air, flapping his wings furiously to keep his hover going.

Then it isn't a problem anymore. A planter with a tree of undeterminable realness collides with my imp, knocking him out of the sky like a blasted game bird. He drops hard to the floor, the planter landing on top of him. A single wing lays stretched out and bleeding beneath.

My concern is there but I can't dwell on it yet. I pull from the depths of my being the energy needed for my next move. I feel my wounds sustained thus far healing up, knowing full well I have a couple more scars now from Squirrelface. The second I feel the last bit of flesh stitch itself up, I am over the balcony, dropping down on top of Dogface, who is crouched over Tandy and tearing into him.

Tandy isn't moving, just twitching from the force of the raking claws with blood surrounding him. I hear a godawful noise that surprises me

163

before I realize it's my cry of anguish at seeing my friend lying dead. I slam into dogface and bury my incisors into his neck. I tear at his back with my claws, shredding the furry muscular flesh. He tries to reach back for me, but my tail slaps his paws away as his blood fills my mouth and courses down both of our bodies.

Then the leech thing rips me away from its sibling or whatever. This sends me into another pillar, making me see stars as I wait for broken bones to heal once more on the floor at the base of the marble post. But it had a desirable effect as well, as I notice that Dogface's neck is now a fountain of blood. And it doesn't look even close to healing anytime soon. After seconds, he drops to the floor, whimpering once before growing still.

They go down easy! Why are we not burning them?
Calm down. There'll be time for that later.

The leech guy picks me up and latches onto my face. It smells *horrible*. A combination of vomit, feces, urine, and swamp, all tied together with the revolting stench of guts rotting in the sun. I can't hold my breakfast down anymore so I puke into its suctioning face. Fortunately, it's not used to its meals yakking into its mouth, and I'm suddenly dropped like a sack of potatoes. I can feel blood trickling down my face in several different places from the mouth full of teeth that was previously latched onto my beautiful mug.

Instead of launching back up at it like I'm wired to do, I exercise some willpower and instead seek out my weapons. They lay where I dropped them after getting mugged by the squirrel-faced prick. I snatch them up and turn around, bouncing back a couple of feet into a defensive position. Good thing too, cause Suck-face is right on top of me, a ropey-fingered hand reaching for me. My sickle is faster.

Four fingers fall to the mall floor, each one making plopping noises as they fall into the blood pool from where Grblyxx had been laying before.

Wait, what? Where did he go?

Suck-face screams through a mouth full of teeth with poor vocal cords. It sounds like the squid-faced guy from *Futurama* choking on a mouth full of (insert nasty comment here). I could do it for you, but you're an adult, I think you can handle it.

Suck-face sucker punches me, sending me flying. Unbeknownst to the annelid mutant, my hammer is not in my other hand. It is being held by my prehensile tail… and rather well, I might add. Especially when I whip it around and embed it into the side of its skull as I sail away from it.

This causes the effect of my entire weight coming to a sudden, vicious stop as the slack of my tail catches up to the tip holding the embedded claw hammer. The action and reaction tears the claw hammer back out of Suck-face's head, taking a generous portion of its skull and brain along with it. The slimy bastard looks at me, dumbfounded, even with shiny, black eyes void of intellect, as I crash down hard from the abrupt stop. Then it pitches forward and lands on top of me. It's a heavy sucker, believe you me. I rest for a second, trying to catch my breath and reassess the situation.

Tandy is sitting on the floor, gun trained on the still smoldering croc-man and Squirrelface. Neither is moving. A fresh pile of worm vomit covers the lower half of each poor bastard. Tandy's unofficial trademark hard at work chewing through *everything*. He told me the story once of the day the worms first came out of him. Not something I'd want to go through. He *used* to have a family. He was suicidal when I found him, running from the cops and horrified by the abomination that he had become overnight.

"Hey, asshole, when were you going to help me?" Grblyxx's voice is surprisingly pleasant to hear, my original concern for his well-being replaced by disdain once more.

I spin around, wicked barb on the tip of my tongue, but then stop. He is limping and only has one wing moving on its own; the other one he is holding in his hand, as it was no longer attached to his back. I don't know if he can heal that one back.

"Look at my wing, damn you!" he yells to me. "This ain't gonna heal, Ploder. You owe me a wing!"

My mind races with guilt and attempts to think of how I can help him. I know a few people who could rig up prosthetics, but I think he will want something of a different, more metaphysical nature, closer to a true replacement wing. Not that I run a body chop shop, nor do I know of one, never mind the imp wing part. I think for a while, going to a mental checklist of contacts, while also verifying that our quarry are all dead.

I'm interrupted by the explosions of the National Guard finally showing up. The main doors at the opposite end of the first floor explode, and a couple dozen soldiers rush in, all oblivious to us in the blue spell Grblyxx has once again applied to the three of us. The corpses of the mutants, however, are very visible, as are Tandy's worms still gnawing away.

I crack a smile at Tandy's grin of satisfaction when many of the guardsmen cry out in disgust at the merciless worms feasting on the fallen mutants. I'm secretly very relieved that my mostly human friend has some strange healing abilities we still haven't figured out yet. But I sure as hell don't tell him as much.

He's not getting that kind of satisfaction from me, dammit. Then Tandy will just think I *need* him or some bromance shit like that. Blecch!

Grblyxx leads the way, hobbling in front until I pick him up and put him on my shoulders. He doesn't complain. We get back to the car without much trouble, thanks to the spell, and enjoy watching the Guard run around like chickens with freshly severed heads. Tandy glares at me before getting in the car. It's a serious look. I help the imp into the back seat and look at my younger ward of sorts, and good friend for the last seven years.

"What? Spill it, Tandy." I keep eye contact, slipping back into human form as I do so. "You've been mean mugging me for a while now."

"Who the hell made those animal freaks, man? That was some serious Dr. Moreau meets Eastman and Laird shit right there." He looks at me with venom, no doubt in response to the surprised look I give him at the comic book reference combined with a movie. "Shut it. Don't even say anything. You're rubbing off on me, ya nerd."

He holds up two fingers. "Second. Why were the armed responses so utterly inept? You would think they would have kicked more ass, considering how easy those freaks went down."

I nod as he says this, his words echoing my own thoughts. "You're right, Tandy. That was ridiculously simple. I thought we were going to be all over that mall. We barely made to the second floor."

"You made to the second floor. I never left the first."

He laughs a little and gets in the car. I get in as well after returning my seat to the correct position. I glance at the imp as I'm doing this. The little guy is snoozing away. I'll be damned if he didn't almost look cute curled up back there.

I start up the car and let it run for a second, thumbing through music on my phone app. A hand flies out and grabs my chest. I recoil from Tandy's grip.

"What the fuck, man?" But his raised finger stops any further protests.

A group of figures stands before us, staring us down. They can see us, there is no question. I look back at the still glowing horns atop Grblyxx's head and frown. The spell is still active.

How the hell do they see us?

Labyrinth spawn! They are labyrinth spawn! Get us out of here, now, you dim-witted fool.

Whoa, that was way too civilized for you, what gives, me?

Look. Again.

I do look again, and my breath hitches in my chest. They are labyrinth spawn. Their half-melted faces shine through the clever veil concealing their true forms. Lycanthropes forged in the depths of Hell. Once I have seen through the trickery, I can't be fooled again. The mangled and deformed creatures are marked with ritualistic looking tattoos and piercings, some with what looks like some kind of dreadlocks.

They point at us, marking us, and the lead creature, a particularly ugly one with three eyes, roars deep and long before they tear off down the street, unseen by the various other people still milling about chaotically in the midst of all of the happenings at the mall.

I turn to face Tandy with a look of dread.

"We are in for some deep doo-doo, my friend."

This was just the beginning of my predicament.

END

GRAVE CONSEQUENCES

Christofer Nigro with JJ Lindsey

September 2018

Um, how do I start this journal? Okay, my name is Hoshi. I already know that, but the readers may not. Unless my name is on the cover of the journal. And it would be, right? Is that how this works? Shit, I'm all stuffed up here!

Okay, let me try again. The event I'm about to describe happened several months ago, but I won't tell you the exact name of my hometown. It happened at a creepy little graveyard in the middle of my hamlet that has acquired no new tenants or maintenance in well over half a century. Well, at least no new tenants of the *buried* sort, that is.

That night, I was to find out that the orderly and logical world I always believed I lived in was… well, nothing of the sort. I found out that the oft-mentioned "things that go bump in the night" are real, and often hiding just outside our immediate field of vision.

However, that wasn't all I learned the existence of during that nightmarish evening; I was also to learn that there are, well, people who are determined to challenge these mostly hidden things that rank above us on the food chain. You see, that fateful night I was also destined to meet one of those people – I guess that's what he was – who actually hunt down and fight these predator abominations. Instead of, you know, looking the other way and pretending they exist nowhere outside the human imagination; or, during the occasions they are directly encountered, running the other way and screaming in helplessness when they corner you.

Those of us raised in the last few hundred years of "scientific rationality" swallow this mental comfort food to keep sane and convince ourselves we live in a world where we, the human race, are top dog on the food chain (considering what I'm about to tell you, maybe that wasn't the best choice of words; but I'll leave it there for now). But some, a notable and frankly incredible few, put all concern for life, limb, and even sanity aside to directly confront these things and not just fight them – but actually blow them the fuck off the face of the planet! Thus, showing us that we *can* resist, and we need not concede the top spot on the planetary totem pole.

Okay, forgive me for being a bit zealous, but after what I saw *him* do that night to *them* – well, less dramatic words and emotions fail me. But how about I just get to what happened instead of belaboring the point and procrastinating any further?

***

So, where do I begin? It occurred about six months ago, back when the world still made sense to me, before reality yielded its ugly truth to me. My long-time friend Anya and I were taking our usual nighttime stroll, gossiping about everyone and everything in our boring but (formerly) pleasant and secure lives. It was about 11 pm in the evening, and even though the night was quiet except for the occasional chirp of crickets and hooting of an owl, we weren't scared. I mean, back then, we thought monsters weren't real. You know, that lie our parents, teachers, and "official" voices have told us all our lives to make our place in the world appear secure according to the rules of scientific materialism? Yes, that one.

We walked a few blocks down the trail leading past that old, wicked-looking church and directly into the middle of that equally old, long abandoned graveyard lying a few meters from the unholy-looking holy building. The metal gates surrounding it have long since succumbed to rust and disrepair, so there is nothing to keep people from just strolling in there anymore. Most folks simply choose not to, finding creepy old graveyards to be a less than agreeable place to wander into at night anyway.

But Anya and I didn't care, so we sauntered into the cemetery without thinking about it overly much. We were blathering and joking and having a good time.

The very last one we would ever have together, as it turned out.

It was after we had walked into the center of the abandoned burial ground that Anya finally reacted to our surroundings.

"Geez, this place gives me the creepers! I wonder if there's ghosts or shit here."

"No such thing as ghosts," I responded in a typically know-it-all fashion. "There's nothing here but a bunch of headstones, rocks, gnarled trees, leaves blowing around in the wind, and—"

"Wait! Hoshi, did you see that?"

I looked around but couldn't see shit. Okay, maybe a stray leaf or two blowing around in the night air, but I don't think that really counts as "something." I presumed she meant something to actually be concerned about.

"No, I didn't. What did you see, and where?"

"Something went, I dunno, scurrying behind that tombstone over there with the angel on top. Something really big!"

"It was probably a rat or a maybe a stray cat or something. Don't worry."

"No, I meant it was *really big*. Like a person. It looked like a *person*."

"A person… scurrying? I thought only rodents do that."

"No, no… it was like a person, but darting behind that tombstone really fast on all four legs."

Of course, I wanted to laugh at Anya. Except that she seemed seriously freaked out. Like she was about to shit her panties or something. But what she said she saw, she couldn't have seen, right?

That was when we heard what sounded like a hiss. Not like a snake or a pissed off cat warning you away. More like an *unearthly* hiss, but most definitely as if the thing making it was pissed off.

Anya looked around and shouted again. "There!"

I turned 180 degrees in a split second. "Huh? Where?"

170

"I saw another one dart behind that big roundish tombstone! I'm not shittin' you, Hoshi! I saw it! Like a person, even wearing some type of clothing. But scampering on all fours, as fast as a rat can go!"

Suddenly, I heard movement behind that gravestone. The name, date, and epitaph were made illegible by the effects of time, wind, and lack of a maintenance staff. Exactly who laid six feet under it didn't matter, however, as he or she was long forgotten. It was what was *behind it* above ground that was our concern.

Just then I heard some noise on the other side of that stone. It was the distinct sound of a twig being broken by someone stepping on it. Then a tall male figure walked clumsily into view.

"See, Hoshi! See! I told you someone was behind that stone!"

I struggled to adjust my eyes in the dark and catch sight of who the guy was. And as my night vision focused, I got a good look. And what I saw was… well, fully human. A young dude that looked completely normal except for some long wizard-like robe he was wearing. His eyes were also wide open with an expression of terror worse than the one Anya was wearing.

"Um, hello?" I called out to him. "Are you okay, mister?"

That question was immediately answered when the guy fell flat on his face without responding. There was a huge bloody hole torn into his back, with something long and glistening wet sticking out of it.

Before Anya or I could react, what I can only describe as a fast-moving humanoid shape shot out from behind the stone and scuttled onto the fallen guy's torn open back. It looked like a man but was dressed in a plain white garment. From what I could tell, its facial features were human-like but with skin a paler hue than its clothing. This humanoid thing then sunk a hand deep into the guy's open back and pulled out what we then realized was his protruding bowel. And the figure began devouring it ravenously, the way a starving man would do with the first meal he had in weeks.

Anya and I heaved forward and upchucked into the grass. Before we could finish our oral bile evacuations a second, similar figure darted out from another tombstone. It looked, and was dressed, similar to the first. It was fully shaped like a human but ran on all fours with a velocity that made you think of a person on film that was speeded up.

171

This second figure scampered over to the fallen man and bit into the back of his skull. It tore out a mouthful of hair, cranium, and brain matter. After chewing up and swallowing the chunk of gore, it repeated the act, devouring the human meat in a revolting variation of what Cookie Monster does.

Anya was finally about to scream. So was I, but I bit my tongue and clasped my hand over her mouth tight enough to leave bruises. I didn't want to risk drawing the attention of that thing to us.

Even before we got the mutual upchucking under control, I grabbed Anya's wrist and tried to pull her in the opposite direction of the carnage. I was hoping to make our way towards the side exit located further into the graveyard as fast and as quietly possible. As we began moving, however, our trek was intercepted by another young man who ran screaming from the path behind the angel statue. Hot on his heels was the first ghoul we saw (subsequent research has made me conclude these things were some variety of ghoul). It was chasing him on all fours as fast as a dog can run.

Just before it left our view the ghoul leapt at him from the ground like a rat! I mean, have you ever seen a rat when it jumps? Well, that is sort of what this thing did, despite being shaped like a human. We should have kept running, but we couldn't help pausing in shock and terror when we saw it jump like that. Its incredible leap was followed by the loud thud that occurred when it landed on the guy it was pursuing and took him to the ground. We stood there shivering in terror as we heard that young man scream along with the sounds of what must have been the ghoul biting and tearing into him.

***

Side note here: As I understand ghouls per some of my research (I mean, I am a college student, so I should be able to do research, right?), their main source of food is human corpses, fresh or rotted; they aren't too picky. This is why when they do manifest, it tends to be in grave sites, preferably the secluded and abandoned variety.

However, the food supply in these places tends to grow sparse over time, especially if more ghouls begin showing up there. If living humans happen to overcome their deep-rooted (and inherently wise) fears about entering one of these forbidden locations when it has additional, unplanned residents feeding there… well, let's just say that the ghouls get mighty irate. And while the flesh of the living is not their preferred choice of cuisine, they are not above killing and eating the freshly dead meat and organs of humans who stumble across them.

There is more than one type of ghoul, and not all of them are the near-mindless sort like this bunch; though it is this variety that tends to go for the abandoned and secluded burial sites. It takes ghouls of the more intelligent varieties, who can sometimes pass for human if necessary, to have the stealth and know-how to take advantage of the culinary opportunities provided by a still operating graveyard.

You know, the type that still receives new permanent "residents" on a routine basis, along with a still living maintenance crew hired to look after it -- some of which, I regret to write, tend to be incognito ghouls of such an intelligent variety. Those bastards can get away with a lot of ghastly shit in these cemeteries, the nature of which I am not going to get into here as I do plan to eat later on (which was probably another poor choice of words). That is, until a monster hunter happens to find out such creatures are on the staff, of course. End side note.

***

Okay, so Anya and I were standing there on the verge of shitting our pants, too terrified to attempt to run for the path that went past the dilapidated angel statue. I think maybe we just didn't want to see exactly what the ghoul was doing to that poor guy it had jumped. I mean, it was bad enough we could hear the man's blaring death screams along with the sound of that thing tearing chunks out of him and chewing. (Who the hell were these other people and what in God's name where they doing there? Well, just keep reading, okay?)

We knew, however, that we had to start moving before the two ghouls behind us were done eating and took notice of our presence. Then there was the one off to the left of the path in front of us; its meal wasn't going to last it forever either. We had to move! No matter how petrified and sick we felt, or what we may glimpse to our left while running by. We had to get out of that fucking cemetery!

As soon as we finally started towards the path while struggling not to scream or vomit again, a fourth ghoul scuttled out from behind the statue a few feet to our right. Its initial intention was likely to try to join in the feast its brother monstrosity was enjoying to our left. However, this one saw us out of the corner of its eye. It turned to face us and made a loud and angry hissing sound. We got a better look at this creature than the others. Its face was human-ish but with ghostly white skin. It had no hair on its head. Its lips, tongue, and the flesh inside of its mouth that would normally be pinkish on a human were an ugly black on this thing. Its teeth looked more human than animal-like, but crooked and a sickly yellow in color.

I must confess what I did – or, rather, *didn't do* – next. I will always be ashamed, no matter how horrified I was at the time. The ghoul that had discovered us lunged forward and leapt at Anya. And… well, I didn't attempt to move and block it in her defense. I just stood completely still, my mouth agape in shock and on the verge of shitting myself. Its powerful jump took my screaming friend to the ground. I didn't know what I should do, and a montage of conflicted thoughts were cascading through my mind.

Should I attempt to pull it off her? Find a rock and try bashing its skull in? What about the others that would soon be finished eating and looking for a new feast?

I cared deeply for Anya and I am not a bad person, but I was no hero nor any kind of warrior. If I tried to help, the end result would likely be both of us getting killed instead of just her. Or, maybe I would get it off her and allow her to get to safety while I got mauled and eaten in her place… but why should I do that? I mean, this wasn't my fault, and it's not like I would be her murderer, right?

I recall ending that quick stream of moral quandaries by turning to *run*. And that was when the decision was taken out of my hands. But not in the way you would think based on everything you read so far. For this is the point in the incident when *he* showed up, and things changed completely. And not just in the direction of the incident, but also the course of my entire life from what it would have been had we not strolled through that gravesite.

***

Before I could leave my friend behind and flee for my life, I was startled by a loud blast, clearly the sound of a high-caliber firearm going off. I could still hear Anya screaming hysterically, and I turned to see her covered with darkish blood and gore that obviously wasn't from her own body. A few feet away lay the unmoving body of her ghoul attacker with half of its head blown off.

That's when I heard an unfamiliar, commanding, fairly youngish male voice shout, "Get back!"

The demand was so authoritative that I involuntarily complied, taking several steps backwards. I did that just before turning to see a man step out of the darkness from the path to my right. Once he was in the moonlight, I could see he was of about six feet in height, of a lean but muscular build, and garbed in a dark t-shirt covered by a black leather jacket with blue jeans and heavy work boots. His hair was dark in color and long-ish in length. He was holding a mean-looking type of gun that was of a model I could not recognize (after all, I was no expert on firearms; but I'm getting there). I was never to find out what type of ammo it had, or if it was in any way special. I simply know that it *worked,* and with great, messy effectiveness.

Then I noticed why he gave me that command. One of the ghouls that rushed off to the left had finished dining and returned to the scene of the commotion. It leapt through the air at me, much as the previous one did to Anya. However, the newcomer blasted the son of a bitch in the head while it was in mid-leap. Chips of its skull and pieces of brain matter spattered over me as it went down a bit to the side of where I stood, its forward inertia being re-directed by the force of the blast.

At first, I was too startled to puke, and the extremely fast series of events came off in my mind as if being viewed in slow motion. I could still hear Anya's screaming behind me, but I perceived it as if it were muted but gradually coming to full audio as I recovered from the moment of shock. Then I barfed again.

That was when the mysterious monster hunter rushed forward and pushed me aside with a powerful shove while I was busy upchucking. His intention was to pull Anya to her feet and check her for injuries.

This was no easy task, since she was still out of her mind hysterical. It was then he noticed that one of her fingers had been bitten off by the ghoul.

"Shit!" he yelled. "I wish I had gotten that mother fucker before it jumped on her. Not good!"

A moment later both ghouls behind the rounded gravestone re-appeared and zipped towards my gruff and very unexpected savior. Before I could shout a warning to him, he reacted to this situation with surprising speed. In a flash of motion, he jumped to his feet, aimed his gun at the ghoul that was furthest from him, and pulled the trigger. The bullet entered its gaping mouth and exited through the back of its skull, taking all the brain matter inside out with it.

At practically the same time, as the closer ghoul leapt at him, a swing of his other arm halted its attack before its outstretched arms or open mouth could latch onto him. He stopped it dead (literally) with some type of bladed weapon that sunk into the underside of its chin. The facially impaled ghoul gagged and choked as blackish blood streamed out of its open mouth. The hunter of monsters then moved his grip in a quick twisting motion so as to pull the blade out in a way that tore the underside of its face open. As the creature fell to the ground writhing and hissing in agony, the hunter clamped his thick-booted foot over the back of its neck to hold it in place. He then blasted its face into bits and pieces with another shot of his firearm, spattering his waders with cranial gore.

The hunter simply grimaced at his gore-drenched boots, as if this sort of thing happened all the time. He then looked around as if scanning the vicinity for signs of other ghouls. He knew there was at least one more in the vicinity. But it hadn't shown itself yet, which implied the undead entity wasn't that mindless after all. It had some degree of strategical cunning, and my "friend" was well aware of that.

After that quick check of our surroundings, the hunter turned to the still screeching and bleeding Anya, and then looked back at me before speaking. "You're not going to like what I have to do now, but don't try to stop me. It needs doing, and right now."

The monster hunter holstered his firearm in his jacket and reached into his pocket to quickly produce a second blade, as large and sharp as the first one. This one, however, did not have ghoul gunk all over it and if I know monster hunters (I have since learned a lot more about them), it was likely heat sterilized.

"This is my backup knife," the hunter explained in an ominous tone. "In case something happens to the first one."

Next, he produced a second, much longer piece of cloth. This one he tied into a tight knot around the still screaming Anya's forearm, obviously creating an improvised but functional tourniquet. He then lifted the second, probably sterilized blade.

When he spoke next, his words cut into me with a sharper ferocity than that blade ever could. "You might want to look away for this part."

I tried to pull my face away, but for some reason I just couldn't. I mean, she was my friend, right? In retrospect, however, I really wish I had taken his advice.

Acting with merciless speed and what looked like practiced efficiency, the warrior sliced off Anya's entire hand at the wrist with a single, quick swipe. She screamed herself raw with agony before the pain caused her to pass out.

"Oh my god!" That was me again.

The makeshift tourniquet would thankfully prevent her from bleeding out, and as I ceased barfing, I noted that he had produced a bottle of what must have been ethyl alcohol from another of his coat pockets. This he soaked onto her stump to slow any possible bacterial infection until I could – hopefully – get her to a proper hospital. I silently thanked our savior for small favors.

The hunter took a few seconds to tighten the tourniquet so there was only minor subsequent blood loss. He then slapped Anya in the face a few times lightly to waken her into an incoherent, pain-addled stupor so he could help her to her feet. "If we get out of this cemetery alive, be sure to get her to a hospital ASAP. They will need to tend to that stump with antibiotics and whatever other shit might be needed to keep it free of infection."

"Oh my god!" I exclaimed a third time before upchucking into the grass once more.

"Told you to look away," the hunter said as he held up the stumbling girl. "Come over here now. I need you to carry her out of here, so my hands are free to—"

We were interrupted as another of the ghouls suddenly rushed out of nowhere and leapt at the hunter. I screamed "Oh my god!" a *third* time as the ghastly thing landed on our friend.

"Shit, I should have been paying attention!" he said aloud, obviously pissed off at himself.

The unnamed monster hunter held the ghoul's snapping mouth from his face with all his might for just long enough to plunge the barrel of his firearm into its maw and pull the trigger. The back of the pallid creature's skull was blown off and Anya and I found each other spattered with blackish cranial fluid. Since my friend was just barely coherent from pain and shock, her only reaction was to briefly wince and gasp. In my case, it was another violent upchuck onto the grass.

The nameless hunter pushed the dead ghoul off him with a grunt, then turned to watch me wipe vomit off my chin.

"You all done, Linda Blair? Because we need to move *now*."

With that command, the hunter started moving towards the other side of the cemetery with me and Anya following closely behind. We knew a path was located there that led to another open-gated exit at the eastern side of the sprawling cemetery. It was roughly a fourth of a mile distant, and our friend and guardian held his firearm in one hand and his fearsome blade in the other as he led the way. His breathing was steady as he moved in a silent but methodical pace towards what we all hoped would be a safe exit. He seemed confidently aware of his environment, but not overly so; much experience had taught him that surprises could still happen, especially in the dark.

I carried Anya with her good arm around my shoulder. She was just lucid enough to walk, but with some awkwardness. It was not enough to slow my pace too much, however. The effects of the drug he stuck her with prevented her from either panicking or passing out from the pain of what he had to do.

Nevertheless, she obviously needed medical attention ASAP, and God only knew how I could explain to the hospital staff how my friend ended up with a severed hand and cauterized stump, let alone pumped up with morphine. As we walked along, I did my best not to panic myself; or, to vomit again from the sight of Anya's wound or the lingering smell of burned flesh coming from her stump. Somehow, the presence of our friend gave me whatever courage and conviction I had to keep going and not collapse into a quivering fetal position to await my bloody end.

The only conversation he made with me as we trudged cautiously amidst the foliage overgrowth and broken tombstones was the following. "I'm sorry about your lady. But she got bit, and that's how these ugly bastards make more of themselves. The hand had to come off or she could start a pandemic of the fuckers. In fact, you should keep an eye on her anyway, and yourself. My advice, if either of you start getting a craving for the flesh of the living..." He didn't finish the sentence but held up his handgun. The implication was clear.

The only response I could give was to nervously nod my head in affirmation.

As we preceded on, I struggled not to hyperventilate from knowing what could be lurking behind any tombstone or one of the knobby, dying trees. The whole graveyard was by now eerily silent, with the only movement being a layer of mist drifting close to the ground (that I prayed wasn't indicative of hostile ghosts manifesting next) and the occasional leaf blowing through the air. The only light we had was a slice of moon in the sky, which wasn't much. I kept silently praying, asking God to speed up time so we could get to the exit faster.

Anya kept moving steadily, her eyes half open and making labored gasps. She said no words, but at one point began quietly singing what I recognized as "It's a Small World After All," her favorite childhood song. I remember briefly having concern about her burned stump, saying further prayers to enable me to get her medical attention before the wound could still get infected despite the disinfectant used on the stump.

I almost soiled my pants again when our monster hunter friend abruptly stopped walking. He looked down, and my gaze followed his to reveal what looked like a pile of human bones. Some of them had a bit of blackened skin on them, with a few wriggling maggots visible on the bones. This made it clear they were from bodies long dead and decayed. Others further along the trail, however, were covered with bits of non-rotted flesh and crimson puddles of fresh blood, with no sign of fly larva infestation. I barely winced, having become almost inured to such a sight within the space of a half hour. Which is good, as my throat could scarcely have handled any more puking.

The hunter of monsters took several more cautious steps before stopping and looking to his left. I caught up to him, carrying Anya unsteadily along with me. I then saw what he was looking at the remains of: yet another recently killed and mutilated young man, this one laying before what looked like some type of wooden altar. It wasn't rotted or weather worn, so it had been erected there in the very recent past. On it were painted a series of bright red sigils along with the melted wax and metal holders of a few doused candles.

"Son of a bitch," the hunter snarled. "Bunch of college kids playing at being occultists, probably trying to impress some goth chick, and waking up some real evil. Don't know why I'm so surprised. I've seen it before. Well, this bullshit's all got to go."

Saying no more than that, the hunter quickly squirted flammable ethyl alcohol onto the table and set it aflame with a small metal cigarette lighter. He also made sure to immolate the remains of those would-be wizards that were close to the altar, since one or more could have provided blood as part of the summoning. That explains what those damned fools were doing there, and why they were wearing what looked like ceremonial robes. I cringed at the thought that Anya and I had wandered into the wrong place at the wrongest time possible.

The hunter then turned to us and spoke firmly. "This has all got to be burned as thoroughly as possible, so hopefully no one calls the damn fire department. And let this be a lesson that dark, forbidden magic is not a fucking toy. Now, we need to..."

Before he could say another word one of the ghouls leapt on him from behind, the force taking him flat on his face to the ground. I screamed in barely audible fashion (my throat was raw and almost swollen at this point) and dropped Anya. She landed on her back, where she stared into the sky with a dazed expression while quietly singing a raspy rendition of "Like a Virgin" by Madonna. I recall being surprised that she was into vintage music, as I never heard her sing or listen to it before that. And why did I even think such a stupid thought at the time?

Anyway, I was certain our monster hunter guardian was finished. I considered that it was only a few hundred yards to the path leading to the side exit. I realized I could lift Anya while the (hopefully final) ghoul was otherwise occupied and try to get us out. There was nothing

I could do to help this hunter of monsters. I was no hero, nor was I a warrior of any sort; I was... *just some fucking guy*.

But I was deeply ashamed for having decided to leave Anya behind earlier. And though I didn't know this hunter of monsters, he risked life and both limbs to protect us and spare the many innocents of my town from having to deal with this horror. I wanted to do *something*, but my instincts and "flight" response told me that I just couldn't; that I owed it to Anya to get her out of there, and I owed it to our families not to have to grieve loss of the two of us.

The matter was decided when, without thinking, I ran over to the struggling duo and kicked the ghoul in the head as hard as I could.

"Get the fuck off him!" I shrieked.

The undead bastard barely seemed to notice, and I am not sure if my attack did much good. Either way, the monster hunter had managed to block its attempt to bite into him by pushing his right arm against its throat. Then with his other hand he shoved his bladed weapon into the side of the ghoul's neck and twisted. This hurt the creature enough that he was able to gain the traction to kick it off him and get back to his feet.

However, the ghoul was back on its feet just as quickly. It hissed at him angrily despite the dark blood seeping out of his neck wound and mouth. Its glaring grayish eyes were suffused with single-minded malignancy. It was obviously poised to attack again, this time on two feet.

"Get back!" the hunter shouted to me a second time that night as he lifted the long leg bone of a severed human leg from the ground.

I did as he said, and a second later the ghoul attacked. The hunter swung the thick bone at the creature's wounded neck as hard as he could. That move stopped it in its tracks, He swung a second time before the thing could regain its senses. The bone broke as it struck the ghoul in the side of the face, knocking out some teeth and likely breaking its jaw, but still not taking it down. Our warrior guardian next delivered a mighty side kick to the staggered creature's diaphragm, sending it off its feet and down atop the burning altar.

"Have a little of this on me, you dick." The hunter took the small container of lighter fluid from his pocket and squirted the remainder of its contents onto the burning ghoul, feeding the flames on the table so they engulfed the creature completely.

The inhuman thing writhed and shrieked like a torture victim as the stimulated flames burned its pale form a dark black. The pain-wracked gesticulations and hissing screeches stopped after a few minutes, and the ghoul did not rise again. I covered my nasal region to spare myself the smell of more burning flesh, but otherwise retained my composure. This time, instead of horror at the sight, I felt a strangely intense form of satisfaction at seeing the horrid creature's fiery destruction.

I looked back to check on Anya. She still lay on the ground where she fell, her eyes partially rolled into her head. This time she was humming a lullaby rather than singing. But she was otherwise okay. Relieved to see this, I walked over, put her arm over my shoulder, and lifted her up again.

"Come on, let's head out now," the hunter of monsters said as he retrieved whatever items he had dropped and began walking again.

He kept both his firearm and bladed weapon wielded as we followed him for the short length remaining to the side exit. The rusted metal gate was half off its hinges, and he directed me to get Anya and myself through it first as he stood guarding the exit area. When he saw we had made it out safely, he quickly slipped through as well. We had now exited the cemetery and the three of us hastened to cross a small wooded island in the middle of the street to further distance ourselves from the grounds. Hence, we were no longer in danger of any possible remaining ghouls and content to know the source that "summoned" them would soon be reduced to ashes.

"Is your cell phone still working? Can you call an ambulance?" the hunter asked me.

I slipped my hand into my pocket and took the small device out. I checked it and it seemed to be in working order, so I nodded an affirmation to him. I answered with a barely audible "yeah" as I logged into the phone.

"Good," the hunter replied. "Then we're done here. And if I were you, I'd keep out of cemeteries and abandoned places at night. Because next time I, or someone like me, might not show up on time. Believe me, even with all this, you're lucky. Not everyone gets saved."

"Can I... can I call someone for you too?"

"No." He turned and began to depart.

"Wait! You saved our lives, and I didn't even get your name!"

"I didn't give it."

"Mine's Hoshi. Hoshi Yano!"

The hunter kept walking, then paused for a moment, seemingly in thought. "It's Dale. Just Dale. You should hope we never have to get more acquainted than that."

He turned away and began to walk again, disappearing into the darkness.

I watched this incredible individual step into the shadows as I dialed 911. The ambulance reliably arrived promptly, and Anya and I received the treatment we needed at the local hospital.

***

At the present time, Anya is doing okay and has gotten used to the prosthesis that now replaces her severed hand. We talk now and then, but not as much as in the past when we were besties. She never mentions the events of this night, and I respect her by not bringing up the subject. I suspect seeing or talking to me may remind her of the evening that cruelly shattered her comfort zone and cost her a hand, which was a very serious trauma to endure. That saddens me, but I realize that I must understand and respect her need for distance.

As for me, well… I did a lot of thinking after that night. This included a strict re-assessing of my place and purpose in the world; not to mention of the nature of the world and the universe itself, of course. I have also been doing a lot of research into some really esoteric subjects, absorbing the info like a sponge and preparing for some serious training.

You see, I have decided to follow in the footsteps of that extraordinary individual who put down those ghouls after they nearly took me and a dear friend from this world. I came to the realization that some people need to do what he does, even if that so happens to be the stuff of nightmares. Personally, I find it rather selfless and heroic, even if he and others like him wouldn't use such words. I also felt a powerful need to not only make up for the bogus "safe" life I once wasted my time leading and my cowardly display that evening (I was going to leave Anya to die!), but also to take control of the reality I now knew I lived in. I needed to be stronger than these dark things that secretly prey on humanity, even as we prey on each other and all the animal species below us.

So, yes. I am planning to become a monster hunter myself. The man who saved us that night and others like him will soon be having a new player on the field, whether they would welcome this or not.

As I close this journal entry, I cannot help but wonder how many other survivors of such nightmarish events have likewise decided to take this leap. Hopefully, I shall meet some of them in the years to come.

Hoshi Yano [signature]

END

REDUX OF THE LIVING DEAD

Kevin Heim

California, 2005

My creator never saw fit to give me a name. That's okay; others have taken that burden upon themselves. Now I have many names. The most popular among them is "Monster."

Santa Mira was supposed to be my retirement home. Large enough that it's easy for someone to go unnoticed, small enough to be able to get some privacy, I had actually deluded myself into thinking this Southern California community would afford me the chance to live the rest of my life unnoticed. But for someone... some*thing* like me, peace just doesn't happen.

It started with an explosion at the HybraDyne plant on the edge of town. As a rule, I do not watch television, as it's too banal, but I do listen to syndicated talk radio. I like "Jung at Heart with Dr Niles" and "The Midnight Hour." Not a big fan of Rush Limbaugh, though, so when they interrupted his program to warn about the fire, loss of life, and rioting, I wasn't too upset.

Within an hour's time, though, enough information had been leaked that I knew there was a real problem. Terms like "bio-weapons," "soldier augmentation," and "military contract" made it past the censors, so I gritted my teeth and waited for the inevitable... "Witnesses described the alleged creatures as RoboCop meets Frankenstein."

There it is. The name that will haunt me till someone finds a way to finally end my existence. Hasn't happened yet, and Lord knows plenty have tried. With my luck, I'll outlive the human race; then maybe I'll get some undisturbed rest, at least until the planet runs out of air. But for now, I have to do something about this mess, before it turns into an angry mob looking for someone to blame. Here's a head's up, in case anyone can't put it together: they always blame me.

I don't own a car. Nothing standard would fit my '7'12", 318 lb. body, and getting something custom built would only draw the attention I want to avoid. But I do have a military issue 1985 Silver Mirage motorcycle, supposedly the only one ever built to support someone with my frame. Naturally, I ditched the sidecar; don't really see much call for a tail-gunner, and it's not like I hang around with… okay, I don't hang around with anyone. Ever.

It takes all of thirty minutes to get across town. All the heavy traffic is fleeing in the opposite direction, and with my leather jacket and helmet on, I'm just another asshole biker riding way too fast. My sense of smell isn't quite the same as it is for humans, so I wind up detecting the acrid vapors from the fire long before I can see smoke, let alone feel the heat.

I can even distinguish one of the chemical agents by odor alone: a nasty concoction called Trilanum that smells a lot like chloroform and remains stable even when vaporized. Those dumbasses must be trying to make another platoon of super-soldiers for Uncle Sam, or else the Ordnance is using the plant as a holding tank for the mistakes they made upstate.

The thing about Trilanum zombies is that they usually retain a lot of their human intelligence. Cyborgs would be a lot easier to handle, since they eventually run out of ammo, and they don't spread by infecting the populace (don't believe everything you see on *Star Trek*). With zombies, rounding them all up is the real chore, and with Trilanum zombies, they can get sneaky.

I'm not fond of using weapons, but I also don't relish getting Trilanum on my jacket, so I grab a broadcast antenna from a disabled news van and start swinging at anything that shambles. As they fall, I make a point of crushing their skulls with my feet. The SWAT team is already on the scene, so I'm not really surprised when they fire a few rounds at me but come on; I'm clearly trying to take these things down.

Blame it on my jaundiced skin, I suppose, or perhaps the fact that I'm made from the parts of fourteen dead people. Why wouldn't they think I'm a zombie? And who's to say they'd be wrong, anyway?

Fine, I hop back on my bike and ride off, looking for stragglers. I don't want to be anywhere near ground zero anyway; the military has a tendency to clean up these kinds of messes by using extreme firepower, as in the kind with a half-life. If I didn't already know I'd survive that kind of explosion I might be tempted to stick around for the fireworks, but the last time I tried that… well, let's just say it didn't help. My heart was in the right place, so to speak, but Tokyo probably disagrees.

I see a truck swerving as it speeds away, not proof that it's being driven by a zombie, but enough to make me suspicious. I ride up alongside it, still wielding that antenna. When I reach the driver's window, the smell betrays the infection in him, even though he's still technically alive. I hold the antenna up over my head and thrust in through the glass. I miss the driver, but I do send him careening off the road and into a tree.

He and his three passengers aren't going anywhere for a few minutes, which is more than enough time for me to set the truck on fire. Two of those passengers are clean, but they wouldn't have lasted too long anyway, and burning to death beats being eaten by the corpses of your friends.

The pick-up truck in flames, I continue my patrol towards town. I see a group of kids talking under a store awning as I get closer to the city proper, but I had better check to make sure none of them are infected. Since they're downwind of me, I must get off the bike and see for myself. My sense of smell may be excellent, but the doctor didn't do such a great job when he set my optic nerves, so I really have to get close if I want to see details. I probably shouldn't complain; I hear my last body is almost completely blind now.

Fastest way to check if the teens still among the living is just to take off my helmet, let them get a good look at me. If they're already zombies, they won't react; and if they're alive, they'll run, which helps to clear the streets. As long as they're the only ones who see me, no one should figure out that I'm in town, and the descriptions from the teens will be assumed to be of a zombie.

Helmet off, I step into the light and growl. It's easier than yelling, more effective, and doesn't hurt nearly as much (that's right, vocal cords weren't Doctor Frankenstein's specialty, either). I get the response I wanted (they run), but I also get a wooden shaft propelled through my chest from behind for the effort.

"He's still standing! What should I do?" a shaky voice called out from across the street.

"Hit him again, I'll get the holy water ready," was the gruff reply, which seems to come from the same spot.

I turn to face my attackers – both thirty-somethings, near as I can tell – as I rip the stake from my heart. Hurts like a bitch, and black crud oozes from the wound. At least they didn't aim for a lung; those take the longest to heal.

"Holy shit! It's the attack of Herman Munster!" one of them yells.

The one with the modified crossbow gets ready to launch another stake, aiming at my head this time. His buddy chucks a water balloon at me. And people wonder why I want to die?

"Gruff" speaks up. "Hold your fire! He's not some goddamned shit-sucking vampire. Must be some other kind of undead."

"Whatever it is, we have to kill it fast," his ally said. "The news said these things were spreading."

"Shaky" still has the drop on me, but there's a better chance he'll shoot me accidentally than actually take the shot.

I take a deep breath so I can speak loud enough to be heard. "Aim for the brain. That's how you destroy a zombie."

My voice is slow, loud, deep, and gravelly, practically a roar. I understand most people find it a very unpleasant sound.

Shaky drops his weapon and looks at his partner.

Gruff tries to console him. "It's not your fault; he pulled a mind scramble on you! He opened his mouth and talked!"

"Zombies. That's the problem here," I reply. "Stop them all or they keep spreading. Fast. And daylight doesn't mean a thing to them."

"What are you, some kind of walking Wikipedia of the weird?" Gruff was recovering nicely, but he was still in shock.

"I'm a monster," I say. "Who would know monsters better than me?"

"Yeah. Yeah, that makes sense," Shaky retorts while keeping his eyes on me.

That makes fumbling through his knapsack much more difficult, but at least he manages to get the crossbow put away. No idea what he hopes to find in there to kill me with, but I'd rather save us the time.

"If you aren't infected, leave," I say. "Zombie plagues don't tend to have many survivors, and I will not be pulling my punches to avoid killing."

The sound of machine gun fire cuts off whatever the duo might have had to say to me. This is turning into a fiasco.

A Jeep M715, an old one used by the SWAT team until recently, comes barreling down the road. Zombies, of course, but zombies dressed as... military cyborgs with guns, missiles, and buzz saws attached to their bodies.

They remind me a little of the Borg. Maybe I need to re-evaluate my opinion of *Star Trek*.

The boys who attacked me start jumping like frogs to get out of the way. Which is about the stupidest thing you can do around zombies, since they're always more likely to see a moving target. So, I rush the Jeep on foot, and give the froggy monster hunters a chance to save themselves.

The impact sends me sprawling backwards, but it also knocks the vehicle out of commission and throws the universal soldiers through the air, right over me. I get a good look at them as they go: a male and a female, both horribly burnt up and bullet ridden. Looks like at least two headshots have already been scored on them, but of course bionic zombies don't have to rely on human brains for mobility. At least they won't be talkers.

I get back on my feet before they do, but they aren't far behind. And those weapons are still active. Who puts a buzz saw on a zombie, anyway?

They're clearly tough, but are they Frankenstein Fucking Monster tough? To find out, I grab the front end of the JM715 with both hands, really digging my fingers into the metal, and heft it at the pair. One of them has just enough time to open fire on it before they both go down. But I can't be sure this will stop them, so it's time to disassemble Johnny-5.

They have the wreckage removed before I reach them. Not much flesh left on them anymore, but they sure do smell like fetid bodies. At least some of their weapons look damaged beyond repair. The male sits up and targets me with a mounted shoulder grenade launcher, but it doesn't fire. The female extracts some shrapnel from her torso, so she can open a cabinet containing… more ammunition. So much for letting them expend their rounds.

"Yo, Terminators!"

Great, my jumpy friends never left.

"Terminate *these!*"

Both of them release arrows fired from compound bows. What that will accomplish, I have no idea. They are great shots though, as both arrows enter eye sockets. Guess they got over their initial twitchiness.

The cyborgs twitch instead, spasming momentarily before falling backwards, sparks crackling from the metal shafts impaling their faces.

"Yeah! Death by Bluetooth!" Gruff cheers.

"I'm not big on computers, but these things have probably been built to withstand an E.M.P.," I note. "I think they will restart soon."

But at least they were thinking. I like that.

Shaky tosses me his belt. "Were they built to withstand grenades?"

"Our contribution to scum-sucking undead birth control!" Gruff looks proud of his quip and high-fives Shaky; hopefully they're still maintaining situational awareness.

I catch the bandolier; the twelve grenades are clipped to a single wire, so I can pull all the pins out at once. I punch open the chest plates on these zombie robots and insert six each. Then I stomp both their heads, just to keep them busy if they reboot before I finish and shove the bodies closer together.

"Run!" I shout, hoping the hunters have already fled too far to hear me.

With a quick tug, the grenades are armed, and I have just enough time to push the Jeep on top of both of them before the explosion.

***

I would like to be able to say that I was knocked unconscious, maybe even killed by the blast. No such luck. The Jeep did its job; directing the blast so none of the force was wasted. All that remains of the zombies is a chuck hole eight feet deep and twenty feet wide, lined with chunks of metal and bone fused to the concrete.

My own twisted visage suffered a major hit. Even my yellow eyes had blisters on them, and every physical sensation was coupled with excruciating pain. But mostly, the explosion just blew me down the street about half a block and left me wide-awake for the whole show. Couldn't see a damn thing for a while, but I smelled oil and transmission fluid nearby. So, I tracked the odors to a nearby garage and hid myself till the flames died down and my corneas healed.

Now I'm on the road again, with nothing but the shredded clothes I was already wearing, a pair of goggles to keep my eyes from getting too dry while my eyelids regrow, and my Silver Mirage, which was thankfully far enough from the blast radius to still be in running condition. Paint job's ruined, though.

No way to know if those awesome monster hunters survived, but they seemed pretty resourceful, so I'm confident they made it. Which will probably suck for me, because they seem ingenious enough to be able to come up with a way to hurt me. Not kill me, of course, but just mess me up for a good long while. And I'd hate to have to kill them for that, but no way could I just let them get away with it.

Maybe it's time I head back East. I enjoyed a bit of solitude on the West Coast, but I've been seen and identified, so it's only a matter of time before either the angry mobs come after me, or the paparazzi do. Just one more thing about living in California that I can't stomach.

END

HORROR HOUSE

Neil Riebe

The morning was cold and damp. Derek liked it that way because cold and damp equated with peace and quiet. People tended to stay indoors. Reaching from his easy chair, he pushed open the window. As he took in the smell of the curling autumn leaves in the chilled outdoor air, he reveled in the silence.

Turning to his book, he slid his finger between the pages where his silk bookmark draped and immersed himself in the words.

A set of footsteps interrupted his reverie. His expression soured as he looked up. There in the doorway of his den stood his brother, Allen.

"I'm leaving," Allen announced.

"For God's sake, Al, this is the third year in a row. I don't even have to look at the calendar to know it's October 12. Why do you insist this house is haunted? Nothing happens when you're gone. Nothing!"

Allen put on a petulant frown. "You forget about my experiences."

"Yes," Derek crooned, "your experiences." He put his book under his chin and moved his free hand over it as though he were playing the violin. "Let's say you did see a ghost. It didn't hurt you, did it?"

"I sensed something malevolent on the landing as I was going up the stairs. Then I heard it, the ghost, walking up the steps ahead of me. It sounded like it was walking barefoot with thick nails on its toes, clicking on the wood. I stopped, then it stopped, and as it stopped...," Allen paused, trying to contain himself. A tear glistened in his eye. "As it stopped," he tried again, forcing the words in a loud voice, "it

192

materialized just as it turned to face me. It looked exactly as Mary Whiteheart described!"

"Mary Whiteheart! Thank small mercies that shriveled up crone is dead and buried. I couldn't believe she wanted to tear down this beautiful house. She had to be nuts."

"Or damned certain of what she believed."

"It's a good thing," Derek leaned back, speaking with an air of superiority, "we made a killing in our respective businesses, or this house would certainly be gone. It goes to show that when money talks, even the decrepit and insane can understand."

Mary Whiteheart, the prior owner of the house, had claimed that something not exactly human and not quite dead was buried in the basement. That was about as coherent a description anyone was able to get out of her, doctors or otherwise. Derek had brushed her off. "Not only has her body gone," Derek had said, for she was confined to a wheelchair, "her mind is gone, too."

Allen was Derek's opposite. Soft hearted, "a ninny," as Derek put it. And he believed something real had disturbed her.

"Besides," Derek interjected, "I thought hauntings were supposed to happen in old, old houses. Ours was built in 1891. That's just twenty years ago."

"Apparently, that's more than enough time."

"Allen, most psychologists today say ghostly appearances are mental projections imagined by people when their emotions are at a peak. In other words, it's all in your head!"

"You forget the scratching I heard at the door."

"Yes, the scratching at your door."

"No! Your door!"

"Yes, my door," Derek corrected himself. "Funny how I didn't hear it."

"That's because you are hard-headed and insufferably callous. That is why you're divorced. That is why when your children call, they ask for me, their Uncle Allen."

"And that's the way I like it. I put up with you because you are my brother. Of course, after all these years, I don't know why that should matter either. I guess some things should be sacred."

"And that is about the only reason why I tolerate you. It is a good thing this is a big house." Allen tightened the belt for his overcoat around his waist. "I'm going to find help. If it means anything to you, I hope you will be safe."

"I'll be right here, reading."

Allen departed.

Derek returned to his book. Out of the corner of his eye he saw his brother outside plop his derby on his head and survey their Queen Anne house with dismay. Their eyes met. Allen looked hurt. Concern underscored his pained stare. Derek raised his book in a show of being preoccupied and did not lower it until he heard Allen start down the walkway.

Allen was forty-eight. Derek would be damned if he was going to coddle his younger brother's feelings anymore. If Allen wanted an excuse to be scared he should stare down the business end of a loaded gun. Derek had that experience when he moved out west thirty years ago. He wanted real work; work that would make him break a sweat, not juggling numbers at their father's accounting business in Manchester.

Derek started out as an extra hand on a ranch. Harley Johnson, one of the men on the cattle drive, thought it would be fun to spook the "greenhorn from New England."

He remembered Harley well, his pockmarked face and the tobacco juice splotched on the front of his shirt.

Derek had his share of fisticuffs growing up. But staring at the hollow eye of a .45 Schofield's muzzle was another matter. His will to live scrambled to find a way out. Then he realized that he wasn't dealing with the revolver. He was dealing with the man, and not a bright one, with the weapon being held within reach.

The thought cleared Derek's head. He snapped hold of Harley's firing hand and twisted down. The Schofield went off. A sensation of heat and pain slashed across his hip. But Derek kept swinging. In one blow he pulped the man's nose, sending him sprawling onto the hard, Texan dirt. In the same move Derek wrenched the gun free and put the sights on Harley.

"All right, kid." Harley held his hands up. His purpled nose made him wince as he spoke. "You proved your point. Hand back the gun."

Derek fired between Harley's legs, sending him scrambling away. The other cowhands laughed.

"You're lucky I'm a bad shot," Derek called after him. "Otherwise we'd be calling you Miss Johnson!"

The hip wound turned out to be grazed skin. It did not even keep Derek from work. As for Harley Johnson, he never came back for his gun. Just as well, because Derek had no intention of returning it. He still had the Schofield to this day.

So, noises upstairs were not going to frighten him, not after being a moment away from having his head blown open to the hot sun. Derek wet his finger and turned a page.

The clock ticked on the wall.

The floorboards creaked in the hall.

Derek looked up from his book. Something had caught his eye, as if something had passed through the doorway.

Then the clock stopped ticking.

Derek frowned. He decided to fix it later.

Next, the room turned cold.

He shut the window. However, the temperature continued to drop. He set his book down and rubbed his fingers.

Coffee would hit the spot.

He brewed a pot in the kitchen and came back to the den with a box of matches. Setting the steaming mug on the fireplace mantle, he struck a match.

The instant the little flame touched the wood a fireball blasted out in a shock of heat. His reflexes saved him from being burned, but the fireball leapt up over the mantle and set fire to his father's portrait on the wall.

To keep the fire from spreading, he wrapped the throw rug around the painting and threw it to the floor. The flames lashed at him as he stamped them into submission.

Stepping away, he wiped his face with a handkerchief. The veins in his neck pulsed from the excitement.

Glaring at the ruins on the floor, he noticed an orange glow creeping through the fibers in the rug. The fire burst back to life and leapt out of the rug to the middle of the room, burning bright and hot on the hardwood floor.

Even though taken by surprise, Derek held onto his wits. He pulled the rug from the portrait in a clatter of broken frame and smothered the wily fire yet again. To be sure, he fetched a bucket of water and doused the rug.

The fire remained extinguished. Derek opened the window to clear the smoke. Worry lines furrowed his brow when he examined the damage. He had to admit he was at a loss to understand what had just happened.

***

After his father had passed away, Allen took over the family's accounting firm. Henry Saward, a prominent industrialist and longtime client of the firm, heard about Allen's problem from the chatter among the secretaries. He had recommended speaking with his daughter, Marcella, as ghosts were her hobby.

As a rule, Allen started with the cheapest services, and since a consultation with Marcella was free, he accepted Mr. Saward's offer. The old capitalist gladly arranged an appointment. October 12, today, was the agreed upon date.

At the Saward's sumptuous estate, a butler led Allen to the library and announced him through the open doorway.

To be honest, Allen expected to meet a bookish schoolmarm with spectacles. Her father had confided that she was unmarried. The fair-haired woman proved to be quite the opposite when she looked up from the work on her desk. Her features were as alluring as a Gibson girl illustration, while her eyes gleamed with intelligence.

The state of the room, however, fit the description of a rat's nest. Books crammed the shelves to overflowing. Boxes of photo albums and stacks of old newspapers covered the floor.

"Mr. Peterson," she left her desk and strode up a path through the stacks of printed material, hand extended. "Thank you for coming."

"No. Thank you." Allen shook her slender palm. "Forgive me for being so forward, but you make me wish I was a young man again with a full head of hair."

She laughed. "Since when did anyone need a reason to wish to be young?"

Allen refrained from making any comments about the room and accepted her invitation to sit in the chair in front of her desk.

Marcella sat down and pulled out a folder from a stack of papers. The label on the file had Mary Whiteheart's name and her address, 2102 Cathedral Lane, which was now his place of residence. Taking the notebook, Marcella flipped to a clean page.

"Mr. Peterson," she began, getting down to business.

"Please, call me Allen."

"Certainly," she said, pen poised and ready. "Tell me about your haunting."

Allen related the scratching at the doors, the feelings of an invisible presence watching him, and the heavy-footed lumbering through the halls upstairs.

"Any physical evidence, such as marks in the wood, damaged property?" Marcella interrupted.

"No." Allen then told her about the ghost appearing on the second floor landing. "Ever since, I refuse to be in that house come October 12."

"Only on that date?"

"Only then."

"Interesting… how long have you been vacating the house?"

"This is the third year."

"Anyone in the house when you're gone?"

"My brother, Derek."

"Does he have any complaints?"

"No."

"Really?" Marcella sounded disappointed.

"You need to add a postscript where my brother is concerned," Allen explained. "He refuses to acknowledge anything is wrong. He's dead set on being indifferent."

"In-dif-fer-ent," she pronounced as she wrote. "If these noises are as loud as you say, I find it hard to believe anyone can be that obtuse."

Marcella asked more about Derek. Allen would rather talk about his problem. He shrugged, humoring her anyway.

"He has been in constant conflict, partly thanks to me. I was a magnet for bullies when I was a boy. Derek was always dishing out black eyes and bloody noses in my defense. He moved out West where he started a barbwire business. I thought it was ironic, prickly as he is. It was a shrewd move. He got into the business when it was the latest thing. But he caught several junior managers embezzling the profits. Since he had made more money than he could ever spend, Derek decided he didn't have to put up with crooked employees and sold the business.

"That infuriated his wife. Her motto was, 'It was the duty of a man of means to expand his means to the fullest of his ability.' She divorced him and took their two boys. Now he lives with me, which is little consolation, I'm sure. I think he's so fed up with people, that if he admits there is a problem in our house, the word will get out and attract attention. I hope I didn't bore you." He ended his story with a sheepish grin.

"Not at all!" Marcella set her pen down and shook the cramp out of her hand. "I need to be sure your brother's experience in the house can't be used to discount yours." She cleared a space on the desk and slid forward a fresh sheet of paper and her pen. "What I would like you to do now is draw a sketch of your ghost."

Allen took the pen, then sat tapping the page, leaving ink dots.

"I'm sorry," he said. "I can see that thing in my mind, but not well enough to draw it."

"Start with an outline. Did the ghost have a head?"

"Yes."

"Arms?"

"Yes, yes, arms, head, torso." He pursed his lips, as digging up the bones of his unpleasant memories unnerved him. Persevering nevertheless, he set his hand to the task.

Allen created a half circle with little dashes, suggesting a head of wild hair. Feral-haired shoulders and arms formed. Large knuckles capped the hands. He drew a long loop for the nose, extending down to the chest, and scribbled in the eyes. Lastly, he marked a series of dashes for the cheeks.

Trembling, he shook his head and threw the pen down. "No more. This is as much as I want to remember."

Marcella studied the drawing. "This is amazing. You don't have a ghost, Allen. You have a goblin!"

"You can't be serious," Allen chuckled anxiously. "As in ghosts and goblins, except, instead of the former it's the latter?"

Ignoring his quips, Marcella fetched a leather-bound tome from the top shelf of the bookcase behind her. She blew off the dust, waving her hand to thin the gray cloud. Her pert nose wrinkled.

"I received this book on sprites from the renowned Baron Vordenburg of Styria. Since he specializes in the undead, he thought I would find more use for it. Personally, I think the baron was enamored with me and hoped I would be charmed."

She paused as if recalling a wistful memory of the baron.

"Anyway," she opened the book before Allen, "this is what I mean. Goblins are akin to elves, fairies, and sprites. However, goblins are the black sheep of their kind."

The book was in German and well-illustrated. Many of the images were of mischievous little characters with toothy grins. Their noses were exaggerated, their ears pointy. Others were frail-looking girls sitting on toadstools, sporting butterfly wings.

The next page revealed a picture that turned Allen's insides. The drawing depicted a man working by candlelight. In his humble surroundings was a black shape peering at him from a dark corner with glaring eyes. The creature had the same wild-haired outline as Allen's sketch.

He snapped the book shut. "How do you get rid of such a thing?"

"I'll cable some friends for their input," Marcella answered. "Your goblin has chosen October 12th to work its magic. We need to find out why the goblin is aggravating you and to what end." She tore her notes out of the notebook and slid them into the folder. "In the meantime, go home. Write down anything strange you hear, see, or smell. To dispel an intruding spirit, knowledge is essential."

Allen agreed to her instructions albeit with reservations.

The overcast broke at sunset, and the spire capping the corner tower of their Queen Anne stood sharp and black against the pumpkin-orange glow on the horizon. A single light shone inside the house. Allen regarded his home with resentment. *A home--hah!* he thought to himself before going in.

Derek told him what happened in the den and showed him the scorched remains of their father's portrait lying on the dining room table.

"I told you!" Allen burst out.

Derek pinched the bridge of his nose, appearing strained. "I don't want to hear any more about ghosts. I'm not happy about losing our father's portrait. It's irreplaceable."

"I'm more concerned about losing my brother who is still alive. You expect me to believe what happened to you was a freak accident? Wood doesn't catch fire that fast no matter how dry it is."

They broke off arguing, scowling from either side of the table.

Allen breached the silence. "At least show me the den."

Derek led the way to the room and turned on the light.

Allen examined the smeary smoke stains on the wall where the painting had hung. So far, the portrait of their mother was unharmed. Allen then noticed the throw rug lying in a charred heap on the floor. He swept the rug aside with his shoe.

"Ah-hah! What do you make of that?"

Derek knelt down on one knee to examine what Allen found under the rug. "Those are an odd pair of burns."

"Oh, please! Anyone can see those are footprints." Allen knelt beside him and pointed out in the two oblong blotches the heels, soles, toes-- and claws. "I said the footsteps upstairs sounded like they had thick nails. See those barbs at the end of the toes? This spirit was trying to assume a form in which to harm you. Look! It was facing your way when you were at the fireplace."

"Enough! Do you believe if we brought in a couple of men from the fire department," Derek said, his voice rising, "they are going to look at those burns and say, 'Oh, yes. You had a hot-footed ghost standing in the middle of your den'? *Do you?"*

Derek stormed out of the room.

Allen stood, thrusting his hands into his pockets. Frustrated, he kicked the damaged rug.

Looking back at the strange burns, he compared them to his foot. If these burns were footprints, the goblin's feet extended three inches longer than his. A shiver skittered up his spine.

"And I thought goblins were supposed to be small," he muttered.

***

After dark, the brothers sat in the parlor. Derek was making up for lost reading time, concentrating on the pages with his usual studied frown, while Allen detailed in his journal his brother's experience in the den.

The clock chimed. It was nine o'clock.

Allen sighed. Three more hours to go before midnight, and another October 12th would be over. Settling back in his chair, he let his gaze roam around the parlor, at the ornamented red carpet and the maple-varnished wainscot.

While he relaxed, the floor creaked. A cold presence pressed upon him and a moist breeze brushed across his cheek, as though someone exhaled with powerful lungs. A feral odor followed, like that of an animal, mixed with the pungent scent of loam. Allen went rigid.

Mercifully, the chilly air and sour smell dissipated as the floor creaked again, further into the room, and then once more near his brother. Allen prayed the spirit would not show itself. He could not bear its horrid visage a second time.

Allen got a hold of himself. He decided this time, come what may, he would not fall apart.

"Phew!" Derek exclaimed, covering his nose. "Was that you?"

Allen rolled his eyes. "Didn't you hear the floor creak?"

Derek shook his head.

"Well, that stink didn't come from me," Allen said.

"It isn't coming from me, either." Derek then reacted with a start. "I can feel a draft, like someone is breathing on me."

"That's because our friend is standing right in front of you."

Derek reached forward, feeling for something he could not see. His hand jerked back. "You know," he intoned cautiously, "you might be right."

He slammed his book shut and swung it through the air, above the spot where the floor creaked, hollering "Scat!" The oppressive presence evaporated.

"The spirit is gone!" Allen exclaimed. "You dispelled it! You, the skeptic." He sank into the chair. "It hardly seems fair."

201

Derek got up and searched the room with his hand extended, circling back to his seat. "Hah!" he snapped his fingers triumphantly. "So much for Mary Whiteheart's vaunted ghost. Your spook is more scared of us than you are of it."

"If you are going to admit I'm right, please don't gloat."

"Oh boo-hoo! You're upset because I don't get worked up like you do."

"It did try to kill you this morning."

Derek tossed his hand at him, dismissing the notion.

The clock chimed. Derek declared the matter settled and headed for bed. Allen closed his journal on his lap. Once again, his brother had proved to be the stronger.

***

The next morning, Derek came down to the kitchen to heat the coffee and fry some bacon and eggs. He could tell by the way his brother was hunched over his oatmeal that he was in low spirits. He asked Allen what was wrong.

Allen stirred his soupy oats, gazing into the swirls. "I imagine after last night you respect me less than ever before."

"You really were hoping that I'd get scared," Derek said with a chuckle, "so we would be on equal footing, weren't you?"

Allen sat with his hand around his bowl as though his breakfast were his only friend.

Derek pulled up a chair. He set his chin on his fist, staring at Allen, wondering what to do with him.

"All right," Derek rapped his knuckles on the table. "Let's face facts. We are never going to get along in any perfect sort of way you want. It's not worth sulking over. We are what we are."

"That doesn't leave much room for self-improvement."

"We're too old to change."

***

In the evening when Allen came home from the firm, they went through their routine of recapping their day over supper and then turned in for bed. Things seemed to have resumed their normal rhythm.

Allen was in his room, asleep, and Derek was about to turn off the light when he had this sensation well up inside him that someone else was close by.

His door was open a crack. From the hall the silence was disrupted by what sounded like a large paw scraping down the face of the door to his brother's bedroom. The bedsprings crunched on the other side of the wall from Allen, making a sudden jolt of movement in his room.

The scraping then erupted into a cacophony of wood being bashed to pieces. Allen screamed.

Derek leapt from under the covers. He bolted to the bureau where lay an electric flashlight, to the closet where his Schofield revolver hung from its holster. Slamming several rounds into the cylinders, he rushed into the hall with the gun ready in one hand and the flashlight blazing from the other.

There in the flashlight beam was a wild-haired, obscene melding of man and beast. It was like a huge mole with well-muscled arms and hands. Its snout was long and narrow like a fox's and barbed with a battery of savage teeth.

The creature crouched on the floor, voraciously chewing the door-- the inch and a quarter thick slab of solid oak--to pieces as if it were a cracker.

"Hey!" Derek yelled to draw its attention.

The beast looked at him for a moment, and then ran for the stairs, making not a sound.

Derek stopped at his brother's room. Allen stood against the far wall in his pajamas, clutching his chest, panting. Before Derek could ask Allen if he was all right a crash resounded downstairs in the den.

Leaving his brother, Derek ran down and burst into the room, scanning all four corners with the flashlight. All appeared undisturbed, but their mother's portrait was now missing.

A deep-throated snarl emitted behind him. He spun and heard a series of padded footsteps thump out into the hall.

He pursued the noise into the parlor where he found the creature facing one of the windows, crouched on all fours. It swiveled around on its haunches toward Derek. Its lips peeled back in a toothy leer, reminding him eerily of a card shark who still had one more trick up his sleeve.

This time Derek did not hesitate to fire. The gun boomed. Glass shattered. When the glare from the muzzle flash cleared from his eyes, he saw the shattered fragments of the window glittering on the floor. The mole-thing had vanished.

Allen phoned Marcella. She assured him she would be there shortly after sundown. True to her word, she came motoring to the house in her white-polished Pierce Arrow.

They gathered at the kitchen table, where, at Marcella's request, he and Derek set down the burnt remains of their father's portrait and the un-chewed portion of his bedroom door. She raised a fragment of the door to the light.

The brothers watched her scrutinize the woodchip with her magnifying glass. Derek had the Schofield belted to his waist while Allen had a Remington hunting rifle cradled across his lap. His knuckles stood out on his hands from clutching the weapon tightly.

"I wish I had a microscope handy," Marcella remarked. "This piece of chewed wood may have traces of saliva stains."

"Saliva?" Allen reacted in disgust. "I never thought that, while we were sweeping up the mess, we could be touching the monster's spit!" He got up to wash his hands.

"How are you going to get rid of the goblin?" Derek asked Marcella. "I hope you don't plan on hanging garlic flowers in all the rooms."

"Only if it pleases you," she retorted. Marcella chucked the gnawed piece of wood into the paper bag containing the rest of the fragments. "I want to explore the premises first, get a feel for the goblin's presence."

Opening her journal, Marcella recorded the date – October 14, 1911, time – 8:40 pm, and wrote, "Quiet. No peculiar sensations. Room temperature—comfortable."

"Right," she slapped her pen down on the open journal. "I need one volunteer to keep watch downstairs and one to follow me upstairs, carrying my camera."

"We should stick together," Derek advised. "If the goblin comes back, we'll have a better chance of blasting it before it can disappear."

"Guns will do no good," Marcella shook her head.

"The beast ran when it saw mine," Derek said. "If it runs, it can be hurt."

"The goblin is a spirit, Mr. Peterson," Marcella explained. "Deceiving is as much its modus operandi as haunting. Now, Allen, would you be a dear and carry my camera?"

Derek snorted. "You said you wanted volunteers."

"I guess she doesn't like you," Allen said softly in his ear.

"Then you and your date have a nice time," Derek rejoined.

"I only work with open-minded men," Marcella clarified with a smile.

With the rifle slung to his back, Allen joined Marcella at the stairs leading up to the second floor. Derek remained at the kitchen table, occupying himself with a deck of cards. His revolver lay within reach on the tabletop. Marcella handed Allen a Kodak Brownie from her leather satchel. She also drew from the bag a crucifix, which she hung about her neck. Its metallic surface caught the light as the cross swung low about her abdomen from a long chain.

Marcella began her investigation at the bottom of the staircase, running her fingers across the wood, searching for any unusual marks or scoring. She banged the handle of the magnifying glass here and there all the way up the steps. At the top of the landing, one of the floorboards made a hollow reply and showed the slightest bit of give.

"Did you know about this?" Marcella asked.

Allen shook his head.

"But here, at the top of the stairs, was where you witnessed your first manifestation."

Allen nodded.

"Interesting." Marcella lifted the hem of her dress and unsheathed a dirk that was strapped to her shin. In one flick of the blade, she popped the board loose, then slid the sharp implement back into its sheath.

Allen blushed at the sight of her exposed leg. Yet he buried his guilty feelings to appear composed.

"Let's see if anything intriguing is in here," Marcella remarked as she reached inside. Her expression turned downcast when she withdrew her arm from the hidden compartment empty handed.

Then Allen smelled that familiar brew of pungent loam and beastly musk. A sultry breath brushed the back of his neck. Fear bound him in its emasculating grip.

Marcella's eyes went wide as she looked past his shoulder. "My God," she said in a soft tone, as if to a pet. "You are big."

She stood, slowly. Not for a moment did she take her eye off her quarry.

Allen spun around and dropped back to Marcella's side. Hunched on all fours, the goblin glared up at them. The charcoal-gray hair was thick, flecked with ochre-hued strands, and stood out on end all over its body, except on the snout. There the hair was short and smoothed back. Every aspect of the creature spoke of a big animal, bar the eyes. Those glistened with some sort of unearthly, non-color, as if they were little portals to the ethereal realm from which the spirit came.

"When I give the word…," Marcella instructed in a hushed voice.

"…run," Allen concluded for her, equally hushed.

"No!" she hissed. "Take pictures."

He looked down at his hand. The camera had escaped his mind. Even so… "You're crazy!"

The goblin clenched its forepaws, digging ruts into the floor with its nails. It bared its teeth. A hiss reverberated within the grotesque entity's throat, hinting at the viciousness pent up as a pressure cooker inside its muscular frame.

Before it could spring Marcella thrust the crucifix into its fox-snouted face. "Take pictures!" she yelled, and then chanted in what sounded to Allen's ears like a Celtic verse.

He stood rooted where he was. Everything was happening too fast.

The goblin recoiled from the cross. It appeared Marcella had the creature at bay.

Then in one swift move the goblin rose to its full height, its head brushing the ceiling, and swiped a small table off the floor, sending a vase and a collection of knick-knacks flying. The table struck Marcella

206

in the side of the face. Her head snapped back as she tumbled down the stairs.

Allen popped to his senses. He rushed down to her inert body at the foot of the stairs and grasped her wrist to check her pulse.

Derek came running from the kitchen with the gun in hand. He looked down at Marcella and then up at the second floor landing. A mixed reaction of awe and anger crossed his face. Before Allen could stop him, Derek rushed upstairs. Shortly he came back down without firing a shot. The goblin had disappeared.

Gently they moved Marcella to a guest room and called their physician, Dr. Morrison. She came to by the time Morrison arrived. He said, at worst, she suffered a mild concussion and asked her to stay put until he checked on her again in the morning. After Morrison left, Marcella sighed.

"It's a shame we didn't get a picture of the goblin," she said. "Collecting photos of spirits is a lot like collecting trophies."

"I'm not putting up with this another night," Derek said. "Whiteheart said something was buried in the basement. You said yourself this thing is deceptive." He jabbed a finger at Marcella, who was holding an ice bag to the swollen bruise on the side of her face. "Why else does it keep appearing upstairs but to draw us away from the basement?"

Marcella agreed with his reasoning.

"But we can't fight an evil spirit!" Allen bleated.

"On the contrary," Marcella said, "I think you two are the only ones who can. The goblin shrugged me off. It knows I'm not an occupant, and therefore it knows I have no right to tell it what to do."

"That's all you have to do?" Derek asked. "Tell it to scoot?"

"Exorcising spirits is a battle of wills," Marcella elaborated. "If you know where you stand you will win. That's the game it has been playing with you. The goblin wants a toehold in the material world. It chose this house. In the spirit plane emotional attachment is equivalent to legal ownership. All the goblin has to do is break your fondness for this place to take possession. That's why you are being harassed--to make this house no longer seem like your home."

What she said made sense. Allen asked Marcella what would happen if their bond with the house were broken.

"You will be driven out," she said, "maybe even killed."

"We should abandon this place," Allen suggested to Derek.

"No," his brother said. "My wife drove me out of my last house. I'm not going to be driven out of this one, and neither are you."

Marcella offered her crucifix. "My crucifix is made of iron. The iron will repel the goblin from touching you, and the symbol of the cross will remind you that you have a higher source of strength to draw from. Find the goblin. Command it to leave. Be firm. If you harbor the slightest doubt, you give it license to rebuff your command."

Allen took the crucifix, stuffed it into his waistcoat pocket.

For her comfort, they left Marcella a glass of Brandy and her journal before going downstairs.

Searching the basement presented one important question. How much damage were they prepared to do to the foundation to find the goblin's lair? They failed to notice anything out of the ordinary when they moved in. Nevertheless, behind a rickety bookshelf, they found a crack in the foundation wall, which began about waist high and continued in a jagged line all the way to the floor. The noxious loam odor wafted in their faces as they slid the shelf aside.

This was as good an indication as any.

Grabbing a pickaxe and shovel from the shed outside, they set to work. The cement proved to be brittle and broke away as easily as chipping teeth from rotted gums. The ripe stench worsened as they uncovered a four-foot-wide hole.

They filled empty jars with kerosene. Allen fetched the acetylene lamp while Derek jury-rigged a torch. When they were ready, Allen wiped his hand on his trousers and extended it to Derek.

"This time I won't fold up on you," Allen said. "I promise."

Derek did not say anything reassuring, but he did shake Allen's hand. "Just pray that whatever we find burns nicely."

He struck a match and lit the torch. Allen picked up the lamp and they descended one at a time down the hole.

Their feet went splat when they hit the earthen floor. The loam odor ripened into something that smelled fruity and thoroughly retching. All about them, gooey globs of dun-colored weeds hung from the walls, looking as though they were about to drip. The brothers stepped carefully, and found their mother's portrait on the ground, among the jelly-like flora, smashed.

"This may be our hairy intruder's nest," Derek remarked. "Whiteheart was right."

"If this is the nest," Allen said, "where's the goblin?"

Without comment, Derek pointed further into the underground. The hole had emptied them into a tunnel.

They proceeded with caution. The earthen floor was hard packed, as though the passage had seen a lot of use. Its alkaline tang tweaked their sinuses, and the damp air turned their skin clammy.

Up ahead, a hulking figure approached them. Its footsteps seemed human, and it seemed to be shuffling, like a person who was carrying a heavy burden. One foot slid forward in the dirt, followed by a pause, and then the other foot slid forward. Allen set the lamp down and shouldered the rifle, while Derek readied one of the kerosene-filled jars. They waited for the creature to come into the light to get a clear shot. Each of them hoped this confrontation would be decisive. For the elder brother, he hoped to end the haunting of his home. The younger sibling wanted something more.

As the shuffling figure drew near, the lamp revealed a disturbing sight. Tentacles squirmed about its torso like earth worms. Its head sagged, as though the bones had gone soft, and stared with hollow eye sockets. Once in the light, the beast did not stop. It kept coming!

A battle of wills, Marcella had said. Allen dropped the rifle and fished out the cross. Shooting would do no good, because even if the bullets killed the fiend, he would not be any braver in his brother's eyes until he conquered his fear.

Derek pulled back to chuck the jar, with its flammable contents, when Allen charged, screaming, "Go! In God's name, get out of here!"

One of the quivering worms snapped around Allen's throat, choking his words. The tunnel monster snatched the crucifix with a second wormy tentacle and popped it into its mouth. The foul beast then swallowed the crucifix, chain and all.

Allen refused to give up. He grabbed the abomination's throat. His fingers sank into the folds of its skin. The slacked jaw kept mouthing its wheezy cries over the top of his hands. His curses spat out between clenched teeth as his cheeks puffed up and turned red. With blood and air pinched off, Allen's body went flaccid in the tunnel monster's grip. It released him, letting the man fall to the ground.

Derek dared not throw the kerosene. His brother lay too close. Instead, he drew his revolver. The Schofield was deafening as it was blinding in the tunnel. Derek unloaded all six cylinders to no effect. It was like hitting dead meat. No blood drained from the wounds. All the Schofield achieved was force the monster back a couple of steps.

The beast narrowed its vacant gaze to a malignant glare and lashed its ropey limbs in rapid strikes. Derek evaded the best his fifty-one-year-old body allowed, which was not good enough. The monster snatched him by the ankle and yanked him to the ground.

Unlike Harley Johnson, he had no idea what he was dealing with. Did the fiend have any weaknesses? Was it mortal? The monster's strength awakened Derek to his human frailty.

In a panic he groped for the rifle. It did not lie where Allen had dropped it. Instead, he found the hem of Marcella's dress. She stood over him, her eye peering at their common enemy through the sight of the Remington.

Marcella fired, cranked hard and fast on the bolt, and fired again, and again. The blows from the rifle rounds sent the monster reeling, releasing Derek.

He scrambled to his feet. "I thought you didn't believe in guns."

"And you want to argue about it now?" she replied incredulously.

Marcella had driven the creature far enough away for Derek to drag his brother back. Once Allen was clear, he and Marcella smashed the jars against the monster's body. Kerosene splashed all over its skin. Derek threw the torch, igniting the combustible juices.

Flames roared to life!

The tunnel monster flailed, wrapped in a consuming blanket of fire. The beast retreated and dropped from sight. Derek rushed to bring the acetylene lamp forward. In the floor of the tunnel he found a hole. Marcella joined him at the rim. The depth of the pit was beyond their imagination, for the flaming monster was still falling, plumbing the depths toward an unknown oblivion.

***

Allen nursed a cup of coffee at the kitchen table. He looked world-weary. Derek stood by with the pot ready to give him a refill. Marcella sat across from Allen suppressing a yawn while the morning sun peeked through the window.

"You probably think I'm a damn fool," Allen said, his throat smarting from speaking, "rushing that monster the way I did."

Derek set the pot down on the table. "Yes, well, there's proving yourself, and there's being stupid. Last night you did both."

"Oh?" Allen straightened up in his seat. "When, in your estimation, did I prove myself?"

"Not once when we went down to the basement did you make one peep," was Derek's complimentary reply. "You didn't whine. You didn't complain."

"You know," Marcella said while examining her reflection in the coffee pot, poking gingerly at the bruise on her cheek, "your goblin friend is probably still at large."

"We set that creature on fire," Derek jabbed the tabletop with his finger. "It fell down that hole."

"That creature was physical," Marcella countered. "It cried out in pain. A goblin would not do that."

"You mean," Allen said, "we have a whole host of monsters down there?"

"It figures we'd kill the wrong one," Derek snarled.

"You may stay at my place, if you like," Marcella replied. "I'm sure my father wouldn't mind putting you gentlemen up for a couple of nights while I try a few things here. First, I want to examine the nest of brown goo, and then explore that tunnel."

"No," Derek said. "We're not leaving. We'll show those critters who haunts this house. Right?" He patted Allen on the back.

"What? Yes, that's right." Allen smiled. He heard respect in Derek's words. Their fight in the tunnel must have helped his brother understand that fear was not a sign of weakness. "In fact," Allen said to Marcella, "we'll go back down into the tunnel with you."

His spirit surprised Derek. Not to be out done, his elder brother said, "Right!" with as much vigor.

For once Allen felt equal to his brother.

END

211

STRAY

Aurelio Rico Lopez III

Iloilo City, Philippines

Jack was a stickler for rules long before the werewolves came to town.

The necessity to follow a firm set of guidelines was wired to his brain. There was probably a medical term for it, he thought.

Jack knew the rules were vital to his survival, so he followed them as if Jesus Himself had climbed off the cross and handed them down.

Rule 1: *Don't get bitten. If you do, you're better off dead.*

Rule 2: *Don't trust anyone.* (This rule was further emphasized by Rule 8: *Everyone's an asshole.*)

Rule 3: *Never let the enemy know where you live.*

There were other rules, of course, but at the moment Jack had more urgent things in mind. He looked both ways before crossing Yuson Street, watching for incoming traffic. He did not need to, however; the streets had been empty for months, but old habits die hard.

He jogged to the curb, grumbling to himself. He should never have fired the shot.

But you did, and you missed. Now it knows where you live, so you have to kill it before more of them find out.

Clutching the shotgun in one hand, Jack stayed low and passed an abandoned Kia that had ploughed into a signpost. Spiderweb cracks fanned across the front windshield, but there was no sign of the driver. When Jack reached the end of the block, he slowed down and peered around a building that used to be an animal clinic. The display window had been shattered, and tufts of fur and feathers clung to cages that had been ripped open. Humans were clearly not the only ones on the menu.

A cold gust of wind sent leaves skittering down the sidewalk. Jack looked up as large, dirty clouds rolled across the late-afternoon sky. His facial expression hardened as he rounded the corner. It would be dark soon. He had to kill the mangy sonofabitch soon, preferably before an entire pack came crashing through his door.

Five minutes later, Jack found himself standing in front of the Museo Artillo, named after the famous city poet John Jeric Artillo. He glanced up and down the street and started up the steps. When he passed by the museum two days ago, the front doors were closed. Today, they were wide open.

Jack wanted to believe survivors had taken refuge inside the building, but he did not know any human who left paw prints.

Rule 5: *Stay alert.*

It probably thinks I can't track it, Jack thought.

He looked up at the sky and realized it was too late to turn back home. A small voice inside Jack's head started to protest. "We're going inside, aren't we?" it asked, already knowing the answer.

It had been a while since he had been inside the museum.

***

Museo Artillo had been empty since the creatures had made their existence known nine months ago. In the grand scope of things, a bunch of paintings and sculptures, a few old coins, Chinese pottery, dusty books and maps, and ancient artifacts did not seem all that important anymore.

No one was looking to get a lesson in culture.

"I don't like this," the voice in Jack's head said. "This doesn't feel right."

Armed with the shotgun, Jack led himself through the entrance into the hallway. He gave his eyes a minute to adjust to the dark. Ambient

213

moonlight cast a silvery sheen on the walls. Dust motes swirled in Jack's wake as if upset by his unannounced intrusion.

The hallway branched in three different directions. Jack turned left. Eventually, his choice led him to a huge, open chamber filled with medieval artifacts. Jack slowly panned the barrel of the shotgun left to right. To the left, behind a barrier which was nothing more than a rope and two wooden posts, along with a wide dusty glass case containing a variety of weapons such as swords, a lance, a shield, maces, daggers, and axes.

Carpets, framed paintings, and maps hung from the walls. A scaled-down model of a trebuchet occupied the middle of the chamber and flanking that was a suit of armor and half a dozen mannequins dressed in attire of the time period.

The room smelled of mold and rat shit.

As Jack crept across the marble floor, his footsteps echoed in the darkness. He considered taking his shoes off but quickly dismissed the idea. He did not want to step on rat shit or anything that might cut him.

But mostly the rat shit.

He looked out one of the windows and gasped. Darkness had finally fallen. Jack's pulse quickened. His quarry now had the upper hand. Their roles had been reversed; he was no longer the hunter.

Jack was about to turn around when he glimpsed movement out of the corner of his eye. He spun around and raised the shotgun, prepared to blast any monster back to whatever corner of Hell it had crawled from.

"Don't shoot!" a man's voice said. "We're human."

"Come out where I can see you," ordered Jack.

"All right," the man answered. "Just don't shoot me, okay?"

The stranger stepped out from behind one of the mannequins. He raised his hands above his head. "Easy now. I'm unarmed," he announced.

Jack looked over his shoulder in case he was being ambushed and the stranger was merely a distraction. An alarm inside his head went off like an air raid siren. *Don't trust anyone.*

"I'm Adrian," the man said.

"What are you doing here?" Jack asked.

Adrian eyed the shotgun. "I... I used to work here as a night watchman. We've been hiding and living here for the past three days. We didn't know where else to go."

Jack sensed no threat from Adrian, but he was not going to let his guard down. "Who is *we*?"

"Me and my son," Adrian answered.

A child appeared from behind the suit of armor. Jack could not see his face, but the boy could not have been more than nine or ten years old. The kid hurried next to Adrian.

"We live four blocks down the street," Adrian said. *"Lived* there, I guess. Not anymore. A pair of those monsters broke into our home, but we managed to escape. If it weren't for Brolly, we'd be dead."

"Brolly?" Jack asked.

"Our dog," said Adrian. "Brolly... he didn't make it."

Jack stared hard at the pair. Finally, he sighed and lowered his weapon. "Name's Jack."

He approached the father and son and noticed a carpet that had been converted to a make-shift bed on the floor behind the trebuchet. A spear lay next to it.

Adrian was not lying. Jack had yet to meet a werewolf carrying a weapon.

"Adrian, I need you to pick up that spear over there," Jack said. "It's not safe here."

"What do you–?" Adrian started.

"There's a werewolf in the museum. Didn't you hear the door open?"

"We thought that was you."

Jack shook his head. "I followed that thing in here."

"Jesus," said Adrian, scanning the room. His son trembled beside him.

"You mentioned you used to work here," Jack said. "How many entrances to this section of the museum are there?"

"Just two. The one you used and another one–"

Adrian did not have time to finish. A dark, menacing shadow rose up behind him. Adrian must have seen the terrified look on Jack's face. He spun around, instinctively jerking his son behind him and saving the little boy from the fatal slash.

The claw tore open Adrian's ribcage before he could even scream.

Jack grabbed the boy by the collar and hauled him backward, away from the beast. As Jack recovered, the werewolf lashed out with a backhand. Jack barely had enough time to block the blow with the length of the shotgun. The force was staggering and pitched him backward onto the ground, sending him sliding across the marble floor.

So much for avoiding the rat shit.

Jack had also banged his head against something solid. Shaking off the looming threat of unconsciousness, he heard a whimper. He turned and saw Adrian's son, eyes wide and face white as a sheet.

"Run! Get out of here, kid!" Jack yelled as he struggled to his feet.

The entire room seemed to tilt sideways, but Jack steadied himself. By some miracle, he had managed to hold on to the shotgun, but the weapon was useless. The impact had dented the barrel.

It was then Jack realized he was standing right next to the glass display of weapons. He raised the shotgun and struck the glass case. On his second try, the pane shattered and rained on the antique weaponry. Jack discarded the shotgun and armed himself with the first weapon he could reach. The long sword felt strange in his hands, but if it had been good enough for some medieval warrior, it was good enough for him.

The werewolf, with its back turned to Jack, feasted on the Adrian's lifeless body, ripping chucks of flesh and clothing with its teeth and claws. It had pretty much forgotten about Jack. In the end, it was just another animal with a voracious appetite to satisfy.

Jack approached the werewolf from behind, both hands tightly gripping the hilt of the sword. He raised the weapon above his head and struck. Time had dulled the blade, and Jack's aim was off. Nevertheless, he managed to hack the right side of beast's back. The sword struck something hard, most probably bone. Vibrations whipped up his arms, causing him to lose his grip.

Sword still embedded between its neck and right shoulder, the werewolf roared and whirled to face Jack. It rose to its full height, dwarfing him by at least a foot. Blood and bits of flesh dripped from the monster's maw. Moments ago, the werewolf had ignored Jacks presence, but now he had its full attention.

Swell.

Christ, he could smell it. Jack had never been this close to a live werewolf before. In the past, he had picked them off one by one with a rifle or a shotgun, and that was it.

Don't get bitten, you fool! That's twice you've missed today. Focus.

Jack jumped back, narrowly avoiding the large claw that swiped the air. He circled around the trebuchet, hoping to put it between himself and the werewolf. That would at least buy him some time to devise a plan. Or, to say a prayer before ending up in the belly of the beast.

The toe of his shoe kicked something on the ground. Adrian's spear! He would only get one shot. He had to make it count.

Jack scooped the spear off the ground. As the hulking werewolf rounded the trebuchet, Jack lunged. The beast's eyes widened as the steel tip plunged through its throat. It collapsed on the floor. As it thrashed about, Jack heard strained gurgling sounds as the monster struggled to draw air.

"I bet that hurts, doesn't it?" Jack asked.

The dark pool of blood beneath the werewolf grew wider and wider until finally, the beast's arms and legs stopped moving.

Silence returned to the museum. The only sound left was Jack's breathing.

Jack looked around. Adrian's son had fled the chamber. After retrieving a dagger and mace, the werewolf hunter found the boy outside the museum, seated on the concrete steps. Jack approached him, unsure what to say.

The kid looked up at Jack. "He's dead, isn't he? My dad?"

Jack nodded.

"Did you kill the werewolf?"

"Yes," Jack said, leaving out all the gory details.

"Good. I'm glad it's dead. I wish I could kill every fucking one of them." The boy sobbed and wiped his nose. "Do you think my dad will get to see Brolly in Heaven?"

Jack cleared his throat. He did not want to lie. "I don't know. I'm sorry."

"I hope they find each other. That would be nice." A moment of silence passed, and tears rolled down the kid's cheek. "Can I please come with you?"

"What's your name, boy?"

217

"Ty," he answered.

Jack was silent for a moment. Finally, he sighed and held out his hand to the boy. "All right, Ty. You can come with me on one condition."

Ty waited for Jack to continue.

"I need you to follow some rules."

END

... AND AN END

Christofer Nigro

Buffalo, New York, a few days before Halloween 2012

This has not been a good week for Michael Alexander Nero, called "Mike" by his friends. Of which he has always had too few to name.

The feeling has always been particularly pronounced during times like this for the monster hunter who also happened to be a monster himself. You see, Mike Nero is a werewolf, though one wouldn't know it to see him in his current human form. He now sat on a Greyhound bus lost in thought as the huge clunky vehicle entered the Queen City. This is Nero's hometown; one he had thought he could leave behind for good. It is a place filled with many memories – some good, many bad, but most quite memorable and formative.

Trinity... was the sole thought that crossed Nero's mind as a tear rolled down his left cheek. He pressed his head against the semi-clean window near his seat to prevent fellow passengers from seeing him emote so sensitively over the love he had just left behind in Michigan. It was one he thought would last forever; yet she still managed to "get away," as the saying goes.

You are such a foolish, naïve asshole sometimes, Nero. He continued leaning against the glass as these melancholy thoughts invaded his psyche. *The wolf dared to dream; and now he walks the lone route again. And finds himself back in Buffalo, of all places.* His thoughts

219

trailed off as the bus pulled into the sprawling station on North Division Street.

Nero trudged down the tiny stairway of the bus and into the station with no duffle bag on hand. He had left behind the few items he brought with him from Buffalo to Michigan, all of which were either expendable or easy to send a courier for. Prior to moving there, something had told him to leave most of the meager items he owned behind in the empty apartment now waiting for him in the Queen City. Something in his portly gut also told him to continue having S.A.V.A.G.E.[3] pay for that ample but unimpressive living space. It was an instinct that had always served him well despite resembling what some might call cynicism.

Despite being past 8PM in the evening, the station was bustling with activity, as it usually was regardless of the time of day. A combination of average travelers who had come to this city for Goddess knows what reason mixed with wayward transients, young runaways, cabbies seeking fares, and outsiders begging for change from strangers. It was an atmosphere that Nero loathed, as he considered it emblematic of the type of society he lived in and what a low regard for human life the system had.

However, Nero was not in the mood for his usual political ruminations this day. Not after finding himself back in the Rust Belt after the happier life he had built over the past year was abruptly sabotaged by a truly capricious whim of fate. Coherent thoughts were not to be found in his frazzled mind right now, though he presumed he would simply return to his writing and monster hunting duties. And the radical politics. Always those damned politics, as his colleagues would often say.

It was then that Nero suddenly caught a disturbing scent. His olfactory capabilities were not at their peak in his human form, but they still covered a greater range than that of typical humanity. And much experience in the vocation of monster hunting had made him sensitive to certain things. Things – or, rather, *individuals* – that, like him, wore the guise of a human being while being something else entirely. That "something else" could be any number of things, many of them inimical

---

[3] S.A.V.A.G.E. = Society for Assessing Viability of Abominations as Good or Evil.

to human life. But what this particular thing in human shape happened to be was quite clear to Nero's nose.

A vampire. A fucking vampire. *Reports from main headquarters had told me that some had migrated from the Big Apple to Buffalo for the purpose of creating a nest here, but...*

Nero did not want to accept that his last year of relative bliss had caused him to overlook and neglect the deadly problem slowly building in his hometown. The Norns had evidently seen to it that he would now be confronting that conundrum head on. The portly man of distinctly Italian features who looked much younger than he actually was turned his head in the general direction he had detected the offensive scent. Nero then sniffed the air again.

Bingo, asshole.

He targeted the source of the distinctive smell of the undead. It wore the form of a young man who somewhat resembled the classic image of a thug. He had dark features and black hair with a red bandana around his forehead and temples. His former human heritage masked the deathly pallor that many Caucasian vampires had. His clothing consisted of blue jeans and a matching denim jacket over a green T-shirt.

Nero moved backwards behind a small congregation of talking people, hoping the vampire would not similarly catch his scent and realize he had serious trouble in his midst. Werewolves and vampires had long been enemies despite their connected supernatural pedigree that was well known to folklorists and monster experts alike. And Nero wasn't just any werewolf. So, if the young vampire detected him, he would surely call for any reinforcements that may be nearby. If none were on hand, the vamp would possibly flee the station and be free to hunt for victims at another time and locale.

Nero couldn't permit that. Now that he was back in Buffalo, this was his responsibility. That, along with the one where he had to confront his grandparents again, the people who raised him; the people who had to deal with the travails he brought down on them (not to mention the entire city) so many decades earlier. That, however, was a lifetime ago. Since then, Nero had chosen the path of protector over bringer of vengeance, and his never-ending quest for redemption demanded that the safety of Buffalo's citizenry be his main priority.

Time to stop feeling sorry for yourself, Nero. You should have known that the gods would never let you keep Trinity. Get her out of your mind and focus on that vampire. You have no idea whose lives, and how many of them, depend on you getting with the fucking program already.

Nero had to utilize stealth to ensure the vampire did not detect his presence in the station for as long as possible, if at all. The monster hunter was impeded by the fact that he could not assume the powerful form of the lycanthrope in such a public setting without scaring the shit out of everyone in the crowd. Moreover, it would likely end up being him, and not the vampire, that the transit police brought their weapons to bear on.

Furthermore, Nero was painfully aware that the main bloodline of vampire from New York City was of the Varnaean strain, to which Dracula himself belonged. Thankfully, most of their number were not nearly as powerful as the Vampire Lord himself and the newbie vampires tended to be little match for a seasoned monster hunter. Nevertheless, they possessed an array of supernatural powers – shape-shifting, mesmerism, animal control, limited weather control – that the great majority of individuals belonging to other vampiric strains lacked. And there could be so many of them in a single nest, let alone in a large city. They did possess the additional vulnerability to silver, rather than only wood and holy relics, but that supernaturally "pure" metal was one that could also be used against Nero and his furry brethren. Hence, he was wary about having some of it on hand.

And, of course, even a single vampire was a major threat to any normal human being, or even a group of them.

I need to get him out of the station and into a secluded part of the neighborhood. But if I approach him, he may realize what I am and either bolt in bat form or call for help. Think, Nero. What would your compatriots in the Boogey Knights, Steven or Dale, do in this situation?

It was then that Nero was startled when a hand came down on his shoulder.

"Are you okay, mister?" asked a transit cop working security, who evinced a tone of both concern and suspicion. "You look like you're looking for someone."

Nero had to accept that his being garbed in a dark leather jacket, black khaki pants, and a skintight black skull cap adorning his shaved head made him likewise fit the stereotypical profile of "thug" as much as his vampiric quarry did.

Wonderful. "Oh, I'm fine, sir," he quickly retorted with a fake smile. "Just got back to my hometown to see some relatives."

The officer raised an eyebrow. "Is that kid over there one of your 'relatives?'"

The security man moved his head to indicate that he was referring to the vampire, whom he had also noticed with suspicion. It was clear what he presumed was going on.

In the immortal words of Lawrence Welk: Oh wonderful, wonderful! *The dude thinks a drug sale is about to go down. He was correct to surmise that kid was trouble, but he's waaayyy off the mark as to what type. How do I get him to drop those suspicions? He's in the way here and fixing to either get himself killed or make me lose the vampire.*

"Him? That guy in the denim jacket, you mean? I have no idea who he is. The relatives I mentioned live several blocks from here."

"Okay. Then why were you eyeing that guy over there, as if trying to figure out if he was someone you were looking for?"

Nero was now desperate, so he decided to grasp a proverbial straw. "I was... admiring his jacket. I thought it would look just as good on me as it did on him. So, I was trying to see if I could figure out what brand it is." This was followed by another fake beam.

The security guard now took on a countenance of irritation. "Mm-hmm. Are you sure he's not a... 'contact,' so to speak? One you arrived here to meet for a business transaction?"

Nero struggled to maintain his insincere smile. "I assure you, officer, if it was anything like that, I would only be buying him dinner and possibly another denim jacket, not handing him cash."

The officer released an exasperated sigh. "I think you know what type of transaction I'm talking about here, wiseass. One that involves powder, not bodily fluids."

Nero decided to resort to another desperate move, one of his typically awkward attempts to soothe a tense situation with a dose of levity.

"Nah. I prefer to buy my Talcum at the local Walgreen's, not from bus station vendors."

Nero's newest bogus beam was met by an expression that betrayed a complete lack of amusement on the part of the guard.

"I don't have time for this shit tonight, mister. Enough has been going on here at this station lately, and I'm getting paid to put a stop to it. So, please come with me."

Shit! "Officer, you have no evidence that I'm here to do anything illegal. Would you like me to call my lawyer now? Because if you don't mind, I have places to be."

Nero turned to see that the young vampire had departed the bus station, likely following an intended easy victim.

Double the shit! I need to ditch this stupid cop and get the Hel out of here.

Unfortunately, the guard noticed that Nero kept his eye on the young man and was displaying alarm at him leaving the premises.

"Something is going on here that isn't good, so, I think I'll take my chances with your lawyer. Now, I'll ask you again, politely, one last time. Will you please come with me?"

"Alright, alright." Nero threw up his hands in a gesture of surrender. "But my lawyer won't be happy about this."

The officer turned to walk towards his mini-headquarters located in the middle of the station. What he didn't realize was that Nero had no intention of actually following him there. After taking a few steps behind the security man as part of a ruse, the darkly attired monster hunter displayed some impressive speed for one so heavy and fled to the revolving doors at the front of the station. The guard noticed several seconds too late.

"Hey! What the hell? Oh, you fuckhead!"

The irate officer grabbed his dispatch radio and called for back-up, despite his realization that to do so was likely futile at this point.

***

Nero rushed out through the revolving doors at the front of the station into the atmosphere of a late October night in Buffalo. The slight chill to the air that one typically felt this time of year served as a hint of the harsh winter that was just around the corner. It brought an immediate sense of familiarity to him. It just didn't happen to be one that he was particularly fond of.

Nero looked around, scanning the dingy urban boulevard of North Division Street. All seemed quiet, a stillness interrupted only by a few straggling people exiting the station behind him and the occasional cab taking off from the curb.

Nero next looked up at the sky and was relieved to see the partial glow of the waxing moon suspended among the stars. It was thus a favorable evening for a metamorphosis if needed. And the power of the lycanthrope would certainly come in handy now, especially the full capacity of that form's lupine olfactory senses.

Thank you, All-Father Odin. As the Brady Kids used to sing: When it's time to change, then it's time to chaa-aa-eenge [the last word in imitation of a pubertal voice cracking]…

Nero also knew he had to dodge any further interference from the transit police that the guard would doubtlessly now be calling. He quickly ducked behind two large SUVs that were parked at the corner, which obscured him from anyone's view and shrouded him in darkness. He then immediately focused and concentrated upon an image of the full moon while simultaneously calling upon the power of the lupine deity Fenris. By this point in time, the skullcap-wearing hunter had conducted this procedure on innumerable occasions. Hence, the waxing lunar energies now bathing the planet augmented the infusion of power from Fenris that permeated every cell in his fragile human form.

In less than thirty seconds, Nero transformed into something decidedly less fragile and much more bestial. His bones and organs re-aligned themselves in an impossible fashion as his body sprouted canid fur and accrued additional mass. His clothing, composed of bio-mimetic material, unraveled into a hardly discernible thin collar around his bulky neck. This left him wearing only his expandable black utility belt, now barely visible under his abdominal pelt of fur; and his distinctive black skullcap, which was made of flexible material that easily stretched to fit the contours of his now wolf-like skull.

Nero had taken on the form of the werewolf he had code-named Beowolf, a permutation of an ancient Norse warrior hero whose legend he had long admired. He raised an extended muzzle filled with razor-sharp teeth and sniffed the air. Quickly identifying the unearthly scent of his undead quarry beside that of an unidentified female human spoor, the werewolf dropped down to all fours. He could move at top speed as a quadruped, and this he sorely needed at the time.

Two armed transit police alongside the first guard rushed through the revolving doors of the bus station just in time to see what looked like a huge canine running from behind a few parked vans. The animal was amazingly fast, and quickly vanished down the darkness of a nearby street.

"Did you see that?" one of the officers queried.

"It looked like a dog or something," another said. "A goddamned huge one, too. But that's not our concern. It seems those suspected drug dealers you spotted are both gone, Ed."

The security guard named Ed nodded reproachfully. "Shit. I thought I had one of those fuckers this time."

***

Beowolf ran on all fours at astounding speed in the direction of the twin scents he had picked up. As he did so, his acute lupine hearing detected the increasingly erratic heartbeat of a person experiencing extreme terror. No screams accompanied it, which actually concerned him all the more.

Additionally, Beowolf knew that he had to focus to maintain control of the animal aspect of the werewolf's persona that existed alongside his human identity when he took this form. It was one that was present to a much lesser degree even when he was in his standard homid mode. Hence, losing control in a fit of anger was something the lycan champion had to constantly guard against. He needed to keep as much of his human persona in charge of things as possible in most cases to get the job done with maximum efficiency and minimal collateral damage (though preferably none of the latter if he could help it).

Within moments the werewolf reached his destination. It was a doorway leading into a dilapidated tenement building located just beyond the limits of downtown Buffalo. He quietly loped up the small stairway and through the foreboding entrance. Inside was a dark hallway filled with the mixed scents of urine, cheap liquor, crack cocaine, bubblegum, and discarded refuse. He shook his huge shaggy head to sift out two particular scents amidst this barrage of mostly unpleasant aromatic distractions.

His eyes then picked up the bright heat signature of a young woman whose body was standing but limp. Her throat was in the steel-like grip of the young vampire he spotted at the station. The recently sired member of the undead had already sunk his fangs into the lady's warm neck and was drinking deeply of the precious red nectar within her veins.

Damn that fucking cop for delaying my hunt!

This pang of anger was accompanied by an animalistic snarl emanating from Beowolf's muzzle. The vampire heard it and pried himself away from his feast to look behind him. The fanged young man's eyes, also keenly attuned to seeing in the dark, gazed upon a massive furry form with pointed dog-like ears as it rose from four legs to an imposing height of seven feet. The shaggy interloper's continual growling and fiery yellow eyes left no doubt to the vampire as to what he was now facing.

"Oh, shit," the vamp said in a slightly raspy voice with a hint of a Hispanic accent. "Look, man, I found this girl first. I'm gonna take what's left of her blood and I'll leave the meat here for you. I don't want no trouble, okay?"

"I'm not here for her," the werewolf grumbled in a scratchy voice spoken through an only partially human larynx. "I came for you."

"Aw, what the fuckin' hell…" was the last words uttered by the vampire before Beowolf barreled into him with an astounding display of speed and strength.

The force of the powerful charge caused the undead youth to drop his victim to the filthy hallway floor as he was battered up against a wall. The cheap stucco caved in as the two supernatural combatants smashed halfway through the material. The vampire was much stronger than human, but he was a rookie to the ranks of the undead. He had not yet learned to transform into mist at breakneck speed as did veteran vampires of the Varnaean strain. His hirsute adversary also had the element of surprise, in addition to a lot of experience battling and slaying those of his blood-sucking ilk. For his part, this vampire had zero experience dealing with threats that matched his own level of power, including werewolves.

As a result, following a fierce but brief struggle, Beowolf managed to sink his razor-like teeth into the vampire's throat and tear it out. A spatter of vampiric blood darkened the floor and stained the front of the werewolf's grayish pelt. As the undead malcontent gasped in agony, Nero's wolfen alter-ego grabbed his adversary's head in his two large furry hands and twisted it to the left with his full strength. A cracking sound, followed by more blood erupting from the vampire's mouth, indicated a broken neck. Beowolf then turned the head in the opposite direction with an equal display of strength. This was accompanied by a similar but slightly louder cracking sound. The vampire spit more blood and his eyes rolled completely into his head.

This signaled to the enraged werewolf that his enemy's vertebrae was completely severed. He then put his canid foot against the wall for support and pulled the vampire's head with all his formidable might. It was torn completely off, ending the creature's un-life. A fountain of blood spurted out of the stump that marked the spot of the vampire's decapitation as the body slunk to the floor. It would soon disintegrate.

The werewolf then extricated himself from the wall and tossed the vampire's head through a hallway window. Its skull cracked in five places as it bounced around the concrete sidewalk like a bloody bowling ball with hair. It, too, would soon disintegrate into ash. This vampire was almost certainly gone for good.

The noise of the brutal scuffle had by now attracted the attention of several people living in the building. One of them, an older man of African American persuasion, ran out of his apartment and into the dank, rancid hallway. His eyes nearly popped from his head as they gazed upon the werewolf standing over the fallen young woman, checking her wrist for a pulse.

Beowolf turned to the astounded man. "This girl is hurt. Suffering loss of blood. Call ambulance. Now!"

The startled man simply nodded his head a dozen times and backed away, struggling not to "dookee" in his pants, as his childhood friends used to call it.

The werewolf then dropped down to all fours and raced out of the building in a grayish blur of motion. Back out on the streets, Beowolf quickly spotted an alley a few blocks away that gave him the several seconds of privacy he needed to revert to human form unseen. His bio-mimetic attire unveiled to surround his portly homid form again as he did so. He then exited the alley and began the walk towards his apartment. Before he could turn his thoughts back to the terrible personal loss he suffered in Michigan again, he heard the chime of the cell phone he kept in one of his belt containers. The caller I.D. let him know that the person on the other line was his grandfather.

It was the first time they had spoken in months, and Mike Nero answered with some trepidation. Those two had never seen eye-to-eye on most things; and despite serving as a father figure to him, James Nero had just as often been a formidable opponent in his own right. The younger Nero was still secretly glad to receive the call, as he was concerned over the 89-year-old man's steady decline in health from the remarkably tough and robust personage Mike once knew and feared.

"Hey," Mike said as he touched the "answer" button. "Long time no..."

"You have a package here," James interrupted his grandson in his usual surly way.

"It turns out I'm back in Buffalo tonight, so I'll drop by and pick it up tomorrow."

"You should come by now. This package is really big."

"It is?"

"Yes, it is. It's some huge wooden crate or something. Delivered in the driveway and it has your name on it. Why did it come here instead of your other apartment or that monster place you run? Or, the place of that girl you shacked up with? Is this some of that 'monster' business of yours? I don't want this here!"

"Okay, okay, chill out. I'll come over there right now and see what it is and get rid of it for you. How have you been, by the way?"

"I've been old. How far away are you? Should I come and get you?"

"No, you don't need to drive if you don't have to. I'm not too far, I'll be there in about twenty minutes."

Mike Nero then ended the call, pocketed his cell phone, and headed towards the home where he grew up. He was admittedly very curious as to what that mysterious crate addressed to him may have been. And frankly, he shared his grandfather's concern that it may indeed be some "monster" business. He obviously didn't want his family to have to deal with anything from that part of his life.

As the monster hunter headed home, he was unaware of a flock of bats in the dark evening sky that were surreptitiously trailing him.

***

A short time later Mike Nero had made his way to the familiar neighborhood of Portland Avenue. He had been here a few times over the past year, and like many revisiting their roots he saw a combination of long-remembered sights and new additions. The old house, where he still maintained the alternate apartment above the one owned by the grandparents who essentially raised him, looked much as he recollected. It stood out from the rest of the homes on the block with its dull blue paint job and the tan pillars that made it truly distinct in the 'hood. The pricker bushes standing behind the front lawn brought back numerous not-so-fond memories of the blood drawn by accidental contact with those lacerating shrubs.

The neighborhood looked quiet save for the short and stocky figure that he instantly recognized standing in the driveway of the Nero residence. The old-style hooligan hat atop the male figure's head, olive green coat, and the cane he held for support in his left hand instantly identified the now fragile form of the elderly James D. Nero.

Time had ceased being kind to the man once he reached his '80s. Mike Nero had always admired the physical prowess and acumen of his grandfather, which he retained for so long into his old age, despite his fear of ending up on the business end of it. This was, after all, the man who had actually flattened his savage lycanthropic alter-ego with several choice blows from a baseball bat back when the younger Nero was just a teen. Mike never forgot the intensity of those blows.

Over the past decade, however, a series of unexpected ailments, including cirrhosis of the liver, had stolen that prowess from James. He had begun to look every bit the extremely aged man he was, and to feel like it too; something he was never hesitant to gripe about over the past few years.

The loss of the elder Nero's physical acumen and mobility had taken its toll on him in other ways too, causing him to sink into a deep depression. His legendary temper was sometimes worse than ever, according to Mike's grandmother the last time he had spoken to her.

Seeing this once warrior-like man so feeble, forced to walk slowly with the aid of a cane on wobbly knees, was heart-breaking to the younger Nero. It was one of the main reasons he avoided visiting his grandfather as often as possible over the past two years in spite of the shame that caused him. He just couldn't stand seeing James in this shape and the depression it caused this proud and once powerful man. Witnessing his legendary strength of mind fail along with his body simply compounded the heartache that Mike experienced.

Though he had trouble admitting it, he still loved this man despite their rocky relationship and appreciated the good he had brought into his life. Mike dreaded the thought of losing him, but he also did not want his grandfather to continue having to deal with living in an aged body that had begun to show so many signs of wear.

James signaled his grandson with a wave of his free hand as he recognized him from a block away. The younger Nero saw the previously mentioned crate beside his grandfather. It had to be around eight feet in height, possibly even exceeding that. Its cover seemed bolted with strong but conventional nails in the front.

What the Hel could that thing be? Just in case anything goes down, I need to cast a potent spell that will prevent anyone living on the block who are inside their houses from hearing anything, including my grandmother. I don't want any of them rushing outside and getting involved or calling the police. I need to deal with whatever this may be alone – without family, other civilians, or cops unprepared to deal with paranormal phenomena becoming endangered or getting in my way.

Mike wanted to be as furtive as possible while taking the few minutes and immense concentration required to cast the spell. This included throwing out the various ingredients from his belt containers to help facilitate it. He was at least thankful that Dr. Enygma, the master mage that often helped him for a price, had taught him this important spell.

The monster hunter and mystic hid behind a large tree at the corner of his block and recited the necessary words, specifically calling upon the *seidr* magick utilized by Odin, Freya, and Norse mystics of the past (and some in the present, like Mike Nero himself). He then tossed out the appropriate tincture of blessed herbs into the atmosphere. The sinking feeling he suddenly experienced indicated that a blanket of silence would now encapsulate the immediate neighborhood for about

231

one hour, which was hopefully as long as Mike would need to deal with any potential problems that may have arisen from the mystery crate. No one in their homes would hear anything that happened outside during the spell's effect.

That done, Mike stepped from behind the tree and approached his grandfather.

"Hey," he said as a salutation.

"Why did you step behind that tree?" James asked him. "Did you have to piss or something? You could have used the bathroom in the house. What if someone saw you? That'll make *me* look bad."

"No, no, I didn't, and don't worry about it." He turned his attention to the crate. "Something tells me that's the package you mentioned."

"I'm glad you noticed it," James replied with acidity. "It's in my driveway and I want it gone."

"Um, it's nice to see you too, by the way."

"If it was, you would have seen a lot more of me during the past year."

"Yea, that stellar personality of yours is absolutely magnetic. Let me get a look at this crate."

Mike inspected both the destination and return addresses stamped in black ink on one side of the large wooden cube. The former did indeed have his name at the top. And interestingly, the latter was a U.K. address bearing the name of that stogie-smoking Englishman's monster hunting organization. The intention was to ship the item to S.A.V.A.G.E.'s main U.S. headquarters. After all, it is always prudent to pass the buck when you "lack the storage space" yourself, right?

Since Mike had recently revived S.A.V.A.G.E. with the blessing of its surviving co-founder and now served as director, he quickly surmised how this mix-up occurred. The address for the revived org, now in New York, had not yet reached the members of the European team who had recovered the object in the crate. Their research uncovered Nero's old home address and they hastily shipped whatever it was there.

"Shit, this is not good," Mike murmured aloud. "Those morons should have known to contact me first. I can't believe they mistook this address for the org's!"

232

"What morons?" James queried as he struggled to move closer on his raggedy legs. "They *must* be friends of yours, right?"

Mike gritted his teeth but elected to spare the old man the full wrath of his tongue… something he now wished he had done more often in the past.

"Colleagues of mine. It was sent to this address by mistake."

"But what the hell is it?"

Mike touched the crate and concentrated, mentally asking Freya for a bit of psychic guidance. The monster hunter detected no untoward impressions to indicate danger, and it seemed to be safe to open. He reached into one of his belt containers and pulled out a small pry bar used for pulling out nails and wrenching open the covers of certain wooden objects such as coffins or crates of this sort.

After a few minutes, the nails were loosened enough that Mike could open the cover and see what was inside. Though he had sensed no danger the sight of its contents nevertheless shocked him to the core.

Mike looked up to see what resembled an eight-foot statue of an intricately carved humanoid figure. It was ornately designed to look as if it was wearing some sort of ancient warrior armor of a culture the monster hunter was surprised he could not immediately identify. It had a grayish color, and closer inspection made it clear this figure was sculpted not from granite or marble but hardened clay. Its countenance suggested a mood of angry conviction with blank eyes that glared at a seemingly non-existent foe.

Mike could scarcely believe what he was looking at.

"By the hammer of Thor. It's… a golem!"

He then realized that his grandfather had managed to scamper over and peer into the crate. "So, this statue is some 'monster' business of yours? What the hell is a 'goch-lam'? It sounds Italian."

"You think everything sounds Italian! No, it's a Hebrew word. A golem is a guardian entity sculpted from clay and imbued with an artificial consciousness. This one is now devoid of a consciousness, though, and I get the… impression, psychically, that it's an empty vessel that can be animated by someone projecting their own psyche into it."

"Sick-ee?"

"Psyche. You know, the mind? Anyway, I'm not sure how it can be done, but that's what this is. A golem can be extremely dangerous in the

wrong hands! I have to get it shipped out of here and into safekeeping at S.A.V.A.G.E. headquarters."

"Yes! Get those weirdos you associate with to get it out of my driveway. I don't want another monster here. It's bad enough I have a grandson that chose to actually become a monster. Because just being a juvenile delinquent wasn't enough."

Mike belayed making the call on his cell phone to address what James had said. "Yes, I made my share of mistakes, okay? But after all is said and done, I do not regret taking on the power of the wolf. I've since used it to do a lot of good. I just saved someone earlier tonight from a vampire."

James stamped his cane on the hard sidewalk. "Of course, you always know where to find other monsters. You even work with a bunch of them who collect shit like this statue! And doing good? You used to hurt people! I had to stomp you with a baseball bat to stop you once!"

"And that was how long ago now? You never let *anything* go. You think I haven't changed and learned a lot since then?"

"No, you *never* change! You never wanted to listen to me or your grandmother. So, you went and made yourself into that thing, so you could use it to hurt other people."

"The reason I originally took the power was wrong, yes. But I did it because others were hurting *me*, and you know that. I wanted to protect myself; I didn't have the kick-ass strength or a bunch of tough-ass brothers or a crowd of friends like you had to protect me."

"Of course, you didn't! You never had friends because of the way you are. No one liked you. That's why everyone wanted to hurt you!"

"Including you in both cases, right? Is that how you justified using me as a target for your own rage and spite? You think you were so perfect yourself?"

"Compared to you I am!"

"Grrr..." *Control yourself, Nero.* "Look, what I did was wrong, but it worked out over the long haul. You never want to hear about all I've done and sacrificed over the past twenty years to redeem myself! Because you could never accept a grandson who wasn't the same kind of person as you! Maybe if you had showed me more support, I wouldn't have sunk to the depths that I did. Maybe, just maybe, that would have been all I needed to avoid sliding down into the dark place that I did. Maybe I could have been on the side of the angels right from the start!"

James inched closer to his grandson's face, as feisty and fearless as ever. "Listen, you ungrateful little son of a bitch! Don't blame *me* for becoming what you did or not doing enough for you! We let you live here after you wouldn't go with your mother. We put up with your shit all those years, including this monster business!"

"And I put up with all of your abuse as part of the price of you taking me in. Did you think that price you demanded couldn't possibly come with a heavy toll for me?"

Mike gritted his teeth again and forced himself to stop when the sight of his grandfather's emaciated form gave him pause. He could not bring himself to carry the anger and spite any further, or to get the old man too riled up. Those days had to end, he realized. The anger, resentment, and other negative emotional baggage had to be let go of, for both their sakes.

He put a hand gently on his grandfather's shoulder. "Listen. I know you and my grandmother did a lot for me all those years. I appreciate it. I'm sorry for the mistakes I made. I've tried to improve even if I didn't in any way that you will accept. But I do not regret what I am, as it's not inherently evil. I don't want us to fight like this anymore, okay? I just experienced a huge loss over in Michigan, which is the major reason I'm now back in Buffalo. So, I have a lot on my mind, and..."

It was then that Mike heard the unmistakable sound of multiple leathern wings flapping in the sky. Despite how hard of hearing James Nero had become, he nevertheless heard it as well and turned to look upwards in concert with his grandson.

"Are those a bunch of... bats?" James asked.

"No," Mike choked out. "Not actual bats. That bastard *did* have back-up, and they followed me here. And because I was so upset, I didn't realize... damn it, what a rank amateur I can be!"

He turned to his grandfather. "Look, you have to get into the house now! I know how bad your legs are, so go into the driveway and in the back door! Don't tell anyone inside what's going on; they won't hear anything happening outdoors, I saw to that! I'll hold those vamps off for as long as I can! Tell my grandmother to keep the doors shut and do not open them for anyone! Vampires cannot enter a home without being invited first. Hurry, goddamn it!"

Mike knew it would take several minutes for his debilitated grandfather to make even the short trek halfway into the yard to get to the back door. The monster hunter realized he would have to fight with a degree of ferocity he never displayed before to give the infirm man the time he needed to get inside the house to safety. And the only hope of doing so was to initiate exactly the transformation that his grandfather dreaded seeing.

"I'm not just going to leave you out here...!"

James Nero's words were cut off as he saw his grandson stand in what appeared to be a meditative posture. It was similar to the "at ease" stance the elderly man recalled from his days as a World War II naval officer. Drawing down the powerful energies of the waxing moon in combination with a desperate mental plea to Fenris, Mike Nero again transformed. It happened within just several seconds.

The elder Nero frowned and grumbled. "Shit. He's becoming the monster again. It figures."

That is when James was treated to a second unsettling sight of bizarre metamorphosis. The seeming swarm of bats descended to just under a dozen feet off the ground in a swift, swooping arc. Upon doing so they speedily morphed into fully clothed humanoid figures by the time they landed. Before the two men now stood twelve vampires all displaying their fangs and ready to drain Beowolf dry in retribution for killing one of their own earlier. They all looked young, a combination of male and female, of a variety of ethnicities and styles of dress.

"I hope none of them are Italian..." James whispered to himself.

"Your blood will taste so fine, werewolf!" the lead vampire exclaimed while pointing a long finger at their hirsute adversary.

"Bring it," Beowolf replied in a deep guttural voice.

Four of the vampires sprinted towards the lycan as the initial attack wave, each of them with their fangs bared and uttering what sounded like serpentine hisses.

Luckily for Beowolf, these were newbie vampires. None of them would be particularly good fighters. But they would be strong, fast, and utterly savage. And they had strength of numbers in their favor. He would have to bring out the baton to have a hope of holding them off long enough to give his infirm grandfather time to get indoors. He was thankful that none of his neighbors would be likely to leave their homes at this time of night, nor to have visitors. And that none of them would hear what was ensuing for the next hour thanks to his spell of silence.

The werewolf quickly reached a hairy hand into a sheathe at the side of his utility belt and brandished a small object. With the touch of a lever a metallic, telescoping baton extended from what turned out to be a rubber-lined hilt. The chrome-colored baton, which had a solid, flattened knob at the top of it, was crackling with what appeared to be arcs of bluish electricity. This weapon, infused with a small portion of the power of the thunder god Thor himself, always came in handy in the face of a monstrous threat. It was Beowolf's prized possession and preferred weapon in most situations.

With an animalistic howl of rage the werewolf swung the enchanted bludgeon at the first attacking vampire. A zapping sound not unlike that of an extra-loud electric bug killer was heard as the head of the undead creature was stuck. The electrical force and hardness of the baton caused the vamp's cranium to shatter in a manner reminiscent of a melon struck by a mallet. One down.

Two of the vampires closed in on Beowolf from his left side as the other in the trio moved in on his right. The werewolf unleashed a powerful side kick at the latter. It connected with the vampire's midriff, knocking the assailant on his back. The werewolf turned in time to smash one of the two vamps attacking on his left side across his jaw with the baton. Another surge of electrical energy crackled as the predator's lower jaw was smashed clean off. As that vampire dropped to his knees in a desperately painful effort to retrieve his lower jaw and reattach it, Beowolf tore out his throat with a slash of his free hand. Two down.

No sooner had the second vampire fallen than the third executed a six-foot leap at the bulky werewolf. Beowolf swung his baton in a swift upward arc so that its released mystical electricity seared the undead creature in half while still in mid-air. The two portions of the corpse landed with a pair of wet thuds, their bowels sliding out onto the sidewalk. He smashed its head into pulp with another swing of the baton to bring it completely out of commission. Three down.

That last move, however, required enough of Beowolf's attention that the vampire he kicked over had time to recover. The vampire leaped onto the lycan's back and wrapped his throat in a vice-like lock with both arms. The nosferatu then moved to sink its fangs into his furry neck. Beowolf quickly dropped to the ground backwards, crushing the vampire with his full weight and stunning it. He then rolled off and tore half its face off with a swipe of his claws and crushed its skull with a downward thrust of his baton. Four down.

Seeing the opportunity to press their advantage, four of the eight remaining vampires rushed in for the kill. They executed spectacular leaps and their combined force succeeded in taking Beowolf to the ground. He dropped his baton, which landed a few feet from the pig pile. The werewolf managed a desperate and powerful swipe of his claw at the lower abdomen of one of his attackers. This successfully disemboweled the vampire, sending his intestines spilling out onto the concrete.

The undead rolled away from the melee screeching in agony and clutching at his dislodged innards. He then took a desperate gambit by crawling over to the dropped baton to grab it and attempt to use it against their foe. Big mistake. Upon grasping its hilt, the enchanted weapon enveloped the injured vampire with a surge of electrical energy that effectively incinerated him. Five down.

The remaining three attackers were quickly overpowering Beowolf, however. He still fought with a relentless degree of grit, but it was a matter of minutes before he would be pinned and his lifeblood drained.

James witnessed all this with dismay. He could not bring himself to attempt to get to the safety of his home's side door without doing something to help the besieged Mike. He could pull out his cell phone and call the police, but it would take a while for them to get there, and they would be as likely to open fire on his wolfen grandson as they would on the vampires. And were regular bullets even capable of stopping vampires?

I have to do something! But what? I'm just a useless old man! But he's fighting to protect me. And he's my flesh and blood, even if he is a monster. I have to... have to...

The extreme determination of James Nero, matched by few in this world, then had a very strange effect. For those who may have witnessed the tableau before them, they would see the extremely aged body of the man slump over to the ground a few feet from the crate. One may have then surmised his elderly heart had simply given out. Such a guess, however logical, would have been wrong.

A second later the sturdy wood of the crate was suddenly smashed to splinters from within. The golem was now somehow fully animate. Its blank eyes looked at the pile of vampires gradually succeeding in their effort to pummel Beowolf's bestial form senseless as a prelude to draining him of blood.

It was then that any observer would be thoroughly startled when they heard the clearly audible words that came out of the golem's mouth in an echoey voice: "Get the hell off of my grandson!"

The powerful synthetic being, now animated by the consciousness of James Nero, moved towards the pig pile before him with a speed and ease that he had been unable to attain for many long years. The clay warrior seized two of the vampires in his immense hands and wrenched them off Beowolf like they weighed mere ounces. The golem then slammed them against the ground head-first with such force that their craniums shattered against the pavement. Seven down in one fell swoop.

James then put the golem's powerful right leg to use by kicking another of the vampires off his grandson, this one a female with long blonde tresses. This succeeded in booting the undead creature over a hundred yards down the street. The vampire's involuntary flight was only arrested when her body struck a neighbor's tree. The she-vampire quickly got back to her feet and rushed to rejoin the melee

Now faced with just one vampiric attacker, Beowolf managed to push his foe away just enough to get his lupine-jointed legs under its abdomen. He then used the talons on his toes to inflict two deep gashes to the gut. The vampire yelled in agony as it bled onto the sidewalk. The werewolf then pushed his opponent's weakened form upwards and seized the undead attacker's throat in his powerful jaws. Biting down with every iota of strength at his disposal Beowolf managed to all but sever his opponent's head, a task he completed with his hands a second later. Eight down.

The werewolf jumped to his feet and noticed the towering gray form of the golem. He had heard the being's earlier exclamation, so he knew exactly who the animating agency was.

"It's good to have you kicking ass again, Papa."

"We have a few more to kick," James replied in the mystic automaton's reverberating voice. He used the golem's right index finger to point at the remaining vampires.

Beowolf snarled in agreement. "Let's get 'em!"

The angry final contingent of vampires were clearly concerned about the turn of events they found themselves confronting.

"This is not going well since that gray giant came out of the crate and jumped in," one of the vamps said before turning to his field leader. "Should we wing it out of here?"

"No," the leader replied. "Better we give this our all and die in the attempt than return to the Master with a report of failure."

As Beowolf realized these last vampires were going to jump into the fray rather than retreat, it mattered not to him if they had been willingly turned or not. They constituted a plague on his city that threatened the lives of every citizen living there. They had to be put down like the monstrous hazards they had become.

Beowolf extended his furry hand and the enchanted baton tethered to his life force swiftly flew back into his grip. He stood side-by-side with the mighty clay giant that was controlled by his grandfather. It was good to see him become a force to be reckoned with once more, now mightier than ever before or than he ever imagined he would be. As a young child, Mike Nero often daydreamed of himself and his tough-as-nails grandfather someday fighting the forces of evil together. Now it was actually happening, and he could not deny the excitement it gave him.

The lead attacking vampire partially morphed into a wolf and lunged at Beowolf.

"Steal my act, huh?" the werewolf said as a few swings from his electrically crackling weapon reduced the creature from undead to truly dead. Nine down.

The returning female vampire then joined a male cohort in an attempt to attack the golem from two sides. As the female distracted him from the front, the male leapt upon the clay warrior's shoulders from behind. He took a huge bite into the jugular region of the giant's throat. That turned out to be another big mistake. Failing to realize that his foe was not flesh and blood, possibly mistaking him for an Earth giant descended from the Nephilim or the Jotuns, the vampire only succeeded in breaking his fangs on the throat's hard, impenetrable clay skin.

James reached up and grabbed the pain-wracked vampire as it dribbled blood onto his slate-colored shoulder. As this occurred the golem once again knocked the Goth-attired female vamp clear across the sidewalk with a mighty kick. This time she landed in the pricker bushes behind the front lawn of his home. The she-vamp struggled and screamed as the wooden particles in the shrub inflicted numerous painful mini-lacerations all over her body.

"I always hated falling into those bushes, too," Beowolf rumbled as he descended upon her. "I can empathize. So, let me put you out of our – I mean, *your* -- misery."

A moment later the vampire's head exploded as the werewolf struck it with his baton. Nine down.

At the same time the mystic automaton grabbed the vampire that broke its fangs on his neck and tore it off his shoulders. He then literally snapped the creature's spine in half over his hard clay knee. Taking the lead from his grandson, James maneuvered the golem into smashing the crippled vampire's head against the concrete, a blow that severed it from the neck and thus ensured that the undead creature would never rise again. Ten down.

Now only two vampires remained. And they were pissed. But no less so than the werewolf and the golem standing before them.

"Want the one on right or the one on left?" Beowolf asked his grandfather.

"I'll take the one on the right," James responded. "I don't like his face. I'm gonna step on it."

The two vampires, determined against even such formidable odds to maintain their supernatural supremacy in the Queen City, moved to attack.

Beowolf pushed his extended baton back into its hilt and sheathed the weapon on his belt. This he wanted to do with his bare claws. He then beckoned to the vampire he faced with a taunting gesture. The undead entity charged at his foe, and the werewolf found himself grappling with a male vampire built like an Olympic weightlifter. He had had obviously been strong while alive and was all the more so while undead. This would present something of a challenge to Beowolf –

which was no major problem to him, as the werewolf sorely desired to work off the remaining fury of his persona's wolfen side.

The two combatants clashed, the werewolf and vampire rolling across the sidewalk then grass as they tore at each other with vicious abandon. The blood of both was shed as they tumbled and bit at whichever limb of their opponent was closest at any given second. It was feral, it was savage, it was horrific… and it was utterly exhilarating to Beowolf. He craved this as catharsis for what he had to leave behind in Michigan, and he was not about to let the opportunity go to waste.

After a few minutes, the iron-muscled vampire lay on the grass in a pool of blood and a pile of viscera. Standing above him was a battered but triumphant Beowolf. A moment later the werewolf sunk the index and middle digits of his right hand into the vampire's eyes, making sure to perforate the brain behind them and tear the gray matter out through the sockets.

"Now that's what I call giving 'im the finger," Beowolf grumbled. And… eleven down.

Concurrently with the above battle, James Nero had the opportunity to put the power of the golem to good use as the final vampire leapt at him. Despite the obvious great strength and ruthlessness of the nosferatu, James was to have no major difficulty with it. Several seconds into the donnybrook he pulled the creature from his barrel-chested clay form and slammed it on the concrete twice. This stunned the vampire sufficiently that he was able to raise the golem's 16-inch foot and bring it down with a single almighty stomp on the blood-drinking predator's face. Its skull splattered into a gory paste beneath the golem's gray heel.

Twelve down… and game.

The job now finished, James turned to see the somewhat smaller form of his lycanthropic grandson standing over the vampire he had just defeated.

"When you said you would step on him, you weren't kidding," Beowolf commented.

The werewolf then sunk his large lupine head in concentration and in moments reverted back to human. Thankfully, the worst of his wounds had healed while he was still in the form of the wolf. He then sauntered over to the golem that now harbored his grandfather's consciousness.

"You were really awesome!" Mike said. "I'm not sure how you managed to project your mind into the golem, but I suspect your indomitable will combined with a surge of emotion to make it happen. Thank you for the help. I wouldn't have survived this without you."

"Yeah," James replied. "You… didn't do so bad yourself. Now, what do I do about this?" He held out the golem's two ultra-powerful arms and looked down at them to indicate what he was talking about.

"Well, it would seem this has given you a new lease on life, so to speak. In this form, you can do the same type of good that I did. I'll have you join the Boogey Knights and train you…"

"No!"

"Huh?"

"I don't want to be a monster… like you became."

"Would you rather transfer back to that aged, feeble body that you were trapped in?"

"No. But… I don't want to be trapped in this one either."

"Look, we'll figure something out, okay? I'll see what some of the experts at S.A.V.A.G.E. can suggest. Just hang in there for now, alright?"

The golem stood completely still. The clay giant uttered no sound and gave no sign of consciousness.

"Alright?" Mike repeated.

James Nero did not answer. The golem remained still. Mike then turned and noted the frail human form of his grandfather laying where it had slumped to the ground upon the moment of transfer. It was just as unmoving as the clay form it had relocated its consciousness to in order to help his grandson during the latter's time of dire need.

It was then that Mike realized what had happened. His grandfather had exercised his resolute willpower one final time, having instinctually realized how to reverse the transfer process. But he did not want to transfer back into that infirm elderly form he left behind. Nor did he want to remain the monstrosity that was the golem, no matter how much power and mobility it granted him. Instead, he focused his will into a third alternative, the only one now acceptable to him.

The elder Nero projected his psyche out into the ether and resisted an automatic transfer back into his original form. He realized that having no place to go, his consciousness would pass into whatever awaited him in the hereafter. James Nero was gone.

"Oh no," Mike said as his mind struggled to force acceptance of what had happened. "C'mon, talk to me, you stubborn old bastard! Don't do this to me! Stop playing around and *talk* to me!"

Mike pounded his fists against the barrel chest of the immobile golem several times as he made those pleas. It remained sessile and silent. He then turned and once again saw the unmoving form of his grandfather's feeble human form. Acceptance was now forced into his already grief-stricken mind.

The younger Nero slumped to his knees at the feet of the golem. He began crying for several minutes, struggling to get all that grief out so he could think clearly enough to conduct the important task that had to be done next.

After his tear ducts were temporarily dry, Mike took out his cell phone and dialed the emergency number of the new S.A.V.A.G.E.

"Eric? You... you need to get a collection wagon here immediately. And... and get a regular ambulance here too, okay? No, I'm okay, I'm okay. Just do it already, alright? I'll... I'll have a full report later."

After he ended the call so his friend and colleague Eric Rebel could do as he was asked, Mike Nero covered his eyes to catch further tears while he awaited the arrival of both the containment wagon and the ambulance. He also said a quiet prayer to Freya to look after the spirit of a certain departed warrior... and another to Balder for providing some peace of mind to both him and the rest of his family.

Mike Nero then stood and wiped his eyes before striding towards a familiar empty apartment that now seemed just a bit emptier. He dreaded having to inform his grandmother and the rest of the family about what had just happened; and that it had again involved what his just departed grandfather derisively referred to as "monster business." The fact that James Nero left the world on his own terms, getting in one last good fight in the process, would have to suffice for the solace his family needed in the days to come.

To the memory of Thomas J. Nigro.

We traveled a rocky road together, but it was a journey I shall never regret taking with you.

END

I hope you enjoyed the first installment of the *Boogey Knights* series! If you did, then please strongly consider saying so with a nice rating and review on Amazon, Goodreads, your personal blog, or anywhere else that allows and encourages such reviews! The more positive reviews we get, the more books we sell, the more visible we get on Amazon, and the more we can afford to bring you quality books of horror like this one at very affordable prices! Remember, we couldn't do this without you, the readers… nor would we want to ☺

ABOUT THE AUTHORS

Ryan George Collins does not like writing about himself, so he is not going to. Instead, he would like everyone to know that if you mix baking soda and vinegar to make a volcano, the least you can do is add orange food coloring to it, otherwise it will not look like proper lava. Authenticity is key to making a proper tabletop volcano, people!

While you're making that volcano, you may also want to read Collins' other books, such as *Operation: Red Dragon: The Daikaiju Wars Part One*; *Occult Mafia;* and *Emerald of Madoc City,* all of which take place in a shared universe. You may also check him out on YouTube as the Omni Viewer. I mean, you may as well, right? You've already come this far.

Aurelio Rico Lopez III is a self-diagnosed scribble junkie from Iloilo City, Philippines. His books include *Not the Forgiving Kind*; *Kaiju Double Barrel*; *Wretched*; *Raising Hell*; *Hangover of the Apocalypse*; *Night Mare*, and many more. He is also the author of the poetry collections *When the Lights Go Out* and *Two Drinks Away from Chaos*. Aurelio's addictions include doughnuts, coffee, books, and horror movies. He can make a half-decent grilled cheese sandwich – a skill which may or may not be useful during an alien invasion.

Christofer Nigro is a lifelong fan of the horror and sci-fi genres, along with comic books, superheroes, and pulp fiction. He has been running the soon-to-be-updated sites The Godzilla Saga and

Warrenverse: The Amazing World of the Warren Comics Characters for years and years. He has had short stories published by Black Coat Press, Pro Se Press, Sirens Call Publications, Pulp Empire, Grinning Skull Press, Local Hero Press, and Horrified Press, with his first two novels published by Severed Press. He is the founder, owner, and editor-in-chief of Wild Hunt Press, which has a growing list of publications behind it, including the *Duel of the Monsters* anthology series and Christofer's *Nero* series of novels dealing with a certain angst-ridden teen werewolf.

Kevin Heim was born in 1969 and began writing fiction shortly after he learned how to read – so, for almost ten years now. In 2012 he contributed two short stories to *Psychopomp*, a defunct ezine, which introduced his version of the Frankenstein Monster and his original character Ivan Ronald Schablotski, both of which have a small but mediocre fan base. Since then, he has submitted stories for a number of Wild Hunt Press anthologies, including *Dorian Gray: Darker Shades* (2018); *Attack of the Kaiju Vol. 2: The Next Wave* (2019); *Boogey Knights: Dark Warriors*; and *Mansion of the Macabre Vol. 1* (the latter upcoming in 2022 at this writing). His most notable achievements are having visited the Elvis American Diner in Jerusalem, Israel, and getting thrown out of St. Peter's Basilica in Vatican City, Rome. Kevin lives in Salem, Massachusetts, where he likes to dress up in costumes and pretend that fictional characters are real people.

Matt Hickman is the product of too much '80s TV. 'Nuff said! (We do not worry about being sued for saying that, because there are no mice around!).

Dustin Dreyling is an avid fan of science fiction and horror, with a soft spot for all things kaiju. Originally hailing from White Bear Lake, Minnesota, he also likes proofreading novels, playing video games both old and new, and taking care of his planted freshwater aquariums. His first published story was featured in Zach Cole's linear horror anthology *The Experiment* from Wild Hunt Press, and his short fiction can also be found in Wild Hunt's anthologies *Attack of the Kaiju Vol. 2: The Next Wave* and *Duel of the Monsters Vol. 1.* His first novel, the debut of his kaiju horror series *Primordial Soup: The First Batch,* was released in early 2020 from Wild Hunt Press.

Dustin is a lifelong native of Saint Paul, Minnesota, where he lives with the love of his life, Melissa. A fan of almost all things Sci-Fi and Horror, he is a devout reader of Jeremy Robinson, Jeff Strand, Brian Keene, and Tim Curran; their work has been a large influence on him. These are in addition to horror greats like H.P. Lovecraft and Stephen King.

Cody Bratsch was born on May 15, 1991, in Washington state (where he still currently resides). From a very early age, he had a fascination with all sorts of creative ventures and forms of storytelling. Classic animation such as the *Looney Tunes* and a slew of '80s and '90s animated series. Epic sci-fi franchises like *Star Wars, Star Trek, Terminator,* and *Planet of the Apes.* Sword-and-sorcery fantasy like *Clash of the Titans, Conan the Barbarian,* and *Lord of the Rings.* Tough-guy action films like *Rambo, Die Hard, Commando,* and *The Expendable.* Terrifying horror found in series like *Halloween, Friday the 13th, A Nightmare on Elm Street,* and the *Living Dead* series by George A. Romero, among other horror franchises. Grand superhero spectacles like the long slew of *Batman* films, the offerings of the Marvel Cinematic Universe, and a great many superhero cartoons on TV throughout the decades. And especially Cody's favorite type of fiction, titanic monster battles of epic proportions find in such franchises as the *Godzilla* series (the longest continually running film series in history).

Exposure to so many different types of fictional genres and forms of storytelling on such an impressionable child made it nearly impossible that Cody would be anything other than a creative type in the wild and fascinating world of writing fiction. Larger than life, creative spectacles are the kind of things Cody lives for the most in storytelling (while still enjoying some calm downtime in his stories once in a good while). All this and more are the kind of things Cody hopes to bring to his works of literature while also hoping the public who reads them will enjoy his own spin on these elements.

So far, Cody's other published works include short stories featured in Volumes 1 and 2 of *Attack of the Kaiju* and *Duel of the Monsters Vol. 1*. He hopes to add many more works to this list before he is done and will stop at almost nothing to see his writing dreams come true.

Zach Cole is the author of the novella *Tsuchigumo* (his debut work), *Kaiju Epoch*, and the Jeremy Walker Thriller series (beginning with *Blue Moon: A Jeremy Walker Thriller*) and is the mastermind behind the multi-author linear horror anthology *The Experiment* from Wild Hunt Press. He was born in Wooster, Ohio, beginning his love of monsters at the age of two after viewing *Mothra vs. Godzilla*. His short fiction has also appeared in *Attack of the Kaiju Vol. 2: The Next Wave* and *Duel of the Monsters Vol. 1* from Wild Hunt Press, which will soon be picking up his Jeremy Walker series, the next novel being *The Secrets of Atlantis* and due out in early 2022. He became a writer around the age of ten, penning Godzilla stories and even comics containing his own monstrous creations. His love of books started with the *Goosebumps* series, reading anything that has to do with monsters, big or small. He lives in West Salem, Ohio with his wife, son, two dogs, and an erratic lizard.

Alex Dumitru is from Northwest, Indiana, where he lives with his family and a very small dog. He was first inspired to write kaiju literature after becoming a fan of the *Ultraman* franchise from Tsuburaya Productions, and this inspired the creation of his own published sentai character, Massive. His debut (and that of Massive) was in Matt Dennion's self-published edition of *Attack of the Kaiju Vol. 1: Age of Monsters*. Alex also made a major contribution to Zach Cole's linear horror anthology *The Experiment* and the horror anthology *Duel of the Monsters Volume 1,* both from Wild Hunt Press. His newest work can be found here in *Boogey Knights: Dark Warriors* from Wild Hunt.

Neil Riebe has been a lifelong fan of Japanese giant monsters since seeing *King Kong vs. Godzilla* back in the '70s. The three-part story "Godzilla vs Atragon," published in *G-Fan* issues #9 through #11, inspired him to write his multi-part Godzilla stories. These tales included "Godzilla vs Super Allosaurus," published in *G-Fan* issues #15 through #17; "Battle of Manazura Island," published in *G-Fan* #25; and "Rodana," published in *G-Fan* #42. After Toho asked *G-Fan* to cease publishing fan fiction based on their characters, Neil posted subsequent stories on FanFiction.net. While writing kaiju fan fiction, he also wrote an article for *Japanese Giants* #10 and the forewords to the *Gfantis vs Guest Monsters* anthology and John LeMay's *The Big Book of Japanese Giant Monster Movies Vol. 1: 1954-1982*.

Neil's work for Wild Hunt Press has included the anthologies *Attack of the Kaiju Vol. 2: The Next Wave* and here in *Boogey Knights: Dark Warriors*.

Little is known about the enigmatic writer **JJ Lindsey**, but thorough investigation has revealed [INFORMATION REDACTED].

MEET THE ARTISTS

Benjo Quinajon started his career as a Final Artist for print production studios and elevated to a Senior Designer employed by reputable design shops and Ad Agencies in the Philippines. His experiences earned during years as a Designer are focused on branding, packaging, and print publication and has handled brands such as Nestlé, Coca-Cola, McDonald's and Proctor & Gamble. His greatest passion is doing manual and digital illustration for clients and personal projects.

Elden Ardiente is an artist based in Sydney, Australia and produces graphic design, illustrations, concept art, and digital sculptures for books, games, movies, and toys. You can see his creations at LDNRDNT.COM.

Glenn Lugapo used to work in advertising as a graphic artist and eventually as an art director. Among clients handled are Alaska, Colt 45, Unilab and URC. Nowadays, he's usually at home with his crazy dogs. Actually, he's visually impaired (low vision), but still tries to draw as best he can.

www.ingramcontent.com/pod-product-compliance
Lightning Source LLC
Chambersburg PA
CBHW020726210626
46807CB00016B/358